THE ADMIRAL'S
SPIES

D. W. Drake

Savanat Press

The Admiral's Spies

Author's Photo by Jane Chouteau

Book edited by Carol O'Donnell

Published by Savanat Press

http:// www.savanatpress.com

Published in the United States of America

ISBN: 978-1-7336163-8-6

TABLE OF CONTENTS

CHAPTER ONE

ALONG ILLINOIS STATE ROUTE 50
THREE MILES NORTH OF MONEE, ILLINOIS
OCTOBER 23, 1936

A small herd of six Holstein milk cows grazed peacefully in their pasture beside the gravel highway, their udders heavy with milk. Tails swished the air above their backs keeping pesky flies at bay. The autumn sun was warm on their flanks and the grass was still sweet so they were content. It was quiet, the only sounds being the occasional buzzing of a passing honeybee, the far off call of a hawk circling high in the sky and the croaking of a bullfrog down in the creek across the road. The animals grazed close to each other, enjoying the comforting presence of their own kind.

This bucolic tableau was disturbed by the faint roaring sound of automobiles rapidly approaching on the road to the north. The leader of the herd, a brown and white cow who the farmer's wife had named Dolly, raised her head and pointed her muzzle toward the sound. Her sisters followed suit because a characteristic of their species was inquisitiveness. They were always curious about what the humans were up to.

The noise rose in volume to a roar as a convoy of three automobiles raced past the pasture on the highway raising a huge cloud of dust. The curious cows followed the moving cars with their heads swinging in unison until they were out of sight. "Dolly," with nary a sound of either approval or disapproval, dipped her head and resumed grazing and the others followed suit. The dust gradually settled and then everything was as it was before.

The lead car in the speeding convoy was an Illinois state police cruiser with four uniformed troopers inside. Whenever an occasional tractor or farm truck was overtaken by the speeding vehicles, the big siren on the fender of the police car would wail and clear the road ahead. Following in the police car's wake were two identical 1935 Chevrolet sedans painted black.

There were ten men altogether in the two black sedans, five in each car. Nine of them were clad in neat dark suits with white shirts and ties and wore their hair short and neatly trimmed. FBI Director Hoover insisted upon it. The tenth man, sitting in the middle of the back seat of one of the Chevrolets, was a little mouse of a man who wore a cream colored suit, with his loud multicolored tie pulled down and askew. He had his hands cuffed in front of him and looked none too happy.

On the floorboards of all three automobiles was a veritable arsenal. There were Browning automatic rifles, Thompson submachine guns and Winchester model 97 pump shotguns.

Piled beside them were web belts with pouches stuffed with loaded magazines and bags of shotgun shells. All these weapons were in addition to the revolver each special agent carried in a holster on his right hip. Counting the FBI agents in the sedans and the troopers in the state police car they had thirteen men to wield the weapons. They would need all of them. They were going after the Baker gang.

While not as famous as Dillinger or the Barkers, the Baker gang was just as vicious and dangerous as their more well-known contemporaries.

Charley Baker, the head of the gang was a psychopath who didn't hesitate to kill anyone who got in his way. Aping Dillinger, their specialty was robbing banks in small midwestern towns and then escaping across state lines. The Baker Gang had murdered eight people so far in the course of their short crime career. Thanks to a fortuitous turn of events, the FBI now knew where they were hiding out.

In the back seat of the second sedan sitting behind the driver, twenty-two-year-old rookie FBI agent Theodore Andrew Miller was struggling with an internal conflict. His hands were trembling slightly, there were butterflies in his stomach, his mouth was dry and he was sweating profusely under his arms. He was thankful that the sweat stains hadn't yet penetrated the cloth of his coat and show his dread for everyone else in the car to see. He was a slim young man with brown wavy hair under his felt hat, expressive blue eyes and a square jaw. His youthful appearance contrasted sharply with the older, harder looking agents in the car. This was his first raid as an FBI agent and he was anxious to do well and impress the others, but the prospect of a gun battle with gangsters terrified him.

The danger he was about to face was real. Two years ago, two FBI agents had been killed in a furious shootout with the notorious "Baby Face" Nelson. Last year, a standoff with "Ma" Barker and her husband Fred had lasted for five hours and thousands of rounds of ammunition were fired.

But while Ted Miller was frightened of the physical danger he would be facing, he was more concerned about the prospect that when the bullets started flying he would show himself to be a coward. Would he dishonor his father's name? Miller's dad had been an Ohio State Trooper killed in the line of duty when Ted was nine. Young Ted had idolized his father and his death had hit him hard. Since then the young man had tried to live according to a strict code of conduct that he thought his dead father would approve of. Sometimes, although he had told no one except his mother, Ted felt as if his dad was somehow watching him and how he conducted himself. Miller's chin dipped and his jaw set in a hard line. He made a resolution. He vowed to himself that no matter the danger, he would do his duty. He would rather die than be disgraced.

Ted's anxiety was also heightened by the speed of the events transpiring around him. Things were happening at such rapidity that it was hard for him to mentally keep pace with them. The raid had been set in motion only a few hours before.

§

Ted Miller had wanted to be an FBI agent since he was a freshman at Ohio State University. One evening he took a date to the movies and saw a newsreel. One of the segments dealt with the FBI's war against the criminal gangs that terrorized the country. Ted was inspired. Some of his friends tended to glamorize the gangsters, Miller didn't. Because of the manner of the death of his father, he thought of Dillinger and Alvin Carpis and their ilk as low life criminals that should be gunned down like rabid dogs. People needed to be protected from them. Sitting in that darkened theater, he decided what he wanted to do in his life. He wanted to bring criminals, like the ones who had killed his father, to well-deserved justice. Last year he had graduated with an accounting degree and instead of sitting for the CPA exam, had applied to join the FBI. To his relief, he was accepted and had breezed through the FBI academy. Four days ago Ted had reported to the FBI field office in Chicago as his first assignment.

He had arrived at the Chicago federal building in a new black suit with a crisp white shirt and muted tie. A brand new Colt .38 revolver nestled in a holster on his right hip under his coat. He was shown into the office of John Hofstetter, Special Agent in charge of the Chicago field office. Hofstetter was a dignified man in his early fifties who gave the new special agent a pep talk about hard work and obedience to FBI regulations. Then he walked Miller into a large room with many desks and introduced him to Special Agent Aubrey Swenson, who had been assigned to train him.

Swensen was a big loud Scandinavian with blonde hair and blue eyes. He looked to be in his mid-thirties and had enormous, strong hands. After a crushing handshake, Swensen sat Ted down in a chair and gave him a more practical talk.

"My job is to train you to be an investigator. Good investigators are born, not made, so we will see if you have what it takes. Most of what we do is boring. We follow up on leads given to us by informants. So forget any romantic notions about being a heroic super-agent."

"There are unwritten rules in this office. Rule number one is not to do anything to make SAC Hofstetter look bad. Do that and your days are numbered. Rule number two is to show up every day. I don't care how sick you think you are, drag your sorry butt down here. Rule number three is to do what I tell you without lip or asking why. If you're not sure about something, ask questions. I'm going to start out teaching you how to stay alive in this job. Believe it or not, there are lots of people who would love to see every FBI agent laid out on a marble slab in the morgue. Just follow my lead and do what I tell you to do. Any questions?"

"No, sir," replied Ted, very eager and anxious to please the older agent.

"You don't have to 'sir' me friend. Only assistant directors and above need to be addressed as sir. If you ever meet Director J. Edgar Hoover though, you must kneel and kiss his ring as well as calling him sir."

"Being a wiseass will get you in trouble someday, Swede," said another agent at a desk nearby.

"Oh, hell, I was looking for a job when I got this one," replied Swensen.

For three days Ted and the Swede spent their time tracking down leads on a continuing investigation of a mob interstate bookmaking operation. The repeal of Prohibition and the conviction of Al Capone had not stopped the organized crime families. They still had their fingers in many less than legal enterprises. Miller wasn't bored at all. He was soaking up all the Swede told him like a sponge. Swensen was a loquacious man with a wry sense of humor. He had Ted laughing all the time. But he also had a full repertoire of dirty jokes that mildly shocked and offended Ted and sometimes made him blush. Swensen also knew the best places to eat.

The big Swede wasn't your typical FBI special agent. He rounded the corners on square FBI regulations when he could get away with it. Nothing illegal or immoral, just minor skirting of the rules. For instance, Swensen refused to carry the standard .38 Special caliber revolver as called for by the Bureau. Instead, he packed an enormous Model 1909, Colt New Service, 45 caliber revolver in a shoulder holster under his left arm. He called it his "hand cannon." During lunch on their second day together, as they were sitting in a bar on Michigan Avenue devouring enormous pastrami sandwiches, Ted worked up the courage to ask the Swede why he carried the big revolver. With a mouthful of pastrami, the big man replied.

"Well, it's like this, young gentleman. If some mutt is trying to kill me, I want a weapon that can answer back with authority. A bullet from that little pea shooter you carry won't even penetrate a car door half the time. The hand cannon uses the same cartridge that Wyatt Earp used to mow down the Clantons at the OK Corral. If it's good enough for Earp and the Lone Ranger, it's good enough for me. By the way, have you

THE ADMIRAL'S SPIES | 11

heard the one about the farmer's three daughters who only had five breasts between them?"

The two agent's routine, established in the first three days, changed abruptly this morning around nine when SAC Hofstetter called Ted and Swensen into his office.

"A flatfoot beat cop on the south side spotted Bennie the Mooch going into a bar. The cop followed him in and collared him. He's at the police station on west 63rd street. Cap Larsen is keeping him under wraps, with no phone calls. Get over there fast and see if you can get a line on the location of the Baker gang," said Hofstettler to the Swede, not giving a glance to Ted.

On the way down in the elevator, the Swede explained all the excitement.

"'Bennie the Mooch' is reliably reported to be the wheelman for the Baker gang. If we can somehow get their location from Bennie, we can mount a raid and get their murdering asses. We have to hurry. The more time that goes by, the more chance that the crooks will be tipped off and they will be in the wind."

It was quicker to hail a cab than check out a car. Swensen's foot tapped constantly on the floorboard of the taxi during the twenty-minute ride. Ted could tell he was excited. When the cab stopped in front of the police station, the Swede jumped out and bounded up the stairs. Ted paid the driver and ran after him.

When Miller arrived at the second floor detective bureau, he didn't see Swensen anywhere in the crowded hallway. Then a uniformed cop behind a counter pointed to a partially opened door midway down a hall. Ted eased through the door, spotted the Swede standing against a wall and joined him. There were eight to ten detectives in the big room, all gathered around a man nicknamed Bennie the Mooch.

The office was the squad room of the Chicago Police Southside Detective Bureau. Like similar rooms in police stations everywhere, it was dilapidated. The paint was peeling from its stained walls and ceiling, the many desks were old and battered and there was clutter everywhere. Ted's nose twitched at the smell. It was a combination of mold, stale cigar and cigarette smoke, unwashed bodies and the sweet aroma of cheap perfume from the two gum-chewing hookers talking to a detective at a desk in a corner. Light flowed into the room through large fly-specked windows. Everyone was smoking so there was a blue haze suspended in the air and the floor was littered with crushed cigarette butts.

Bennie was sitting in a scarred oak office chair with each wrist cuffed to a chair arm. He was small and scrawny with a narrow face and eyes that darted from detective to detective standing around him. To Ted, he resembled a trapped rat. He was dressed in a light-colored suit with a loud tie. The small gangster's face was a picture of defiance as he looked up at the policemen crowding him. A big Chicago detective stood about three feet in front of Bennie. The cop was stout and middle-aged and his jowly face and big nose were shot through with little purple veins. He was wearing a rumpled gray suit with the vest unbuttoned. The Swede leaned over and whispered to Ted.

"That's Cap Larsen, Chief of Southside detectives."

"Come on Bennie, tell us where the Baker gang is. You know you're gonna' tell us in the end. Why make it hard on yourself?" asked Larsen. His gravelly voice echoed through the room.

"I ain't tellin' you bastards shit. You can beat on me all night an I still ain't gonna' tell you shit. I ain't no squealer. I want my phone call. You bulls have to give me a phone call," blurted out Bennie in a high and reedy voice.

The detective reached in his pocket and came out with a pair of brass knuckles. Bennie eyed them warily. Larsen slipped the knuckles onto the fingers of his right hand.

"One last chance, Bennie," said the Captain.

"Go fuck yourselves!"

With speed and power and with all his weight behind it, Larsen delivered a punch to the left side of Bennie's chest, right on the ribs. It was a solid blow and Ted winced when he saw it. He was surprised and a little shocked that the detective captain would hit a handcuffed prisoner like that. Ted looked over at Swensen, who just shrugged. Benny said nothing. The detective hit him again, but the little man only grunted and stared back defiantly. Cap Larsen stood back with his hands on his hips. "This is getting us nowhere. Bill, slide that other chair over here."

Another detective brought over a chair and placed it about two-and-a-half-feet from Bennie's knees. The cop bent down and grasped Bennie's ankles and put his feet up onto the other chair. The gangster was now sitting suspended between the two chairs with nothing below his knees but air. With a sigh, Larsen sat down on Bennie's knees, bending them backward. The small man remained silent, but Ted saw him grit his teeth and screw his face up in agony.

'Why do they call you Bennie the Mooch?" asked Larsen. "I've heard that it's because you never have your own cigarettes and mooch off everyone else. Is that true?"

Bennie didn't answer the question. Sweat was pouring off his face. He also turned bright red. Little groans escaped his lips and saliva dribbled down his chin from the corners of his mouth. Larsen had been sitting on his knees for about fifteen seconds when Bennie, at last, threw back his head and screamed.

"Alright, alright, I'll spill. Just get the fuck off me!"

The detective got up and Bennie lolled back in relief. His mouth was wide open, breathing in gulps of air. He gradually recovered himself and spoke.

"Charley and four other gents are holed up in a farmhouse down south of the city near a little burg called Monee. He sent me inta' the city to get some booze and a particular hooker he likes."

"When is he expecting you back?" asked Larsen.

Now that Bennie had started to talk, it was as if he had crossed an invisible line. He gushed forth anything the officers wanted to know.

"If I'm not back in a coupla' hours, Charley will start to get antsy. It's all the fault a that whore Charlene. If she hadn't made herself so hard to find, I wouldn't be here. An' ya' never woulda' got me if that flatfoot hadn't been so sneaky. He snuck up behind me an' laid a sap 'side my ear."

With this new information, a raid was hastily organized, consisting of all the special agents SAC Hofstetter could round up on short notice. Most of the Chicago detectives wanted to go, too, but Captain Larsen adamantly refused.

"I'm not prepared for the shit storm from the Chief I would be in for if one a my boys gets killed outside the city limits. Call the state police. They got nothing' better to do anyway, sittin' out in the country waitin' for the weeds to grow up their asses."

§

The plowed fields and cow pastures abruptly gave way to the town of Monee. The state police car braked hard and turned left onto the main road through town. Ted caught sight of a sign that said the road was Court Street. The middle car, containing SAC Hofstetter and Benny the Mooch, pulled over and stopped in front of the town hall with its sign that read POLICE. Ted's car stopped behind them. The state police car continued on for a hundred feet, then stopped and reversed back to where the other cars were parked. The two black sedans were covered in a thick coating of dust from following the police car all the way from Chicago on the dirt and gravel highway.

All four doors of the SAC Hostettler's car opened and the occupants got out. The group of agents began leading Bennie toward the town hall. Hofstetter waved at the other vehicles with a come-on gesture. The Swede, Ted and the other three agents as well as the uniformed cops also got out and followed, leaving their long guns in the car.

The town police chief was there to greet the group when they walked in the door of the one-room police department. He was about sixty with long grey hair and was wearing a khaki shirt with a gold badge pinned on his left breast. The shirt was tucked into brown farmer's pants held up with wide, white suspenders. Strapped around his waist was an old cowboy style Colt revolver.

"Mornin' gentlemen. I'm Chief Roger Dalls. How kin' I help you?"

"Good morning Chief. We are FBI agents," Hofstetter retrieved his credentials from his breast pocket and showed them to Dalls. "We have information that leads us to believe that a dangerous criminal gang is hiding out near your town."

The Chief's bushy gray eyebrows shot up. "In Monee?, Hell, nothin' ever happens in Monee."

Hofstetter jerked Bennie forward. "Tell the chief how to get to the farmhouse," the FBI agent said.

Looking at the floor, Bennie haltingly explained the twists and turns to the hideout of the Baker gang. By his halting speech and shifting eyes, it appeared he was starting to have second thoughts about his cooperation.

"Why that sounds like the old Benson place," said Chief Dalls. "They went bust in thirty-two. The place belongs to the bank now I suppose,"

"Chief, we don't need your assistance in tackling these gangsters. We have brought sufficient forces. If you could lock this man up in one of your cells until later today, I would much appreciate it," said Hofstetter as he pushed Bennie forward.

The Chief looked relieved. Maybe he didn't relish doing battle with dangerous men using his ancient firearm. "Yessir, I kin' do that," replied Dalls and led Benny to one of two cells that lined the west wall. Taking out an enormous brass key, he locked the criminal in and replaced the key in his trouser pocket.

Hofstetter then gave his instructions for the raid. "The farmhouse is in a grove of trees surrounded by open fields, so there is almost no chance of sneaking up on the gang. Our best bet is to roar in there and get the place surrounded before they can react. Be prepared for them to start shooting the moment they see us."

"You state troopers cover the south side. Block the road in with your police car. Swede, Miller and Jackson, take the east side. Johnson, Murphy and Gerard cover the north side. I will take the west side with Noyes and Smith. You agents assigned to the north side, ride my running boards. I will drop you off on the way to my position. Don't hesitate to shoot to kill. The Baker gang is gonna' be stopped here. Any questions?"

The agents and the troopers remained silent. They ran back to the cars. Two of the agents from Ted's car positioned themselves on the outside running boards of Hofstetter's car. Each hung on to a doorpost with one arm while clutching a long gun in the other. All three automobiles roared off east on Court Street. The convoy made several zigzag turns and covered about two miles of dusty country roads. Finally, Ted could see the farmhouse with its grove of trees in the distance. It was mid-day, so the house was completely shaded by the leaves of the overhanging trees. The land around the house was flat fallow farmland stretching off into the distance.

The house with its access road faced south. Agent Jackson who was driving followed Hofstetter's car as it swung wide around the house bumping over rutted, weed-choked fields, stirring up clouds of dust. Jackson stopped the car about a hundred feet from the east side of the farmhouse and the agents piled out with their firearms. Jackson, Ted and the Swede separated. They could see the bottom half of a window set amid the weathered clapboards of the house below the low hanging branches of the trees. Various items of rusty, broken farm equipment littered the yard amid the weeds, the detritus of a failed farming enterprise.

The Swede motioned to Ted to come closer to him. Ted obeyed instantly and ran up to Swenson while looking around, his heart pounding with fear and excitement. There was no cover anywhere near to shelter behind. The Swede had noticed it too.

"Stay close to me, don't get too far away. Head for that ditch," said Swensen and pointed to a shallow, weed-choked irrigation ditch about fifteen feet behind them. They had just gained the dubious protection of the ditch when all hell broke loose.

The glass on the window facing them was smashed, and a fusillade of gunfire was directed at the three agents. Ted could see continuous muzzle flashes and the ground around them danced with spurts of dust from bullet impacts.

"That fucker's got a BAR! Return fire! Shoot!" shouted the Swede.

Ted Miller crouched in the ditch. He had a Winchester Model 97 pump shotgun in his hands. He worked the slide and chambered a shell. Pointing in the general direction of the window, he fired. The recoil of the weapon slammed the stock into his shoulder like the kick of a mule. Ted didn't even notice. Pumping the slide, he fired again and again until the trigger clicked on an empty chamber. He dug in his pocket for more shells and slid them into the bottom of the weapon, his fingers shaking badly.

Ted was terrified. Feeling appallingly exposed, his first instinct was to drop his gun and run away. He almost did in the first moments of the furious action. What stopped him was the resolution he had made to himself in the car on the trip down from Chicago. "My father didn't run away and neither will I," he told himself. "I asked to do this and I will finish it." He gritted his teeth and choked down his fear. Ted was aware of Swensen beside him, banging away with an M1928 Thompson submachine gun. Suddenly, it stopped firing.

"Fucker's jammed!" said the Swede and he threw the heavy weapon down to the ground in front of them. Swensen pulled out his "hand cannon" and started blasting away at the window. Ted noticed that the fire from the window was slackening and then it abruptly ceased. A few moments later he heard car doors slam and an engine starting up. A big black Packard sedan emerged from the shade of the trees, its engine roaring. It was accelerating right toward Ted and the Swede. A member of the gang was leaning out of the passenger window, firing a Browning automatic rifle at them.

Ted Miller wasn't a soldier, but the combat he was experiencing was just as furious as on any battlefield. Experience in America's wars has shown that young men going into battle for the first time react in different ways to the horrors of combat. More than a few of them, sad to say, freeze up in terror and cower at the bottom of a foxhole or try to run away. Most of the rest somehow conquer their fear and do their duty, but no more. But a tiny minority, no more than one in ten thousand somehow rise to the occasion and perform extraordinary feats of valor. These brave young men are almost never the cocky loudmouths that brag beforehand about how tough they are, but the quiet little guys that no one pays much attention to before the shooting starts. As unlikely as it seemed, Ted Miller, the hesitant son of a murdered state trooper, turned out to be one of these extraordinary young men.

As the gangster's car burst from the trees, a change came over the young agent. His fear was instantly replaced by a towering rage. With the onset of the anger, his mind suddenly became crystal clear and sharp. He saw immediately what he had to do. Throwing away the shotgun, He quickly bent and picked up the discarded Thompson. He remembered in detail the firearms instructor's lesson at Quantico on how to clear a jammed Thompson.

Ted hit the magazine release catch and the heavy, circular, one hundred round drum magazine slid sidewise from the weapon. He cradled the magazine under his arm while he yanked back on the charging handle on the top of the gun's receiver. A ruptured cartridge fell out of the breech and to the ground. He slid the magazine back onto the weapon until he felt it click into place. Since the Thompson fired from an open bolt, it was ready to fire again.

The gangster's car was almost upon them. Ted had only seconds. He stood, ignoring the sound of bullets zipping by, and brought the Thompson to his shoulder, lining up the sights. He rested the forward grip on the palm of his left hand.

"Short bursts or you will lose control," the instructor at the FBI academy at Quantico had said. Miller ignored the gangster firing the automatic rifle and instead aimed at the driver of the car. He pulled the trigger briefly and the heavy weapon spewed out four bullets.

The windshield in front of the driver shattered with multiple impacts. The car slewed around to the left and rolled to a stop, presenting a broadside shot to Miller. Next, he aimed at the gunman with the rifle. He pulled the trigger again and the powerful weapon spoke. Ted saw at least one of the big .45 caliber slugs strike the gunman's head. The wounded man dropped the automatic rifle. Ted detected movement in the back of the big car and he put burst after burst into the rear seat area until the Thompson's bolt slammed forward on an empty chamber.

Rookie Special Agent Theodore Miller stood still, holding the smoking Thompson submachine gun to his shoulder. The acrid smell of burned gunpowder was strong in his nostrils and his hearing was muffled by the noise of the gunshots. His rage subsided as quickly as it had arisen. The other agents came running to the car from their positions on other sides of the house. All five members of the Baker gang were dead, including Charley Baker himself, shot to pieces by Miller's fire. The Swede rushed over to Ted and clapped him on the back.

"Hot damn, you sure earned your wings today boy. Agents will be talkin' 'bout you from Kansas City to Washington. Let me shake your hand!"

Ted ignored the Swede's hand and, still holding the Thompson, walked toward the bullet riddled car. He could see Charlie Baker hanging half out of the front passenger window. Most of the right side of his head was gone, and a stream of bright red blood ran down the side of the car and dripped onto the dirt of the farmyard. The driver was slumped over the wheel with a neat hole in his forehead. Three other men, shredded by bullets, with weapons clasped in their lifeless hands, were sprawled across each other in the back seat with blood everywhere.

Ted told himself that he should feel regret, or something, for what he had done. He had just snuffed out five lives. But the only thing he felt was triumph. Men such as these had killed his father. A sergeant from the Ohio state police had told Ted's mother on that fateful day his father was killed that Trooper Miller had waged a courageous battle against the hoods that killed him, reloading twice before he was cut down. Ted looked briefly up in the sky and wondered if his father was watching him and approved of what he had just done. A feeling of calm assurance washed over him. He knew that he had changed. The events of this fateful day had transformed him into a different person from the scared youth he was a few minutes ago. His fellow agents instinctively noticed the difference too. They stood and gaped at him with expressions of awe and wonder on their faces. Ted's body started to tremble, the after effects of the adrenaline rush kicking in. The Swede gently took the Thompson from his hands and sat him down on the shiny fender of Charlie Baker's bullet-riddled Packard.

"You done good today, son, really good," said the Swede. "From now on I'm gonna' call you Machinegun Miller."

CHAPTER TWO

WHEELER'S MILL
INDIANA
MAY 22, 1937

S pring had finally come to the sleepy little town of Wheeler's Mill. The sepia tones, blowing snow and freezing temperatures of winter were now just a memory. On this day in May, the bright Hoosier sun bathed the land in its golden rays, white cumulous clouds propelled by the steady breeze out of the flatlands to the west drifted overhead and cast moving shadows across the area's small farms and patches of woods. Amid the green riot of new life, yarrow, thimbleweed and false indigo were in prodigious bloom and along the banks of the streams the magenta spikes of butterfly milkweed bushes poked proudly toward the sky. Songbirds wheeled and soared and gave voice to their joy at being alive. It was the creator's spectacular annual display of the renewal of life and great beauty was on display.

Most people feel better when surrounded by nature's beauty. It tends to lift their spirits, brighten their outlook on life and acts as a counterbalance to the ugliness they encounter. Not just physical ugliness, but the ugliness of mind and spirit that too often plagues human society. But most people also more often prefer the sensational and transitory to the timeless. That's why many more of them are seen sitting in movie theaters and attending sports contests than taking quiet walks in the countryside. So it was in this small Indiana prairie town in the fourth decade of the twentieth century.

Every year from April to September the males of all ages in town, as well as a good many of the women and girls, would go crazy for baseball. They were about evenly split between fans of the Cubs and the White Sox. In the evenings they would huddle around their radios listening to broadcasts from WIND or WGN of reenactments of major league games played earlier in the day. Wherever men gathered, there would be lively discussions, and sometimes physical altercations, about Babe Ruth, Lou Gehrig and the fantastic Yankees second year center fielder, Joe Dimaggio. A small minority of the townspeople who didn't care about baseball and wanted to talk about boring things like President Roosevelt running for a second term in the upcoming Presidential election, the Great Depression that seemed to go on and on and the Spanish Civil War were shunned like Puritans living in sin.

Very few of the local baseball fans had ever seen a big league baseball game in person. Their love of baseball was tempered by good old midwestern thrift. Times were still hard and they didn't have the money to go gallivanting up to Chicago to watch a baseball game. Fortunately for them, there was an alternative. The local high school had a baseball team that was a perennial contender for the county title. Whenever there was a big game, the town would empty, commerce would grind to a halt and the folks of Wheeler's Mill would flock to the high school baseball diamond.

It was the first game of the year between Wheeler's Mill High's Pawnees and their long-time rivals, the Valparaiso Vikings. At the end of the twelve game season, one of these teams would take the county title, have their team name engraved below the prior year's winners on the big brass trophy and display it at their school for the next year. The Pawnees and the Vikings were the powerhouse teams of the county. None of the other schools had a chance. Valparaiso had won the trophy last year and the Pawnees were out for revenge.

The Baseball field at Wheeler's Mill High School was in rough shape. The town was a poor community of small subsistence farmers and workers from the steel mills in Gary, ten miles to the north, and there wasn't much money available for repairs. A section of the right field bleachers was roped off because it was too rickety to support the weight of people. The bases were old flour sacks filled with corn cobs and anchored with long iron spikes. The rest of the school was in similar disrepair. The high school principal and his teachers labored at near starvation wages to educate the children of the area. They succeeded for the most part, every year graduating literate young men and women prepared to take their place in society.

The player's shabby clothes also testified to the fact that it was a poor community. Each Wheeler's Mill player wore a team jersey with his name and number on the back above a notice that said, DONATED BY JOHNSON'S HARDWARE. The boys wore their own trousers and shoes. There was hardly a boy on either team that didn't have frayed cuffs or patches sewn to the knees of his britches. A few of the poorer boys played barefoot.

It had been a good, scrappy game with the score seesawing back and forth. Now it was the bottom of the ninth inning and Valparaiso was ahead by one run. But Wheeler's Mill had rallied after two outs in the inning. Tommy Phillips had walked, Elmer Johnson had hit a two-bagger and, just like that, the Pawnees had men on second and third bases. The bleachers were full and everyone was on the edge of their seat. Would the Pawnees be able to pull it off? The fans in the crowd supporting Wheeler's Mill were many more in number than the people from out of town supporting Valparaiso and they yelled their support. Pawnee fans felt encouraged because their star player was on deck. If anyone could do it, it was Fritz Hofmann.

The crowd roared as Fritz walked confidently to the plate. He was tall and slender. His shoulders and arms were more muscular than the usual seventeen-year-old due to his after school job of loading and driving a delivery truck. The veins stood out prominently on his forearms. Fair hair poked out from the band of his blue Chicago Cubs baseball cap. The lips on his open, handsome face wore a confident smile. Oh, he's a cool one, thought the fans. The pressure didn't seem to bother him at all.

It was all a front. Fritz was trembling slightly as he squared off at the plate. He felt faintly queasy in his stomach. He glanced over at the part of the stands where Gladys Murphy was standing, looking gorgeous in her pink sweater. She hadn't known he was alive when school started last September. Now, thanks to his position as captain of the baseball team, he had a date with her tonight. He had to take that back. He might have a date with her tonight if he didn't blow this chance. If he hit an anemic ground ball or struck out, she probably wouldn't have anything more to do with him.

Fritz looked at the pitcher. His name was Bill Smith. He was Valparaiso's ace. His heater was sneaky fast and his curve dived like it was dropping off a table. Fritz had faced him three times today. In his first two at-bats, he had struck out on curveballs. In his third, Smith had brushed Fritz back with some chin music, then came back with another fastball low and outside. Fritz had hit a little dribbler to the first baseman and had been out at first by twenty feet.

The umpire pointed to the pitcher and Bill Smith wound up and fired a fastball right down the middle. The bat stayed on Fritz' shoulder.

"STEERIKE ONE!," called the umpire.

Smith smiled and wound up again. This pitch was a curve. It broke low and outside.

"BALL, ONE AN' ONE"

Smith stood on the mound and rubbed the ball with both hands as he studied the catcher intently. He nodded and wound up again. This one was a heater aimed at Fritz's chin. Dropping his bat, Fritz fell backward and sprawled on his butt in the dirt. He got up smiling, dusted himself off, picked up his bat and reentered the batter's box. It wouldn't do to let Smith know he could be intimidated.

"BALL, TWO AN' ONE," said the ump.

Fritz studied the pitcher and had a sudden thought. I wonder if he is going to try to get me out with a fastball low and outside, like the last time. The count favored Fritz so he decided to sit on heat, low and outside. Smith wound up and threw the ball.

Fritz had guessed right. A fastball soared in just where he was expecting it and he swung mightily. He didn't try to pull the ball but went with the pitch. The barrel of his bat made solid contact with the ball and there was a loud crack. Fritz hit a rocket line drive, about six feet off the ground and toward right field. The ball was hit so hard that the Valparaiso second baseman had very little time to react. He leaped to his left and as his feet left the ground, he extended his glove to his maximum reach. Almost miraculously, the ball sailed into the pocket of his glove. The infielder hit the ground on his belly, then scrambled to his feet and lifted his glove with the ball high in the air in triumph. The roaring crowd suddenly fell silent. Fritz had taken two strides toward first base when he saw the catch. The Valparaiso fans let out a collective whoop. The Viking's bench cleared and the second baseman was mobbed by his teammates with congratulations. Fritz lowered his head and shuffled toward the showers.

It was very quiet in the Wheeler's Mill locker room. The other boys on the team avoided looking at Fritz and spoke only in monosyllables.

There was none of the usual joking and horseplay. Fritz knew his status at the school had just gone from the pinnacle to the depths with one pitch of a baseball. Everyone took cold water showers and left quietly, one by one. When he emerged from the building, there was no one there to greet him. Even Gladys had deserted him. I guess that's over too, he thought.

Fritz was walking with his head down as he approached his home. He lived in a section of Wheeler's Mill that had seen much better days. It wasn't the kind of place where you brought friends home to see where you lived. The houses, shacks really, had been thrown together in 1910, at the height of the steel boom, to provide housing for workers at the US Steel plant in Gary. None of the houses Fritz passed had felt the caress of a paintbrush since. There were no sidewalks on his block, so he walked at the edge of the road, avoiding the deepest mud sumps in the dirt. He passed weed-choked planters and overgrown yards, carrying his bat over his shoulder with his catcher's mitt tucked under one arm. Fritz waved at his next-door neighbor, the Widow Wilson, who was seated on her front porch, still in her housecoat in the late afternoon.

As he approached the front entrance of the place he called home he heard angry raised voices through the torn screen door. He recognized the voices. They were those of His younger brother and his father. Fritz groaned. His bad day was about to get worse. He didn't go in right away but stood and listened.

"You are German. You have Aryan blood running through your veins!" yelled Fritz's father Engel in German.

"I am an American, and my blood is no different from Mario Delvecchio's who's Italian or Mike Murphy who's Irish. Hell, it's probably the same as Sol Green who's a Jew," replied Eb in English.

Fritz winced. There was nothing that would anger his father more than for his son to compare himself to a Jew. Engel Hofmann hated Jews. He blamed them for the death of his wife, the Great Depression and every other calamity he could think of. He was a member of the German America Bund, and he came back from their monthly meetings railing against the Jews. Fritz didn't care for Jews either, but he didn't hate them like his father.

"How dare you compare your sacred blood to that of a Jew! I guess I will have to beat this nonsense out of you. You have insulted your race!" The German words came out slurred.

Drunk again, thought Fritz.

"Stay where you are, old man. The days are past when you can get drunk and beat on me. If you come over here I will fight back, and I might just knock you on your skinny ass."

Fritz reached for the rusty handle of the screen door and yanked it open. He had better get in there and try to quiet the situation down before the argument turned physical. He stepped into the tiny foyer and a stale beer smell mingled with human body odor and the stench of spoiled food, assaulted his nostrils. His father and brother were standing about five feet apart in the small cluttered living room, glaring at each other. Fritz's father dropped the empty Pabst Blue Ribbon beer bottle he had been holding. The bottle landed with a clunk, rolled across the old slanted floorboards and came to rest against five or six other empty amber bottles. Engel Hofmann caught sight of Fritz and gave him a boozy smile.

"Ah, Friedrich, my good son. Tell this ungrateful pup that he should not disparage his heritage. Germany is a land of greatness. Greatness!"

Engel swayed for a moment, then sat down heavily on the filthy sofa. He was a dissipated looking man, in his early forties, with a weak chin and a receding hairline. His clothing was a baggy pair of grey trousers and an undershirt that once had been white but was now stained with spilled beer and food. His face was flushed from all the beer and he wore the out-of-focus expression of the chronic drunk.

Maybe he is the way he is because of what has happened to him in his life, thought Fritz. He knew the pitiful story by heart because he had lived through most of it. Engel had come home from the Great War to his native Munich to find Germany in turmoil. He couldn't find work and he and his wife, Greta, were starving. Greta was in contact with her sister Frieda who had emigrated to America early in the century and done well in their new country. Aunt Frieda had offered to sponsor Engel and Greta as new American immigrants. They had jumped at the chance. When they arrived at Ellis Island in March 1920, Greta was big with child. Fritz had been born shortly thereafter. Frieda's husband got Engle a job in the US Steel mill in Gary Indiana, and the family rented a house in Wheeler's Mill. The next year Greta presented Engel with another son. They named him Eberhard but called him Eb.

Fritz remembered the years before he turned eleven as the happy time. His mother had been a warm, affectionate and practical person who kept the family on track. Then in 1931 the family's luck turned bad. Engel was laid off from his job at US Steel because the demand for steel had plummeted due to the Great Depression. Try as he might, Engel couldn't find another job. Things became desperate. Greta found work scrubbing floors in a Gary office building at night. With the pittance she made, they were able to eat more or less regularly, though they ate a lot of beans. Fritz and Eb worked odd jobs after school to contribute to the family's income. Fritz's father started swilling beer all day and complaining about the raw deal he had received from the Jews at US Steel.

Four years ago, in June of 1933, Fritz's mother detected a lump in one of her breasts. She ignored it. The family didn't have money for doctors. By the time she finally sought treatment at a charity clinic, the cancer had metastasized and spread. The doctor who gave her the bad news was a Jew, Dr. Gold. He said there was nothing he could do, the cancer was too advanced. Greta died in October. Fritz's father spiraled down further. He said that the Jew at the clinic could have saved his wife if he had wanted to. Bitterness ruled his life. He hadn't even looked for work since, relying on county dole payments and the money the boys earned with after school jobs. Greta's sister and her husband had tried to reason with him but were angrily rebuffed. They didn't come around anymore.

Fritz felt frustrated with his father and a little angry at his brother. Why does Eb have to push back so hard against father? Why doesn't he do what I do and ignore the crazy things the old man says. Fritz was reminded again how different he was from his brother.

He was easy going and respectful and didn't like confrontations, while his sixteen-year-old brother was belligerent and hot-headed and thrived on conflict. Besides personalities, there were physical differences as well. Though a year younger than Fritz, Eb was the same height but outweighed him by twenty pounds. The shabby clothes he wore couldn't disguise that he had a very powerful body. Without saying another word, Eb brushed by Fritz and went into the tiny bedroom the two brothers shared.

"Friedrich, I have news, wonderful news" said his father from the couch. "I have received a letter from your Uncle Anton. He has sent us money for passage back to Germany. The Fuhrer has transformed it into a paradise. He has kicked the Jews out of power and given new life to the country. We will go back and be a part of the new Germany."

Fritz was shocked. He didn't know what to say. He opened his mouth to ask his father what had brought this up all of a sudden but was interrupted by his brother reentering the living room. He had a rucksack slung over his shoulder along with his heavy jacket. Fritz caught his brother's arm.

"Did you know he wants to move back to Germany?"

"Yeah, I know what he wants to do. That's what started the argument," said Eb looking over at his father in disgust. "Well, I'm not going to Germany. I'm going out on the road on my own. I have had about enough of his bullshit."

Engel Hofmann got shakily to his feet. He pointed his finger at Eb.

"Eberhard, You will do as I say. I am your father."

"Goodbye father. Bye Fritz, I will see you sometime," said Eb. He hugged Fritz briefly, put on his cap and strode out the door. The screen door banged against the frame after him. Fritz's father sat back down on the couch and hung his head.

"First my Greta and now Eberhard. Are you going to leave me too, Friedrich?" asked Engel in a whining voice.

Fritz didn't know what to think. His family was breaking up before his eyes. He was torn. What should he do? It would be the easiest thing in the world to quickly pack his things and run to catch up with his brother. A part of him wanted to do just that. He had no wish to leave America. Fritz was well aware that his father was using guilt and pity to get him to agree to accompany him to Germany. It was the usual way the old man manipulated him into doing what he wanted. But, in spite of all that and the wreck his father had become, Fritz still felt a measure of loyalty to him. He couldn't leave him all alone.

'Nein vater," said Fritz sadly.

CHAPTER THREE

HAINSTRASSE 5
LEIPZIG, DEUTSCHLAND 12 NOVEMBER, 1938

Leipzig was the largest city in the German province of Saxony. Located at the confluence of three navigable rivers, it had been an important trade center since the time of Charlemagne. The city was a picturesque place, known for its art, literature, friendly residents and bustling commerce.

All that changed when Adolf Hitler and the National Socialists came to power in 1933. Now the city was grim, full of strutting packs of brown clad SA stormtroopers and more sinister black-uniformed SS men. Flags and banners were everywhere, bearing the bent armed cross of the Nazi swastika symbol. It dominated every public space like a malevolent spider. The only music allowed was either martial or classical and had to have been composed by white Aryans. Laughter and light banter once heard in the cafes and streetcars had given way to rude, vulgar expressions of racial hate, looks of suspicion and stiff-armed Nazi salutes. People had to be very careful about what they said. Opinions that varied from official dogma were considered an insult to the Fuhrer.

It was now three days since the nationwide anti-Jewish riots of 9 November, the Night of Broken Glass, or Kristallnacht as the Germans were starting to call it. Organized gangs of Nazi toughs had descended on Jewish businesses, synagogues and even some well to do homes in an orgy of looting and arson. Those Jews who rushed to defend their property were beaten senseless by brown-shirted SD storm troopers and then arrested by the police. All of Leipzig's synagogues were looted and then gutted by fire. Priceless Torah scrolls, many quite ancient, were consumed in bonfires. The next day a huge collective fine was assessed on the Leipzig Jewish community. They were accused of causing the riots. It was all very lawful because Jews had no legal protection in Germany. The 1935 Nuremberg Racial Laws had seen to that.

In the Jewish quarter of Leipzig, the residents huddled inside their homes behind bolted doors and closed shutters. It was very dangerous to venture out. In a house on Hain Strasse, a Jewish fur dealer, Yakob Rosen, looked at his seventeen-year-old daughter Hannah. She was standing in front of him swiping tears away from her eyes with her fingers.

"But, I don't want to leave you and mama. Please don't make me."

"You must go, Hannah. It will be dangerous for you to stay. We don't know what the Nazis will do to our people next."

"Why can't you and mama come too?" pleaded Hanna, as more tears welled from the corners of her eyes. She was a lovely, young girl with jet black hair framing a perfect oval face and large dark eyes. Her skin was flawless and the color of fresh cream. Even weeping, with her eyes red and swollen, she was beautiful. Yakob Rosen couldn't bear the thought of what the brown shirts and SS thugs would do to her if she fell into their grasp.

"It is not possible my liebchen. I wish it was, but it is not."

Until yesterday, Rosen had owned a fine fur store on Katherinestrasse. Then the Nazis had seized his shop and bank accounts. Why they had bothered to seize the shop he didn't know. It was a gutted and looted building. During the recent riots, he had lost all his beautiful furs to Nazi thieves.

Rosen's family had been in Leipzig for centuries. His family's business had centered on furs for many generations. In 1933, when Hitler and the Nazis came to power, his brother Moshe, who had emigrated to America in the early twenties, had urged him to flee with his family to the United States. Like a fool, Yakob had continued to believe that the persecutions would lessen and things would get back to normal. Instead, they had become worse and the window of opportunity to get out of Germany had slammed shut. It was virtually impossible now for a Jew to get out of the country legally. Only the ones who were very wealthy could afford the huge bribes that would have to be paid to Nazi officials for exit permits.

Rosen wasn't a wealthy man. He had been well off but not wealthy. He had, however, a little hoard of gold, enough to pay a smuggler to get his only child out of the prison that was the new Germany. It would involve a perilous journey across the country hidden in the back of a cargo truck. Once across the Belgian border though, it was on to the United States and freedom. His beloved daughter had to leave tonight.

Just after full sundown, a large goods truck with a canvas cover over the bed stopped on the street in front of the Rosen home and a man appeared at their door. He was a stocky, rough-looking man in dirty workman's clothes. He wore a cloth cap that he had pulled down to obscure the upper part of his face.

"We must hurry before an SD patrol comes by," said the truck driver to Yakob Rosen.

Hannah watched her father hand the man a blue velvet sack, with the drawstring at the top pulled tight. The man hefted the sack measuring its weight, then opened the top and looked inside. Satisfied, he put the bag into his jacket pocket.

"Get the girl, one suitcase only. We must hurry."

Hannah hugged her parents one last time and followed the smuggler outside. She looked back and saw Yakob and Anna standing in the darkened doorway. She could barely make out the grief written on their faces. The man boosted Hannah into the bed of the truck. He shone a small electric torch at the cargo. The bed was loaded with large wooden crates.

The smuggler jumped up after her and muscled one of the crates to the side, revealing a narrow space about one and a half meters square. There was a dirty blanket, water bottle and a bucket inside the cramped space.

"Get in there and be quiet. No sound, especially when the truck is stopped, if you don't want us both to be caught by the Gestapo. If you have to relieve yourself, use the bucket, but only when the truck is moving," said the man.

Hannah crawled into the space and the crate was replaced behind her. The pitch darkness was frightening. After a few moments, she heard the whine of the vehicle starting up and felt it move. Hannah sat on the blanket with her back against the wooden side of a crate, bracing herself against the swaying motion of the truck with her legs curled under her. When the truck first started out, she heard the muffled sounds of the city, automobile traffic and, once, the clanging bells of a fire engine. Gradually the sounds diminished and there was only the steady roar of the truck's engine and the rushing of its tires on the pavement.

Sitting in her dark little hideout, Hannah had ample time to reflect on the life she was leaving. She was the only child of well-to-do parents. As a consequence, she had grown up pampered and cosseted by her parents, especially her father. She remembered frilly dresses and mounds of presents on her birthdays. Her parents did not practice Judaism and considered themselves assimilated Jews. This caused many of the orthodox and conservative Jewish families to shun them socially. The Rosens were forced to live in the Jewish quarter of the city. Although tolerance of Jews by the German public had increased since the turn of the century, that tolerance didn't extend to having a Jew live next door.

Living in the Jewish quarter, but being shunned by many of their neighbors resulted in Hannah having a wider range of friends than most Jewish girls. She had many gentile friends. Because she was precocious and beautiful as a child, she was a popular playmate and was invited to all the parties.

Hannah remembered the feeling of security she had when she was little. When there was a storm or she had a nightmare and was frightened, she would creep to her parents' bedroom and her father would lift her onto the bed with his strong arms and nestle her between him and her mother. She would burrow under the covers and revel in the feeling of absolute safety.

Everything changed when the Nazis came to power. Yakob Rosen's shop had its windows defaced with painted Stars of David and the word, JUDEN because Hitler had declared a boycott of Jewish businesses. Jews began to be beaten and humiliated on the streets by brown-shirted SA stormtroopers and it became very dangerous to travel anywhere in the city. The Jewish residents spent most of their time behind bolted doors.

In the spring of 1933, when Hannah was eleven, she went to school one day as usual. Before class started, the teacher rose before the students and read a proclamation from the Fuhrer. Henceforth, all Jewish children would be forbidden to attend public schools. The teacher then shouted, JUDEN RAUS!, Jews out! Hannah's classmates, many of whom she had known and played with since age six started to chant, JUDEN RAUS!, JUDEN RAUS!, JUDEN RAUS! Hannah fled the school and ran home to her family. Her father held her in his arms as she shed hot tears of shame. She continued her schooling in the nearby home of a professor who had been ejected from Leipzig University because he was a Jew. Remembering all this caused Hannah's already crushed spirit to descend even further and she began to cry, careful to emit no sound.

Several times the truck stopped and Hannah heard conversations between the truck driver and, she presumed, police at checkpoints. Each time she would sit, her heart in her throat, until the truck started moving again.

After about twelve hours of traveling, the truck came to another stop and she heard muffled voices outside. Hannah put her ear to a crate to try to make out what they were saying but couldn't. Then the voices got louder and were coming from the rear of the truck. Hannah could understand the conversation now.

"What are you carrying?" said one voice.

"Machine tools, just like it says on the export papers in your hand," said a voice Hannah recognized as the truck driver.

"Don't get smart with me, or I'll find some excuse to deny your exit from the Fatherland."

"I'm not getting smart, I just have a long way to go and I'm tired," said the driver.

"Bring out a couple of crates and open them."

Hannah was terrified. She was shaking violently. Was she about to be discovered? She put her hands over her mouth to muffle any sound if she involuntarily cried out. The driver spoke up; his voice sounded exasperated.

"Each of those crates weighs several hundred kilos. I don't have time for this. I apologize for my remark. I will give you ten marks if you will just let me go on my way."

"Alright, give me the money, but if you ever backtalk me again I will make you unload your truck. Is that clear?"

"Ja, again I apologize."

"Heil Hitler."

"Heil Hitler."

Hannah heard the sound of the cab door slamming. The truck started up again only to stop again a minute later. There was another illegible conversation outside the truck and then it started to move again. About five minutes after that, the truck slowed to a stop again. She heard the door to the cab open and close and after a minute, the crate locking her in was moved aside. Fresh air flowed in and Hannah was blinded by bright sunlight. She put her hand in front of her eyes to shield them. The smuggler was standing beside the moved crate.

"It's alright now. We are in Belgium. You can come out now and ride in the cab of the truck. My destination is Antwerp but I will let you off at the American Embassy in Brussels."

Hannah gratefully crawled out rubbing her bruised backside. After the hard bed of the truck, the padded seat of the cab felt unbelievably luxurious. The truck driver handed her some bread and cheese, which she devoured hungrily after her twelve hour fast. The smuggler became talkative and spoke to her in a friendly voice for a time. He then took his right hand and put it on Hannah's thigh. She moved his hand away, but he put it right back. She began to cry and the truck driver cursed and took his hand away for good. He was silent after that.

Since the age of twelve when she had started the transition from a girl into a woman, Hannah knew that men of all ages treated her differently than other girls her age. They would smile and lift her chin and comment on her beauty. But she didn't like the look in their eyes, behind the mask of cordiality. As she grew, Hannah began to detest the attention she received from men. She came to look upon her beauty as a curse rather than an asset.

She was trembling and feeling lonely when at about two in the afternoon, she walked into the American Embassy in Brussels carrying her one suitcase. She was greeted by a slim young man in an ill-fitting suit, who addressed her in French. Hannah didn't speak French and replied in German. The young man handed her off to a woman seated at a desk behind the counter, who spoke German.

Hannah showed the woman her German passport with its big red "J" stamped on the cover and a letter from her Uncle Moshe in America offering to sponsor her in the United States. The woman, who identified herself as Miss Kunsler, leafed through the pages of Hannah's passport.

"Fraulein Rosen. You have no exit stamps from Germany and no entry visa for Belgium. You entered this country illegally. These are crimes in both Germany and Belgium. These issues, as well as the restrictions enacted in the U. S. Immigration Act of 1924, disqualify you from receiving a visa for entry into the United States."

Hannah was vaguely aware of a well-dressed older man who had come to stand behind Miss Kunsler but took no notice of him. What would happen to her now? Would she be turned over to the Nazis? She was a frightened, exhausted teenager who faced certain arrest by the Gestapo if she was returned to Germany. As her spirits sunk to a new low, she hung her head and thought about her bleak future. Huge tears rolled down her cheeks and off the end of her nose. She had never felt so alone.

The man standing behind Miss Kunsler looked at the weeping young girl. His name was William Steiner. He was a Wall Street lawyer by trade and a special political friend of President Roosevelt. He was wealthy, sophisticated, world-wise and a ruthless opponent in a courtroom. But beneath this cosmopolitan veneer he was a good man with a kind heart. The weeping young girl reminded him of his daughter Madeline.

In 1919, during the Spanish flu pandemic, he had held his three-year-old daughter, Maddie, in his arms as she died burning with fever and gasping for breath. He cradled her small limp body for hours afterward as an unbelievable sadness consumed him. Since then, there was a hole in his heart that would never heal. Maddie had been a beautiful child with dark hair and huge brown eyes. This young girl standing in front of him was the image of what he imagined his Maddie would now look like if she had lived. His heart went out to the weeping girl. She was so sad and lonely looking.

Steiner's success in the business world was due to his ability to quickly size up a situation and come to a quick decision. Once a decision was made, he was tenacious in the defense of his position. Looking at the pitiful young girl, he decided that he was going to help her. The U. S. Congress had shut off immigration to the United States in 1924, but he failed to see how the nation would be harmed by letting this child escape the Nazis and enter America. If he had to, he would move heaven and earth to get her granted resident status in the United States. He would do it for Maddie. Steiner cleared his throat and Miss Kunsler turned around and looked at him.

"Mr. Ambassador, I didn't know you were there," said the woman deferentially.

"I will handle this one, Miss Kunsler," said Steiner. He turned to Hannah, "Fraulein, please follow me to my office upstairs." His German was very good.

The Ambassador strode up the stairs to his private office with Hannah meekly following behind. He sat her down in a chair across from his desk, took his seat behind the desk and began to question her. The questions seemed endless. After a half hour of asking her things and writing them down in a small book, Steiner nodded, excused himself and left the room.

He returned a few minutes later with a tall regal looking woman. The ambassador introduced her as his wife, Geraldine Steiner. She was very elegantly dressed for so early in the day, wearing a long gown of green satin material. She wasn't beautiful but wasn't plain either. Her hair and makeup were perfectly done. When she spoke to Hannah there was very little warmth in her voice.

"My husband tells me that you are to be staying with us until he sorts out your situation. Come with me and I will show you to your room."

Mrs. Steiner abruptly turned and the Ambassador indicated with a gesture that Hannah was to follow her. She was led down an elegant hallway to a bedroom. It was large with tall windows looking out on the city. The furniture was of light-colored wood, intricately carved.

"I hope you will be comfortable here," said Mrs. Steiner. Her German was stilted like she had learned it in school but rarely conversed in it.

"Oh yes, danke. It is very nice."

"I should think so. This must be heaven for a penniless Jew just off the streets." Her voice turned very cold. "My husband is something of a soft touch. He is too gullible for his own good."

Later that evening the Ambassador came to Hannah's room. With sadness in his eyes, he explained about his wife.

"You must excuse the way my wife spoke to you. The death of our young daughter many years ago had a profound effect on her. It has made her bitter. She used to be such a happy person."

Hannah stayed in the embassy for almost two months while Ambassador Steiner used his influence with the American immigration authorities. He would have a kind word for her every day. Mrs. Steiner, however, avoided her like the plague. Hannah took her meals in her room and most days just sat and stared out the window worrying about her parents.

She felt very lonely and homesick and cried herself to sleep at night.

In early February 1939, the Ambassador summoned Hannah and told her that everything was arranged. She could start her journey to America. He took her to Antwerp in the embassy limousine. At the gangway of the ferry boat to England, Steiner turned to Hannah. She could see tears in his eyes.

"Have a wonderful new life in America," he said and smiled.

Hannah was so grateful to him that she broke protocol and flew into his arms, kissing him on the cheek and expressing her thanks. As the ferry boat sailed out into the channel, Hannah could see the tall dignified man waving from the dock.

Upon arrival in England, Hannah booked passage to America on the Cunard White Star line's HMS Britannic, using almost all the money her Papa had given her when she left Germany. She could only afford a berth in third class. She stayed in a cheap Liverpool hotel, skipping many meals until the ship departed.

She sailed from Liverpool on a cold frosty morning in March 1939. It was a rough, stormy crossing. Hannah slept in a room that held six bunks, but she had the room all to herself. She took her meals in a large dining room with metal tables bolted to the floor. There were only four other women in the room. Hannah tried to strike up a conversation but discovered that the other women spoke only French. Apart from some of the crew flirting with her, it was a lonely crossing. Because of the rough seas, she was violently ill for three days. Then her body adjusted to the motion and she was fine. The Britannic docked in New York harbor in the middle of the night.

Early the next morning she boarded an open boat that took her to Ellis Island for processing of her immigration papers. She walked through huge rooms built to accommodate thousands of people, but which were now empty. Her footsteps echoed in the cavernous buildings.

Hannah was examined by a doctor who poked and prodded her and asked about childhood diseases. He signed her exam form after concluding she was in good health. Next, she was directed to a lectern with a man in a green uniform standing behind it. He was tall, wore a mustache and spoke to her in German with an Alsatian accent. He stamped her entry form with a rubber stamp and handed it to her.

"Fraulein Rosen, welcome to the United States of America," he said with a smile.

It was raining when Hannah Rosen stepped off the boat from Ellis Island and into New York City. She had no raincoat or umbrella and as a result, she was soaked to the skin. She was exhausted from worry about her parents and three months of waiting and traveling. She hadn't slept well on the ship. Her life seemed to be a disorganized mess. The lack of order bothered her.

She set her lone suitcase down on the wet pavement and looked for her Uncle Moshe. The area where she was seemed to be a park. She was eighteen now and in spite of her hair being plastered to her head and her dress wet and sagging, several male passers-by gave her smiles and tried to attract her eye. She ignored them. She spoke no English, so the signs posted everywhere made no sense to her.

She heard a shout and looked to her left. She caught sight of Uncle Moshe. She recognized him from a photograph her father had shown her. He and Aunt Rachel were hurrying toward her sheltering under one umbrella. They were both short and stout and the dance they performed under the umbrella to escape the rain was the first amusing thing Hannah had seen in a long time. Her face lit up with a smile, and when Hannah Rosen smiled every male within a block perked up.

Her aunt and uncle embraced her in turn. Uncle Moshe brought her into the shelter of the umbrella. Its circumference wasn't large enough, however, to keep the rain from striking Hannah's shoulders and running down her back.

"We would have been here much sooner but your aunt went off without the subway fares," said Moshe in German.

"Now Moshe, why is it my fault? You could have remembered to pick up the nickels as well as I," replied Aunt Rachel, with a bit of irritation in her voice.

"You always get the subway fares. I must keep my mind on important things," said Moshe, getting annoyed.

"So now I am only fit to get subway fares. My brain is not fit for important things?" said Aunt Rachel, her voice rising.

"I didn't say that. Don't get emotional."

"Emotional? Emotional! I will show you emotional when we get home."

Hannah was dumbfounded. She was huddled under an umbrella in the rain with two arguing people. This was her first inkling that the relationship between her aunt and uncle had no middle ground. Either they were going at it like two gamecocks or they were cloyingly sweet to each other.

Finally, it dawned on Moshe and Rachel what they were doing. "What are we standing here for? Come, let us go to your new home," said Hannah's uncle and the three began to walk toward the nearest subway station. Uncle Moshe gallantly abandoned the umbrella to the two women. He turned up the collar of his suit and braved the rain.

They rode the subway from Bowling Green to the 168th Street station. When she emerged from the underground station to street level, Hannah saw a different world. The rain had stopped, and the air was crystal clear and fresh. The street was lined with small shops. Each had a Jewish name proudly displayed on the storefront. Some of the signs were in Yiddish, which she could read. There was an open-air produce market in progress. Pushcart vendors haggled with housewives over tomatoes and beans. For the first time since leaving her parents in Germany, Hannah relaxed. She was back among her own people.

Uncle Moshe led the way up the steps of the building where the Rosens had their apartment. It was on the second floor. The apartment contained a living room, bathroom, kitchen, and two small bedrooms, one of which was to be Hannah's. Aunt Rachel had spruced up her new bedroom with flowers to welcome her. There was a narrow bed, a small writing table with a wooden chair and a four drawer dresser. A window on the far wall let out onto a fire escape. When Hannah saw the room she cried with happiness and hugged Aunt Rachel, who began to blubber herself.

"Hannah, it is so very good to have you here with us. Think of this as your home for as long as you want to stay. Ach," Rachel wiped away the tears from her face. "Dinner will be ready in an hour. Why don't you rest for a while?"

Alone in the room, Hannah stripped off her wet dress and hung it on the window sill to dry. She put on her one change of clothes from the suitcase and reclined on the bed. She began to weep. She wept from missing her mama and papa and ached to see them again. She wept for her life in Germany before the Nazis. She wept because the loneliness lay on her soul like a stone. Then, gradually, her tears subsided, and she sat up and dried her eyes. A look of deep determination came on her face. You must stop acting like a helpless child and start behaving like a grownup, she thought. This is no time for girlish weakness. Mama and Papa sacrificed themselves to get you this far. You will not let them down. I don't care what you have to do, you will succeed in this new place and find some way to save them.

The next day Aunt Rachel took Hannah shopping, after concluding that the two outfits she had brought from Germany were not enough. Midmorning found them in a southbound subway car on the way to Herald Square and Macy's department store. The car was crowded as usual and the two women had to stand in the aisle holding on to leather straps suspended from the ceiling. With the swaying of the car, Hannah found herself inadvertently bumping into the person standing behind her. Each time it would happen she would cringe away. Having so many people so close to her, jabbering away in a language she didn't understand, made her very uncomfortable. She was relieved when the train pulled into the 34th Street station and she could get off. On the station platform, she was almost knocked down by a bearded man running to catch the departing train. Aunt Rachel firmly took her hand and led Hannah through the crowded station and up the stairs to street level.

When she emerged into the daylight, the scene she encountered frightened her more than the subway. Tall buildings towered over her and busses and taxicabs crept by on the street to the accompaniment of loud honking horns. But it was the sidewalks, packed with a solid mass of humanity that scared her the most. Like milling ants, people were walking in both directions adroitly dodging each other. The totality of the scene was so alien to Hannah that it was as if a giant hand had plucked her out of a safe existence and set her down on a chaotic otherworld planet. She stopped dead in her tracks, dragging Aunt Rachel to a stop beside her. The foot traffic flowed around them like water around a boulder in a stream. Aunt Rachel saw the fear on Hannah's face and smiled.

"Do not be frightened; you are in no danger. Just hold on to the back of my collar and don't let go."

Off they went with Hannah's aunt expertly weaving through the crowds and Hannah bringing up the rear with a death grip on her collar. A few blocks later they entered the huge Macy's department store. It was much less crowded inside and Hannah felt better.

In the ladies wear department, Rachel combed through the sale racks for inexpensive, practical clothing. Every so often she would pull a garment from the rack and hold it up in front of Hannah. About the fifth time she did this, a middle-aged blonde woman struck up a conversation with Rachel. Hannah couldn't understand what they were saying but she surmised that the woman was giving Aunt Rachel advice about the suitability of the clothing. This struck Hannah as outrageous. In Germany, one didn't approach and speak to a stranger without a good reason.

Safely back in her room that afternoon, Hannah reflected on her outing. Tears came to her eyes. She knew she had resolved not to cry anymore like a child, but she couldn't help it. She didn't think she was going to like it here in New York. She fervently wished that the Nazis would be kicked out of power and she could go home.

CHAPTER FOUR

BRAVES FIELD
COMMONWEALTH AND BABCOCK STREETS
BOSTON, MASSACHUSETTS
SEPTEMBER 25, 1941

Braves Field was the home of the Boston Braves of the National Baseball League. Located only a mile west of Fenway Park where the Red Sox of the American League played, it was the National League's premier pitcher's ballpark. Almost all the bleachers were located in foul territory and the tall fence in center field was five hundred feet from home plate. These factors combined to make a home run in Braves Field a very rare event.

Angelo Scatano was a sportswriter for the New York Herald Tribune. His view from the press box high above home plate was splendid. The sun was bright, the stands were full of fans milling about and banners were flapping in the breeze as he took in the unique American spectacle of a major league baseball game. The contest was between the Boston Braves and the Brooklyn Dodgers. The sportswriter sat behind a big black Underwood typewriter with a sheet of foolscap paper all spooled up and ready. His hat was pushed to the back of his head and his suit jacket was draped over the back of his chair. Of middle age, he was a short, square bodied man with a swarthy complexion inherited from his southern Italian forebears, who habitually had a cigar clenched in a corner of his wide mouth. His last name wasn't really

Scatano. It was actually Sciacchitano, but when his father was being processed through Ellis island in 1900, the Immigration clerk was tired and didn't feel like writing out all those letters, so he had shortened the name. The family had been Scatano ever since.

Angelo was very perturbed, bordering on being angry. It was the beginning of the eighth inning of the game and the Dodgers were ahead five to zip. And to make matters worse, if Brooklyn won this game, they would clinch the National League pennant. He detested the Dodgers team, but his hatred for the Brooklyn manager, Leo Durocher, was passionate. The manager and the sportswriter had been feuding for over a year.

It had all started in August of 1940. Scatano had been covering the Dodgers and traveling with them for some time with no incidents. Then one day Durocher pulled his pitcher, Luke Hamlin, in the seventh inning of a tie game against the Cardinals. St. Louis rallied off his successor and won the game. Angelo had written what he thought was an amusing article criticizing Durocher's decision and inferring that the manager didn't know what he was doing.

A couple of days later Scatano went to Toots Shor's nightclub, on West 51st Street which served as a hangout for New York sportswriters. He was sitting with some of his colleagues enjoying a drink when Leo Durocher approached his table. The Brooklyn manager was wearing a flashy suit and had a good looking woman on his arm.

"Listen you greasy little wop," said Durocher. "What do you know 'bout baseball? I've forgotten more about the game than you'll ever know. The next time you write one a yer' cutesy stories 'bout me, I'll kick yer' ass."

Angelo was shocked and his face reddened. "I got a right to write what I want," he replied.

"Right to right, huh. What gibberish is that?" said Durocher and started to take off his coat. "Come on you little prick. Let's go outside and settle this."

Despite Scatano being beefier than Leo, he backed down. Angelo remained seated and stared at his drink until Durocher swaggered away. Angelo felt the eyes of all the people in the barroom on him and imagined their pitiful, disdainful looks. The Brooklyn manager had brought out into the open the sportswriter's darkest secret. Since he had been a kid, Angelo had been a coward, afraid to fight with his fists. For exposing his shameful secret, Scatano would never forgive Durocher. Mild disdain turned to outright hatred. He decided to get even using the only way open for him, with his pen. He started slanting his favorable stories toward the New York Giants, the other New York National League team and penning scathing criticisms of Durocher's handling of the Dodgers. At the same time, he stayed away from bars frequented by the Brooklyn manager.

The Trib's sports editor, Stan Woodward, was at first irked at Scatano for his hit pieces against Brooklyn. Then he noticed that the people who read his sports pages seemed to love them. There was nothing better than a vendetta full of back and forth rancor to sell newspapers, so the feud was allowed to continue.

Angelo watched Cookie Lavagetto walk to the plate to start the eighth inning. Tom Early was pitching for the Braves. Cookie worked him for a walk. Peewee Reese was up next. The Dodger shortstop slammed a three-one pitch into right field for a single. Lavagetto ended up on third base. Mickey Owen then hit into a double play, but Cookie scored on the play, causing Scatano to groan.

Damn, he thought, the Dodgers got another run. They are ahead now by six runs. It will take a miracle for the Braves to come back. What's this? Durocher just stomped onto the field to argue with the umpire who had made the call of the second out at first base. Look at him, the little asshole is right up in the umpire's face arguing. Angelo shook his head as the stadium erupted in boos from frustrated Boston fans. Scatano wanted to yell, too, but it would be a violation of reporter decorum so he remained silent. After two or three minutes Durocher ambled back to the dugout with a scowl on his face and the game resumed.

Whit Wyatt, the Dodgers pitcher, was next up to hit. Angelo watched him walk to the plate. He was Brooklyn's ace pitcher this year, winning twenty-one games so far. Tall and lanky, he was mild-mannered off the field, but a fierce competitor when pitching.

During the beanball war with the Cardinals earlier in the season, Angelo remembered that Wyatt had cheerfully bounced balls off Cardinal batters' heads right and left. To top it off, that asshole Durocher gave Whit a cash bonus each time he beaned someone. But Wyatt wasn't very good with the bat and went quietly, grounding out to third base.

During the last two innings of the game, Angelo watched in mounting frustration as the tall Dodgers right-hander mowed down the Braves batters one by one. He had pitched masterfully throughout the game, only giving up five hits and no runs. Finally, it was down to the last Braves out. Max West strode to the plate and set himself against Wyatt. On a 2-1 pitch, he hit a weak ground ball to Cookie Lavagetto at third base. Cookie fielded the ball and gunned it to Dolph Camilli at first base for the final out, and the Brooklyn Dodgers were the 1941 winners of the National League pennant.

Whit Wyatt and Mickey Owen, the catcher, met between home and the pitcher's mound and gave each other a bear hug. All the rest of the Dodgers players converged on them and formed a big blue and white ball on the grass. All, except for Leo Durocher. Angelo saw the cocky bastard stand alone in front of the Dodgers' dugout with his hands on his hips and chin high, savoring the moment. He was acting like he was the king of the world. At that moment, watching his enemy's triumph, Scatano's hate for Durocher was a white-hot thing.

There was quiet in the stadium as the Boston fans turned and made their way out of the stadium, disdainful of their Braves. They had failed to stop the Dodgers from clinching the pennant in their own home ballpark. They were losers. Americans hated losers.

Angelo threw his cigar to the concrete floor angrily. After retrieving his coat, he turned his back on the celebration on the field and made his way toward the exit. He shuffled instead of walked, with his head down. The sportswriter was mulling over in his mind how he was going to cover Brooklyn's triumph. Maybe I'll write that the Dodgers winning of the pennant was just dumb luck, and not from any prowess on their part or of their manager, Mister Leo Fucking Durocher, thought Angelo. I'll say they don't have a snowball's chance in hell against "Joltin' Joe DiMaggio," and the rest of the mighty Yankees in the World Series.

CHAPTER FIVE

BERLIN DEUTSCHLAND 22 JUNI, 1942

Berlin was the capital of a nation at war, but one would be hard-pressed to find any outward sign that this was so. Unlike London, Berlin's public buildings weren't protected by walls of sandbags. At night the street lights shone brightly and the headlights of the automobiles weren't shrouded. The population of carefully certified Aryans didn't carry gas mask canisters with them on the streetcars and in the cafes. Reichsmarschall Goering had promised that his mighty Luftwaffe would protect the city from enemy bombs, and the people believed him. Sure, there had been some minor nocturnal British air raids early in the war, but these were mere pinpricks.

The only apparent difference in the city from peacetime was the presence of so many military uniforms on Berlin's streets. And, like in every German city, but especially here, all public buildings and most of the private ones were festooned with the symbols of the National Socialists.

The people of Berlin were pleased and proud. The Third Reich was at the zenith of its power. Its armies had conquered almost all of Europe and it appeared that the mighty Wehrmacht was unstoppable. The war had brought with it unbelievable prosperity. Luxuries available only to the rich before the conflict were flowing in from captured lands and were available at bargain prices, caviar and vodka from Russia, fresh fish from Norway, high-quality meats from Poland and the Ukraine and fine wines and perfumes from France. Berliners were happy and satisfied and they knew who they had to thank for their good fortune, Adolf Hitler. Whenever the Fuhrer made a public appearance, the people of Berlin would express their gratitude with spontaneous stiff-armed Nazi salutes and shouts of HEIL HITLER.

In the Tiergarten district, just south of central Berlin, there was a huge ugly complex of buildings called the Bendleblock. Built of light grey stone in the neoclassical style, it was the headquarters of the OKH, the High Command of the German military. The main entrance bustled with high ranking Wehrmacht officers and their aides, coming and going in long, black Mercedes and Maybach limousines. Rigidly erect sentries in dress uniforms flanked the wide entrance. The lawns and shrubs were perfectly maintained by work details of young enlisted men. The grounds even included a stable and thoroughbred horses so senior officers could ride for pleasure along the forested paths of the nearby Tiergarten.

Inside the complex, the German general staff formulated plans for the conduct of the war. Since 1939 it had become a frustrating exercise. Adolf Hitler thought he was a better general than his most senior professional soldiers and would make decisions according to his whims and the fantasy world he had constructed in his mind.

In the southern section of the complex, on the top floor and down a dark hallway, there was a glass-paneled door. Written in gold on the glass was one word: ABWEHR. Inside the door sat a female receptionist in a naval uniform. Flanking her were two alert Naval petty officers holding MP38 machine pistols up and ready for action. If a visitor was fortunate enough to make it past the receptionist, he or she would see several hallways branching off the reception area. In rooms off these hallways, dozens of men and women in uniform worked diligently.

Some were analyzing information sent from spies around the world. Some were forging foreign documents. Still others were updating maps with the latest enemy dispositions to be sent to the front. There was a tailor shop where clothing with foreign labels was fashioned. A locked steel door led to an armory stocked with weapons and ammunition. There was a radio room, manned round the clock, where coded messages from around the globe were relayed from the big listening station in Hamburg. The purpose of all this was to support global spy operations. The Abwehr was a spy agency, the Military Intelligence arm of the Third Reich.

At the end of the center hallway was another steel door, guarded by two more armed Naval ratings. Inside, a neat young man in the uniform of a Hauptmann in the Wehrmacht sat at a desk in a spacious office. He was secretary and aide to the head of the agency. Behind him was another door. It was of ordinary varnished wood and led to the private office of the Director of the Abwehr, Admiral Wilhelm Canaris.

The Admiral was a small man in physical size. He was in his mid-fifties with becoming gray hair and a face that looked younger than it should at his age. In his younger years, women had found him quite handsome and dashing. In his manner of dress, he favored neat single-breasted suits and muted ties. He was never seen out of doors without his Homburg hat, grey calfskin gloves and silver-handled walking stick. If one were to observe him out walking his constant companions, two wire-haired Dachshunds named Sabine and Sepple he would appear to be perhaps a low-level diplomat or a university professor. However, in this case, looks would be very deceiving.

Canaris was a man of high intellect. He spoke and wrote five languages and could converse intelligently on hundreds of subjects. But his bright mind was tempered with just the right amount of deviousness and cunning that allowed him to run rings around the world's intelligence agencies and his rivals within the Nazi government. He had enjoyed a full career within the Kriegsmarine and still held the rank of Admiral, but his true talents lay in the shadowy world of espionage.

Besides his intellect, Canaris had another enormous advantage. Since his appointment as Director of the Abwehr in 1935, he had the ear of Adolf Hitler. The official German civilian foreign intelligence agency was the AUSTLAND-SD, part of the huge Security Service bureaucracy. This agency had shown itself so full of incompetence and cronyism that the Fuhrer distrusted it and relied almost exclusively on the Abwehr for foreign intelligence.

This trusting relationship with the Fuhrer attracted enemies. Power-hungry Heinrich Himmler, Chief of the SS, and up until recently his deputy Reinhard Heydrich, wanted control of the Abwehr. They were eagerly waiting for a stumble by Canaris that they could use to undermine the agency in Hitler's eyes. Also, they were constantly trying to plant spies there. So far, Canaris had remained one step ahead of them.

Himmler and Heydrich would have been thrilled to discover that Wilhelm Canaris was playing a double game. He harbored a deep, dark secret that, were it to be exposed, would earn him a one way trip to a basement liquidation cell. He was no longer a supporter of Hitler and his homicidal henchmen. In fact, he was a bitter foe, albeit a clandestine one.

How he had come to hold such dangerous views had to do mostly with the Fuhrer's treatment of the Jews, gypsies, and mentally ill people.

When Hitler had come to power in 1933, the anti-communist Canaris was an enthusiastic supporter. The Admiral saw the charismatic Hitler as a bulwark against the Bolsheviks. Then came the government-orchestrated hate campaigns against the Jews and gypsies. Canaris thought the racial theories of the Fuhrer were idiotic and he recoiled in disgust at the treatment of the innocent Jews and other minorities of Germany.

The Admiral began to get disquieting reports about something called the T-4 Euthanasia Program. Old people, cripples, the insane and even mildly retarded children were being murdered in special centers all over Germany. He was shocked. Then came the 1935 anti-Semitic Nuremberg Laws. The instituting of these outrageous laws and the 1938 Crystal Night riots that came three years later were making Canaris a disillusioned man.

As news of each new Nazi outrage crossed the Admiral's desk, his conviction grew that his support for Hitler had been a terrible mistake. At heart an honorable man, he felt that the things the Nazis were doing were not just wrong but ghastly. But he did nothing. He had sworn an oath of absolute fealty to Adolf Hitler. To break this oath would compromise his personal integrity and brand him as dishonorable. Canaris seriously considered resigning his position as head of the Abwehr.

In 1939, after the invasion of Poland, reports began filtering in from Abwehr agents of what German forces were up to in the conquered country. The SS had formed special killing groups called Einsatzgruppen, or Special Action Groups. All over western Poland these groups were murdering Jews and other Poles in large numbers and burying them in pits. The reports seemed too fantastic to be believed, so the Admiral decided to personally investigate. He got on a train headed east. In Bedzin, Poland, Canaris witnessed the SS round up two hundred Jews, including women and children, and herd them into the village synagogue. The building was then set on fire and the Jews inside roasted alive. Those that tried to escape the flames through the windows were shot down by the SS. As Admiral Wilhelm Canaris stood watching that synagogue burn, his outlook was forever changed. All loyalty to Hitler and the Nazis left him. He came to the opinion that the Fuhrer was an insane monster and was leading Germany toward disaster.

But what to do about it? Canaris could take the safe path by keeping his head down, continue as before and ignore what he had come to regard as barbarism. But his personal integrity precluded following this path. The question of the oath he had sworn to the Fuhrer became moot. An oath to a madman who was destroying Germany wasn't valid.

Taking enormous risks, the Admiral began to subtly work behind the scenes to thwart the aims of the Nazis. In order to do this, he had to remain in his position. To keep his job he had to maintain the output from the Abwehr of very high-quality intelligence.

In his office, which was Spartan, Canaris leaned back in his chair. He took off his pince-nez glasses with one hand and rubbed the bridge of his nose with the other. There were problems in all the Abwehr departments. Russia was a particular thorn in his side. But a special problem in 1-H-West now occupied his mind. This department was engaged in intelligence gathering in Great Britain and the United States. Specifically, the Admiral was worried about his espionage network in the United States of America.

One of the courier agents for the network was under surveillance by the American FBI. These courier agents were vital to the operation of the network. They collected the information that his agents in place obtained and conveyed it to the base. The courier agents had to be people who had a legitimate reason to travel around the country from city to city.

The Abwehr's courier agents in America were Anton Dietrich and a renegade Irishman named Michael Flynn. Dietrich was a traveling salesman for a woman's cosmetics firm in New York City and was a naturalized American citizen. Flynn was an airline pilot based in New

York and a citizen of Ireland.

Anton Dietrich had made an incredibly foolish mistake. On the evening of 11 December, the day the United States declared war on Germany, he had gotten drunk in a bar in New York. Some American servicemen near him were bragging that they were going to poke Adolf Hitler in the anus or some other such nonsense. Due to the alcohol, Anton had lost his temper and loudly voiced the opinion that Germany was going to win the war. The bar went deathly quiet. Suddenly sober, Anton realized his mistake and left immediately. He must have been followed though, because he had sent a detailed letter to the other courier agent reporting what he had done and that he was being shadowed everywhere he went. He dare not go anywhere near any of the Agents' dead drops or the base. It was bad but not disastrous. Canaris knew that Dietrich was only suspected of un-American sentiments, and not of being a German spy. He knew this because he had an agent in the New York office of the FBI.

Obviously, Dietrich would have to be replaced. They dare not use the traveling salesman ruse again. It was too risky. If or when the Americas got serious about counterintelligence, traveling salesmen in their country would be obvious targets of scrutiny. The Abwehr would have to think of something else, and soon. The network was compartmentalized, so Canaris had no fear for the Spaniard Carlos Breyer, a vital agent to the operation. He had diplomatic immunity. The agents in place were also safe. They were above suspicion. All of them were Jews.

When Canaris took over the Abwehr in 1935, he was shocked at how amateurish the German espionage activities were in the United States. The operation was run out of the German embassy and was headed by a man named Frederick Duquesne. The agents were all German immigrants or the children of immigrants. Most of the spies were also members of the German American Bund and other subversive far-right organizations. But, the Admiral discovered that the operation didn't need to be professional. This was because the United States had no counterintelligence apparatus at all! An American Secretary of State, Henry Stimson had declared in 1929, "Gentlemen don't read others mail." With this attitude prevailing, the Americans were terribly vulnerable and didn't know it. Canaris was astounded at how naïve they were. He knew, however, that should war ever come between the Americans and the Germans, this situation wouldn't last long.

In 1940, when it became a real possibility that the two countries might go to war in the following years, Canaris quietly began to build another network. This one was to be very professional and deep undercover. The existing network would be left in place as juicy plums to be later picked by the American FBI, which happened the next year.

The Admiral decided to use a unique pool of people for his agents, refugee Jews. When the Nazi regime began its persecution of Jewish people, many had fled the country. Because the Nazis made it hard to leave, and expensive, many Jews fled but left close family members behind. These Jews, now living in the United States, were an untapped pool of potential agents if they could be made to cooperate.

The Admiral sent agents all over Germany looking for a remote location where a hundred people could be housed discreetly for a long period. From these agents' reports, Canaris selected an unoccupied, isolated Jagdschloss, or hunting lodge, deep in the forest near the small town of Suderburg, about 100km south of Hamburg. The building was old and in disrepair. Workmen descended on the place, converting rooms into barracks and installing foodservice equipment. A generator was installed and a fence of electrified barbed wire was erected around the perimeter. Lastly, a detachment of Kriegsmarine troops was detailed as a guard. The capital ships of the German Navy were rotting in their ports, blockaded by the British, so there were naval troops readily available.

Next, the Admiral directed subordinates to comb through emigration records to find Jews who had been let into America but had close relatives still in Germany. He also had agents cull public American records for other Jews who had sneaked out of Germany without permission. Every month, the American Immigration Service published a list of those who had been allowed into the country. Thanks to the German penchant for record-keeping and the American's foolishness, the task wasn't hard, just time-consuming. In one month's time, Canaris was handed a list of almost a thousand names. From this list, he culled the names of only those who had more than one close family member still trapped in Germany. He ended up with two hundred and ninety-four names. Next, he carefully reviewed the occupations of the 294. Canaris chose women who were secretaries and men who were scientists or highly skilled technical workers. He ended up with twenty-three names.

The relatives of the twenty-three were quietly rounded up without violence and taken to the lodge at Suderburg. Some of them had to be plucked from various concentration camps and ghettos. The Admiral gave strict orders to the naval officer commanding the guard at the lodge that the Jews were not to be mistreated or even insulted. They were to be allowed adequate food to cook for themselves and to freely associate within the camp. But, under no circumstances were they to be allowed to escape.

Each detainee was required to write a letter to their Jewish relative living in America urging him or her to cooperate and stating that if he or she refused, they would be turned over to the SS and put in a concentration camp. A photograph was taken as proof of life.

In mid-1941 Canaris sent five agents to the United States

supposedly as tourists. These agents quietly contacted each of the Jews on the list and showed them the letter and photograph from their relatives. The Admiral was apprehensive. This was the obvious time for the operation to fail. If one or two on the list balked and contacted the FBI, then the whole endeavor would fall apart. To his relief, nineteen agreed to work for the Abwehr. Two couldn't be found and two adamantly refused to be spies but agreed to keep silent about the offer to protect their loved ones being held in Germany.

Ordinarily, when an Abwehr network was set up, Canaris would turn it over to control officers to see to day to day operations. With this one, he didn't. He wanted to keep this network close to his vest. Perhaps he had a hunch that the information his Jewish spies would provide would be special. In any case, Canaris decided that only himself and his deputy, Hans Oster would be privy to the network's output.

Using these people like this was distasteful on its face, but it had two advantages. First, it would give Canaris cover. If the Nazi hierarchy discovered that he was using Jews in this way, it would bolster his outward facade as a loyal Nazi. Secondly, he would be able to shield a hundred innocent Jews from the murderers of the SS. No harm would come to these people. The Admiral would see to that.

There was a knock on his door and Canaris looked up.

"Geben sie!"

The door opened and General Hans Oster, Deputy Abwehr director, walked in. He had a big smile on his face. The two men liked and respected each other. While the Admiral preferred to wear civilian clothes at the office, Oster was never seen out of his Wehrmacht General's uniform. A tall, totally bald man in his forties, he was carrying a folded newspaper under his arm.

"Guten morgen, Herr Admiral. I have the honor to report that

Heydrich is still dead. He did not rise from his casket after three days as some anticipated."

The two men laughed out loud. Oster was referring to SS-ObergruppenFuhrer Reinhard Heydrich, head of the Security Police, and one of the Admiral's main rivals within the government. He had been wounded by Czech partisans in Prague on 4 June. After being shot, Heydrich had lingered near death for days. Canaris had discovered that Heinrich Himmler, the SS head, had sent his personal physician to Heydrich's bedside with orders to make sure he didn't survive. Himmler thought Heydrich was getting a little too powerful.

"What about operation Pastorius?" asked Canaris.

"The agents have all finally been caught," said Oster.

Canaris nodded. Operation Pastorius was a diversion operation intended to distract the American FBI while a very important transaction was occurring in Buffalo, NY. The Abwehr was going to buy a complete set of plans for the new American P-59 experimental jet fighter from a corrupt worker at the Bell Aircraft defense plant. Operation Pastorius, a group of German agents landed on the east coast of America by a submarine, was meant to be a failure.

The Admiral had selected eight fanatical Nazis out of new Abwehr recruits. Each one spoke English and had spent time in the United States. They were given a short, three-week sabotage training course, told to wreak havoc in America and loaded aboard two U-Boats for transport to North America. They were split into two teams, one was to land on Long Island and the other in Florida. Unknown to the men on the mission, their leader, George Dasch, was a long time Abwehr Agent. Dasch was under scrutiny by the Gestapo for making anti-Nazi statements to a girlfriend, who had turned him in. Canaris had to get him out of the country. Canaris told Dasch to make sure the operation was blown and discovered by the Americans as soon after landing as possible.

"Why did it take so long?" asked the Admiral.

Oster's smile got wider. "It was a comedy of errors. Herr Admiral. As soon as the agents landed at the beach on Long Island, they encountered a uniformed sentry and Dasch approached him. It was a young Coastguardsman who didn't even have a weapon! With the other agents watching, Dasch gave the youngster a wad of money and told him to forget what he had seen. The young Guardsman ran away. Dasch was sure that an alarm would be raised and they would be caught, but it didn't happen. The agents boarded a train and ended up in New York."

"Both teams successfully infiltrated?"

"Ja, it appears so, Herr Admiral. The incompetence of the Americans was staggering. So, to continue, Dasch decided that the only way to expose the operation was to turn himself in and confess that he was a spy. He went to the FBI New York headquarters and told the American agent at the reception desk that he was a German spy. Our agent in the FBI has told us that he was passed from office to office and no one would believe him. Finally, he was seen by the assistant director of the FBI in charge of the office. The man listened to Dasche's story, then called him a crackpot and was going to throw him out! Dasch remembered the briefcase he was carrying and the money it contained. He dumped out 84,000 dollars on a table in front of the assistant director. Then they believed him and started a manhunt for the other agents."

"That is amazing. Maybe we are overestimating our American adversaries," said Canaris with a broad grin.

"And now to the reason I have interrupted you on this busy Monday morning," said Oster. "I think I might have found a way to replace our compromised courier agent in America."

With a flourish, Oster whipped the magazine from under his arm and placed it in front of Canaris. It was a copy of the American magazine, News of The World, the issue of 8 June 1942. An article was outlined in red. The magazine was in English. This was no problem for the Admiral. He was fluent in five languages, including English.

The article detailed the woes that the war had brought to American major league baseball. Almost all of their good young players and prospects had left, or would soon leave, to enter various branches of the military. The sport had to rely on older players called out of retirement and young men with draft deferments. They were holding tryouts, open to anyone to try to find players.

Canaris looked up from the magazine. He didn't know anything about American baseball. "Would one of these baseball players be able to travel around to many cities?" he asked Oster.

"Oh Ja, between April and September each team travels to all the major cities on the eastern seaboard and the midwest. It would be the perfect cover for our courier agent. But, between October and April, he would have to find some other excuse for traveling around the country, maybe an extended holiday? Even if our man is not selected as a baseball player, he could still find some other job with one of these teams that would allow him to travel with them to various cities. It would be the perfect cover for a spy. The Americans hold professional sports players in such high regard, that they would never be remotely suspected."

"Fine, comb the immigration records for young men who lived in the United States in the 1930s and who have played this game of baseball." said the Admiral. Thanks to the German penchant for documenting everything, each ethnic German who had come home to Germany in the 1930s had been interviewed about his or her activities while in exile. The results had been cross-referenced and cataloged in the Interior ministry. On the third day of searching the files, Abwehr agents came upon the name of Friedrich Hofmann.

CHAPTER SIX

STADTRAND VON ROSTOV ON DON IM SUDEN RUSSLANDS

22 JULI 1942

A weary Fritz Hofmann watched Luftwaffe Stukas dive-bomb and strafe the southern Russian city of Rostov on Don in the distance. From his position in the dubious shelter of a muddy irrigation ditch he saw the stubby planes dive in turn, their sirens wailing and release their bombs. He felt the concussion of the exploding bombs first, then heard the thunder-like sound a few heartbeats later. Clouds of black smoke billowed into the air over the devastated city.

Though Fritz was only twenty-two, he looked older. The constant strain of combat had caused worry lines to form around his eyes and mouth and his skin to take on a pasty, unhealthy appearance. The hair under his helmet had been crudely shorn close to his scalp. He was clad in the standard German infantry uniform of gray-green wool, officially called "feldgrau." Around his waist was a wide, black leather belt supported by straps over his shoulders. Pouches on this belt held five-round clips of 7.92 mm ammunition for his Model 98K Mauser rifle as well as a bayonet and grenade canister. His trousers were tucked into calf-length black, leather boots with hobnails protruding from the soles for traction. On his head, he wore a steel helmet in the shape of a coal scuttle. Fritz's uniform looked much different now than when it was first issued. After over a year of combat, it was stained, torn and filthy.

THE ADMIRAL'S SPIES | 69

His helmet was scratched and dented and the German eagle emblem on the side had lost one of its wings.

The other members of Fritz's company were spread out on either side along the ditch. Other companies were also deployed on each side, extending the German line. Fritz clutched his rifle to his chest and scanned the skies for the Russian aircraft that he knew the Stukas would inevitably draw like flies to a dead horse. His unit, the 29th Motorized Infantry Division of the Wehrmacht, was waiting for the order to make the final push into the city on the Don River.

Fritz's stomach was sour and grumbling from the morning meal of stringy horsemeat and stale black bread, the same meal the troops had eaten twice a day for the past week. When he wolfed down his ration this morning, he detected a whiff of decay coming from the meat. He thought at the time that the horse meat was starting to turn bad and would soon be inedible. Fritz sincerely hoped that food poisoning wouldn't be added to his long list of miseries.

Fritz Hofmann was glum. He hated being a soldier. He abhorred combat with its horrible noise, constant lack of sleep and the overall dread of being maimed or killed at any minute. He also hated sleeping in his clothes, eating rancid, half-cooked food, squatting over a hole in the ground to shit and constantly scratching at the lice that infested him, particularly in the armpits and groin. His hatred of what he was doing was sharpened by the realization that he no longer believed in the cause behind it. His superiors told him and the other soldiers that they were seizing more living space for the German people. Fritz didn't care about that because he didn't consider himself German. Down deep inside, though he could never tell anyone, he was an American. He missed the United States and was deeply saddened that his country was at war with Germany.

Taking his eyes off the burning city, Fritz turned and scanned the area behind him for the hulking figure of his platoon non-commissioned officer. Sergeant Schultz was on him continually about his performance. Schultz was a big, raw-boned, ill-tempered man with close-cropped hair and small beady eyes that missed nothing. The Sergeant had somehow sensed that Fritz's heart was not in any of this and had become his tormentor. He gave Hofmann every punishment detail from digging latrines to toting extra mortar shells on the march. Fritz thought that any Russian son of a bitch who managed to kill Schultz would earn his undying gratitude. He would kiss the Bolshevik bastard on his vodka soaked lips and maybe even give him some tongue.

The Sergeant didn't seem to be around at the moment and Hofmann relaxed a little. Exhaustion gradually overcame him. He had had no sleep for thirty hours. Despite the noise of the distant bombing, Fritz was so tired his eyelids slowly closed and he dozed. As he dropped off to sleep an image came to mind of him standing near the stern of a ship and watching the Statue of Liberty recede in the distance.

§

When Fritz and his father had arrived in Germany from the United States, they had stayed with Fritz's Uncle Anton in Munich. The boy and his father were treated like what they were, poor relations. Uncle Anton was a big blunt faced, arrogant man who was a mid-level supervisor in a Munich munitions factory. He presided over his dinner table like a king over his court. His wife, Aunt Frieda, was small and prim and had aspirations above her station in life. The couple had a son, also named Anton, who was two years younger than Fritz and a small daughter named Gertrude.

Uncle Anton and his family were staunch supporters of Adolf Hitler. Anton and his wife were Nazi party members and young Anton was in the Hitler Youth. Portraits of the Fuhrer were prominently displayed in almost every room of their home in addition to Nazi flags and other regalia. A tall Nazi banner hung on the front of their middle class house.

Fritz's uncle promised Engel a job at the factory, but Aunt Frieda had something else in mind for Friedrich. The family had a cook but no other domestics. Fritz was given a white shirt and black trousers and turned into a servant. He was expected to serve the family's meals while they sat at the big mahogany table in the dining room. Aunt Frieda would scold him sharply if he made a mistake while serving or set the tableware in an incorrect position. In addition to waiting at the family table, Fritz was expected to make the beds and clean the house. He had to rise before everyone else to light the fireplaces when the weather turned cold. Given a small room in the attic that was bare except for a lumpy bed and battered dresser, Fritz began to adapt to his new life. His tiny room was alternately boiling hot or freezing, depending on the weather. He was given no salary, so he had no money for any kind of entertainment.

Because of his easy-going nature, Fritz could probably have coped and made the best of the situation were it not for young Anton. The fifteen-year-old would strut about the house in his khaki Hitler Youth uniform and make life a misery for Fritz Hofmann. Anton would go out of his way to humiliate his cousin. He would do things like kicking over the pail of water that Fritz was using to scrub the floor and then lecture him about being careless. Anton would summon him from a distant part of the house to get him something that was only a few meters away. He humiliated Fritz in front of guests to the house, calling him his American lackey.

The situation came to a head in December of 1937, about six months after Fritz came to Germany. He was returning to his attic room after helping the cook wash the dinner dishes. When he entered his room, he saw Anton standing in front of his dresser. The top drawer was open and the boy was holding the catcher's mitt and baseball that Fritz had brought with him from America.

"What the hell are you doing here?" asked Fritz.

"I am inspecting your room for subversive materials. This American crap has no place in our Fatherland. I am confiscating it and will burn it in the incinerator," replied Anton and started to walk past Fritz, carrying the ball and glove.

Fritz was at the tipping point. It took a lot of abuse to finally make him snap, but now rage boiled up in him. The little tyrant was stealing the one link he had to a happier life in America. His right hand formed a fist and flew at Anton's nose of its own accord.

The blow landed with a splat and the boy was knocked backward and onto the floor. He got up and rushed out, with blood streaming from his nose.

He was back within five minutes with the elder Anton, Aunt Frieda and Fritz's father. Fritz noted that his father was barely able to stand, drunk again. The elder Anton's face was red with anger.

"What is the meaning of this outrage? You have assaulted my son."

"He was going through my personal possessions without permission. He was going to burn my baseball things," replied Fritz.

"I will ask you to remember that you are a guest in this house. If you cannot refrain from striking my son, you may leave," said Uncle Anton haughtily.

"Fine, I will leave," replied Fritz, and started to pack his meager belongings in his battered suitcase.

Aunt Frieda, no doubt thinking she would have to start cleaning the house again, spoke up. "No, Friedrich must apologize to Anton. He must stay."

Fritz looked at her. He didn't want to stay now. "No, I will not apologize, I will go. I will make my own way, perhaps go back to America."

"You are forbidden to go!" shouted Aunt Frieda

As Fritz was striding away from the house, the shrill voice of his aunt, ordering him back followed him down the street. There was no goodbye to his father. Fritz had had it with him too. The old drunk was the reason he was in this awkward position. If his father hadn't dragged him back to Germany, he wouldn't be homeless now.

For the next two months, Fritz existed by doing odd jobs around Munich. He had it in his mind to make enough money to buy passage back to the United States. His plan was hopeless. All the money he made had to be used to buy food and shelter during the harsh winter. But, living on the streets gave him a unique perspective on German life. The prosperous upper-class Germans ignored the poor people around them. Christian virtues like helping the poor and compassion had gone out of fashion. The people seemed to worship a doctrine of the superiority of the strong over the weak. If one was poor or unable to find work, it was a sign of weak character.

Several levels below the poor in their treatment were the German Jews. The public at large was outright hostile to them. On more than one occasion, Fritz was obliged to lower his trousers and prove he wasn't a Jew to stormtrooper patrols. He didn't hate Jewish people, but he didn't especially like them either, he was just indifferent. He was very glad, however, that he hadn't been born a Jew. They were excluded from the rights of German citizenship. Their businesses were constantly vandalized and they were forbidden from all professions that made a decent living. A constant stream of government anti-semitic propaganda kept the people's anger against them stoked white-hot. Almost daily, Fritz saw Jews beat up and humiliated on the streets by SA brown shirt patrols.

On a freezing day in mid-February 1938, Fritz was stumbling down Lindwurm Strasse, weak with hunger. He hadn't eaten in two days. He was debating with himself about going back to Uncle Anton's and asking forgiveness. He saw a Wehrmacht recruiting station. The people inside appeared to be warm and well-fed. A soldier in uniform looked at him through the window and beckoned him inside with a hand gesture. Within thirty minutes, Fritz allowed himself to be talked into joining the German Army. He raised his hand and swore eternal loyalty and obedience to Adolf Hitler.

During the first year-and-a-half of Fritz's army service, Germany was still at peace with its neighbors. Fritz learned about how to be a soldier. His days were a whirlwind of marching, inspections and weapons training. Given his compliant nature, he turned out to be a good soldier. He obeyed orders without hesitation and kept within the strict boundaries of proper conduct.

Concurrent with military training, there was an intensive program of political indoctrination. The soldiers listened to hours of recordings of the Fuhrer's speeches. Propaganda films were shown to them, prominently featuring martial music and strong handsome people marching to a bright future carrying Nazi banners. The troops were lectured about the superiority of the white German race and it's right to rule over lesser, inferior races. They were told over and over that it was the Fatherland's destiny to recover territory lost in the Versailles Treaty and punish the Jewish bankers who had profited out of the defeat of Germany in the Great War.

Fritz was caught up in the excitement and, for a while, believed the propaganda. His heart thrilled to the vision of Germany's bright future outlined in the Fuhrer's speeches. He finally saw himself as German. His upbringing in America began to fade from his consciousness.

The propaganda worked so well on Fritz because of his personality. He was by nature one of those agreeable people who smile and want to be just part of the crowd. This character trait made him fairly easy to be manipulated. But all the carefully instilled Nazi ideas would be wiped away by shocking events in Poland.

On 1 September 1939, Friedrich Hofmann invaded Poland as part of the 29th Motorized Infantry Division of the Wehrmacht. The well trained and led German forces easily sliced through the gallant but weak Polish resistance.

Fritz's newfound pride in being German was tested on the third day of the invasion. His platoon was ordered to halt because of a blown bridge ahead of their line of advance. They stopped in a tiny village in the middle of nowhere. There were only about ten families in the village and they were dirt poor. Accusing the villagers of destroying the bridge, Fritz's platoon commander ordered the men to be shot. They were lined up against a mud-brick wall and gunned down. The German soldiers then began to rape the younger women in front of their children. When they had sated their lust, the women and children were also shot. Fitz was horrified. He took no part in the massacre, but just stood there with a look of revulsion on his face. All the Nazi propaganda in the world couldn't convince him that such actions were justifiable. How could supposedly civilized men do such a thing? It was impossible for him to be inspired by Nazi slogans while stepping over the bodies of machine-gunned children.

On 8 September in the small village of Dabroka, near Ciepielow, a German regimental commander was shot by a Polish sniper. Fritz's platoon was ordered to round up three hundred Polish prisoners of war.

They were lined up in a ditch and Fritz was among the soldiers that were ordered to shoot them. He did what he was told, but contrived to miss with most of his shots, firing over the Polish prisoner's heads. All traces of German pride in him evaporated. He thought of deserting but where would he go? From then on Fritz kept to himself and did the minimum necessary to satisfy Sergeant Schultz, who had already marked him out as a shirker.

A week later Fritz's platoon was detailed to assist an SS unit for an operation. They were ordered to surround a Jewish village while the SS troops went in and rounded up the people. Fritz saw the SS march six hundred people into the woods near the village. The Jewish men were ordered to dig a deep trench. When it was completed, the six hundred people were ordered to disrobe and were systematically shot, including women, small children and babies, their bodies filling up the trench. As he was watching the executions from a distance, Hofmann went down on his hands and knees and vomited in the grass. He was convinced that he was the only sane person left in the world.

Everyone else had gone crazy with sadism. He wanted to shout to the SS that this was madness but knew it would only draw a bullet from Sergeant Schultz.

In 1940, Fritz's unit participated in the Battle of France as strategic reserve. They had garrison duties in eastern France until early 1941. This was an easier time for Fritz. The army and the SS were not as brutal to the French as they had been to the Poles. The food and wine were good, but the people, especially the women, were hostile. Fritz didn't blame them. If they had invaded his country, he would be hostile too.

In early 1941, the 29th Motorized Infantry Division was shipped east to become a part of Operation Barbarossa. On 22 June 1941, the Germans hurled over a million men and their machines against the

Soviet Union. It went well for six months but then the terrible winter and stiffening Russian resistance began to take its toll. The high command decided to concentrate its offensive power in southern Russia.

§

Fritz was jolted awake by the scream of an incoming artillery shell. It sounded oddly like the cry of a woman in pain. The ground about fifty meters in front of the ditch erupted in a geyser of black earth. Fritz Hofmann felt the now familiar grip of the terror. It came over him every time he was in active combat. Like an ugly, menacing, malevolent beast, the fear crawled up his spine and consumed him in almost paralyzing panic. "RUN AND HIDE!," the beast would shout into his ear. Its urgings turned his bowels to water, fogged his mind, slowed his reaction time and gave him an almost irresistible urge to flee or throw his arms over his head and cower on the ground. But in this savage war against the Russians, there was nowhere he could go that was safe. Whether it was a steel shard from an artillery shell or a bullet in the back of the head from Sergeant Schultz's pistol, there wasn't anywhere that death couldn't seek him out.

The first time Fritz had felt the fear, in his first combat, he had frozen up and presented a perfect, stationary target for the enemy, which had almost cost him his life. This time he ducked below the lip of the ditch and tried to squirm into the Russian mud as deep as he could. The earth was the infantryman's friend. Get deep enough into it and one was safe. He jammed his helmet down on his head and held it there with all but two fingers. Those he put in his ears to muffle the incredible noise. The concussion from the exploding shells buffeted him and jarred his teeth. The shells that landed close by squeezed the air out of his lungs, causing him to lie there fighting for breath.

More screams and more shells followed, landing all over the

German positions. Above him, the air was filled with millions of lethal, white-hot shards of steel, moving at incredible speeds, of which even a tiny piece could kill a man. One of the big Russian shells impacted in the drainage ditch about twenty-five meters down the line from Fritz. Feldgrau clad bodies and parts of bodies flew into the air. The shelling went on for what seemed to Fritz an eternity but was probably only about five minutes and then the bombardment ceased.

Fritz lifted his head out of the mud and looked down the ditch. His nostrils were filled with the strong chemical smell of the explosives used in the artillery shells, mixed with the coppery reek of fresh blood and exposed guts of a slaughterhouse. Greenish gray smoke hovered in the air for a few moments until it was blown away slowly by the breeze.

Fritz gingerly lifted his head a little higher and peered over the lip of the ditch. A long way away across the waving grass of the plain, he could see what looked in the distance like a line of brown beetles advancing toward him, accompanied by swarms of brown ants. Shit! It was a Russian counter-attack! The fear that had lessened for a moment came back, but not quite as bad. Facing bullets was not like being under artillery fire. Artillery was a bitch.

Fritz jumped up, waved to Sergeant Shultz and then pointed at the advancing Russians. After making sure the sergeant had seen the enemy, he crouched back down under the cover of the wall of the ditch and extended his rifle out over the edge toward the enemy.

The Russians were getting closer. The beetles and ants gradually transformed into T-34 tanks and Russian infantry in brown uniforms. Sergeant Schultz walked back and forth behind the line shouting for his troops to hold their fire until the enemy was closer. Groups of soldiers were hustling forward carrying extra boxes of ammunition for the machine guns, on stretchers. The German line began to take long range machine gun fire from guns atop the advancing tanks. Sergeant Schultz ignored the zip and snap sounds of passing bullets and continued to stroll calmly back and forth beside the ditch. Fritz had long since given him up to be insane.

Fritz took the two stick grenades he carried tucked under his belt and laid them on the mud beside him ready for instant use. They consisted of cylindrical steel cans of explosives attached to slim wooden handles. In a recess in the base of each handle was a little porcelain ball attached to a string. To use one, you pulled the ball and string to activate the fuse and then threw it within five seconds. If you didn't throw it quickly enough, you died.

The Russians didn't fool around with fancy tactics in their attacks. They used brutal frontal assaults. Their commanders didn't seem to care how many men they lost. Fritz and his comrades killed them by the thousands, but they always seemed to have thousands more in reserve.

When the line of tanks was about three hundred meters away, the Company commander gave the order to open fire, which Sergeant Schultz echoed. Fritz heard the loud, tearing paper sounds of multiple MG-34 machine guns start firin., There were nine of them in Fritz's company alone, each firing at the rate of 900 rounds per minute. The Russians were attacking into a kill zone where nothing human could survive, but still, they advanced. Interspersed with the machine-gun fire were the individual bangs from the rifles of the soldiers. Fritz fired his rifle as fast as he could work the bolt. Every five shots, he took a clip from his leather ammunition belt and replenished his rifle's magazine. He didn't have anything against the Russian peasants charging toward him but if he didn't kill them, they would most certainly kill him.

Over the terrific noise of battle, he heard a peculiar whang sound beside him. He looked over at his squadmate Willi Klemper, who up until a second ago had been at his side firing at the Russians. He was younger than Fritz and quiet, always wearing a sad, sardonic expression and keeping to himself. A Russian heavy machine gun bullet had entered the side of Willi's helmet and exited out the other side leaving a jagged bloody hole. He must have had his head turned to the side for some reason, thought Fritz. Willi's body was slumped forward. Fritz turned him over and saw to his horror that the boy's eyeballs were dangling out of his eye sockets, forced out by the overpressure of the large-caliber bullet passing through his head. Fritz's terror came back full force and he froze, his hands shaking.

Over the din, Fritz caught snatches of an angry voice shouting behind him, and then a savage blow to the back of his helmet. He looked up and behind him into the angry, intense little eyes of Sergeant Schultz. His mouth was open, yelling and he was drawing his right boot back for another kick. Fritz grabbed his rifle and resumed firing. Out of the corner of his eye he saw Schultz dragging Willi's body out of the ditch.

The Russian infantry was falling in heaps, their brown clad bodies sprawled on the grassy ground. The tanks continued on in a straight line, without deviating from their course, and were beginning to fire their main guns at the Germans. Fritz became concerned. The infantry had no weapons capable of reliably stopping the enemy tanks. Abruptly, one of the Russian beasts exploded, its turret and gun cartwheeling into the air. A battery of 88mm guns behind the German line had taken the Russian tanks under fire. The 88 was originally designed as an anti-aircraft gun, but combat in Russia had shown it to be a superbly effective tank killer. One by one, the Russian T-34s were all hit and stopped. Some of them were on fire. They sat there inert with plumes of smoke rising into the blue sky. Every so often the ammunition in a burning tank would cook-off and explode in a huge orange fireball.

The smoke was getting thick around the Russians but Fritz could make out the thinned ranks of the infantry. They kept coming and were close enough now for him to discern individual figures. As they advanced into the murderous fire, Fritz saw whole swaths of them mowed down. The depleted Russian formations were whittled from battalion-sized to that of companies, to that of platoons, then squads. Finally, there were just individual soldiers running forward.

One Russian was thirty meters away, coming straight at Fritz. He was a big man with a beard, wearing a cap with a large red star on the crown and carrying a rifle with a bayonet attached to the muzzle. His mouth was open and he was yelling, his face twisted in hate and determination. Fritz took careful aim and shot him in the chest. The Russian soldier staggered a few steps more, then fell to the ground. As Fritz lowered his rifle, a tear rolled down his cheek. He quickly wiped it away. Oh God, how he hated this!

Then it was over. The weapons stopped firing and there was silence. The quiet seemed weird and alien after the storm of sound during the battle. Fritz looked out over the ground at the carpet of Russian bodies and burning tanks, his hearing muffled from the noise of battle. He glanced down the ditch. There were German bodies too, lots of them. He had a sudden premonition that he would die here in Russia. It was only a matter of time. He imagined that everyone on both sides of the savage conflict would eventually end up killed in battle. The last Russian and German would kill each other in a last savage battle for supremacy. It was pointless to have any hope of survival. Fritz's natural pessimistic nature was working overtime.

His mouth was dry and he pulled out his canteen, took a drink and let the lukewarm water trickle down his throat. After slaking his thirst, Fritz put his rifle aside, flopped over on his back in the mud and looked up into the blue sky. The soldiers around him were bringing out cigarettes and lighting them with shaking hands. Fritz didn't smoke. He couldn't stand the taste. The few times he had tried cigarettes, the smoke made him gag.

Neither Fritz nor the other soldiers stirred to go and look for Russian wounded and give them aid. They knew the German NCOs would soon be walking among the piles of corpses, searching for Russians who were still alive and shooting them in the head. Fritz began to tremble as the adrenalin in his blood was slowly absorbed. Once again, exhaustion overcame him and he drifted off to sleep.

He was awakened by a soft kick in the side from one of the other soldiers. He heard his name called. "Hofmann! Hofmann, you piece of shit. Where are you?"

It was the voice of Sergeant Schultz. Fritz jumped up and trotted over to the big man.

"The Company Commander wants to see you. Why would the Hauptmann want to see a worthless slacker like you? If you have done something to make me look bad, I will kick your ass from here to Kiev."

I don't know, Herr Sergeant," replied Fritz.

"Well, what the hell are you standing here for? Move!" shouted Schultz.

Fritz trotted a hundred meters back to the company command post. He saw Hauptmann Proust, the Company Commander, standing in a group of other officers studying a map and reported to him.

"Hofmann, I don't know what this is about, but I have orders to send you back to Germany, to Berlin. Here are your travel orders and the address where you are to report. Dismissed."

Fritz took the orders from Proust's hand and saluted. He was astounded but his spirit soared with hope. Anything that would get him away from the Eastern Front was welcome. That afternoon he sponged the mud off his uniform and boarded a train back toward Germany. The accommodations were crude, just the hard floor of a freight car, but Fritz didn't care. He luxuriated in being out of the front lines for the first time in a year. Three days later he reported to the Abwehr Headquarters in the Bendleblock in Berlin.

He was kept waiting for over an hour, then was shown into an office. Sitting behind a desk was a tall bald man in the uniform of a General in the Wehrmacht. Fritz jumped to attention and saluted. He was terrified, he had never been in the presence of a General before. With a gesture, the officer ordered him to sit in a chair across the desk from him.

"Friedrich Hofmann. Born in Amerika. Played the game of baseball. Is that true?"

"Ja, Herr General"

"Were you proficient at this game of baseball?"

"Ja, Herr General, I was very good. At one time I thought I might try to do it professionally." Fritz was mystified why the General would be asking him about American baseball.

"From now on we can drop the 'Herr Generals', just answer yes or no. I have a proposition for you. You must volunteer. We are not going to force you. I am with the Abwehr. We are an espionage agency that collects intelligence about our foreign enemies."

"We have an espionage network in the United States. We need someone who can move freely between major American cities, collect reports from other agents and carry them to a base of operations. We want to send you to America and for you get a job with a professional baseball team and use it as a cover to be our courier agent. If you cannot get hired as a player, get some other position that would allow you to travel with them. You appear to be qualified for this assignment. We have studied your Wehrmacht record. You seem to be a good soldier and patriotic German."

Fritz was dumbfounded. This was insanity. "But, Herr General, professional baseball players are the elite. Only one in ten thousand people can play at their level. I was only a high school player."

"American professional baseball is bereft of good players right now. All their good, young, prospective players are being inducted into the military. They have been forced to use old retired players and young unknowns with draft deferments. It is worth the effort to try. We have arranged for an ex-professional baseball player to coach you. Will you do it? If you decline this assignment, you will be sent back to your old unit."

Fritz looked down at his hands and thought about going back to combat in Russia. Anything was better than that. If he went back there, he would surely die. The General's offer promised, at the very least, a reprieve from death.

The General sat back in his chair.

"There is something I must warn you about. You were born in the United States. If you accept this assignment and are caught by the American FBI, they will execute you as a traitor."

"Ja, I will do it," replied Fritz.

CHAPTER SEVEN

FBI NEW YORK FIELD OFFICE
500 PEARL STREET
MANHATTAN
NEW YORK
JULY 25, 1942

A
ssistant Special Agent in Charge, Milton Turley put his hand on Hannah Rosen's knee and gave it a little squeeze.

"That's all, for now, sweetie, but I may have some more dictation later."

He called Hannah "sweetie" or "honey" more often than he called her by name. Turley was in his early forties and was big and beefy with close-cropped hair and bushy eyebrows. Today he had his coat off and was wearing wide suspenders to hold up his trousers and a bow tie on the collar of his white shirt. When he talked, he breathed out volumes of air that smelled of rotten teeth and the foul aroma of the cheap cigars He habitually smoked. The almost overpowering smell made Hannah want to gag.

Special Agent Turley fancied himself as quite the lady's man. He was continually smiling and touching Hannah but remained just under the threshold of being overtly objectionable. Besides Hannah, there were three other women in the secretarial pool serving Turley, the other supervisors and the Assistant FBI Director in charge of the field office,

Matthew Byrnes. Because she was the best looking, Turley usually picked Hannah when he needed clerical help. She didn't like the way he treated her but there was nothing she could do. Women who worked outside the home were expected to put up with such nonsense. She got up to leave Turley's office but as she neared the door, he called her back and handed her a thin stack of papers.

"File these reports, will you honey?"

Hannah left his office with relief and headed toward the file room. It was down a long hallway from the secretarial pool. When she entered, she saw that the room with its rows of file cabinets was deserted. She ducked behind a pillar that hid her from the doorway and scanned the reports Turley had given her for any information that might be of interest to her German masters. She had been told by the Germans that someone was watching her so she dare not withhold anything from them. Her parents' lives depended upon it.

The reports Hannah scanned were concerning citizen reports of suspected Nazi spies in New York. The Bureau got hundreds of them every week and all were investigated. None of the reports in the stack were of sufficient value to tell the Germans about. She leaned back against the pillar and closed her eyes. How have I got myself in such a horrible position, she asked herself. I thought I had problems when I first came to America but now they seem so trivial.

On April 6, 1939, her third day in America, over breakfast, Uncle Moshe announced that he had found a retired school teacher from the neighborhood who had agreed to teach Englishto Hannah for a very reasonable fee. Annie Levine turned out to be a prim woman in her sixties with kind eyes. For five months she guided Hannah in her quest to learn English. It was difficult at first. English is a very difficult language to learn. By the end of their sessions together, however, Hannah could speak and write rudimentary English. She still made many gaffs and her accent was heavy, but Mrs. Levine said she was ready for instruction in a more formal setting. She recommended that Hannah enroll in a secretarial college after she expressed an interest in clerical work.

This first six months in America were very lonely for Hannah. She was studying hard but otherwise had no life. About the only reprieve from the sadness came in the form of tattered letters from her parents, smuggled out of Germany every couple of months. When Hannah would receive one, she was elated. At least she knew her mama and papa were still alive. The letters were full of banalities and assurances that everything was fine. She didn't believe what her parents wrote. She was sure they were keeping things from her,. But she had no way of replying to ask questions about how they really were.

Living with her aunt and uncle presented some challenges. First, the pair had frequent spats, and they weren't just calm disagreements, but screaming matches with dramatics worthy of Sarah Bernhardt. Hannah often confined herself to her room to escape the shouting.

Another problem was religion. Rachel and Moshe were observant Jews. They honored Shabbat, kept kosher and attended synagogue every week. They expected Hannah to participate in the weekly rituals and attend synagogue with them. Hannah's family in Germany had been assimilated Jews and didn't practice Judaism. Nevertheless, Hannah went along with what her relatives wanted, though she was somewhat uncomfortable with the rituals and wasn't sure if this was the way God wanted to be worshipped.

She believed that there was a God. There was too much order in nature for there not to be. But what was he really like? Every sect, in every religion seemed to have its own views of who God was,and his attributes. Some said he was fierce and unapproachable. Others said he was soft and sappy with love. Still others said he required rituals to placate him. Who was right? The more time Hannah pondered these questions, the more uncertain she became. When she thought too hard on this, she would usually end up forcing thoughts about God from her brain in frustration.

The thing that caused her the most distress in living with her relatives had nothing to do with weighty issues. Hannah was one of those people who have an innate need for cleanliness, neatness and order. As a little girl, her dolls had been lined up in her room with military precision. It bothered her when her surroundings were untidy. With Aunt Rachel, on the other hand, keeping the apartment clean and neat wasn't a top priority. Not that she was slovenly, but beyond a thorough weekly cleaning for Shabbat, she pretty much let things slide.

Uncle Moshe was no better. Three or four times a week he would sit in his favorite chair in the living room after dinner, smoke a cigar and read the sports pages of the newspaper. Hannah hated the aroma of burning tobacco; she always had since she was little. She couldn't go to her room to escape because the foul cigar smoke filled the whole apartment. But it wasn't just the smell that drove Hannah to distraction. Uncle Moshe would flick the ashes from his cigar at a small ashtray on a table three feet from his chair. Most of the ashes would miss the ashtray and fall on the tabletop or the floor around the table. Each clump of white ash that missed its mark was like an affront to Hannah. She would sit across the room anxiously waiting for Uncle Moshe to get up and leave the room so she could clean up the mess. Her aunt and uncle had been kind to her and she loved them, she didn't want to hurt their feelings with her obsession. So she waited until she was alone in a room to surreptitiously wipe the kitchen counters, sweep up crumbs, or dust the furniture. She also kept the bathroom spotlessly clean. Hannah's room was her haven. It was squeaky clean and in perfect order, the way she liked it.

By September 1939 Hannah was a different person from the timid creature she had been when she first came to America. She no longer cringed at the teeming millions of people rushing around New York. She could travel all over the city on the subway with never a care. Human beings usually adapt to their surroundings. Hannah was no exception. She found herself not only tolerating the hustle and bustle of the city but actually enjoying it. She discovered that New Yorkers, under their gruff and wisecracking exterior, were with some exceptions mostly kind people willing to help a stranger. Without Hannah realizing it, America was winning her over.

Using money borrowed from her uncle, Hannah enrolled in night classes at the Eastern Secretarial College on West 54th Street. Then she went in search of a day job to earn money to pay her uncle back for his kindness. She applied at Macy's, the first place Aunt Rachel had taken her to in New York.

The man assigned to interview her was bright and young and had a carnation stuck in the buttonhole of the lapel of his suit. He asked Hannah about experience. Her heart beat faster and she almost panicked. She had a sudden urge to jump up and leave because she didn't know what to say. She had no employment experience. She nervously mumbled something about being willing to work hard. It turned out she could have said she was a circus acrobat or an arctic explorer. The young man wasn't listening, he was too busy staring at her legs.

The interviewer hired her and asked for a date in the same sentence. Hannah politely declined the date but took the job. She was put to work as a salesgirl in the Macy's Ladies Wear department for the princely sum of twelve dollars a week. The supervisor of the department was a pinch-faced old spinster named Miss Gates who was partial to severe woman's suits and no-nonsense discipline. She wasn't impressed by Hannah's beauty one little bit. Miss Gates gave her a lecture about fraternization with male employees and proceeded to watch her like a hawk. In spite of her efforts, the male employees found ways to flirt with Hannah. As usual, she ignored them. She was too busy for that.

She met a friend, a fellow employee of Macy's. Her name was Betty French and she was a tall, blonde, wise-cracking native New Yorker about Hannah's age. Betty had three passions--young men, swing dancing and club sandwiches. She became Hannah's co-conspirator in outwitting Miss Gates. Most days the two young women ate their bag lunches together on the Macy's roof. Betty's lunch was usually a club sandwich, but she made it differently than anyone else. She substituted a second portion of bacon for the turkey to go with the lettuce, tomato, mayonnaise, and toasted bread.

It wasn't long before Hannah was eating them too. At first, she felt very guilty about eating pork. Though her family in Germany had been assimilated Jews, they had never stooped to eating the flesh of pigs. For a Jew, it was the ultimate taboo. Hannah felt regret that God had forbidden his chosen people to eat such tasty meat. If he had said not to eat mutton, she would be okay with that and only too happy to obey. But she was very careful to keep from her aunt and uncle her newfound vice. She thought that if they knew, they would toss her out on the street.

Betty also introduced Hannah to swing music and jitterbug dancing.

One Saturday night, Betty took Hannah to the Roseland Ballroom on West 52nd Street and she heard her first swing band. As she listened to Benny Goodman and his orchestra play "Stompin' at the Savoy," "Don't Be That Way," "Flying Home" and others, she was immediately hooked. The only music allowed to be played in Germany was either martial or classical. All other kinds of music had been ruthlessly suppressed. Goodman's music opened up a new world for her.

Betty taught Hannah how to jitterbug in the parlor of her rooming house to the accompaniment of a windup record player and other tenants banging on the walls demanding quiet. They both laughed until their sides hurt. On weekend nights when Hannah had no secretarial classes, the two young women would dress in outfits obtained for almost nothing from the Macy's sale rack using their employee discount. With male employees from Macy's as escorts, they would head to the Onyx Club, Roseland Ballroom or any one of a number clubs on West 52nd Street. They would dance the jitterbug until they were physically exhausted and just couldn't do another aerial or breakaway.

Hannah often used a store floorwalker named Will Peters as a dance escort because he was a wonderful dancer. After two dates, though, Will got a little fresh. He wanted more than dancing. Hannah had to sit him down and tell him that the only time he was allowed to touch her was on the dance floor.

In March 1941 Hannah received a proficiency certificate from the Eastern Secretarial College. She had worked hard to learn what she needed to know to be a secretary. She had been in the United States for almost two years. Her spoken English was very goodand her word selection almost perfect, but she still spoke with a pronounced foreign accent. Thanks to the college, she had also mastered written English.

She had come to America as a frightened girl but was now a self-assured young woman. Although she was only a resident alien, she now considered herself an American. New York had worked it's magic. She loved it there and didn't want to be anywhere else. A nagging worry about the safety of her parents in Germany was always with her, but the letters from them still came every few months so she knew they were still alive. She longed to be able to bring them to this wonderful city to be with her. Hannah applied for work at several big insurance companies, assuming they would employ many secretaries. She ran into an unexpected problem. When she was granted an interview with the Allied Casualty Insurance Company on East 36th Street, she found herself sitting across from a stern-faced, nervous man who looked down his nose at her.

"Miss Rosen, the Allied Casualty Insurance Company doesn't hire employees of the Hebrew race," said the interviewer.

She ran into the same problem at the next three big companies where she applied. At two of them, she wasn't even allowed to submit an application. She began to get discouraged.

What Hannah was experiencing, was the result of a huge increase in American anti-semitism that had arisen during the Great Depression of the 1930s and still hung on. It would seem that visceral hatred of Jewish people is a monster that lurks unnoticed in the human psyche until times of economic distress or other calamities, when it comes roaring out, gnashing its teeth. While anti-semitism was common in New York, it was nothing compared to the rest of the country. In a 1939 Roper Organization nationwide poll, fifty-three percent of respondents agreed with the statement, "Jews are different from ordinary Americans and need to be restricted." Virulent anti-Jew organizations operated openly, among them the Silvershirt Legion, the German American Bund and the Defenders of the Christian Faith. A Catholic priest, Father Charles Coughlin, had a popular radio program dedicated to the vilification of Jewish Americans.

Finally, Hannah had an idea. It was fairly devious but she decided to try it anyway. She would drop the "n" from the end of her last name and become Hannah Rose. On applications where they asked for "race," she would list "Caucasian," instead of "Jewish." Her plan worked. At the Guardian Casualty Insurance Company on 7th Avenue, she passed the initial interview and was shown into the office of the Personnel Manager for a final interview. The man took one look at Hannah's face and figure and hired her on the spot. "You're worth the salary for me to just sit and look at you all day," he said.

Everything was looking up. Hannah now had a good job paying twenty-four dollars a week. She was able to start paying Uncle Moshe for her room and board, support herself and save a little each month. She would have felt secure except for one serious problem. The letters from her parents in Germany had stopped coming. By October 1941, not having heard from them since April, Hannah was frantic with worry. On a fateful day in early November, she found out why the letters had stopped.

On her way home from work, she had just emerged from the subway near her uncle's apartment when a man fell in step beside her. He was of slight build wearing a long brown overcoat. He was utterly ordinary looking except for his small intense eyes. He stopped Hannah dead in her tracks when he spoke to her in German.

"Hannah Rosen? I have news about your parents."

She whirled on him. "You have news? Are they alright?"

"Not here, follow me," said the man and turned back the way they had come. He led her to Mitchel Park which was near the subway station and the two sat on a bench near some trees. The bench was of wrought iron, painted black with wooden slats on the seat and back. The man in the overcoat looked all around, then handed Hannah a letter addressed to her. She became excited when she saw her father's handwriting on the envelope, she tore it open and started to read.

21 July 1941

My dearest daughter, my Hannah.

Your mother and I are in prison. We were arrested late at night and taken a long way to a building deep in the forest somewhere. There is an electrified, barbed wire fence surrounding the building, so there is no doubt that we are prisoners. The guards are from the German Navy and have treated us well. Thank God they are not SS brutes. I don't know how long this good treatment will last. Hannah, if they mean to hold us hostage to get you to do something for them, refuse. Forget about us. Live your life.

Your loving parents, Yakob and Anna.

Attached to the letter was a grainy photograph of her parents that showed them clinging to each other with fear on their faces. They looked much older than the last time she had seen them. Hannah lowered the letter and photograph to her lap and looked at the man in the overcoat.

"Fraulein, I work for a German intelligence agency. We need agents in America. I am going to put a proposition to you. Work for us and your parents remain safe. If you refuse or betray us, your loved ones will be turned over to the SS and sent to a concentration camp. Terrible things are happening in the camps. You have one minute to make up your mind."

She didn't need the full minute. "Yes, I will do anything you say."

The man handed her an object. Hannah looked at it nestled in her hand. It was a small, metal, rectangular box with a sliding lid. Glued to it were what appeared to be magnets.

"Underneath the bench you are sitting on is a box identical to the one you are holding. Retrieve the box and check it for messages from us at least twice a week. Do not open the box here but take it to a place where you cannot be observed. If we have an urgent message for you, you will receive a letter signed "Uncle Moses." If you receive such a letter, check the can immediately. Remember, the lives of your parents depend on your cooperation. We will have people watching you to make sure you comply. If you go to the police, or anyone else, not only will your loved ones suffer but we will kill you too. Good day."

He got up and walked away. Hannah didn't know whether to laugh or cry. She had to work for the Nazis and it was abhorrent to her. But her parents were alive! Her parents were alive!

Six days later she checked the can and found a message ordering her to apply for a job within the Office of Naval Intelligence, the New York office of the Federal Bureau of Investigation, U.S. Immigration Service or the Harbormaster's office. She applied to all four. The only interview she got was with the FBI. The agent that interviewed her seemed more intent on impressing her with his physique than asking her questions. She was required to fill out a long questionnaire about her background. A week later two FBI agents interviewed her aunt and uncle and their neighbors in the building. They asked if Hannah had ever made any statements to them favoring communism, or the Soviet Union. Because she was Jewish, they didn't even ask about the Nazis. A week later she was informed by letter that she got the job and was to report on the next Monday morning to the FBI field office on Pearl Street. Since then, Hannah's life had changed for the worse. She had no social life. She lost touch with her friend Betty French and quit dancing.

After leaving the file room Hannah went back to her desk. She began typing the correspondence of Assistant SAC Milton Turley. As if she hadn't enough complications in her life, Hannah had added another one; her feelings for FBI special Agent Ted Miller.

Hannah was under stress. The double life she was leading ate at her insides. She was a spy against the country that she had come to love and she hated herself for it. The only thing she could console herself with was that, so far, the only things of importance she had passed along to the Germans was information about a man named Anton Dietrich who was under FBI surveillance and what had happened to their spies that had landed by submarine in America.

With all this on her mind, she had no time or inclination for a relationship with a man.

Her mind was full of worry about her parents and she distrusted men. Because she was good to look at, she was bombarded on a daily basis with advances from men. In the high testosterone world of the FBI, where all agents thought of themselves as manly heroes, the rooster's dance was something to behold.

Ted Miller was in Counter-Espionage, the most glamorous of Bureau assignments. Hannah had first seen him about six months ago, a couple of months after the attack on Pearl Harbor. Ted had just been transferred from Chicago. AD Byrnes had called a meeting of all counter espionage agents in his office. About thirty agents attended. Ted Miller had appeared at the secretarial pool door and asked directions to Mr. Byrne's office.

He was tall and thin with a square jaw and wavy hair. He was ruggedly handsome, like Clark Gable, as opposed to pretty like Robert Taylor. He had beautiful expressive eyes and an aura about him of great strength. He looked her in the eyes and then looked away, showing a little shyness. Hannah thought he was the most beautiful creature she had ever seen.

She was unprepared for her physical reaction. Up to this point, Hannah had been totally immune to male advances. She didn't trust men and didn't want to be involved with them. She was experiencing a feeling she had never had before and it scared her a little. She was almost overpowered by a rush of attraction for the tall agent. Her face blushed a deep scarlet and her breath quickened. Their eyes met again but this time it was she who looked away. When Ted went off to the meeting, it took several minutes for Hannah to compose herself. When the meeting ended, Ted walked by her door again. He stopped, waved and smiled at her. He had a lopsided grin that made him all the more appealing to her.

Hannah began quietly asking the other female workers about Special Agent Theodore Miller. She learned that he had distinguished himself on his third day as an agent in a shootout with a criminal gang. He had shot all five of the criminals himself. His work since then had been excellent, and as a reward, he had been assigned to Counter-Espionage. She also learned that he was single and had no steady girlfriends.

By coincidence, Special Agent Miller found himself walking by the clerical pool door on almost a daily basis. He and Hannah would chat about mundane things like the weather and the war news. Hannah noticed that Ted didn't flex his muscles or brag about himself like the other agents that flirted with her. He was a little shy with her and smiled his lopsided grin. She began to look forward to seeing him. When they talked, her face would get warm and she would get butterflies in her stomach. Hannah began to check her appearance in a mirror frequently throughout the day; something she had never done before.

The other secretaries smiled. They had seen Hannah attract scores of men since she had come to the office. Although the three other women in the office were happily married and liked Hannah, each of them harbored just a little bit of jealousy of her beauty. They knew what was going on here and rubbed their hands together in glee. Hannah was about to fall. This was the mating dance of "Machine Gun Miller," and "Hannah, the ile Princess."

It is a curious phenomenon that individuals in military organizations and paramilitary ones like the police and FBI readily make up nicknames for each other. It has been going on for a long time. No doubt during a ninth-century Viking raid to the Irish coast one Norseman had said to another, 'Look, there goes priest sticker, Sven.'"

Ted Miller was lucky. He had earned his nickname by an act of extraordinary courage. His partner, Bill Parker, was not so fortunate. He had been a Chicago policeman before joining the Bureau. He was known as "Apple Stealer Bill." Another agent in the office, Kurt Jones, had the misfortune of being born with large ears. He was known as, of course, "Dumbo Jones." One day that week "Apple Stealer Bill" and "Dumbo Jones," got together at the water cooler and started an office pool on when the shy "Machine Gun Miller," would ask the "Ice Princess," for a date.

CHAPTER EIGHT

519 W. 151ST STREET
APARTMENT 1D
MANHATTAN
NEW YORK CITY
JULY 31, 1942

" **I** know he's a Nazi. He looks just like Conrad Veidt, and what about that locked room in the basement. He could have set up a secret transmitter. For all I know he could have Japs hidden down there as well," said eighty-two-year-old spinster, Heloise Farmer. Conrad Veidt was a Hollywood actor that usually played a villain in movies, often as a sinister Nazi spy. Special Agents Ted Miller and Bill Parker were sitting across from Miss Farmer in her parlor. It was full of heavy, ornate Victorian furniture with lace doilies on every horizontal surface. Every square inch of wall space was covered with paintings and old photographs depicting long dead relatives. Most of these pictures, however, were obscured by the many potted plants in the room which were the size of small trees. The leaves of one plant poked Ted in his ear every time he turned his head in the old lady's direction. It was like conducting an interview in the Amazon jungle. Miller was waiting for monkeys to appear, swinging from branch to branch above him. He could see that the old woman was getting more agitated. Miss Farmer had the hard-eyed, fanatical stare of one that was either very old and losing it, or nuttier than squirrel feces.

"Miss Farmer, your super, Mister Schultz, isn't a Nazi spy," replied Parker. "We checked him out. His family has been in New York for a hundred years. He keeps his supply room locked because the neighborhood kids were stealing his light bulbs and selling them."

"You're wrong, young man. The man has sinister eyes. We should lock up all these Germans the same way we did the Japs. We'll see about this. I will take this up with President Roosevelt personally," declared Miss Farmer, pointing a bony finger at the two FBI men.

As his partner talked to the crazy old lady, Ted let his mind wander. He knew that Miss Farmer was suffering from what had come to be known as Pearl Harbor Psychosis. Before the war, most Americans thought of the Japanese as small, bumbling, non- threatening little men with thick glasses. After the Japanese sneak attack and their rampage through the Philippines and the Dutch East Indies, they became like supermen in the minds of some Americans. One congressman had recently taken to the floor of the House of Representatives and actually advocated abandoning the West Coast and making a last stand at the Rocky Mountains. It was all very amusing, but Ted remembered that he had been shocked and a little panicked on the day of the PearlHarbor attack himself.

Ted remembered the events of that day like they had happened yesterday. He had just returned from church. Ted was a Methodist and attended services whenever his job permitted. He didn't consider himself a good Christian by any means, but like his mother, he believed in the creed of the church and subscribed to the vision of morality expressed in the Ten Commandments. To honor the memory of his mother and father, Ted tried to live a life guided by high moral principles. As a result, he sometimes came off to other people as a little pompous, self-righteous and stuffy. If he hadn't already earned the nickname, Machine Gun," his FBI colleagues would probably have dubbed him "Preacher Miller," for his oft voiced opinions about morality and his tendency to weigh every action by a black and white standard of right and wrong.

Noon on Sunday found Ted sitting in his favorite chair reading the Sunday Chicago Tribune and smoking a Lucky Strike cigarette. He had his radio on and was listening to a football game between the Chicago Bears and the Chicago Cardinals. The Bears were ahead fourteen to ten in the second quarter. Ted's FBI partner, Aubrey Swensen, and his wife Ruth had invited him over to their apartment that evening for Sunday dinner. He was trying to think of something appropriate to take with him when the radio announcer suddenly broke in on the broadcast.

"From Washington, we bring you a special bulletin. President Roosevelt has just announced that Japanese aircraft have attacked our naval base at Pearl Harbor Hawaii.First reports indicate there is a heavy loss of life. Stay tuned to this station for further bulletins."

Ted stared at the radio. At first, he wondered if the announcement was a fake, like the Mercury Theater broadcast of "War of the Worlds." Then he quickly realized it wasn't. The implications of this were vast. His country was at war. Yesterday, over half the people in the nation were against getting involved in the war raging in Europe and the Far East. Ted wondered how they felt now.

Miller jumped up and ran down to the lobby of his building to the pay telephone. He picked up the receiver, put a nickel in the slot and asked the operator to connect him with the FBI field office in Chicago. The line was busy. Miller tried several times in the next ten minutes with the same results. He went back to his apartment, grabbed his hat and coat and clipped his revolver onto his belt. He rode the elevated train to the FBI office. The emotions of the other passengers on the train were written on their faces. The women were weeping and dabbing their eyes with handkerchiefs. The men were red-faced and angry with their jaws clenched. At the FBI office, he walked into a scene from Bedlam. Everyone was excited and shouting at each other. More agents were arriving every minute, including Ted's FBI partner, Aubrey Swensen.

The big Swede entered the room hurriedly. Miller could tell that he was angry. His face was red and his jaw was set in a hard line. Swensen spotted Ted and came over to him.

"Well, we are knee-deep in shit this time," said the Swede. "Don't worry, before this is over we're going to beat the little yellow bastards like a red-headed stepchild at a family picnic."

SAC Hofstettler emerged from his office and called for everyone's attention.

"I have just spoken to Director Hoover. He told me that the United States is now at war with Japan and very possibly will be at war with Germany and Italy very soon. He told me to tell all of you to get prepared, that we are going to be very busy for a long time. Starting today we start picking up all male aliens of Japanese, German and Italian origin. We are compiling lists of aliens as we speak. Speaking personally, I want to emphasize that we are now soldiers in a war we didn't seek but will finish victoriously."

The public mood became ugly very quickly. People who the day before looked on the wars raging in Europe and Asia as someone else's problem now expressed their outrage at the sneak attack by the Japanese. Anyone on the street who even looked vaguely Asian was in physical danger of assault. Ted shared their anger but held his emotions rigidly in check when doing his job.

Hoover had been right about the FBI being very busy. Miller and Swensen logged sixteen-hour days in the next few weeks. Because Japanese people were about as rare as twelve toed albinos in the midwest, the Chicago agents went after the Germans and Italians with a vengeance. Ted couldn't help but feel sorry for some of the aliens, the Italians especially.

One of the men he detained was named Mario Carona. He was a young guy in his twenties who worked as a bricklayer. He had a wife and three young kids. When Ted and the Swede came to his dingy apartment and put the cuffs on him, Carona had begged for a reprieve. His wife didn't work and there was no one else to provide food for his kids. Though he felt pity for the man, Ted gritted his teeth and hauled him in. Orders were orders. He couldn't let personal feelings interfere in his duty. In the midst of all this ado, Miller was abruptly transferred to Counter-Espionage and sent to New York.

At the bottom of the front steps of Miss Farmer's building, Ted took a deep breath and let it out slowly. What a colossal waste of time, he thought. He was assigned to Counter-Espionage, the plum job in the Bureau. There were agents who would prostitute their wives to be assigned here. But so far all he had done since Pearl Harbor was investigate spy sightings.

Most of the tips were from well-meaning people. Ted and his partner, Bill Parker, did about ten of these investigations every day. Most involved the tipster hearing someone speak German on the subway or in their apartment building. That they would hear German spoken was understandable because New York was home to many German-speaking neighborhoods, including Little Germany on the lower Eastside and Yorkville on the upper Eastside. There were also Jewish refugees from Nazi tyranny. Crown Heights was full of them.

Then there were the nuts and crackpots. One lady had called the FBI office and said an entire Jap division had just landed on Long Island. The agent that took the call asked her how she knew this, as she was calling from Queens. She replied that she had seen it in a "vision" and they had better act quickly because her visions were never wrong. Another investigation involved mysterious lights; they got a lot of those. A man had called and said Nazi spies were signaling U-boats with blinking lights from Staten Island. This onehad led to a very wet and uncomfortable night in a rowboat for Ted and his partner.

Actually, U-boats didn't need Nazi spies signaling them with blinking lights to find ships to sink. The lights of New York shone as brightly as in peacetime. The bright skyline perfectly silhouetted ships going in and out of New York harbor for the German U-Boats. There were so many ships being torpedoed that the Navy pleaded for blackouts in New York and other coastal cities. Influential business interests were adamant that the lights remain on. They wanted people to shop and spend money and they couldn't do that stumbling around in the dark. Businessmen leaned on the politicians and the lights remained on and merchant seamen died needlessly. When he heard about this, Ted was so angry he could spit. "Greedy bastards," he muttered to himself.

Ted Miller was getting discouraged. His job had turned into the constant placating of hysterical and crazy people. He didn't think he was doing enough for the war effort. Ted wondered if he should resign from the FBI and join the Marines. There he could make a greater impact, an active one, with a rifle in his hands.

The war news was bad from all fronts. England was still under siege, with a German invasion expected at any time. The Nazi hordes were still unchecked in Russia. The German Africa Corps had pushed back the British in North Africa. In the Pacific, the Japs had overrun the Philippines and the Dutch East Indies and were threatening Australia.

In the first half of 1942, there had been only two bright spots. In January the Marines on Wake Island had repelled a Japanese invasion force. Afterward, when asked what they needed, the Marines had replied, "Send us more Japs." The four-word message was on the front page of every newspaper in the country. Marine Corps enlistments had jumped thirty percent.

The second bright spot came in April. Word had flashed to the world that Colonel "Jimmie" Doolittle of the Army Air Forces had led an air raid on the Nippon home island with medium bombers. President Roosevelt, when asked where the bombers were based for the raid had replied, "Shangri-la," which was a mythical kingdom in the 1935 novel, "Lost Horizons."

Ted felt that he would probably accomplish more as a Marine than an FBI agent, but there were a lot of reasons for not resigning from his job as an agent. First off, he was a trained agent and was needed here. But the real reason, which he wouldn't admit to himself, was that he was smitten with a secretary in the FBI office.

Ted had always thought that love at first sight was a myth, fodder for cheap romance novels. But when he first met Hannah Rose and looked in her eyes, he was intensely attracted to her. He didn't know if it was love but it was something special.

He had been called to the Assistant Director's office to attend a meeting on counter espionage. Just having been transferred from Chicago, he had stopped in at the secretarial pool to ask directions. Hannah had been sitting at the first desk. Their eyes met. Ted felt something like an electric shock pass between them. Her eyes were big and dark brown, and he couldn't take his gaze from them. They stared at each other and a rosy blush spread on the creamy white skin of her cheeks. Someone laughed out loud in the hallway behind Ted and it broke the spell. He averted his eyes.

During the counter-espionage meeting, Ted stood near the back of the room while Mr. Byrnes talked. He nodded his head when the other agents did and laughed at the AD's jokes with the others. In reality, he didn't hear a word that was spoken. All he could think about were those amazing eyes, framed by an oval face, with a perfect nose and red lips. Ted realized he had only looked at her face and not her body. She might be shaped like a Navy blimp. He determined to try to get a peek on the way out.

After the meeting, Ted once again made his way to the secretarial pool. Looking in through the doorway he saw Hannah again. She was standing in profile retrieving typing paper from a shelf. She was wearing a light green dress of some knit material that conformed to the contours of her body. It had high sleeves with white cuffs and little red buttons. Her waist was slim and she had a shapely backside. Her legs were long. Everything was in perfect proportion. Hannah's head turned and their eyes met again. Ted smiled and waved at her and she waved back. Embarrassed by his thoughts, he made a hurried exit.

Since then, Ted had made a daily excuse to stop by the secretarial pool. The FBI was a bureaucracy like most entities in the federal government. If you walked around carrying a piece of paper and looked determined, you could go anywhere and no one would stop you. For six months he had chatted with Hannah every working day, usually about mundane things like the weather or the bad war news. Ted still hadn't asked her for a date.

As he and Bill Parker rode the subway back to the office from Miss Farmer's apartment, Ted chain-smoked Lucky Strikes and thought about Hannah. Six months was a long time. He had better ask her out soon or some other guy would slide in ahead of him. But her manner toward him was so changeable. One day she would be bright and sunny and the next day aloof. Even on the good days, every time he started working up the courage to ask her out, Hannah's demeanor toward him would change. She would become cold and curt and turn away from him to her typewriter. The way she acted toward him was beginning to cause him some worry. He wondered if maybe she was one of those schizophrenics he had heard about, with two personalities in the same body. Maybe there were two Hannah Roses. Maybe she had a twin sister. They shared one job, and one sister didn't like him. That was a lot of maybes. Maybe he should just can the maybes.

This has got to stop, thought Ted. I will ask her out this afternoon, as soon as I get back to the office. If she rejects me, then at least I will know where I stand. Back at the office, Miller's palms were sweating and his heart pounding as he neared the secretarial pool door. He lit up another Lucky to steady his nerves. He entered the door and there she was, sitting at her desk, typing.

"Hannah, I have something to ask you."

She turned toward him and her face lit up with a smile. His heart skipped a beat. She was so beautiful.

"Today is Friday I was wondering if you would like to go to dinner tonight and maybe see a movie? "Mrs. Miniver" is playing at the Casino Theater on 86th Street. I have heard it's good," said Ted, and waited expectantly.

Hannah stared at him for a few moments. A look of uncertainty crossed her face and she bit her lip. It looked like she was torn about what to answer. Then the smile was back.

"Yes, I would love to have dinner with you. I live at 521 W. 168th Street, Apartment 2C. I will be ready around seven if that is alright." replied Hannah. Ted found her foreign accent delightful.

Ted felt faint with relief. He stood and grinned at her for a few moments, looked down at his shoes for a few more and left with a parting, "See you at seven."

Two of the three other secretaries in the room grinned broadly. The third cried because the scene was so romantic. One of the grinners jumped up and hurried out the door to spread the word. Harvey Jenkins won the office pool. His guess was the closest to the six months it had taken Ted to ask.

At the stroke of five, Ted was out the door. He rushed home to his small apartment in the Bronx, took a bath and carefully shaved. He put on his best suit, a dark grey single breasted. Once dressed, he ducked out, found a florist and bought Hannah a bunch of carnations. Miller agonized with himself about when to arrive at Hannah's door. If he was early, he would appear too eager. If he was late, Hannah might think him careless.

Ted rang the doorbell precisely at seven. A small sign above the bell said, "Rosen." Ted had thought Hanna's name was "Rose." He figured it out pretty quick as he was standing there waiting for the door to open. Hannah was Jewish. Ted asked himself if it mattered. No, it didn't matter at all was his answer. Hannah's uncle, Mr. Rosen, a short, stout and bald little man, greeted him politely. He also met her Aunt Rachel, also short and very nice. She took the flowers and went to find a vase. Then Hannah emerged from a bedroom and Ted's mouth dropped open.

At the office, Hannah eschewed makeup and wore her shoulder-length dark hair pinned back, away from her face. This was a different Hannah. She had applied makeup and lipstick. Her hair was done up over her head with a large curl at the front and smaller curls across the crown of her head. She was wearing a rose-colored, flowing dress that accented her shapely figure. She looked dazzling. Hannah saw his look of awe and responded with a wide smile.

Ted splurged and they took a taxi to Little Italy. They ate in a little Italian bistro on Mott Street. The food was standard Italian fare but there was romantic violin and accordion music playing in the background. After dinner, Ted pulled out his pack of Luckies and prepared to light up.

"Would you mind not smoking. I hate the smell. I have always hated it, even as a little girl."

Ted shoved the pack back into his pocket. He resolved to stop smoking then and there. If Hannah didn't like it, he would never smoke again.

They talked about their lives. Ted told her about growing up in Ohio. He talked about the day he came home from school and learned his father had been shot and killed by criminals. As he told the story a tear rolled down Hanna's cheek. He reached for her hand and held it and she didn't pull it away. Ted told her about college and joining the FBI. He told her about the shootout with the Baker Gang, and then how a week after the shootout, his mother had died from appendicitis, leaving him alone in the world.

Hannah, in turn, told about her early life in Germany, before the Nazis. She and her parents had a good life. Then Hitler came to power with his hate for Jews and everything changed. She told Ted about being smuggled out of Germany, and the pain of having to leave her parents behind. Strangely, Hannah then clammed up. She wore a worried expression. It was if she had let out a secret without intending to.

The movie, "Mrs. Miniver," was about a family of upper-middle-class Englishmen living in a village outside London and their trials during the Blitz. Hannah cried when one of the characters, a young woman, was killed in an air raid. Ted put his arm around her and she nestled closer to him.

When they arrived back at Hannah's apartment building, they exchanged telephone numbers. Ted told the cabbie to wait and escorted Hannah into the foyer of her building. She turned to say goodnight.

Their eyes met. As if it was the most natural thing in the world, she was suddenly in his arms and they were kissing. Her lips were soft and yielding and the feel of her body against his aroused him. Suddenly, she hugged him tighter and crushed her lips against his. He could feel her breasts pressed against his chest. Their mouths were open so Ted moved his tongue forward until it made contact with hers. Hannah paused for an instant as if surprised, then her own tongue became the aggressor. She ground her pelvis into his, causing his body to respond mightily. Ted reveled in the sensations. He had had experiences with other women but it was never like this. He decided that he wanted this woman for his own.

Abruptly, Hannah went rigid. She pulled away without a word and ran up the stairs. Ted took the cab home and bounded upstairs to his room, whistling. He was elated and couldn't wait for their next date.

A little while later, there was a knock on Ted's door. A neighbor said he had a telephone call. Ted rushed down the stairs and put the old fashioned earpiece to his ear.

"Hello."

"Ted," It was Hannah's voice! "Ted, this will not work out. We have no future together. Please do not come by my desk anymore."

"But Hannah, Why?"

"It is for your own good. There are things you don't know about."

Ted started to respond but it was no good. She had already hung up.

CHAPTER NINE

BERGHOF BAYERASCHEN ALPEN
BERCHTESGADEN, DEUTSCHLAND 10 AUGUST 1942

Until the mid-nineteen thirties, the Obersalzberg, in the Bavarian Alps just above the alpine town of Berchtesgaden, about 130 kilometers southeast of Munich, was an exclusive retreat. The elite of Bavarian society would spend their summers there, to escape the heat and bask in the spectacular mountain scenery. Many opulent vacation homes once clung to the picturesque mountainsides.

Now only one resident remained in the Obersalzberg. The rest of the people had been bought or forced out and their homes demolished to provide concentric rings of security for that person. Alert, black-uniformed SS troopers manned sentry posts and roved the area in patrols to keep him safe. That person was Adolf Hitler, undisputed dictator of Germany and conqueror of a huge chunk of the continent of Europe.

Built-in 1935 using royalties from the sale of his book, Mein Kampf, Hitler's Berghof was a huge, ugly, boxy structure painted stark white. The house had an expansive stone terrace attached to one side for viewing the magnificent mountain scenery. The Fuhrer's architect had designed the house to be a larger than life projection of masculine power, at the expense of any charm or grace. Hitler, who prided himself on his "artist's eye" and knowledge of architecture, had enthusiastically approved the design, proving he had neither.

The only access to the Fuhrer's aerie was via a narrow mountain road that ascended from Berchtesgaden below. Invited guests would first have submitted to screening at an SS checkpoint in the gatehouse down the mountain. A second checkpoint was located midway between the gatehouse and the Berghof.

A large, black, Horch limousine flying Nazi flags on its front fenders ascended the road just past the second checkpoint. It hadn't even slowed down at the checkpoints. The SS troopers manning these posts, upon seeing the car, had come to attention, rendered the Nazi salute and waved the automobile through. The reason for this deference was sitting on the plush rear seat of the big car.

Reichfuhrer-SS Heinrich Himmler, chief of the SS, looked out of the side window of the moving car. The window was spattered with raindrops and ominous dark clouds threatened a downpour at any minute. Himmler disliked the mountains. Goring, Bormann and Speer had all built houses in Berchtesgaden to be near the Fuhrer, but Himmler hadn't. His constitution wasn't strong and the altitude bothered him. But when the Fuhrer summoned most of the leadership of the Third Reich for a meeting, he had no choice but to attend, if only to protect his interests.

He wasn't physically imposing. Of only medium height and build, he wore wire-rim spectacles and sported a mustache only a little wider than Hitler's. A weak chin destroyed any illusion of Nordic manliness. When he spoke, his voice was high pitched and squeaky. In ordinary circumstances, he would be regarded by most people as a very nondescript man.

The impeccably tailored uniform he wore wasn't black but gray-green. At the start of the war, he had ordered the SS to put away their black uniforms and wear feldgrau in solidarity with the Wehrmacht. The only ones exempted from the order were Waffen SS tank crews and SS-Liebstandarte Adolf Hitler, the Fuhrer's personal bodyguards.

When the big car came to a stop in the courtyard of the Berghof, Himmler's aide, who was sitting in the front passenger seat, scampered out to open the rear door for the Reichfuhrer. Followed by the same aide, Himmler ascended the steep stairs to the entrance hall. Once inside he was informed by the chief of the guard detail that the Fuhrer had moved the location of the meeting from the terrace to the Great Room due to the rainy weather. Himmler was pleased. The huge scale of the terrace and the grandeur of the surrounding mountains tended to make him look small and insignificant, and anything that appeared to diminish Himmler made him very angry.

Hitler's guests gathered in the great room. Which was huge in scale. The walls were painted a light shade of Jade green and the ceiling was coffered into squares of varnished wood. Paintings from Hitler's private art collection were displayed on the walls. A fire crackled in the large fireplace with its red marble mantel. The many bulbs in an outsized, circular chandelier flooded the room with light. The senior leadership of the Third Reich seated themselves on plush sofas and armchairs around a low table in front of the fire. No alcohol was served and smoking was forbidden. Coffee and fruit juices were available but no one partook.

Besides Himmler, the guests included fat Reichmarschall Herman Goering, Deputy Fuhrer and chief of the Luftwaffe; Club footed Dr. Joseph Goebbels, Nazi Propaganda Minister; General Alfred Jodl, Chief of the Operations Staff of the Wehrmacht high command; and Admiral Wilhelm Canaris, Director of the Abwehr. Just the sight of the little Admiral made Himmler angry.

Himmler sighed and settled back in his chair. He had gathered immense power to himself within the Third Reich. At the time he was appointed the head of the Schutzstaffel or SS, as it was usually called, it had been only a small part of the SA brownshirts organization, serving as a small elite guard for Hitler and other party leaders. Under Himmler's leadership, The SS had grown to be the most powerful entity in Germany. Himmler not only ran the SS, but he was also chief of all the German Police, Reich Commissioner for the strengthening of German Nationhood and the director of the Reich Main Security office, controlling the courts and concentration camps. His control of the security apparatus of Germany was total except for the Intelligence arm of the German General Staff, the Abwehr. The Reichfuhrer wanted to control that too but so far, Hitler had refused to hand it over to him. It galled him immensely.

Himmler's ambition knew no bounds. He thought he was destined to rule the world. That in due time he would supplant Hitler to be the ruler of Germany and later the globe. He didn't know what means fate would use to install Him as Fuhrer, but Himmler had no doubt that it would happen. He was a master of eliminating people who stood in the way of his destiny. Ernst Rohm, the leader of the stormtroopers and Reinhard Heydrich, Himmler's deputy in the SS, had both stood in his way. Now both were dead.

"Mein Herren," said Hitler, "this will not be a formal meeting but just a little chat about the state of the war." He was dressed in a cream-colored tunic, with the Nazi eagle emblem embroidered on the left breast, brown trousers, white shirt and tie.

Himmler saw that the Fuhrer was in a jovial mood. When he wasn't, these little chats often became angry rants.

"Herman, what is the state of the Luftwaffe? asked the Fuhrer. Goering was one of Hitler's oldest friends, hence he called him by his first name. The grossly obese Goering, in his garish Luftwaffe uniform festooned with medals and decorations, stood and came to attention clicking his heels. No easy feat for a man as bloated and disgusting as he, thought Himmler.

"Mein Fuhrer, we have more than made up our losses in the England operation. Once our jet fighters begin production we will sweep the skies of enemy aircraft. Thanks to the Abwehr, we know that American jet research is years behind ours."

"Good, that is good," replied Hitler.

"If we were allowed to develop four-engine jet bombers, we could get even with the English, and even bomb New York," added Goering.

"Nein, nein," said the Führer. He punched his right fist into his left palm. "We need fighters more than bombers. How many times do I have to tell you? Don't bring this up again." The Fuhrer's voice rose. Goering had obviously broached this subject before and been rebuffed, and Hitler didn't like him bringing it up again. The Fuhrer's affability was starting to crack.

"General Jodl, what is the situation in Russia?" asked Hitler. His eyes had started to take on the intensity that they showed when he was agitated.

"Our armies are advancing all along the front. At Kharkov we encircled four Soviet divisions and wiped them out. In July we launched Operation Blue, an attack to capture the oil fields in the Caucasus. The offensive is progressing well," said the tall aristocratic-looking general. Himmler looked on Jodl as a spineless toady who always told Hitler what he wanted to hear. Therefore, he was no threat to the SS head's power.

"Splendid, it is only a matter of time before the entire Russian front collapses," said the Fuhrer brightly. His good humor had returned.

"Herr Reichfuhrer, what of the SS?" asked the Fuhrer.

Himmler stood and drew himself up to his full 1.74-meter height. The light from the chandelier reflected off his spectacles.

"We have made solid progress in our goal of making Europe Jew-free. Three extermination camps are operational. at Belzec, Treblinka and Sobibor. When the huge new facility at Auschwitz comes onto line......"

Himmler was interrupted by Goebbels.

"Nein! Nein! Nein! The Fuhrer is not to be told of these things!"

'Quite right, Joseph. I am not to be informed about those things," Hitler said, with a wink at Himmler.

There was a pause in the conversation and the Reichfuhrer decided that this was a good opportunity to diminish the Abwehr in the Fuhrer's eyes.

"Mein Fuhrer," asked Himmler, "might I be allowed to ask Admiral Canaris a question?"

"By all means," said Hitler, and Himmler turned toward Canaris.

"What actual benefit are your spies to the Reich. I mean, how does it help us to know that American factories produce x number of tons of steel or farmers in England grow y tons of grain?"

For the first time Canaris spoke. He didn't stand as the others had done. "Suppose, Herr Reichfuhrer, that the Americans develop a revolutionary tank armor that is impervious to our anti-tank guns. If these new tanks were ever deployed against us, they would crush the Wehrmacht. But what if one of the Abwehr's agents discovered the secret of this new armor and sent the information back to us. Our engineers would then have time to develop new weapons to counter it."

"Quite right, Herr Admiral," said Hitler, chuckling, "Herr Reichfuhrer, he has got you there."

Himmler stared at Canaris with thinly disguised hatred. How dare you show me up in front of the Fuhrer, he thought. I will destroy you. I have had my doubts about your loyalty for a long time. Sooner or later you will make a mistake and I will put you in a casket.

"Herr Admiral," the Fuhrer continued, "you have served me brilliantly. Last year you came to me and said that the Russian defenses were weak but getting stronger and advocated an early strike against them. My generals, with their mighty brains, cautioned against attacking the communists. They said that Russia was huge and had too many resources. Well, the generals were wrong. My soldiers sliced through the Russians like a hot knife through butter. In a short time, the Russians will be conquered and I can turn my attention to England and America."

After the meeting with the Fuhrer, on the perilous drive down the mountain seated alone in the back of a shiny black Daimler, Wilhelm Canaris thought about Hitler's compliment to him and smiled. The arrogant monster didn't know that attacking Russia was the worst mistake of his life. The evidence that it was a mistake had already begun to surface. In December 1941 the German forces had suffered a massive defeat at the gates of Moscow and all along the front, the forward progress was slowing. The reason for the Admiral's smile was because he was responsible for the invasion of Russia.

In late 1940, the Admiral began to intimate in his intelligence reports to Hitler that the Soviet Union only appeared to be abiding by the nonaggression pact with Germany. Subtly, Canaris intimated that Stalin was secretly assembling vast armies far away beyond the Ural Mountains that would one day emerge to attack Germany without warning, while the Wehrmacht was occupied on the Western Front. Stalin hoped to stab Germany in its unprotected back. Canaris also suggested that Russian preparations were in their early stages, so the Soviet Union was very vulnerable to attack.

It was all a lie. The Abwehr's networks in Russia were in a shambles. Most of the agency's spies that had tried to penetrate the Russian government had been caught by the NKVD and shot. Canaris had no idea what was going on in Stalin's inner circle.

The Admiral's aim was for Germany to fight the communists and blunt its offensive power on the vast steppes of the Soviet Union. It would then be much less of a threat to the rest of the world. In the process, the Russians would also be weakened. Canaris looked upon Stalin as just as bad as Hitler. The spy master's only regret was for the thousands of young German men who were to die, but it couldn't be helped. Hitler took the bait. In June 1941, he sent the Wehrmacht crashing into western Russia.

Canaris felt this disinformation campaign was not only necessary but vital. The Nazis had to be stopped. The whole gang of them were monsters. Hitler and Himmler's smugness during the meeting about murdering tens of thousands of people had turned the Admiral's stomach. They were joking about killing innocent civilians. They couldn't be allowed to win the war.

But he had to be very careful from now on. Canaris had made a greater enemy of Himmler today and the Reichsfuhrer would double his efforts at infiltrating SS spies into the Abwehr. He had thwarted their efforts so far. Himmler was as cunning and dangerous as an adder, but he was at heart. a fool. His question about intelligence gathering had shown that. Himmler didn't realize that conducting a modern war was impossible without intelligence as to the enemy's capabilities. Information on industrial production as well as the number of men in

THE ADMIRAL'S SPIES | 119

uniform and the state of their training was vital in determining what the enemy was capable of accomplishing militarily. It was then up to the generals of the High Command to make educated guesses as to how the enemy would use their capabilities.

Canaris then turned his mind to the secrets he was keeping from the Nazis and chuckled out loud. The glass partition between Canaris and the driver slid down. "Did you say something to me Herr Admiral?" asked the SS driver.

"Nein."

So the rear seat of this automobile had a listening device and the driver could hear everything that was said. Canaris noted this for future reference.

Yes, Canaris knew things that would surely cause Goering's straining buttons to give way and fly across the room. The Admiral knew that British codebreakers had cracked the German Enigma machine code in 1941 and were reading most of the military and diplomatic messages of the Reich. This gave the Allies a tremendous strategic advantage, though so far it hadn't helped. They were in retreat across the world. Canaris knew about what the Allies called Ultra because a certain Brigadier General in Intelligence at the War Department in Washington was prone to drinking too much during lunch and then trying to impress his pretty Jewish secretary about what an important man he was. The secretary was an agent of the Abwehr.

From the same source, the Admiral also knew about the Manhattan Project. The Americans were expending vast resources toward the development of a very powerful weapon, an atomic bomb. Canaris was dubious that such a weapon was technically possible but had thought long and hard about what to do with this information. If the Abwehr succeeded in stealing the secrets of an atomic bomb and through misfortune the information wound up in the hands of Hitler and Heinrich Himmler, the consequences would be too horrible to contemplate. Canaris had, after much consideration, urgently messaged the courier agent and the agent in place who had uncovered the information to drop the line of inquiry and say nothing more about it to anyone.

The quality of intelligence from the American network was first-rate, surpassing all his other sources. The ability of the Admiral to keep certain intelligence secret was due to the way Canaris had set up the network.

Because of the distance between New York and Hamburg, Canaris ruled out using wireless to communicate with the network. Instead, instructions to the agents were sent to the Spanish Consulate in New York. A Spanish diplomat there, Carlos Breyer, received the orders from the Abwehr to the agents in the Spanish diplomatic pouch and would take them to a certain photography shop in New York. The shop was owned by one of the Abwehr's Jewish agents. Two courier agents operating separately would retrieve the orders from the shop and put them into the agent's dead drops in cities around the country. For responses, the process acted in reverse. When the responses reached Barcelona, they were intercepted and forwarded to the Abwehr in Berlin. The code used was a modified book code that the Admiral considered unbreakable. There were special procedures for urgent messages. Only Canaris, his deputy, Hans Oster, and the courier agents in America, knew the code that was used. It was a simple, elegant system.

The young American baseball player was completing his training and would soon be inserted into America to replace the compromised courier. Things were progressing well if only he could keep Himmler at bay.

CHAPTER TEN

ABWEHRKAMPFSCHULE QUENZGUT
BRANDENBURG, DEUTSCHLAND, 10 SEPTEMBER, 1942

His name was Toshiro Watanabe, but Fritz called him Tosh. During the late thirties, he had been a pitcher for the Osaka Tigers in the Japan Baseball League. To hear him tell it, he was a pretty good one too. He told Fritz that during a game against the Tokyo Giants in 1938 he had struck out thirteen batters. Or so he said, Fritz, didn't know if he was telling the truth or fudging a little. Now, four years later, Tosh found himself in the Imperial Japanese Navy with the rank of petty officer, helping to guard the Japanese embassy in Berlin. Every afternoon for a month, Tosh had been throwing fastballs by Fritz. Lately, he was succeeding less and less.

Fritz Hofmann didn't know how the Abwehr had found Watanabe and didn't care. It felt good to be facing a pitcher again with a bat in his hands. Tosh wound up and fired a fastball, grunting as he threw. Fritz swung his bat and made solid contact. Like a frozen rope, the ball streaked out in the open field behind the pitcher. Fritz gazed at the flight of the ball against the blue of the lake in the distance. The lake was called Quenzsee and it was on the outskirts of Brandenburg, twenty kilometers west of Berlin.

He was on the grounds of the Abwehr training school for agents. It had been modeled on the British SOE training schools. Once the country get-away for a wealthy Berliner, the manor house and grounds had been taken over by the Abwehr training staff and various temporary looking outbuildings were erected.

From dawn to dusk, agent trainees were taught the art of being a spy. There were classes on tradecraft, like how to pass messages by brushing up against a fellow agent in a crowd. They were taught about invisible inks and codes and a hundred other subjects necessary for being a spy. The trainees were taught how to kill with a gun, knife and bare hands. Defensive hand to hand combat and intensive weapon take away techniques were also emphasized in order that the trainees wouldn't be killed with a gun, knife or the enemy's bare hands.

Fritz did well in most areas of his trainingwith the notable exceptions of surveillance and counter-surveillance. Try as he might, he was unable to shadow someone without the target spotting him. No matter how he tried, he always managed to stick out like a sore thumb. Likewise, he was incapable of spotting someone following him. No matter how much his instructors railed at him, he just couldn't pick up the technique. His most spectacular failure came on a Berlin street when Fritz had four men closely following him but failed to spot a single one. His angry instructor said he was recommending that Fritz be rejected from the training program. Fritz expected to be on a train back to Russia shortly. As the weeks went by and it didn't happen, he relaxed.

His schedule was different from the other trainees. Most mornings, he attended the same classes as the others. In the afternoons, however, he was to be found on a makeshift baseball diamond in the middle of an open field by the lake. Fritz would practice batting until he had no energy left to swing the bat, or Tosh's throwing arm gave out. When that happened, after a short break, the Abwehr instructor, who knew nothing about baseball, would make him don his catcher's gear and practice throwing the ball to each of the bases.

The pain in his feet didn't help his performance. When he first came to the school, Fritz had endured a painful operation on his feet. The bones of his arches were broken and reset to give him flat feet. The operation had kept him in bed for two weeks and even now the pain was bad.

At the end of each day, though dead tired, he would have a few glasses of beer in the canteen with Tosh after evening mess and the two would talk baseball. As instructed by the Abwehr, they would speak only English. Watanabe had learned the language in the late thirties because he had aspirations of moving to America one day. His English was pretty good, but he had a hard time pronouncing words containing the letter "L."

Tosh wound up again and threw. Fritz thought the ball was high, out of the strike zone, and didn't swing. At the last second, the ball dropped to the middle of the plate and knee-high and rolled against the pile of pallets serving as a backstop.

"Strike!" yelled Watanabe, "that was a beautifur' curveball, you Yankee bastard. You could not hit that one in your dreams."

Fritz felt a little frustrated. He had trouble hitting the off-speed pitches. It was a problem he had always had, all through high school in America. He choked up on the bat.

"Throw me more curves. I have to work on this," yelled Fritz.

Tosh threw him ten curveballs in succession. If Fritz knew it was coming, he hit the curve well. The trick was in recognizing them just after they left the pitchers hand. Fritz was concerned. His inability to hit the curve consistently would make his baseball career very short.

For the next three days, Fritz had Tosh throw him alternate curve balls and fastballs. He concentrated on the split second before the ball left the pitchers hand. At first, he saw only a blur. Then at the end of the second day, Fritz detected a slight difference in the blur of Tosh's hand when he threw the curveball. On the third day, he was hitting both pitches well.

Today had been particularly tiring. Fritz was picking up his baseball gear in preparation for the long walk back to the barracks and a hot shower. They would be serving the evening meal soon. He was ravenously hungry. The food here was good and the training, while mentally taxing, wasn't very strenuous. This was much better than Russia, with its mud, blood and sleep deprivation. And there was no Sergeant Schultz around to make his life miserable.

A short, fat Navy Seaman, one of the ones the school used for messengers, chugged up to him and told Fritz that he was wanted urgently in the Manor House. Still, in his sweat-stained workout clothes, he hurried to the building. He was shown into an empty office and told to wait.

The same bald Wehrmacht General he had spoken with before strode into the room carrying a heavy satchel. Fritz leaped to his feet and came to attention. The General put the satchel on the top of the desk and sat down in the desk chair.

"At ease, sit down." said the officer and Fritz complied, but he eyed the General warily.

"Your training is at an end. Starting tomorrow you will go operational. There are things you need to know, so pay attention."

"Ja, Herr General," replied Fritz.

"Your assignment in the United States will be to act as a courier agent between agents in place and a base. You will, with a few exceptions, never meet the agents in place face to face but will use dead drops."

Fritz nodded his head. He knew all about dead drops from classes at the school. They were locations where one agent could secrete messages that another agent could pick up at a later time.

"Your headquarters in New York will be Stein's Camera Shop, at 447 West 46th Street. Mr. Stein will be the only agent you will deal with face to face on a regular basis. He is working for us under duress, so bear that in mind when you deal with him. In fact, all the agents in the network are Jews except Michael Flynn, the other courier agent. We are holding our agents' relatives hostage to ensure their cooperation."

"That brings up another of your possible duties," continued the General. "You are an experienced soldier with combat experience. There is a small possibility that you would be ordered to enforce discipline if one of the Jewish agents ever got out of line. If one of them was about to blow his cover, for instance, you might be required to neutralize the threat. Do you understand me?"

Fritz looked at the older man, his mind clicking into overdrive. "Neutralizing the threat"could only mean killing. Well, I have had enough of that in Russia. I will never kill another human being as long as I live if I can possible help it, he thought. Out loud he said, "Ja, Herr General."

The Abwehr man then removed two cameras from the satchel. One was a small 35 mm. the other was a larger format with a viewfinder on the top.

"Both of these cameras are American made. You will use a supposed photography hobby as a cover for visiting the shop so often. Our instructions to the agents in place will be sent to the camera shop. You don't need to know how. You will take the messages we send to our agents, decode them and deposit them in the appropriate dead drops.

Each agent will be identified by a number, one to nineteen. Here is a list of the locations of the dead drops and alternates for each agent."

The General retrieved a manila folder from the satchel. Inside were about five sheets of paper. He handed it to Fritz.

"Use this list to find the drop locations. After a while, when you become familiar with the locations of the drops, destroy this list. Also included is another list. On it are the agents' names and addresses. In the event we have an urgent message, you will send a letter to the appropriate agent containing pleasantries and sign it, "Uncle Moses." The General looked at Fritz with a steely gaze. "Under no circumstances are you to let these lists fall into enemy hands. Do not keep them on your person but hide them in a safe place."

"The messages you receive from us will be in code. You will decode them and encode the return messages from the agents using this." The General once again reached into the satchel, this time retrieving a thick book and handed it to Fritz. Hofmann saw that it was a copy, in English, of <u>Northwest Passage</u>, by Kenneth Roberts, first edition, published in 1937.

"We have an identical copy at Abwehr headquarters. Here is how you will use it. Suppose the first word of an agent's message is 'ship.' You will look through the book and find this word. You write down the page number and then a slash. You will count the lines of the page down until you reach the line containing the word. You will write the line number after the page number followed by another slash. Next, you will count the words out from the left until you have reached the word 'ship.' You will write this figure after the line number followed by another slash. You then continue on to the next word and follow the same procedure."

"If you have to spell out a word, follow the same procedure, only with letters instead of words. Instead of a slash, use a star. Do you understand what I am saying?"

Fritz looked at the General. He understood perfectly. It was a book code, modified slightly from the norm. He had learned all about secret codes and ciphers at the school.

"Ja, Herr General."

"Once you have encoded the messages from the agents, you will give them to Mr. Stein. He will send them to us. If you must pass along photographs or diagrams, Herr Stein will reduce them to microfilm and hide them under the stamp on his communication with us. The General sat back in his chair. Do you understand all my instructions?"

"Ja, Herr General."

"You must not allow yourself to be taken by the enemy alive. You will be certain to be executed in any case, so if you are cornered and capture is imminent, use this."

The general retrieved a small box from his pocket and handed it to Fritz. He opened it and saw a small capsule inside.

"It is a Cyanide capsule, you will be dead ten seconds after you bite into it."

"Ja, Herr General," said Hofmann out loud, but he thought, LIKE HELL I WILL!

The General's face then turned hard.

"One more thing. We are also giving you a lot of money to be used for expenses. If you should get the urge to just disappear in America with our money, think again. We have enormous resources, more than you know. If you should suddenly disappear, we will send agents after you. We will also tip off the Americans. So you will have the American

FBI after you and they will hang you as a traitor. If our agents find you, you will get a bullet in the back of the head. Do I make myself clear?"

"Perfectly, Herr General.

Things moved fast after the interview. Fritz was outfitted with clothing with American labels. The next morning, he boarded a train carrying a suitcase and headed west with a uniformed German naval officer as an escort. There was very little conversation between them on the trip. The officer had been instructed not to converse with Fritz. When they reached Lorient France, he was taken to a huge waterside bunker-like building with a concrete roof many meters thick. Inside, he saw a dock and a submarine moored there. U-584 was painted on the side. The naval officer gave Fritz a large sealed envelope. He was hustled aboard and the submarine sailed at nightfall.

He was given a berth in the stern torpedo room. The Captain and the other officers were annoyed. Until they delivered Fritz to his destination they could not attack enemy shipping. The enlisted crew loved him for it. His presence meant they would be safe from depth charges for a while.

When the submarine dived for the first time, Fritz had an attack of claustrophobia and had to be held down. The interior of the U-Boat was incredibly cramped, with pipes and equipment jutting out everywhere. He had never liked close places and the foul smell of diesel fuel, sweat and cigarette smoke only added to his panic.

After a day or so Fritz adapted and his fear at submerging receded. He passed the time reading the big book the General had given him. He ate, slept and read about Roger's Rangers. He had no duties to perform on the submarine.

He also had the time to do a lot of thinking and soul searching. Thoughts tumbled through his brain: All my life I have allowed others to talk me into things. That time when I was a kid in Wheeler's Mill, Eb talked me into letting the air out of the tires on a car belonging to Mr. Ham, the math teacher. But Eb got away and I was caught and had to take all the punishment. Then there was my father talking me into returning to Germany, the Wehrmacht recruiter talking me into joining the army, and now the Abwehr talking me into becoming a spy. Each time digging me deeper into a hole. What next? Will I be asked to volunteer for a suicide mission? Maybe it's time for me to take my life in hand and think for myself. From now on I will question everything anyone tells me to do. I will do what's best for me. Screw the German Abwehr.

The conditions aboard the submarine were appalling and Fritz wondered how they got men to volunteer for this life. There were no facilities for bathing. To keep clean, Fritz was only allowed a few centimeters of tepid freshwater in a basin every other day. After the third day of the voyage, the crew member's bodies got very ripe. Combined with the fuel oil smell, it caused Fritz to want to gag. The food was dreadful, consisting of mostly canned fish from Norway. To make matters worse, Fritz's bunk in the aft torpedo room was directly under a torpedo. When he slipped into his bunk, there were 1528 kilograms of Hexanite explosive, twenty centimeters away from his face. If the torpedo were to suddenly explode, he would be blown into such tiny bits as to be food for only the small baitfish that shared the sea with the submarine. He tried not to dwell on it.

About three times a week in the middle of the night, the crew members, including Fritz, were allowed on deck for a half-hour of fresh air and exercise. After the confinement in the submarine hull, the freedom was heaven.

One afternoon, about two weeks after he boarded the submarine, a crew member shook Fritz awake. The Captain wanted to see him. They were nearing the American coast. A burst of excitement enlivened Fritz but was quickly replaced by trepidation. What awaited him on the beach?

Fritz dressed in his American made suit and shoes, picked up his suitcase and went to see the Captain.

CHAPTER ELEVEN

MITCHEL SQUARE PARK
W. 166TH STREET AND BROADWAY
WASHINGTON HEIGHTS
NEW YORK CITY
SEPTEMBER 10, 1942

It was a beautiful Thursday evening in New York. The leaves on the trees in the park were starting to turn various shades of red and yellow. It was a harbinger of an early fall. The sun was setting behind purple clouds and the temperature was a perfect sixty-nine degrees. The people who lived in the area were taking advantage of the beautiful weather so the park was more crowded than usual.

Hannah Rose was not enjoying the beauty around her. She was tired and her feet hurt and she wished the damn sailor and his girl sitting on her bench would finish their business and move along. She had made two circuits of the park already and didn't relish a third.

She had seen Ted today at the canteen during the lunch hour. She was walking back to her desk after eating. She had looked up and there he was. Their eyes had met. The look of hurt and sadness on his face had almost broken her heart. She wanted to rush into his arms and hug him around his neck. She wanted him to kiss her right there in front of everybody. Instead, she had lowered her eyes and walked past him.

How had she let her feelings for Ted get so out of hand? At first, though she had been extremely attracted to him, Hannah had thought she could handle the situation. What was the harm, she had told herself, in going out with him and talking? She had miscalculated badly. She looked back and pinpointed the exact moment when the scales were tipped and Ted had become more to her than a good looking man.

It was at the restaurant and he was talking about the murder of his father and the years that followed. Hannah had suddenly seen Ted Miller for what he was, a good, decent, compassionate man who was immensely strong, both physically and in his character. His strength was very attractive to her because she was lonely and feeling very vulnerable. But he was tender too, holding her hand gently as if it was made of porcelain and would break. At that moment, the strong physical attraction Hannah felt for Ted combined with a stronger emotional one. Having never experienced anything like what she felt, she didn't quite know what to think. Was it love? She was pretty sure it was.

When they had returned to her apartment house after the date, Hannah planned to shake Ted's hand and tell him she had a nice time. Instead, she found herself in his arms and they were kissing. When their lips met she experienced such a rush of desire that it shocked her. It was something she had never felt before. She pulled him tighter to her. When Ted touched her tongue with his, she had been driven even wilder with desire. It was as if she was rushing headlong down a steep slope with a precipice at the end. Suddenly she had stiffened. What are you doing?, she thought, This is crazy. With the force of her will, she halted her slide down the slope and backed away from the cliff. Hannah broke the embrace and fled up the stairs to her room, where she sat on her bed for a half-hour shaking and trying to bring her emotions under control. Hannah had lost her heart to Ted Miller and what made it so tragic was that the relationship was impossible.

Because she cared deeply for Ted Miller, she couldn't have him. She was a German spy. If she were ever caught and they were together, then he would suffer. At best, he would be branded a fool. At worst, the FBI might think he was complicit. Even if he proved his innocence, Ted's career would be ruined. He would carry the stain for the rest of his life.

Hannah couldn't do that to him. She cared too much. It was much better to think of Ted as this impossible thing she could never have. Thank God he had given up on the telephone calls and the letters. He had also given up trying to talk to her at work and coming to her desk.

She was miserable and Uncle Moshe and Aunt Rachel had seen the change in her. They had been treating her extra nicely and they seemed genuinely concerned about her. She longed to tell them the reason for her distress, but she dared not. She couldn't tell anyone. If she did, her parents would die.

The Bureau had recently come into possession of intelligence, including photographs, of the atrocities that the German SS were committing in Poland and Russia against her people, the Jews. She had read the reports and looked at the pictures. Whole villages of people made to dig their own graves and then shot. Hannah couldn't let her parents fall into the hands of killers like the SS. She would do just about anything to prevent that.

She reflected on the cleverness of her German masters. They had gotten her, and presumably other Jews, to spy for them by threatening their families in Germany. Now, even if they had second thoughts, they couldn't turn themselves in without facing the electric chair. If they should come forward, the authorities would ask why they didn't come to them in the beginning when first approached by the Germans. The American government wasn't in a forgiving mood right now regarding Nazi spies. Now the Jewish agents were in too deep and were well and truly trapped.

Finally, the sailor and his girlfriend got up from the bench and strolled away. The sailor's right hand, which had been around the girl's waist, drifted down and came to rest on her bottom. She didn't make him move it. Hannah envied the girl. Damn the war! Damn the German Secret Service! Damn Hitler and his murderers!

Hannah sat down on the bench. She was here because she had received a letter yesterday from Uncle Moses. Not HER Uncle Moshe, the other one. It was getting dark so there was less risk of someone seeing her retrieve the box from under the bench. She sat sideways to shield her left arm from view and freed the box. A few minutes later, in the privacy of her room, she slid open the lid of the box. There were five twenty Dollar bills inside and a slip of paper. When she finished reading the note she let out a sarcastic laugh. What next? she thought.

Hannah was ordered to learn to drive an automobile and get a New York driver's license within two weeks. She didn't understand why the Germans wanted her to know how to drive but figured that it wouldn't be anything good.

She looked for driving schools in the yellow pages of the phone book. Her eye caught an ad for "Herb's Driving School. Learn to drive in three easy lessons. It's cheaper than you think." She wrote down the address and took the phone book back to the hall and put it beside the phone. Hannah heard Aunt Rachel's call that dinner was ready and left the room.

The next morning at seven, Hannah called Special Agent Milton Turley to tell him that she was ill and wouldn't be in the office that day. Turley was very solicitous.

"Hannah, sweetie, what's wrong with you?"

"Nothing too serious, Mr. Turley, just some female complaints. If you like I will explain them to you."

"Oh no, no, no, Miss Rose. That won't be necessary. I hope you feel better tomorrow."

"Actually, it may be a few days, it has to do with my…"

"That's okay," interrupted Turley, "take all the time you need."

Even though she was very stressed, Hannah had to laugh. It was a trick taught to her by the other typists in the office. If you wanted a day off, just mention female complaints. The big, tough FBI men got very uncomfortable hearing about menstrual cycles and pap smears and would ask no questions.

She dressed in what she would have worn to the office. A knee-length floral print dress. The weather was still good, so she didn't need a coat as she walked to the nearby subway station. Forty minutes later she was standing in front of 74 West 125th Street. It was smack in the middle of the business district of Harlem. A steady stream of colored people passed her on the sidewalk. She looked up at the building. Painted on one of the second-story windows was "Herb's Driving School" in gold letters. Hannah walked up the stairs and found the office. She entered without knocking.

A light-skinned black man was sitting behind a desk. He looked up at her when she entered. He was about thirty years old, with wavy pomaded hair. He was in his shirt-sleeves, with his suit coat draped over the back of the chair, and was using a rag to polish a cream and brown, wingtip shoe.

"How kin' I help you, ma'am?"

"Yes, I am looking for Herb's Driving School," replied Hannah.

The man jumped up and hopped on one foot while he put his shoe back on. He donned his suit jacket and extended his hand.

"That's me. Herbert Johnson, at your service."

"I need to learn to drive right away," said Hannah as she shook Johnson's hand.

Johnson frowned. "Ma'am, this is Harlem. And I'm colored. You need to go uptown to one of the white schools."

"That's ridiculous, what has color have to do with learning to drive?"

"If I'm seen driving around town alone in a car with a white woman, it could be dangerous for both of us," said Johnson.

"I don't have time to find someone else. Please help me."

"You talk funny. Where are you from?"

"I came here from Germany almost five years ago."

"Ooooooh no! I ain't getting mixed up with no Germans. 'Sall I need, ridin' round with a white woman that's a German. The white cops would love that," said Mr. Johnson, and sat down heavily in his chair.

"Mr. Johnson, I am a Jew. I came here to escape prejudice."

Herbert Johnson's face softened. "Well. . . I dunno."

"How much do you charge to teach someone to drive? And how long does it take?" asked Hannah.

"I charge forty-seven fifty. That includes the cost of the license. It usually takes 'bout three, four-hour lessons."

Hannah put five twenties on top of the desk. "Mr. Johnson, I will make a deal with you. If you can teach me to drive and get me licensed in three days, I will give you this one hundred dollars."

Johnson eyed the money for quite a while, then scooped it up and put it in his pocket.

"Alright, I'll do it, but first you have to promise me that you don't have a father, brother or boyfriend that owns a shotgun," Johnson said, only half in jest.

"I promise."

Herb escorted Hannah downstairs to an automobile parked at the curb in front of the building. The car was a 1935 Studebaker Land Cruiser, painted jet black. It was spotlessly clean and shiny. Hannah could tell it was Johnson's pride and joy. He opened the rear door for Hannah.

"Better you sit back here. People will think I'm your driver."

Hannah got in and Johnson drove off. He told her he was taking her to the parking lots around Yankee stadium. The Yanks were out of town that week and the lots were empty. It was a good place to learn the fundamentals of driving. Herb tuned the radio to a swing station and the two listened to numbers by Count Basie, Glenn Miller and Tommy Dorsey.

As they were crossing the Harlem River on the Third Avenue Bridge, a cop on a motorcycle pulled up alongside them and gave the eye to Johnson and Hannah in the back seat. Herb gave him a big smile showing dazzling white teeth.

Once in the stadium parking lot, Johnson told Hannah to take over and she slid behind the steering wheel. Herb walked around the car and seated himself on the passenger side. The instruction began. Hannah caught on pretty fast, but she had a little trouble mastering the clutch. For the first two hours, the car lurched around the parking lots like a rhumba dancer. Johnson proved to be a patient teacher but got a bit excitable at times. On the first day, Herb started to scream when she was careening toward a brick wall at fifty miles per hour. "BRAKE! BRAKE!," he shouted and the car skidded to a stop four feet from the wall. At the end of the third day, Herb and Hannah arrived back at the 125th Street address. She had a brand new, New York driver's license in her purse. During their three days together, she and Herb had become friends.

CHAPTER TWELVE

There had been great strength in Elaine Miller all along, although early on she didn't realize it. In 1924 she was twenty-seven, lived in Dayton, Ohio, and was married to an Ohio State Police Trooper named Edward. They had a nine-year-old son named Ted. She happily fulfilled her role as a housewife and mother and deferred important family decisions to her husband. Life was good. One day she watched Ed put on his uniform. He kissed her goodbye, requested pot roast for dinner that evening and walked out the door. He never returned. Instead, the familiar figure of Ed's Sergeant, Hal Venti, appeared who told her that Ed was dead, killed in a shootout with two low life hoodlums. Hal said that her husband had put up a mighty fight against the criminals who shot him, killing one of them.

When her son, Ted came home from school, she didn't try to keep anything from him. She told him his father was dead and the circumstances. They were a church-going Christian family and Elaine took down the family bible and she and her son sat together on the couch, and tried, like thousands before them, to find comfort in the scriptures. Young Ted was devastated. He and his Dad were close. His eyes brimmed with tears and he kept wiping them away with his fists. Elaine told him it was perfectly appropriate to cry in mourning for a man as fine as Edward Miller. The two sat on the sofa in their little house and clung to each other weeping, their tears falling on the pages of the bible.

In the following days and weeks, Elaine was devastated and didn't know if she could go on. If it hadn't been for Ted, she might have given up on life. But every day she somehow managed to get out of bed and go forward. She drew from a well of strength she had no idea she had. Maybe it was a gift from God, or maybe it was the inherited grit and toughness passed down to her by her Scotch-Irish forebears. She didn't know where the toughness came from.

Out of necessity, she cast about for a means of supporting herself and her son. She had been a whiz at sewing throughout her marriage, making clothing for her family. She opened a small dress shop in her home town of Dayton. It was tough in the beginning, but after a few months she had a respectable number of women who patronized her shop. She eked out enough to live on. Elaine received a six thousand dollar life insurance payment for her husband's death which she put away in a special bank account for Ted's college education.

Elaine Miller decided she was a one-man woman. Although still young and attractive, she had no wish to be the wife of another man. Besides, men like her husband were few and far between and it wouldn't be fair to the other man. She would always be comparing him to Ed. She resolved that she would devote the rest of her life to raising her son to be the kind of man Ed Miller would have wanted him to be. She would live through her son. She would do nothing without considering its effect on him. As the boy grew, Elaine would look at him with love mingled with sorrow, he looked so much like his father.

From her conservative Christian upbringing, Elaine looked at life in pretty much black and white terms. She believed that people's actions were either right or wrong; there were few gray areas. She didn't believe in situational ethics. She imparted these views to her son. While most people who hold such a rigid outlook on life tend to be self-righteous and judgmental, Elaine Miller wasn't like that. Her rigidity was softened by two qualities she possessed in abundance, compassion and a genuine love for people. She never lacked for friends.

As the boy grew into his teens he developed into a young man she could be proud of. He was polite and respectful and never rebellious. He got good grades in school. But it was his tenacity that surprised her. When something was important to him, he had an iron will. Whenever he set a goal for himself he was single-minded in accomplishing it. He was like a bulldog that once he had sunk his teeth into something, he wouldn't let go.

Young Ted, for his part, saw the grief on his mother's face and resolved to do nothing to cause her more sadness. He would be the perfect son. Ted set impossibly high standards for himself to honor his dead Father. When he would inevitably fail, and commit some minor sin, he would berate himself for days. His childhood wasn't much fun. The other kids considered him a goody two shoes.

When his father was killed, Ted had been very angry at God. How had He let this happen? His father's death was the most unjust thing that he could contemplate. Although he eventually made peace with his deity, he was changed for life. It had been demonstrated to him, in the worst way possible, that there were bad people in the world and injustice was commonplace. Ted grew to hate unfairness in any form. He thought that there had to be individuals who dared to stand up and protect innocent people from the bad elements in the world.

In 1930, Ted was sixteen and in high school. There was a student, Danny Phillips, who had contracted polio as a child. He survived the disease but had to wear metal braces and crutches to walk. There were two other boys in the school who would taunt and harass the crippled boy on a regular basis. One day Ted was walking down the school hallway and saw the two harassers trip Danny and cause him to fall on the tiled floor. He cried out in pain as his tormenters laughed.

Ted was outraged and lost his temper. He ran toward the two offenders with his fists flying. One of the boys suffered a broken nose and the other was sent fleeing with a torn shirt and a fat lip. The Principal hauled Ted into his office and gave him a lecture about violence never being appropriate to solve disputes. Ted remained silent and respectful but he knew in his heart that, just as with his father's murderers, violence was sometimes the only way to correct an injustice. He was suspended from school for a week. He figured it was worth getting suspended to keep those two jerks from messing with Danny again. Ted Miller didn't realize it at the time, but he was already positioning himself as a watchman on the wall, guarding his people against the barbarians.

LIBERTY AVENUE AND 9TH STREET
PITTSBURG, PENNSYLVANIA
OCTOBER 1, 1942

The Bureau had been conducting surveillance on Anton Dietrich since late December 1941. They had been expending all the effort because Dietrich had expressed pro-German, anti-American sentiments. He was a naturalized American citizen of German descent and was a former member of the German American Bund.

The surveillance of Dietrich had been ordered from FBI headquarters in Washington during the chaos in the Bureau following the attack on Pearl Harbor. Perhaps they had forgotten they ordered it. But, AD Byrnes was a very obedient agent and terrified of Director Hoover. He would keep his mouth shut and continue the surveillance until orders came for it to stop.

The original team of agents shadowing Deitrich had been relieved. Around-the-clock surveillance was hard work and following Anton around the country had kept them away from their families for too long. Ted Miller and Bill Parker and another team comprised of Sam Winston and George Smith had taken over in early September.

So far, all Deitrich had done was travel from city to city and make sales calls at dime stores, hawking lipstick from the company he worked for, Lady Liz cosmetics.

At their briefing, before starting the assignment, Byrnes had told the agents that the surveillance of Anton was just a precaution. They didn't suspect him of being a spy, only a German sympathizer. There were no more German spies or saboteurs operating in the United States. Director Hoover had said so. The same went for Japanese spies. All the Japs in Hawaii and the West Coast had been rounded up and sent to camps where they couldn't spy.

Ted was not so sure. Yes, Mr. Byrnes had said that the FBI had caught all the spies, but how could he be so sure they had caught them all? It was dangerous to assume something like that. He said nothing however. Contradicting his boss wouldn't be a wise thing to do.

The method the agents used to tail Dietrich was a simple one. One agent would tail him from behind and another agent would be ahead of him across the street. One more agent would parallel them in an automobile one street over. The fourth agent would be resting, it was his job to watch Dietrich at night. The agents switched positions frequently. They had tailed him to many cities. Today they were in Pittsburg. Ted didn't mind the assignment. It kept him busy and was better than talking to crackpots. And it kept him from thinking about Hannah.

For weeks after their date, he had made call after call to Hannah's apartment. Each time, either her aunt or uncle would tell him Hannah didn't want to talk to him. He had written numerous letters to her but didn't get a response. When he ran into her at work, she was cold and wouldn't look him in the eye. It made him miserable. He didn't sleep well and had lost his appetite.

One evening in Philadelphia, over dinner, Ted had opened up to his partner, Bill, about his Hannah problem. Bill, who had minored in history in college, had given his advice.

"Ted, maybe the problems between you and Hannah stem from her religion. The Jews are an ancient people. They have maintained their racial identity despite the fact that they haven't had their own country for two thousand years. How do you think they managed to do that? They refused to allow their sons and daughters to marry anyone but another Jew. They are really strict about that. Maybe her family has forbidden her from seeing you."

Ted sat back in his chair and considered Bill's comments. Could this be the reason Hannah had suddenly turned on him? The more he thought about it, it made sense. If Bill's theory was true then her coldness had nothing to do with him but some religious taboo. Ted knew it should make him feel better, but it didn't.

Ted thought again about enlisting in the Marines, but he never did. He threw himself into his work. Instead of investigating ten crackpot tips per day, he did fifteen. It was driving Bill Parker crazy. Ted's partner was relieved when this assignment came up.

Up ahead, Dietrich went into an independent five and dime store. Ted leaned against a parked car and lit up a Lucky. He hadn't kept his promise to quit smoking. Without Hannah, there was no point.

Ted looked around. There seemed to be less and less automobile traffic on the streets these days. He guessed the rationing of rubber and gasoline were really taking their toll. Miller didn't own a car. He saw no reason to own one in New York City. Maybe after the war when the restrictions are eased he might consider buying one, he mused. What kind do I want? Everybody seemed to own a Ford so he didn't want one of them. Too ordinary. Chevrolet was the same. Too common. Maybe a Buick. That's it, a long, black Buick convertible, with white sidewall tires. Ted imagined himself out in the country at the wheel of his new car with the wind blowing through his hair.

Ted was so intent on his daydream that he almost missed Anton come out of the store carrying his samples case and head northeast on Liberty Avenue toward 9th Street. Ted snapped back to the present and followed.

Suddenly Dietrich bolted. He ran northeast on Liberty and right on a small side street called Smithfield. Ted signaled to Bill and the agents gave chase. Miller rounded the corner onto Smithfield and just caught sight of Dietrich turning right onto Sixth Avenue.Ted was pounding after him and starting to breathe hard when he heard tires squeal and a heavy thump around the corner on Sixth.

When Ted rounded the corner he saw a green Ford Model A pickup truck stopped in the middle of Sixth Street. Sprawled on the pavement in front of it was Dietrich. Ted caught sight of the bright red of fresh blood. He ran up and saw that Anton's right leg was almost severed just below the knee. It was only connected to the upper leg by strings of white ligaments. Spurts of bright red arterial blood came from the stump. The pickup truck was missing the front bumper and the sharp bumper brackets stuck out. This was what had severed Dietrich's leg. The driver of the truck was standing with his hands on his knees and looked like he was going to be sick.

"He came out from between two parked cars. I couldn't stop in time," said the driver, and vomited onto the pavement.

Ted knelt next to Dietrich, whose skin was the color of old parchment. The FBI agent stripped off his belt and put it around the stump to try to make a tourniquet. He couldn't exert enough pressure and the blood continued to flow.

Ted looked up and met Dietrich's eyes.

'You will never catch them. No one will ever suspect them," said Anton and smiled.

As Ted watched, the life left Dietrich's eyes and he died.

On the train back to New York, Ted struggled to write his report. Bill Parker was slumped in the seat across from him, asleep. Ted's mind was a jumble of thoughts. Anton must have known that they were tailing him and the pressure built until he snapped. Dietrich's last words had been heard by only him. Bill had arrived a moment later. What did it mean? "You will never catch them" implied there was someone to catch. It dawned on Ted that there must be other Nazi spies operating in the United States. It was the only conclusion one could draw. The second part of Anton's last speech, "no one will ever suspect them," could only mean that they were buried so deep, or in such high positions, that they would never be suspected of spying

What Dietrich had told him was above Ted's pay grade. He must get this information to his superiors as soon as possible. He wrote down his conclusions in his report. His eyelids grew heavy and he joined Bill in slumber.

The next morning around nine-thirty, Ted was summoned to AD Byrnes's office. When he entered the room Miller saw that in addition to Byrnes, Assistant SAC Turley was there. They were hovering over Byrnes's desk where Ted's report sat front and center. A fan labored in the corner to push the hot air around and the window was open. Byrnes was a distinguished older man and something of a clotheshorse. He favored custom made double-breasted suits. He was wearing one now despite the heat while Turley was in shirtsleeves. Their eyes swiveled to

Ted. From their expressions, he could tell they were not pleased.

"Good morning Ted. I want to talk to you about this report. You maintain that there are undiscovered German spies in the country?"

"Yes, sir, I do. The suspect's last words make that clear."

"I wish to make you aware that Director Hoover has told me personally, that it is his opinion that there are no more enemy spies operating in the United States," said Byrnes emphatically.

"Yes, sir, I appreciate that, but what if it isn't true? What if there is another spy ring? Dietrich's last words indicate that it is composed of people who would never be suspected. Surely we would want to catch them."

Byrnes and Turley exchanged a look.

"Milt, will you excuse us for a moment?" asked Byrnes and Turley left the room, closing the door behind him.

"Ted," said Byrnes, "you are a fine agent. You have a bright future in the Bureau if you don't do any stupid things. The stupidest thing you could do would be to contradict the Director. If J. Edgar Hoover says there are no more spies in America, then there are no more spies. Do you get my drift?"

"I'm sorry, Mr. Byrnes, but what if a ring of well-placed enemy agents are stealing vital secrets and getting soldiers and sailors killed?" asked Ted.

"There hasn't been one documented case of sabotage in the United States since the start of the war," said Byrnes. He was getting a little annoyed.

"Maybe it's strictly an espionage ring. Please, sir, let me follow this up. I want to search Dietrich's room in the Bronx."

Byrnes looked down at his desk, clearly tired of talking about this.

"If you want to search Dietrich's room, go ahead, but get a warrant."

Ted hurried back to the counter-espionage office to write up an affidavit for a search warrant. The office was a room only about twenty-five feet square. There were fifteen wooden desks crammed into it. With thirty agents assigned there, the room was incredibly cramped. Ted had to turn sideways and inch along in the narrow aisles between the desks. He sat down at the desk he shared with his partner, Bill, and filled out the affidavit containing his probable cause to search Dietrich's room. It didn't have to be very solid. Judge Potter was a sure thing.

Elderly Hiram Potter had been appointed to the federal bench in 1908 by President Teddy Roosevelt. He was possibly the most pro-law enforcement federal judge in history. In his career of thirty-five years, Potter had never refused to sign a search or arrest warrant for the FBI or other federal law enforcement agencies. He loved to take a break from his other business and listen to windy stories from G-men about their work.

When Ted was ushered into his chambers, the old Judge looked at him with his watery eyes.

"Well, 'Machine Gun' Miller. What can I do for you?"

"Hello, your honor. I have a search warrant for you to sign."

The old judge reached for the warrant and signed it without a glance.

"Tell me the story again about the shootout with the Baker gang."

Miller spent five minutes re-telling the story. He made wild embellishments to the tale just to please the old man. Judge Potter had a big smile on his face when Ted left.

It was afternoon before Ted and Bill reached Dietrich's rooming house in the Yorkville section of Manhattan. It was a lower middle-class neighborhood. Clotheslines had been strung between buildings and drying clothes flapped in the breeze. Ted showed the landlady his FBI credentials and the search warrant. She was scandalized but let them into Dietrich's room with her passkey. Bill went door to door in the house to interview any of the other tenants who were around.

It was a bare looking room containing a single bed, a battered dresser, and a sagging overstuffed chair. There was a small closet and a window that looked out on a fire escape. There was no bathroom or kitchen. The house provided the meals and residents on each floor shared a bathroom.

Ted found a brown leather valise on a shelf in the closet. He opened the top and saw that it was empty. However, it weighed a surprising amount for an empty valise. He examined it more closely. He stuck his hand inside and measured its depth. It appeared to be too shallow. Ted hunted around the inside bottom until he found a little leather tab that had been tucked into the bottom seam. He worked it free and pulled on the tab. A false bottom came away revealing a four-inch-deep space. The space was packed neatly with banded stacks of ten-dollar bills. Ted dumped it out onto the bed and counted the money. There were six thousand, four hundred and thirty dollars.

Ted was gratified. This went a long way to prove his theory. Who else but a spy would have this much money in a false bottomed case in his closet? He anticipated what Byrnes would say. Maybe he was a gambler or a loan shark. There was no way to tell where the money came from. Ted, however, was now convinced that Dietrich had been a German spy.

There was little else. In the bottom dresser drawer, he found some pre-war literature from the German America Bund. Ted put the literature and the money into the valise and prepared to leave. On his way out of the room, he saw a book sitting on top of a foolscap pad on the floor beside the chair. It was a copy of <u>Rabble In Arms</u>, by Kenneth Roberts, published in 1933 by Doubleday. Ted remembered reading the book in his college days.

The presence of this book struck Ted as incongruous. Why would a German spy, a traitor, want to read a book about the American Revolution? He put the book into the valise and examined the pad. It was a five-cent pad of cheap paper sold in every dime store. He turned it to catch the light and saw that there were impressions on it. To his eye, they looked jumbled but he could make out a long series of numbers and dashes. Ted shrugged and put the pad in the valise too.

Back at the office AD Byrnes was not impressed with their finds. "Maybe it was the guy's life savings. Look, I think you are giving too much weight to the ravings of a delirious man who just had his leg cut off."

Ted bundled up the items seized at Dietrich's room and sent them to the FBI crime lab in Washington. Two weeks later everything came back to him, minus the money of course.

The report said the money was genuine, printed in 1938, but untraceable. The book was just a book. There were no traces of secret inks, pinholes or things hidden in the binding. The top sheet of the pad was more interesting. The impressions were jumbled but appeared to be just long lines of numbers broken up with slashes. Miller thought it might be a code, but when he showed the report to Mr. Turley the big man balled the paper up in his hand and threw it into his waste can. "Could be anything, even a golf score."

Ted sat at his desk. He didn't know how to proceed. Without backing from his superiors, he was at a dead end and it was frustrating. But it had to be investigated. There was something fishy here, he was sure of it. At the same time, he was chiding himself for his stubbornness. Why do you have to be the one to buck the system? he asked himself. Any other agent would just forget the whole thing. Why can't I just let this go and go along with what Byrnes says?

CHAPTER THIRTEEN

LONG ISLAND SOUND
ONE KILOMETER OFF MATTITUCK INLET,
LONG ISLAND, NEW YORK
12 OCTOBER, 1942
0234 HOURS.

I t was chilly and dark on the water. The waxing crescent moon and the stars appeared only as blurry, faint blobs of light through the night mist and shed little light on the sea. The water was calm, with only small ripples on the surface caused by the onshore breeze. It was quiet and peaceful save for the squawking of some seagulls circling high overhead.

The serenity of the night was broken by a sudden disturbance in the water. A vertical metal rod poked above the surface and moved west, leaving white foaming water in its wake. The conning tower of a submarine appeared and rose out of the sea, followed swiftly by the rest of the boat. U-584 was painted in light grey on the side of the conning tower. The submarine glided to a stop with decks awash.

A hatch popped open and three men emerged and posted themselves on the tiny deck at the top of the conning tower. Two of the men were lookouts. The third was the vessel's captain, who raised a pair of Zeiss binoculars with special lenses for viewing in low light conditions. He focused on the shoreline a kilometer away. All he could see was a thin line a little lighter than the sea that marked the beach. With the night glasses to his eyes, the captain made a slow, three hundred and sixty-degree circle looking for threats to his boat and crew.

The sea off the northern coast of Long Island wasn't patrolled by the Coast Guard as frequently as the more populated southern coast. The American Navy thought that the many underwater obstacles between Little Gull Island and Fishers Island at the entrance to the sound would deter submarines from entering. The German Commander, a daring and resourceful man, had done the unexpected. He had gone through the gap on the surface, in the dark of night and only dived when he reached deeper water.

The captain leaned down to the hatch at his feet and whispered orders for the submarine to ease in toward shore. At one hundred meters from the beach, he ordered his helmsman to swing the submarine parallel to the coast. He watched the shore scroll by. When he saw the faint outline of the opening for the Mattituck Inlet, he leaned down again, ordered all stop on the engines, a rubber boat to be launched and the "special cargo" to be landed.

§

Fritz Hofmann stood at a hatch that led to the deck at the base of the conning tower. He was wearing a dark-colored American made suit. In his wallet were a draft card, Social Security card and a New York State driver's license, all in his own name, all forgeries that he would replace with genuine ones later. He carried a brown leather suitcase containing some clothing, a book, two cameras and twenty thousand American dollars. Two German sailors stood beside him, each carrying a short paddle. At the captain's order, the three burst from the hatch and out on the deck. Two other sailors were lowering a rubber boat into the water. One of them held a rope that kept the boat snubbed against the side of the submarine. The two sailors accompanying Hofmann jumped into the boat with the deftness of men who make their living on the water. They each grabbed one of Fritz's arms and helped him down the sloping side of the submarine and into the unstable boat. Once they got him seated, the sailors began to paddle like mad for shore.

A short few minutes later, the boat plowed into the sand of the beach with a groan. The sailor up front jumped out, grabbed the bow rope and pulled the boat further up on the sand. Fritz stood and stepped onto the beach without getting his feet wet. He walked a few steps inland and turned to wave goodbye to the sailors. They were already several meters away, paddling rapidly back to the submarine.

Fritz looked to his left. It was very dark but he could just make out where Mattituck Inlet dumped into the sound. According to the sealed orders he had received upon sailing there was supposed to be a dirt parking lot at the top of the dunes, just to the west of the inlet. His orders said there would be someone there to meet him with transport. If there wasn't, he was in big trouble.

Fritz trudged up the sand dunes. His palms were sweating and his heart pounded in his chest. This had all sounded so simple when he read it on a piece of paper. Now that it was the real thing, he was terrified. He expected searchlights to snap on at any minute and pin him in their glare and machine-gun fire to cut him down. He reached the top of the dunes without incident, however, and in the dim light spotted an automobile with its lights off parked in the dirt lot.

The car was parked with its rear to the sea so Fritz approached it that way. It was a dark-colored sedan. As he came near, the car's engine fired up. Whoever was in the driver's seat was alert and had seen him approach. Fritz opened the rear door, threw his suitcase in the back seat, opened the front passenger door and slid in.

"Sie sind der Deutsche spion?" asked a female voice.

"Speak English, you fool!" Fritz shot back in a hoarse whisper. "Yeah, I'm the guy you're waiting for."

Hofmann saw that it was a small woman behind the wheel. She snapped on the headlights, pushed in the clutch pedal, put the car in gear and drove smoothly out of the parking lot. The car followed a dirt road leading away from the beach. After about a kilometer and some sharp turns, they came to a paved road. The woman turned right on the road and accelerated to forty mph. They had the highway to themselves, with no other traffic. Only the lights of distant farmhouses pierced the darkness.

Fritz looked over at the woman driver. The light from the instruments on the dash wasn't enough to make out the features of her face very well. In his packet of instructions was an admonishment to Fritz that he was positively, under no circumstances, on pain of punishment, forbidden to converse with the person who picked him up or ask about that person's identity. Screw the orders, he thought. It might be important for him to know who this woman was.

"Who are you?" He asked.

"You know very well. I am a dirty Jew who you have forced to work for you by threatening my parents who you are holding hostage in Germany."

Fritz was surprised by the venom in her voice. He also knew she wasn't native to America. She had a pronounced foreign accent.

"Is this your car?"

"No, it is hired."

"What is your name?"

"I am Hannah Rosen. I am your spy at the FBI in New York."

Fritz was shocked. The Abwehr had an agent inside the FBI? Holy shit!

"First off, don't get on your high horse and get mad at me. I'm in the same boat you are. I was born in America. My drunken father dragged me back to Germany in nineteen thirty-seven. I ended up in the German army. Before I was offered this job I was fighting in Russia. You have no idea how savage the fighting is there. If I didn't get out of there, I was going to die," said Fritz, with an edge on his voice.

"I don't believe you."

"Well, believe me or not it's true. Look, you say you are a Jew, fine. But you are a Jew living in America. Your parents are hostages? At least they are alive. Do you know what the SS is doing to the Jews in Poland and Russia? They round up whole Jewish villages, make them dig a trench and then shoot then and fill up the trench with their bodies."

Hannah looked over at Fritz in the darkness. He could sense her eyes on him.

"You have seen this?"

"Yes, I have seen it."

They fell silent after that and Fritz concentrated on the road. He figured they had come about twenty kilometers. He caught himself. Time to start thinking like an American. That means ditching the metric system. Let me see, a kilometer is six-tenths of a mile. Then twenty kilometers would be about twelve and a half miles. The map he had studied showed his landing site was about ninety miles from New York City. They had a long way to go. About thirty minutes later Hofmann saw a sign that said New York was sixty miles away. Hannah was driving a steady forty mph. Then she broke the silence.

"There are lights behind us, coming up rapidly."

Fritz turned on the seat and looked through the rear window. It wasn't a car. The lights didn't maintain a constant distance from each other. There were two motorcycles approaching fast. That could mean only one thing, Cops! Fritz slid across the seat and put his arm around Hannah.

"What are you doing," she asked.

"Just relax. If we are stopped, let me do the talking. That accent of yours might make them suspicious," replied Fritz.

The lights did indeed turn out to be two policemen on motorcycles. They hung back about a car length for a few moments then the lead officer turned on his red light. Hannah immediately pulled to the side of the road. The cop who approached the driver's door was a large man dressed in his New York State Police uniform with a pistol in a flap holster on a wide belt and a strap across his chest. The other officer remained astride his motorcycle. Hannah cranked her window down.

"Gimme' your driver's license. What are you two doing out here in the middle of the night?"

Hannah handed the officer her license. She started to answer but Fritz began talking first.

"Well, Officer, it's kind of a delicate matter. We have just come from a friend's fishing cabin. I have to get back to New York. I have to work tomorrow. The lady is not my wife and. . . well. . . you know," said Fritz.

"And, who are you, Bub?" asked the officer.

"Name is Fred Hofmann. Here's my identification." Fritz handed him his phony driver's license.

The officer studied the licenses for a few moments, then handed them back.

"Alright, you can go, but you two should be ashamed of yourselves."

The officer walked back to his machine, mounted it, kick-started the engine and the two cops sped off in the direction they had come. Hannah roughly pushed Fritz back to his side of the seat.

"How dare you! Making that man think I was having some dirty affair with you. I was so embarrassed," Hannah said angrily.

"What would you rather have, a little embarrassment or be dangling from a rope?"

Hannah accelerated back onto the blacktop and they continued their journey. It wasn't until they were entering Queens and the sun was coming up that Fritz realized how beautiful his driver was. He looked at her in profile. Each component of her face by itself was attractive but put them all together and the result was spectacular. She was gorgeous.

They entered Manhattan via the Queensboro Bridge. Hannah turned north on 3rd Avenue. As they approached 3rd Avenue's intersection with 60th Street, Hannah pulled to the curb. She looked at Fritz but said nothing. Once again he was impressed at how beautiful she was. He got out and retrieved his suitcase from the back seat. Fritz stood on the sidewalk and watched her drive away.

Fritz was ravenously hungry. He walked north but within a minute, his feet began to hurt. He spotted an all-night diner ahead. He went in and settled himself on a stool. It was a little after six-thirty in the morning so everyone in the place was eating breakfast. The counter waitress sat a glass of water in front of him.

"What kin I gitcha, hon?"

Fritz ordered three hamburgers, French fries and a chocolate malt. The waitress gave him a strange look, but then shrugged and put in the order. When the food came Hofmann attacked the meal. He was in heaven as the dimly remembered tastes exploded in his mouth. It felt good to be back where he belonged. He had never cared for the diet of the Germans, especially the slop he had eaten on the submarine. After eating, he paid his bill and walked outside. The bill had come to ninety-five cents.

His feet were aching badly. He hailed a taxi and asked the cabbie to take him to a good clean boarding house. He offered the driver three dollars extra for his trouble. The cabbie took Fritz to 1567 Sheridan Avenue in the West Bronx. It was an old Victorian home.

There was a sign in the window, ROOM FOR RENT. He paid the cab driver and rang the bell on the house.

The woman who answered the bell was in her early fifties, had her grey hair pulled back into a bun and was drying her hands on an apron tied around her waist. She was very severe looking but friendly enough in manner. Fritz inquired about the room and was told the rent was eleven dollars a week including meals, first two weeks in advance. He accepted, paid, and the woman showed him to a room on the second floor and handed him a key. She said dinner was promptly at six-thirty. She added that he had to eat what was offered. She didn't cook special meals.

Fritz found himself alone in the room. It was small but looked comfortable enough. The bed wasn't too lumpy and there was ample space in the dresser for his things. He sat down in an ugly, flower print chair and thought about his options.

The way he saw it, he had three. First, he could go to the FBI and confess. He could tell them he didn't want to be a spy but was forced to do so by the Nazis. This was very risky because the Americans had shown no mercy so far to Nazi spies. The Abwehr had told him how the last Germans landed by submarine had gone to the electric chair.The second option was to take the Abwehr's money and disappear. This alternative was very tempting, but Fritz remembered the bald general's warning and decided it was too much of a risk. The third option was to do what the Abwehr sent him to do. For now, he decided, he would follow that course. Maybe later a way of escape would surface.

He walked down the hall to the bathroom to urinate. After doing his business, and still standing in front of the toilet, Fritz carefully took out the suicide pill the Abwehr had given him, threw it into the toilet bowl and flushed. He eyed the cyanide pill as it circled the bowl and then went down the drain. He smiled wickedly and gave a middle finger gesture towards the east, toward Berlin.

§

U. S. IMMIGRATION AND NATURALIZATION SERVICE

500 12TH STREET S/W

WASHINGTON, DC

OCT 12, 1942

A clerk in the file room of the Immigration and Naturalization Service stayed behind when the other clerks went to lunch. This wasn't unusual. She often ate a bag lunch she brought from home. She waited until she was sure everyone else had gone, especially the head of her department, Miss Pettibone. The clerk retrieved a sheet of paper from her purse and walked over to a particular filing cabinet out of hundreds. She opened the middle drawer and pulled another sheet of paper from a file. She replaced the paper with one that was identical to the first, with one exception. It omitted the notation that one Friedrich Hofmann had left the United States on June 16, 1937, bound for Germany. She walked back to the table where her lunch was laid out and put the original record in her purse.

Her name was Esther Cohen and she was an Abwehr spy.

CHAPTER FOURTEEN

1567 SHERIDAN AVENUE
WEST BRONX
NEW YORK CITY
OCTOBER 13, 1942

When Friedrich Hofmann awoke on his bed in the rooming house, his first thoughts were not on his mission for the Abwehr or the dangers he would face. His first thoughts were about Hannah Rosen. He had dreamed about her the night before. He only remembered snatches of the dreams but those bits he recalled had been erotic. Fritz pictured her face in his mind as she had looked at him before driving away.

Fritz violently shook his head. What the hell are you doing? he berated himself. You have no time for this. Mooning about some woman could cause you make mistakes and get caught. Keep your mind on what you need to do to keep out of the electric chair.

Fritz quickly washed his face and shaved in the bathroom at the end of the hall. He dressed in his one suit and went downstairs to the dining room where the other roomers were gathered around a large oak table. Breakfast was oatmeal with milk but no sugar. One of the other tenants told Fritz that since sugar was rationed in June, Mrs. Taylor the landlady guarded it like her daughter's virginity.

While eating, Fritz asked the other tenants for a good place to buy a suit. A man identifying himself as Jack told him that Gimbles in Herald Square was having a sale. He gave Fritz directions to the department store.

He left the rooming house and walked south for two blocks, west for a block and then south to the 170th Street subway station. He went down the stairs to the platform, put a nickel in the slot and passed through the turnstile. The place was packed with people. He squeezed onto the first train going toward lower Manhattan, which took him south for a while, looped east across the Harlem River and then south again. The seats were all taken, so he had to stand, holding on to a strap. Fritz got off at the 33rd Street station and climbed the stairs to street level.

The sidewalks were crowded with people moving in all directions. They seemed adept at dodging each other. Uniforms were everywhere, representing all the service branches. Fritz weaved his way north for a few blocks to Herald Square and saw the Gimbles Department store building. He entered and went to the third-floor men's wear department.

There was indeed a sale going on. Hofmann chose suits in the mid-price range. He would have loved to buy high priced ones. He had plenty of the Abwehr's money. Fritz, however, wanted to save as much of that money as he could. He might have a use for it later on if he had to flee. High priced suits would also make him stand out in a crowd and he didn't want that. He chose two suits, one a solid grey wool and the other a blue pinstripe. Both suits were single-breasted and without vests or cuffs on the trousers. The salesman said it was because of cloth rationing. Fritz didn't really care about the cuffs and the vests. He had another problem. He had broad shoulders and a narrow waist. To get a coat that fit, he had to go to a size forty-two. But, the trousers that came with the forty-two coat had a size forty-two waist. They hung on him like a tent. Fritz shrugged and took the suits as well as six white dress shirts, five ties, a felt hat, two pairs of shoes and ten pairs of argyle socks. As he was paying the grinning clerk, he asked directions to the nearest tailor shop.

Fritz emerged from Gimbles with his arms loaded with packages. He walked the four blocks to the tailor shop, dodging other pedestrians and crazy New York cabbies at the intersections. The tailor, a bald man wearing a yarmulke with a cloth tape measure hanging around his neck, altered the suit trousers to fit while Fritz waited. Fritz studied the Jewish tailor while he worked. It was strange to be this close to a Jew. The last ones he had seen were naked and stumbling to their executions. He discovered that he had no enmity toward the Jewish tailor. His feelings were neutral. It was like he was looking at a lamp or a chair or some other object.

Wearing one of his new suits, he walked across the street to a five and dime and bought a cheap tablet of lined paper and a box of pencils. When he came out of the store, Fritz stopped. After standing on the subway and all the walking his feet felt like they were on fire and he really didn't want to brave the subway again with all these packages. He decided to take a cab. He could afford it and after all, he was using Hitler's money.

Back in his room in the West Bronx, Fritz hung his suits in the closet and put the other things in the dresser. Sitting down on the chair, he sharpened a pencil with his pocket knife and wrote a message to his Abwehr masters. HAVE ARRIVED. NO INCIDENTS. ROOM AT 1567 SHERIDAN AVE. AWAITING FURTHER INSTRUCTIONS. Fritz then took his copy of Northwest Passage and painstakingly encoded the message. When he was through he had a piece of paper with long lines of numbers, broken up by dashes and stars. He wadded up the paper with the plain language message and put it in his pocket. He would dispose of it in the toilet.

A little after two that afternoon, Fritz walked into Stein's Camera Shop at 447 West 46th Street. It was a dim little place with a glass display case containing many new and used cameras. Behind the case was a curtained off doorway leading to the back room and photo laboratory.

Standing behind the counter was a tall slim man with stooped shoulders. He looked to be in his fifties. He had bushy eyebrows and a mustache brushed down so it completely covered his upper lip. A yarmulke was perched on the back of his head. His face was lined with worry and his eyes were sad.

"Yes, sir, may I help you?" asked the man in a heavy German accent.

"I would like to own a Leica with a 1.7 lens, but I can't afford it," said Fritz, giving the code phrase he had been told to provide in his packet of instructions.

The proprietor's eyes changed from sad to angry. His face screwed up into such an expression of hate that Fritz was taken aback.

"Save your money and maybe someday you can," said the man behind the counter, giving the correct response. He said "follow me" and ducked through the doorway and Fritz followed.

In the backroom, Mr. Stein whirled and stuck his finger under Hofmann's nose.

"I don't know how much longer I will be able to do this and put up with you bastards. If you weren't holding my sister and her children, I would kill you."

He said it with such vehemence that Fritz put up his hands, palms out.

"Wait a minute mister, I'm no Nazi. They are making me do this too."

"You are a Jew? They are holding your relatives also?"

"No, I'm not Jewish, but it was either do this job or get killed. It amounts to much the same thing," replied Fritz.

The man looked at him for a full ten seconds but then relaxed. He seemed to deflate and he became sad once more.

"What do you need?" asked Stein. "Outgoing message," replied Fritz and handed him his message to the Abwehr.

Stein went to a cabinet and unlocked it with a key from his pocket. He put the message inside and relocked the cabinet.

While waiting for a response to his message to the Abwehr, Fritz got genuine papers to replace the forgeries he came off the sub with. He already knew how to drive from his teen years driving a delivery truck at his after school job. Fritz needed a car to take the driving test for a driver's license. He called a driving school and made a deal to use one of their cars for the test. Their driver drove him over to the Motor Vehicles Department.

All went well and he walked out of the building with a valid New York driver's license. Fritz next went to the Social Security office in the Federal building and got a new Social Security card.

When Fritz went to the draft board headquarters and asked to register for the draft, he met unexpected resistance. An angry faced official looked at him with suspicion.

"Why are you just getting around to registering now? You should have done it in 1940 with everyone else."

"I was on the road, living under bridges. I didn't know about it until this year," replied Fritz.

The clerk looked skeptical but then shrugged.

"I think you have been trying to dodge the draft. But it doesn't matter now. You will be immediately inducted," said the draft board official. He filled out a form and walked Fritz downstairs for an induction physical. The doctor took one look at Hofmann's flat feet, spoke to the official, and thirty minutes later Fritz walked out of the building with his draft card. The classification on it was 4F. This classification meant that he wouldn't be called up until there were German tanks rolling up Fifth Avenue.

Fritz's last stop was the St. Agnes Public Library on Amsterdam Avenue. He looked for the dustiest and most unused part of the building. He found it on the third floor. At the tail end of one of the stacks, he pulled a book out. Entitled, "Twenty Puritan Sermons, 1630-1690." The book was dusty and looked like it hadn't been taken down since it was put there years ago. Using his body as a shield, Fritz put the folded list of agent's names and addresses between the pages of the book and started to return it to the shelf. He hesitated for a moment, then retrieved the list and looked up a particular name. After memorizing an address, He put the list back in the book and slid it back in its slot on the dusty shelf. He then went home to the rooming house.

That night he studied the list of dead drops the Abwehr had given him. From footnotes on the list, Fritz discovered that the drops were listed according to their priority. There were three levels of priority, A, B, and C. Those with an A beside them were to be serviced weekly. Those with a B, monthly. Those with a C were all in smaller midwestern cities and were to be serviced whenever possible. All the drops with an A were in New York, Philadelphia and Washington. Fritz looked down the list. The dead drops were mostly in graveyards. He thought about that, then he realized the reason. No one questioned seeing a person kneeling over a grave. After almost two weeks, Fritz received a message from the Abwehr. He hurried home to his room and laboriously decoded the message.

GOOPERATIONALSERVICEDEADDROPSNEWYORKPHILADE LPHIA WASHINGTONADVISEIFYOUGETBASEBALLJOB, it read.

Using his list of drops, Fritz went about doing as instructed. He was very careful not to establish patterns in his travels between cities. He would alternate between busses and trains and wear different suits. A few times he rented an automobile. He knew he had no valid excuse for the travel, so he kept to himself and didn't have conversations with anyone. It would be safer when he got a job that gave him cover to move between cities. Fritz was still skeptical that anyone in the major leagues would hire him as a baseball player.

The messages he received and encoded from the agents were varied. Most of them were incredibly mundane, factory production figures, ship sailings, topics of boring government conferences. There was even a long message about crop failures last year in eastern Iowa. A few of the messages were more interesting. From an agent in Washington, Fritz received the order of battle for an entire American army corps being sent to England. Fritz didn't try to encode this massive document. He had Stein photograph it and reduce it to microfilm and sent it glued under the stamp on a letter to Madrid.

In his travels, Fritz was intrigued by the bustling activity that was going on all around him. He saw factory after factory, belching smoke and with armies of workers coming and going. Everywhere it was the same, industrial production must have quadrupled since he left the United States. The busses and trains were packed with purposeful people all going about their business.

One day while he was on a train to Washington, Fritz was staring at a framed poster hanging between two of the windows of the train car. The poster showed drawings of Mussolini, Tojo, and Hitler with their hands cupped to their ears. The caption at the bottom read: ENEMY EARS ARE LISTENING. Fritz looked at the people sitting around him. The poster was warning them about people like him. It made him feel a little ashamed.

The public attitude was unbelievably hostile to the Germans and Japanese. The crazy thing was that Fritz agreed with them. He hoped the Allies won the war, yet here he was spying for the Nazis. The utter incongruity of the situation caused Fritz to chuckle out loud, drawing a curious glance from a woman sitting across from him. From what he had seen of industrial production and the anger of the American people, Fritz had a feeling that the Germans and the Japanese had been very foolish to start a war with the United States.

CHAPTER FIFTEEN

ABWEHR HAUPTSITZ
TURPITZUFER 76-78
BERLIN, DEUTSCHLAND 2 FEBRUAR, 1943

The weather in Berlin was brutal, very cold with a thin coating of ice covering everything. It was dreary and depressing for the city's inhabitants. The mood of the people matched that of their Nazi leaders, but for a different reason. Hitler and his minions were reeling from the news that Feld Marshall Von Paulus had just surrendered the remnants of the German Sixth Army to the Russians at Stalingrad. Ninety-one thousand exhausted scarecrows went into Russian captivity, all that was left of the mighty force that had attacked the city six months ago. It was the first time in history that a German field marshall had surrendered. The Nazi leaders suppressed the news. Dr. Goebbels's propaganda machine continued to spew out stories about the heroic battle on the Volga.

Admiral Wilhelm Canaris sat in his office and reflected on the debacle. During the height of the battle, Von Paulus, watching his troops being encircled, had begged the Fuhrer to be allowed to retreat and save his army from annihilation. Hitler had thrown a tantrum, refusing Von Paulus permission to retreat an inch and ordering him to fight to the last man. The loss of so many young German soldiers could be laid at the feet of only one man, that Austrian Corporal who thought he was a better strategist than his generals. On the other hand, the debacle weakened the German war machine and that was a good thing.

The Admiral heard band music outside. He walked to his window and looked out. He saw a long column of soldiers, marching four abreast and following a small marching band. The banner they carried identified them as being from the Das Reich division of the Waffen SS. In spite of there being no waving and cheering Berliners lining the street, the SS men, in Feldgrau marched proudly. No doubt they were on their way to Russia to murder more Jews, thought Canaris. With great sadness, he walked back and sat down again at his desk.

The Admiral picked up a folder. It reported on the SS activities in Poland and Russia concerning Jews, Gypsies and others they considered untermensch. Mass shootings of Jews by SS death squads were continuing. More frightening, the SS had set up factories of death, extermination camps, at Belzec, Treblinka and Sobibor. Thousands of people were being murdered every day. A huge new killing center had opened since last summer on the grounds of the slave labor camp at Auschwitz. Tens of thousands were being gassed daily. Something must be done.

Canaris was aware that resistance conspiracies were forming within the German officer corps. His own deputy, Hans Oster, was quietly assembling a group of disaffected officers prepared to risk death in stopping Hitler. Oster thought he didn't know.

Wilhelm Canaris was considering a step that could profoundly affect his well-being, as well as that of his family. He considered it carefully. Similar to Caesar's crossing of the Rubicon, once this decision was made, there would be no going back. The Admiral was still for a long time. Finally, he nodded his head and flipped down his intercom switch.

"Ja, Herr Admiral?" asked his secretary.

"Please tell General Oster I want to see him in my office."

Five minutes later, Oster walked into the Admiral's office and closed the door. He was wearing his usual relaxed smile.

"Good morning Hans, please sit down."

Oster settled himself, crossing his legs and placing his hands in his lap.

"Hans, I know all about your efforts to organize a resistance movement against Hitler," said Canaris.

As the Admiral uttered this, the smile slipped from Oster's face and was replaced by one of fear for a few seconds. Then his expression turned cold.

"I admit it. The Nazis have been a disaster for Germany. You know Admiral, what the SS is doing to the people, especially the Jews in the conquered territories. We are going to lose this war and the crimes of the SS will make it impossible to negotiate an honorable peace. The Fatherland will be conquered and ground into powder" said Oster with heat.

"I agree with you," said Canaris. "That is why I am going to join you in your efforts."

Oster's face registered surprise but he remained silent. He thought that the Admiral might have more to say. Indeed, Canaris did have more to say.

"You know, Hans, there are great risks in this undertaking. If we fail or are betrayed, everyone will say we are traitors to Germany. We will be called dishonorable for breaking our oath of obedience to the Fuhrer. All our property will be forfeited and we will be executed. Our families will also be in danger. After deep consideration, I have decided that the cause is worth the risk."

'I think so too, Herr Admiral," said Oster.

"The only hope for Germany is to negotiate an armistice with the western Allies. Peace with Russia is impossible after how the SS has behaved in their country. Before we can negotiate an armistice, we must assassinate Adolf Hitler."

Both men lapsed into silence, shocked by the gravity of the last three words the Admiral had said.

CHAPTER SIXTEEN

SPANISH CONSULATE
150 EAST 58TH STREET
MANHATTAN
NEW YORK CITY
FEBRUARY 15, 1943

Asistente Concillor Carlos Breyer, a minor diplomat for the Kingdom of Spain, was sitting at his desk, feeling very offended. He often felt that way because he usually walked around with a chip on his shoulder. A fluke of heredity had made him short in stature, which was a problem in a culture that equated height with manliness. In his stocking-clad feet, he was exactly 150 centimeters tall. Measured using the English system, he was four feet, eleven inches. Carlos was very touchy about this. He did everything he could to look taller. He wore platform shoes and styled his hair into a bouffant mass on top of his head. His efforts only made him look silly. The female consular workers called him, "el pequeno pavo real," (the little Peacock) behind his back.

All the teasing he had received over the years had made him react strongly when he thought he was being slighted. Born in 1912 to a German father and Spanish mother, Carlos lived in Dresden, Germany, for the first eight years of his life. In 1920 his parents divorced and he went to live in Spain with his mother but spent two months every summer with his father in Dresden. In his early teen years, both in

Germany and Spain, he was subject to merciless hazing about his height.

In 1933, when Hitler came to power, Carlos, now twenty-one, came under his spell. Like many powerless and afflicted people, he had seen the Fuhrer's charismatic power and been attracted to it. He became a fanatical supporter of Hitler and his ideas, including the Fuhrer's hatred of Jews.

When Carlos was in his teens, his mother had married a wealthy mid-level official in the Spanish government. He was therefore educated at the best schools and had his pick of careers. He chose the diplomatic service because diplomats were powerful people who commanded respect.

In early 1941, shortly after his posting to the Spanish Consulate in New York, Breyer was approached at a cocktail party by a representative of the Abwehr. The Germans wanted him to spy for them against the Americans. Carlos was thrilled. Spies were dashing, manly people. He accepted the offer readily. The man from the Abwehr told him that he would be the most important element in the spy operation. It was said by way of flattery to clinch the deal. Although the spy recruiter never said so, Carlos got the impression that he would be the spymaster. He had visions of beautiful female spies looking up to him and waiting in awe for his orders, barely containing their lust for him because of his power. The reality of it was so much different and that was why he was feeling offended.

All Carlos was required to do was receive the Abwehr's messages to its agents in America in letters addressed to him in the diplomatic pouch without the Consul's knowledge or consent. Twice a week, using the cover of a supposed photography hobby, Carlos would take the messages to a camera shop on West 46th Street and hand them over to a Jew. A Jew! He would receive letters addressed to a mail drop in Madrid going the other way and send them out in the diplomatic bag. He was nothing but a glorified courier. Carlos had opened one of the letters containing a message. There were long streams of numbers. He could make nothing out of it.

The resentment had built up over a long period of time. He felt that the Abwehr had lied to him and not showed him respect. The spy agency should allow him to run the operation and the messages should come to him. He would decide what was passed on to Berlin.

Through all of this, it never crossed Carlos's mind to wonder why the Abwehr would entrust a valuable espionage network to a foreign runt, with no training or experience at spying.

Carlos had a sudden thought and snapped erect, his mind confused. What if there is something fishy going on here. Why would the Abwehr be dealing with a Jewish camera store owner? Was it possible that this supposed spy network was actually a front for traitorous activities against the German Reich? In a few days, Carlos was due to depart on his annual leave to his home in Madrid. Maybe he would make some inquiries at the German Embassy when he was there.

CHAPTER SEVENTEEN

204 GRAND STREET
MANHATTAN
NEW YORK CITY
MARCH 3, 1943

FBI Special Agent Ted Miller walked through a doorway that had a sign above it that read KINGSTON WHOLESALE MEATS. A pretty young woman greeted him at the reception desk.

"I'm here to see Mr. Jessop. Tell him William Price wants to see him," said Ted.

The woman ducked through a door and returned a few moments later accompanied by a dark-complexioned man with a hangdog, jowly face and shifty eyes. Jessop made eye contact with Ted, who he knew as William Price, and signaled him to follow. Miller followed Jessop through the door, down a short hallway and into a cramped, cluttered office. There was only room for a desk and two chairs. Jessop gestured Ted to sit in a chair and took a seat behind the desk.

The meat wholesaler retrieved a piece of paper from somewhere in the clutter.

"Okay, I have twenty individual five-pound beef rib roasts, each separately wrapped, that would be perfect for your restaurant. This is high-class midwestern beef, not that stuff from Mexico. The price is two hundred dollars," said Jessop, with an avaricious smile.

Ted had been posing as the owner of a restaurant in midtown Manhattan. He looked at the meat wholesaler. The price he was asking was over six times the official controlled price of beef rib roast. Ted was outraged, You rotten bastard, he thought. While young soldiers are dying all over the world, you undercut them because you're a greedy piece of shit. But he betrayed nothing of what he was thinking and smiled back at Jessop. He took a big wad of bills out of his breast pocket and peeled off ten twenty dollar bills. Jessop's greedy eyes watching the count intently. He didn't know that most of the wad was composed of one dollar bills with larger denomination bills on the outside for show. Then Jessop scooped up the money and shoved it into a back pocket.

"Pull your truck up to the side door on Mott and we'll load you up," said Jessop.

Ted went outside and slid behind the wheel of a 1940 Ford panel truck. He started the engine and drove around the corner on Mott Street. He saw a roll-up door that was slowly opening and backed the truck up into the doorway. Ted got out and met Jessop and a stooped old man at the rear of the truck.

Sitting just inside the door was a pallet stacked with packages, neatly wrapped in pink butcher paper. Jessop moved to open the rear doors of the panel van. Ted stepped back, drew his revolver and pointed it at the meat wholesaler and the old man.

"FBI!, You are under arrest for violating OPA rationing regulations."

Bill Parker appeared around the other side of the van, pointing a twelve-gauge shotgun at Jessop and the old man, whose face suddenly turned ashen. Bill had been slumped down in the passenger seat the whole time. Seeing that Parker had the suspects covered, Ted holstered his gun and handcuffed the two men. Jessop's face was red with anger.

"Listen, you son of a bitch, I have important friends in city hall. You are going to find yourself in a lot of trouble. Ten minutes after we arrive downtown, I'll be walking out the door, a free man," said Jessop through clenched teeth. Ted just smiled at him.

"Some of my customers are powerful men in this city. You will find yourself transferred to some hick town down in Georgia," said the red-faced man, still trying to bluff but getting more desperate.

Ted didn't reply. Having tried bluster and threats, Jessop tried another tack.

"Hey, mister,this will ruin me. I will lose my business. What will I tell my friends and the people at my lodge? I have a nephew in the army. If we could make a deal, I would make it worth your while. Say I just give you back the two hundred and a hundred more and we forget about this whole thing?"

"You just added another charge. attempted bribery of a federal officer. You heard him didn't you, Special Agent Parker?"

"Yup, I did," said Bill.

Jessop said nothing more until an NYPD paddy wagon arrived to take the prisoners away. The old man was blubbering and protesting that he had nothing to do with the black market meat. He just worked for Jessop. Miller changed his mind and let him go.

Unlike earlier in the war, Ted and Bill spent a lot of their time investigating black market operators like Jessop. Rationing had begun with sugar in mid-1942 and soon was implemented to cover meat, coffee, automobile tires, gasoline and a host of other commodities. Everyone was given a ration book. Each rationed item was given a point value. Each person was given a set number of points to last them for the month. It was up to each individual as to how they used the points. Some people augmented their rationed food by planting victory gardens to grow fruits and vegetables. They were all over, in vacant lots, rooftops and terraces.

As a result of rationing, a robust black market had sprung up, which the FBI was tasked with suppressing. Ted liked going after the black marketeers. These were real investigations and not like chasing phantom Nazi spies. Crackpot spy sightings had tapered off sharply as the war situation had improved. Things were looking up for the allied cause all around the world.

By March 1943, Rommel's Africa Corps had been defeated at El Alamein, the Allies had landed in North Africa and the Russians had given the Nazis a crushing blow at Stalingrad. In the Pacific, the Japs had lost four carriers in the Battle of Midway and the Marines had landed and defeated the nips on Guadalcanal. Ted, like most Americans, felt a growing optimism about the outcome of the war.

If only he could see room for optimism in his personal life. Ted still couldn't shake his sadness over the lost relationship with Hannah. No matter how he tried to erase her from his mind, at odd times he would suddenly think about her face as he had bent to kiss her on their only date. Her eyes had been locked on his and her lips were slightly parted in anticipation. At such times, Ted would shake his head and berate himself. Stop it!, It's over and she doesn't want anything to do with you. Despite the self-flagellation, he still couldn't stop thinking about her.

He had tried dating other women. It wasn't hard to find female companionship in New York. He had gone out with two women, but the dates were unfulfilling, and he hadn't asked either one out again. He was always comparing any woman he was with to Hannah. The woman he was with would quickly sense that Ted was in love with someone else and didn't like it. He finally decided he would live like a monk for the rest of his life. It was easier. He just couldn't get excited about any woman but the beautiful Jewish girl.

He often reflected on what a lonely life he led. He would bust his ass at work, often working late into the night. But on the nights he wasn't working, although sometimes he had drinks with other agents, he usually ate alone, the blue plate special at some little café or diner. Going home to his empty apartment, he would listen to music or sports on the radio or read the sports pages of the newspaper or books he had checked out of the library, before going to an empty bed. Lately, he was getting concerned that he was turning into a loner. He went around with a nagging feeling that something was missing from his life. He knew what was missing, it was Hannah.

Ted was starting to rationalize away his earlier suspicions about there being more Nazi spies operating in the United States. He told himself that he was making too much of a dying man's last words.

Since he joined the FBI, Ted had high respect for FBI Director J. Edgar Hoover. That respect had taken a beating in late 1942. Don Singleton was a Special Agent on temporary duty in New York from Washington. He and Ted had taken a liking to each other right away and formed a friendship. They were drinking in a bar one evening, Ted had decided that it wasn't a sin to drink alcohol as long as you didn't get drunk and lose control of yourself, despite what some preachers said. The two agents became a little tipsy and began to talk the way men do when their inhibitions are dulled by alcohol and secrets spill out. The subject of J. Edgar Hoover came up. A smug little smile formed on Singleton's lips.

"Do you know that our great leader lived with his mother until he was forty years old?

The son of a bitch is a fanatic about cleanliness, making his maid change his bed sheets twice a day, and ordering everyone around him to wash their hands before handling a paper he would have to touch. And not only that, Me and the rest of the guys in Washington are convinced that J. Edgar and his second in command, Clyde Tolson, are secret nancy boys and are carrying on a homosexual affair. They are touching each other all the time and are together constantly, even going on vacation together. One of the agents has a confidential informant, who has been reliable in the past who swears he saw Hoover at a sashay party, dressed up in woman's clothes."

Singleton paused, took another sip of Scotch and continued.

"My advice to you is to keep your head down and away from Hoover's attention. He is a vindictive bastard and keeps an enemies list and has loads of damning information about powerful people in his safe. He has been known to ruin an agent's career on a whim. He's not the kind of guy you fool with. That's all I'm gonna say. I've said too much already."

The revelations had hit Ted like a thunderbolt. Though he trusted Singleton and didn't think he was lying, he couldn't take his word alone for something like this. There was another agent who had worked in the Washington headquarters of the bureau for years, before being transferred to New York. His name was Fred Griffin. Ted got him alone by the water cooler and repeated Singleton's allegations against Hoover. He asked him if all of this was true. Griffin looked very uncomfortable and swiveled his head around to make sure no one else could hear the conversation. He looked Ted in the eye and nodded.

This information changed Ted's whole outlook about his superiors and the bureau itself. He decided that he had best keep his mouth shut about his theories on Nazi spies. He would do his job and let the German spy thing go. Within ten minutes of making this decision, something happened that fired up his imagination again and forced him to abandon his resolution.

He was sitting at his desk, writing up his arrest report on Jessop. When it was completed he would send it to the U.S. Attorney's office. One of the other agents walked by his desk and threw a report on his desk.

"Hey Ted, did you see this?"He picked up the report and began to read.It was an account of the arrest of a woman named, Rachel Greenbaum.

Two boys searching for worms for fish bait had turned over a flat stone in Georgetown's Waterfront Park. The stone was just off a path in the middle of a grove of trees. The boys found a metal tube. Looking inside, they saw a sheaf of rolled-up papers. There were formulas and diagrams of machines and words the boys couldn't understand. They took the papers home to their parents, who called the FBI.

The Bureau staked out the location. A week later, Rachel Greenbaum, an employee of the Office of Scientific Research and Development, was observed lifting the stone. She was immediately arrested. The information discovered by the boys was determined to be from on a highly secret scientific project related to the development of a revolutionary new fuse for artillery shells.

Miss Greenbaum, upon questioning, refused to provide any information. She was being held in solitary confinement pending further investigation. The woman was a refugee from Germany, entering the United States in 1939.

Ted looked at the report. It fired up all his old suspicions about spies. He knew this new information was important. Could Rachel Greenbaum be a spy for Germany? It seemed ridiculous. The woman was Jewish, at least her name indicated she was. Why would a Jewish refugee spy for the Nazis? Unless she wasn't spying for the Germans. Maybe she was an agent of our allies, the Russians. It was a possibility. A fair number of Jews in America were left-leaning. Ted decided to think about all this some more before he discussed it with anyone. He didn't want to become the office gadfly and have Hoover hear about it and ruin his career.

CHAPTER EIGHTEEN

BEAR MOUNTAIN INN
BEAR MOUNTAIN, NEW YORK
MARCH 21, 1943

An icy wind was blowing across the crudely prepared baseball diamond and ominous clouds threatened snow as the pitcher wound up and threw the ball. It flew in a perfect arc and dropped into the catcher's mitt.

"Pretty good changeup," said Leo Durocher, the manager of the Brooklyn Dodgers. "Now let me see your best fastball."

He was calling to a gangling red-haired teenager with a long beak nose, a cowlick that stood four inches high, a long neck and no behind. He looked like he had just come in from slopping the hogs.

"That wuz mah fast bahl, suh," said the boy in a thick southern drawl.

"Git yer hillbilly ass outa here," yelled Durocher. "I got a pistol in my pocket an' I'm gonna pull it out in ten seconds an' start shooting. If you are around here then, you are what I'm gonna' be shootin' at." Durocher's voice had increased to a bellow as he was stalking towards the pitcher's mound. The young pitcher fled in terror, his shirttail flapping in the cold air.

Derocher turned, kicked at the frozen dirt and walked back to the sidelines. He wasn't a big man, only five foot ten and 160 pounds, but he could be very intimidating. It came from the force of his personality and the fact that he spent his life in a continual state of angry frustration. His formula for winning an argument was not to reason but to yell louder than the other man. He was supremely confident that he was smarter than every other son of a bitch in baseball.

Right now, in spite of the heavy parka, he was wearing over his Dodger uniform, the Brooklyn manager was freezing as well as pissed off. The Commissioner of Baseball, Kennesaw Mountain Landis, had decreed that all major league teams must have their spring training near their home fields and not in sunny, warm Florida. The Commissioner said it was to save space on trains because of the war and how baseball was patriotic and all that shit. Leo thought the idea was nuts. Durocher reckoned that with a name like Kennesaw Mountain Landis, the commissioner had been pounded on by bullies so much as a kid that his brain was probably damaged.

So here I am, thought Leo, up in the mountains freezing my balls off and not in sunny Florida where the dames walk around with their nipples trying to poke through their thin dresses. Here in Bear Mountain, all the women were bundled up in heavy coats looking like the Eskimo ladies he had seen in National Geographic magazine. But the weather and the dames were the least of his problems. He had to come up with a major league baseball team for the 1943 season and most of his regular players were in the service, playing for a bunch of fat generals. What the hell was he gonna do?

Leo Durocher had broken into the big leagues with the Yankees in 1928 as their starting shortstop. His fielding was pretty good but his batting was only so-so. His cocky, combative nature made him a favorite of then Yankee manager, Miller Huggins. Not so with his teammates. Babe Ruth didn't like Durocher and dubbed him "the all American out." He didn't endear himself to the Yankees general manager either by writing a series of bad checks which the team had to make good. After demanding a raise in a noisy scene, Leo was traded to the Reds in 1930. In mid-1933 he was traded again. This time to the Cardinals, partly because he couldn't get along with some of his Reds teammates.

In 1938 Durocher signed with the Brooklyn Dodgers as their starting shortstop. At the end of that season, Brooklyn's erratic new general manager, Larry MacPhail made him the player/manager of the Dodgers. All the local sportswriters thought the decision was crazy.

It was as a manager that Leo Durocher came into his own. He had enjoyed baseball as a player but had chafed at being forced to obey the orders of managers he considered dumber than he was. Now HE was in charge, and those sons of bitches on the team had better do what he said. He gave up the shortstop position to Pee Wee Reese and never looked back.

§

As Durocher stood on the sidelines watching a bunch of young men not good enough for the army make fools of themselves on the diamond, he was feeling sorry for himself. Why me?, he silently asked God. Couldn't you have left me one good left-hand pitcher? Oh, for the glory of the 1941 season when I took a ragtag group of scrappy players and we clawed our way to the top. My Dodgers won the national league pennant but then lost to the Yankees in five games in the World Series when the baseball gods suddenly turned against us.

After the attack on Pearl Harbor, Durocher had been surprised that major league baseball wasn't suspended for the duration like in the First World War. Commissioner Landis was going to do just that, but then-

President Roosevelt told him that he wanted professional baseball to continue to entertain the public. It was a good thing, Durocher needed the money. He had a very extravagant lifestyle. He liked flashy clothes and even flashier women. Baseball was something he did to make money so he could pursue his real vocation, drinking and chasing dames.

His general manager, Branch Rickie, was pressing him to find talent. What was it about baseball that attracted people with weird names? Leo asked himself, Kennesaw Mountain Fuckin' Landis, and now Branch Rickie. Rickie's name sounded like the name of one of those cocktails the broads drank down in Florida, with celery or pineapple sticking out of the top of the tall glass. But hell, Rickie was better than his last GM, Larry MacPhail. That son of a bitch was crazy.

In his frantic search for players, Durocher had coaxed some older players out of retirement. He figured he would have to hire some stretcher-bearers to carry them off the field after the first real workout. He had advertised in the New York, Philadelphia and Boston papers for aspiring baseball players to come to public tryouts. That was what he was doing today. What he had seen so far really depressed him.

He was done with pitchers. He didn't see anybody he could use. For the next hour, he looked at outfielders. They all looked like the Marx Brothers in the outfield, running into each other and dropping "can a corn" fly balls. Durocher was getting more and more pissed off at the waste of his time.

Catchers were next. There were three candidates. One couldn't make it to second base with a throw. The best he could do was one hop. Durocher sent him packing. The next guy had a pretty good arm but was old and had bad knees. He grunted with pain when he squatted behind the plate. Leo told him to go find a rocking chair somewhere and take it easy. The third guy was different; he had a rocket arm, but what was even better was that he was accurate. Durocher liked him even better when he found out he was 4F. He wouldn't have to worry about him getting drafted. He told the guy to stick around for batting practice.

Two hours later Durocher had five men from various positions who had performed well enough in fielding. Batting was next. If we even get to that, thought Durocher. Those dark clouds promise a fuckin' blizzard any minute. The snow held off long enough for the batting tryouts to begin. The third guy up was the young catcher with the rocket arm. Leo watched as he settled into the batter's box. If he can hit, he thought, I will hire him.

Johnny Allen was pitching. He was thirty-nine years old, ancient for major league ball. His heater wasn't so fast anymore but he still had a good curve. The first pitch was a fastball. Leo heard the crack of a solid hit and the ball rocketed into left field. The next pitch was a ball, out of the strike zone. The batter held up. Allen threw another fastball and the young catcher had another solid hit. Leo was impressed. Durocher then signaled for a curve and everything fell apart. The guy swung and hit nothing but air. The next pitch was another curve. The swing was mighty but still hit nothing and the ball dropped into the catcher's glove.

Durocher sadly shook his head. Too bad. That was why major league players were paid so handsomely. The ability to hit an off-speed pitch. Only one in ten thousand guys had the eagle eyes to detect the spin of a curve when it came out of the pitcher's hand. Leo signaled Allen to stand down and walked to the batter's box.

"Sorry, bud. I don't think I can use you."

Durocher walked away a few steps, then had a thought and turned around. "I need a bullpen catcher and general gofer. My last one just got drafted. The job pays forty bucks a week, and you gotta' help the equipment guy load and unload all the team gear when we're on the road. Jobs yours if you want it. What's your name anyway?"

"Fred Hofmann, Mr. Durocher. I'll take the job"

CHAPTER NINETEEN

WARSCHAUER GHETTO WARSCHAU, POLEN

20 APRIL, 1943

It was the second day of the uprising of desperate Jews in the Warsaw Ghetto. They had decided that rather than meekly submitting to death at the hands of the SS, they were going to resist. For months they had been smuggling arms and ammunition into the ghetto through the sewers. The resistance leaders dispersed their young underground fighters on strategic rooftops and secretly fortified bunkers. Every one of the fighters knew it was a suicide mission, but they stood to anyway. They would sell their lives dearly and take some Germans with them into the abyss. Yesterday when the Nazis came in force they were ready.

In October 1942, Heinrich Himmler ordered the liquidation of the Warsaw Ghetto. All able-bodied Jews would be sent to slave labor camps. Those unfit for work, old people, young children and the infirm would be transported by train to the death camp Treblinka and gassed. In late 1942 and early 1943, the SS conducted numerous raids into the ghetto, snatching Jews where they could, and organizing for a final push.

On 19 April 1943, the final liquidation began. The SS had gathered what they thought were sufficient forces, consisting of the veteran Jew killers of the Einsatzgruppen augmented by SS auxiliaries, mostly Ukrainians. They marched boldly and proudly into the ghetto. Among their number was SS-Untersturmfuhrer Franz Keller, aged twenty-three. They were met by a hail of gunfire from hidden bunkers and rooftops.

The SS was stunned. The Jews were usually so compliant, walking meekly into the gas chambers. This was something new. The resisters must be gangsters, the depraved of the depraved. The shocked SS troopers retreated, dragging twelve dead Germans and Ukrainians with them.

Today the Nazis were back in force. They were going systematically from house to house rooting out Jews. Untersturmfuhrer Keller moved northeast on Pawia Street leading a mixed force of ten SS and twenty Ukrainians. Emaciated dead bodies lay sprawled here and there on the sidewalk victims of starvation and the smell of rotting human flesh was terrible. Keller could hear explosions and see smoke rising in the sky to the north. Waffen SS units had been brought in to assist in the push and were pounding the central part of the ghetto with mortars and tank fire.

A figure suddenly darted out of a doorway up the street from Keller's men and ran toward them. It appeared to be a skinny girl of about sixteen, dressed in a dirty blue smock with a white scarf tied over her head. She had a wine bottle with a flaming wick protruding from the neck in one of her hands. The girl threw the bottle toward the group of Germans and was immediately cut down in a hail of bullets. The bottle wobbled through the air and landed at the feet of a Ukrainian SS Auxiliary. The bottle shattered and showered the man with petrol. With a whoosh, the benzine ignited and the auxiliary stumbled around screaming, engulfed in flames. A couple of his comrades beat out the flames with their jackets, but it was too late. The Ukrainian was dead.

Keller walked to where the girl lay crumpled on the pavement. She was still alive, but barely. He looked down at her emaciated face and she returned his gaze with a look of naked hatred in her hollow eyes.

"Damn you. Damn you to hell," the girl uttered in hoarse German.

Keller raised his pistol, smiled and shot her in the head.

A little while later Franz and his men entered a house on the south side of the street. In pre-ghetto days it had been a large private home, but the Jews had since partitioned it off into many small living spaces. Keller stepped over the decomposing body of a small child in a hallway. He breathed through the left sleeve of his tunic because the death stench was so strong it was triggering his gag reflex. Franz was wearing his Feldgrau SS uniform, polished black boots and a visor cap with its silver death's head badge.

He was just above medium height and stocky, but his face was what his victims recoiled from. He had a heavy brow with intense, angry eyes set too close together, a prominent nose and a cruel mouth that had a habit of smiling just before he executed his victims.

He came to a closed door. Drawing his pistol, he wrenched it open. It was a small closet, and huddling together on the floor was an old man and an old woman cradling a small boy about three years old. They looked up at him in fear. Keller smiled and the little boy smiled back at him. Franz shot them in turn in the head, saving the child for last. Keller did so with no more thought than if he was stepping on a cockroach. For to Franz Keller, that's what Jews were, vermin.

He hated three groups of people passionately-- Jews, Americans, and Russians, in that order. By contrast, his greatest loves were Adolf Hitler, the German nation and his mother, in descending order. Keller's hatred of Jews was the result of a steady diet of anti-Semitic propaganda instilled in him by his mother and stepfather from an early age. His hatred for Russians was due to their slaughtering of thousands of German soldiers on the Eastern Front. His hatred for Americans had more curious origins. Born in Munich in 1920, Keller's father had died when he was very young. His mother had remarried a man named Herman Lang. Lang had been an original member of the Nazi party and was with Adolf Hitler in his abortive 1923 Munich Beer Hall Putsch. He had emigrated illegally to the United States in 1927, taking his wife and young Franz with him.

The family had settled in New York City in a neighborhood on the border between Spanish Harlem and an Irish enclave. Being young, Franz learned English quickly but because of his heavy German accent the Irish boys had been merciless to him, beating him up and stealing what little lunch money his mother gave him. Keller was forced to seek protection from a group of Puerto Rican boys who took him into their gang for unknown reasons, but probably just for an excuse to beat up on the Irish. As a result, by the time Keller was in his teens, he was trilingual. He spoke his native German, perfect American English and a Caribbean dialect of Spanish. Keller would probably have eventually blended into the melting pot of America, but an event occurred that prevented that and changed his destiny.

In 1939, Herman Lang, Keller's stepfather, by then an American citizen, was recruited at a meeting of the German American Bund to spy for the German fatherland. He was of particular interest to the Germans because he worked at the Carl L. Norden Company, the developers of the top-secret Norden bombsight. The spy ring, headed by a man named Frederick Duquesne, was penetrated by the FBI in late 1940. In 1941, when Keller was twenty, members of the ring, including Herman Lang were rounded up and charged with spying for a foreign power.

While Lang was awaiting trial, the American Immigration authorities abruptly deported Keller and his mother, who had neglected to become American citizens, back to Germany. They arrived in Hamburg penniless. Ever since then, Keller had nurtured a white hot hatred for Americans.

After a rocky start, Keller and his mother ended up being treated very well. Herman Lang was considered a hero in Germany. Keller joined the SS and because of his stepfather's notoriety was sent to the SS Officers Training School. Since being commissioned an Untersturmfuhrer, the lowest SS officer rank, he had been killing Jews relentlessly in Poland and Russia.

At the end of the second day of the uprising in the ghetto, some progress had been made.

Keller had killed many more people. When they came upon individual Jews or even small groups, they were summarily executed. Larger groups were herded out of the ghetto to waiting trains bound for Treblinka. Exhausted after a hard day of ridding the world of the Fuhrer's enemies, he and his men were standing outside the ghetto gate waiting for transport to their billets. A black Mercedes open touring car drove up and stopped. A tall SS-Hauptsturmfuhrer got out and approached Keller. Both gave the stiff-armed salute and they Heil Hitlered each other. The officer, superior to Keller by two ranks, ordered him to accompany him. Obeying instantly, he got in the back seat of the Mercedes, followed by the Hauptsturmfuhrer, and the car drove away.

They were driven across Warsaw to SS headquarters. Keller was shown into the dining room of a magnificent house, once owned by a wealthy Pole. The huge dining room now had a large portrait of the Fuhrer prominently displayed on one wall. In the portrait, the Fuhrer was wearing an army greatcoat. He was standing and looking into the far distance. There was an expression of calm confidence on his face as if he was assured of Germany's bright future under his leadership. The pose was a particular favorite of Hitler's and thousands of copies had been produced and distributed around the Nazi empire.

Sitting under the picture at a large, finely carved table was an SS-

Standartenfuhrer in full uniform. He was slicing sausages on a plate in front of him and feeding them to a large shorthaired dog sitting beside his chair. Franz came to attention and gave the Nazi salute.

"Heil Hitler, Untersturmfuhrer Keller reporting."

"Keller, I have had a message concerning you. It is from Reichsfuhrer Himmler's office. You are to report as soon as possible to the Ostland-SD Department at SD headquarters in Berlin. Your train leaves in thirty minutes. Be on it," said the seated officer.

§

The name Sicherheitsdienst was too big of a mouthful for everyday conversations, so everyone called it the SD. It was a big part of Heinrich Himmler's empire within Nazi Germany. It controlled everything to do with security in Germany and the occupied territories. The police and courts were a part of the SD as well as foreign espionage.

The department of the SD that concerned itself with foreign spying was called Ostland-SD. It ran its operations out of German embassies in neutral countries around the world. Their agents, however, were chosen more for national socialist purity than for competence. They were very often heavy-handed idiots who had a habit of bungling their assignments and embarrassing the Reich. They fooled almost no one. In Lisbon, for example, cab drivers and hotel waiters knew who they were and accepted bribes from the British for keeping tabs on them. The German military and the government leadership, including Hitler, knew they were worthless and ignored almost everything they said. The offices of the organization were in the SS complex on Prinz-Albrecht Strasse in Berlin. This is where Franz Keller reported two days after leaving Warsaw.

Keller was shown into a large, lavish office. Crossed swastika flags were arranged as a backdrop to the huge desk. Sitting behind that desk was a man in the uniform of an SS-Standartenfuhrer. He wore an Iron Cross First Class pinned to his left breast. Otherwise, he was an ordinary-looking man in his thirties. Keller snapped to attention and gave the Nazi salute.

"Heil Hitler. Untersturmfuhrer Keller reporting."

The Standartenfuhrer waved his right hand casually to return the salute. He didn't ask Franz to sit.

"Keller, my name is Schulenburg. I head the Ostland-SD Department. We are charged with foreign espionage. I know you haven't been trained as a spy but there is a situation in which you might be useful. You do speak Spanish?"

"Ja, Herr Standartenfuhrer."

"It seems the Abwehr, they are military intelligence by the way, have a spy network in the United States. A member of that network, a Spanish diplomat in New York, has told us that he has been handing over messages from the Abwehr to a Jew who runs a camera shop in the city. Now, we both know that Jews are our mortal enemies. It seems suspicious. We need someone to travel to New York and investigate the situation. We have chosen you. If the Abwehr is playing a double game here, consorting with our enemies, then you are to report back to us. Are there any questions so far?"

"No, Herr Standartenfuhrer."

"You were selected for this assignment first of all because your loyalty to the SS is above question. Second, you grew up in the United States and know the language and culture. Third, you speak Spanish. You will have a cover as a minor diplomat at the Spanish Consulate in New York. Reichsfuhrer Himmler has taken a personal interest in this case and has spoken directly with the Spanish Foreign Minister, who has agreed to give you diplomatic credentials. You needn't fear arrest. You will have diplomatic immunity.

Go to New York and find out what is going on in this Abwehr spy ring. My assistant will give you more details. Do not fail us, Untersturmfuhrer Keller."

"I will not fail, Herr Standartenfuhrer," said Keller with a stone face. Inside he was excited. This was his chance to go back to America and pay back the bastards that humiliated him and his mother. He would accomplish his mission, but he had some private scores to settle too.

CHAPTER TWENTY

500 PEARL STREET
MANHATTAN
NEW YORK CITY
APRIL 30, 1943

At precisely five o'clock pm, the Manhattan Federal Courthouse and office building began to disgorge people in a gush. Someone watching the building spew out people would almost expect it to deflate, like in a Mickey Mouse cartoon. With significantly more haste than they had shown when they went in nine hours before, people hurried home to their dinner tables, or maybe a nice little neighborhood bar.

Hannah Rosen was among them, although she moved much slower than the rest. She was depressed. All she had to go home to was an apartment containing her aunt and uncle, who had been involved in a silly argument for three days. The disagreement had started when Uncle Moshe had made a contribution to a Zionist organization. Aunt Rachel had shouted that he had given too much, and the fight was on. It was similar to a boxing match. First a period of yelling at each other, then the two would retire to their respective corners and a phase of hostile silence would ensue. Then the yelling would begin again for another round.

The stress was getting to Hannah. It wasn't just her relatives fighting, they did that all the time. It was everything, being forced to spy for a country she hated, worrying about her parent's treatment by the Nazis and thinking about Ted Miller.

The subway was crowded and she was forced to stand as usual. About midway in her commute, a sailor in uniform got up and offered his seat to her. As she was about to take it, a stout older woman with a black mole on her cheek pushed her out of the way and took the seat. The woman glared at Hannah in triumph for the rest of the way to her station.

What a miserable day, she thought, as she got off the train at her station. She began walking up the stairs to street level, not knowing that her very bad day was about to get worse, much worse. Hannah emerged from the stairway and began walking east on168th Street. She sensed a presence on her right side. She looked over and saw a man walking beside her, keeping pace.

"Hi, remember me?"

Recognition dawned on her, oh my God, It was the German from the submarine! Hannah stopped in her tracks and turned to face the man.

"What are you doing here? What do you want?" said Hannah, close to panic.

"Now, hold on," the German raised his hands, palm out. "Don't be scared. I'm not going to hurt you. I just need to talk to you."

"Not here, follow me," said Hannah

She led him to a bench in nearby Mitchel Park. She chose one that was out in the open. She felt pretty safe as there were plenty of people around. They both sat. Hannah kept as far away from him as she could.

She looked the man in the face.

"What more do you want from me? You threaten my parents and force me to do your dirty, filthy work. What's next? Do you want to sleep with me? I am a virgin. I have never been with a man. I will not sleep with you."

"Hold on," said the man, "I have no intention of forcing myself on you. I just want to talk. I'm lonely and I want to be your friend."

"My friend! Do you realize how stupid that sounds? If my parents were free I would yell for a policeman right now."

"Look, I was just hired by the Brooklyn Dodgers. I make a hundred and sixty dollars a month. I have no one to spend it on. I thought we could go out on the town and dance and have some fun. I'm not a Nazi. I was forced into doing what the Germans wanted. I'm in the same situation as you."

Hannah stood. Her cheeks were red with anger. "Just leave me alone. I don't want anything to do with you."

She walked away, leaving the man sitting on the bench, and continued home close to tears. When she arrived at the apartment she discovered that the boxing match was over. Instead of a "useless bum," Uncle Moshe was now, "my darling Moshe." Aunt Rachel was now, "my treasure." Hannah picked at her dinner and went to bed early.

She was awakened by her aunt and uncle's noisy lovemaking which she heard through the wall of her room. Hannah lay on her back and began to imagine what it would be like to make love to Ted. She had never been with a man but her friend Betty at Macys had told her all about sex. She became very aroused. Abruptly, she turned over and struck her pillow with her fist. She forced the images from her brain. I must never think about this again, she thought. What is wrong with me.

Have I turned into one of those wanton women I have heard about, who can't control their lust? The way I acted when Ted kissed me, grinding my body into his was disgraceful. The thoughts made her blush deeply in the dark of her bedroom and brought the lustful thoughts back again. She slept very little that night.

The next evening, Hannah got off the subway with trepidation. The German was nowhere to be seen. She thought back, what had he told that cop his name was? Then she remembered, Fred Hofmann. She climbed the stairs to the street and still didn't see him. Hannah took a deep breath and expelled it with relief. He must have gotten discouraged by her hostility and given up.

Before going up the front steps of her building, Hannah took a peppermint Lifesaver from her purse and popped it into her mouth to cover any lingering smell of the bacon from the sandwich she ate for lunch. She was greeted at the door by Aunt Rachel.

"Hannah, why didn't you tell me that you were having a young man over for dinner? I would have had something better than latkes."

Hannah was puzzled until she walked into the living room and saw The German spy from the submarine sitting on the sofa, talking to Uncle Moshe. She inhaled sharply and choked on her Lifesaver. After a fit of coughing, she recovered from her surprise and became angry. She was about to explode on the spy when she hesitated. Not in front of my aunt and uncle, she warned herself. Hiding her anger, she said hello and went to her room and closed the door. She sat on her bed and brooded and didn't emerge until dinner was served. Hannah almost gagged on her food. Her anger had morphed into a feeling of helpless frustration.

The spy and Uncle Moshe had a spirited conversation about baseball after the visitor revealed that he worked for the Brooklyn Dodgers. Uncle Moshe was a Yankees fan. After the modest meal, the German stood up.

"I don't want to eat and run, but Hannah and I have reservations, and we have to hurry," he said.

Hannah was still a little numb when the German spy escorted her down the front steps of her building. She began to cry.

"Why are you doing this? Why are you torturing me?

The man took a folded handkerchief from his pocket and gave it to her. "Hey there, don't cry. I just thought we would go dancing. I don't want anything from you except companionship."

The German hailed a cab and took a sullen Hannah to the Onyx Club on West 52nd Street. Hofmann had reservations and they were soon escorted to a small table. After asking Hannah to call him Fred, he ordered a Tom Collins and Hannah a glass of water.

Duke Ellington and his band featuring the fantastic saxophone player Ben Webster were playing. Without realizing it, her foot started to tap under the table, in time with the swing rhythm. Hannah hadn't been dancing since she started spying for the Germans and she suddenly realized how much she had missed it. Fred took her onto the dance floor and they danced for the next two hours. In spite of her inner torment she soon realized that she was having fun.

CHAPTER TWENTY-ONE

EBBETS FIELD
55 SULLIVAN PLACE
FLATBUSH
NEW YORK CITY
MAY 4, 1943

Ebbets Field was the most intimate baseball stadium in the National Baseball League. Though the park had a capacity of thirty-five thousand people, its two-tiered design and construction allowed the Brooklyn fans to be very close to the action taking place on the field. Usually, this was a good thing. But there were times when having fans so close to the players was not so good. If a visiting team did something to arouse the ire of the Dodger fans, their outfielders would become the targets of an incredible array of flying objects, from flashlight batteries to false teeth.

Brooklyn fans were considered by most opposing players to be the most raucous and partisan in the league. Calling their beloved team "dem bums," there was no doubt as to what they thought of the other teams in the league. They were in rare form today and the noise level was high though the players had not yet taken the field. Hot dog, beer and peanut vendors walked up and down the aisles, hawking their treats to a full stadium. The beer vendors were careful to dispense the amber liquid in paper cups. Beer bottles would also be perfect missiles for worked up Brooklyn fans to throw at the umpires or opposing players.

Fritz Hofmann was jogging on the grass down the right-field line toward the bullpen. Rube Melton, today's starting pitcher for Brooklyn, was a few steps behind him. Fritz already had his catcher's gear on except for the mask and mitt, which he carried in his hands. Both were wearing Brooklyn's home game uniform. It consisted of a jersey and knee-length pants in white cotton. Both garments were loose and blousy to give maximum freedom of movement. Embroidered in blue across Fritz' chest was the name "BROOKLYN," in cursive. Dark blue socks covered his legs below the knee. On his head, he wore a cap of the same dark blue with a large "B" embroidered in white on the front.

Fritz squatted behind one of the two bullpen plates and Rube Melton stood on the pitching rubber sixty feet six inches away. Melton wound up and lobbed a ball into Fritz's mitt. He threw it back. The pitches would get harder and faster as Rube warmed up. He was a huge man, six foot five inches and two hundred and five pounds. A country boy from North Carolina, he was easygoing off the field but a fierce competitor during a game. He threw extremely hard but could be a little wild. He had led the league last year in walks and wild pitches. Rube had been friendly toward Fritz since he came to work for the Dodgers.

In fact, most of the players were friendly. They considered themselves just regular guys. They were decidedly blue-collar in their outlook and distrusted the stiffs in the front office, General Manager Branch Rickey, bankers, politicians and millionaires. In short, the players were pretty much like their fans in the way they looked at the world. But Fritz was surprised at some of the crazy habits of his teammates.

Every Sunday when the Dodgers were at home, they were required to attend a chapel service. The preacher who conducted the service was a Methodist minister, the Reverend Ralph Crawford. He was a severely dressed man in his fifties with a wonderfully sonorous voice, whose sermons were part Christian doctrine and part positive thinking pep talk. He was utterly ordinary looking except for one thing. He had a lazy eye. As he talked, his left eye would swivel around the room of its own accord.

Outfielder Paul Waner was convinced that the preacher was giving him the evil eye. Wherever he sat in the room, Crawford's wandering eye would swivel around, land on Waner and stay there. Paul got so nervous that he took to carrying around two rabbit's feet and a lucky quarter. When he went into a batting slump, Waner even visited a fortune teller in Queens who advertised an antidote for the evil eye. He wasn't alone. Fritz was amazed at how superstitious baseball players were. One would walk backwards to pick up his bat before going to the plate to hit. Another would swing his bat in the on-deck circle exactly seven times before walking to the plate. Still another refused to get rid of a tattered, worn-out ball glove and played with it even though the padding was all gone. There were lucky amulets and charms galore. Fritz heard about one infielder, who is 1938 had a string of thirty errorless games while playing second base. At the start of the streak, the player became convinced that the uniform and underwear he was wearing were lucky. He refused to change out of the clothing for over a month. Finally, his teammates, tired of the smell, held him down, stripped off the offending garments and burned them in a trash can. The player went out that day and muffed two easy ground balls.

Fritz loved his job. His duties were few and the pay was good. He only had to catch for batting practice before the game and warm up the starting pitcher and any relief pitchers later on in the game. He also ran errands for Durocher when needed., since he was hired, Fritz had gotten to the ballpark two hours before he was required to on every game day. He would volunteer to help the equipment man with getting the gear ready for the game. His enthusiasm had made an impression on Durocher. The fiery manager seemed to like him. When he was at the ballpark, Fritz could almost forget that he was a traitor to the United States and would fry in the electric chair if his spying activities were ever discovered. But, everything considered, he felt pretty good about his present situation. At least he was alive.

Back on a day in early February, Fritz was standing in a barbershop waiting to get his hair cut and idly thumbing through the pages of a newspaper. An article about the German debacle at Stalingrad caught his eye. Reading further he learned that the entire German Sixth Army had surrendered to the Russians. The blood drained from his face, his hands shook and he got lightheaded. His old unit in Russia had been part of the sixth army! He found a place to sit down and read further. Only ninety-one thousand German soldiers had survived to be taken prisoner. Mental images of some of his old comrades slipped through his mind. He wondered who had died and who had survived and been captured. Fritz wondered which was worse, death or Russian captivity. After the way, the Germans had behaved in the Soviet Union, and the Russian reaction to it, he probably would have preferred death. Sitting in the barbershop, Fritz felt a rush of gratitude to the Abwehr wash over him. They had saved his life.

His newfound gratitude to the Abwehr didn't prevent him from disobeying their orders in one specific area. Fritz knew he would be in a lot of trouble with his superiors if they ever found out he was socializing with another agent, especially one that was spying on the FBI, but he couldn't help himself. She was the most beautiful woman he had ever seen. Ever since she had picked him up from the submarine, he couldn't get her out of his mind, even though she was Jewish. All his early life, Fritz had been told by his Father that Jews were evil bloodsuckers responsible for almost everything bad that happened. Hannah wasn't like that. She was good and decent.

She had made Fritz change his attitude. All that stuff his father and the Nazis had said about Jews was just bullshit. They were just lies that were told to blame other people for their own mistakes. Fritz was now convinced that most of the things that people in authority had told him were bullshit. Fritz Hofmann was utterly smitten with the young lady. He had tricked Hannah into going out with him, but he got the feeling that she enjoyed their evening together. He really did.

After about ten pitches, Rube's fastballs were zipping in nicely. They would smack into Fritz's mitt with a loud bang that echoed around the stadium. After ten more throws, Melton put his hands on his hips, signaling he was ready.

The announcer's voice on the P.A. system echoed through the stadium, telling everyone to rise for the National Anthem. Everyone rose and put their hands or hats to their left breast as the Star-Spangled Banner was played. The military personnel in uniform in the stands came to attention and saluted. It was a patriotic time and any man in the stands who didn't show the proper respect for the flag and anthem would find himself flat on his backside with a sore jaw.

"Play ball!" yelled the home plate umpire and the game started. Rube Melton started out strong, mowing down Philly's batters. But Jack Kraus, the Philly's pitcher was just as good. At the top of the second inning, the Phillies threatened to score with two men on base, but Rube got out of the jam.

At the bottom of the second, Dolf Camilli got caught looking at a third strike and made the second out of the inning. Dolf started to argue with the umpire. Durocher came storming out of the Brooklyn dugout. He got right up in the umpires face. From his seat on the dugout bench, Fritz was able to hear clearly what Leo said to the umpire.

"The whorehouse called. You left your seeing-eye dog there and they want you to come to pick it up."

"Don't give me any a yer lip, Durocher. Scram or I'll throw your ass out of the game," shot back the umpire.

"That 'strike' you called was so wide that it almost hit my Aunt Minnie, sittin' back a' first base."

"Are you gonna get back in the dugout so we can get on with the game, or will I have to throw you out?"

Durocher stalked back to the dugout grumbling and looking angrily over his shoulder at the home plate umpire. Fritz sat in the dugout and watched his manager. He was the most competitive man Fritz had ever seen. He didn't just want his team to win, he wanted the Dodgers to go out and murder the other teams. His players were forbidden to slide coming into home plate. They were told to knock the opposing catcher down whether he had the ball or not. If Durocher could have gotten a win by taking out a tommy gun and mowing down the opposing team, Fritz thought he would do it.

At the top of the seventh inning, Earl Naylor came to the plate for the Phillies and hit a home run into the left field stands. The next batter, Pinky May grounded out to second base. Mickey Livingston then hit another ground ball to second base. The Dodger' second baseman, Alex Kampouris bobbled the ball and Livingston reached on the error. Durocher was livid, pacing up and down the dugout, swearing.

The next batter was Jack Klaus. He struck out on five pitches. That made two outs. If Rube could get the next batter, then Brooklyn would get out of the inning only one run down.

Danny Murtaugh came up and hit a fly ball down the right field line that landed fair and bounced around in the corner. Livingston trotted home for the second Philly run. Danny Litwhiler then struck out to end the inning.

When Alex Kampouris came into the dugout after the third Philly out, Durocher glared at him angrily. It was a habit of Leo's. He did this to players that struck out or made an error. It was a violation of baseball etiquette and the players hated it.

The score remained two to one until the top of the ninth inning. In the eighth, Durocher told Fritz to go to the bullpen and warm-up relief pitcher Newt Kimball. He was going to pull Rube Melton. However, Newt didn't endear himself to his manager when he gave up a third Philly run in the top of the ninth. Brooklyn got one run back in the bottom half of the inning, but walked into the locker room after the game losers for the day.

About twenty minutes after the game ended, the players were lounging around talking and smoking, getting ready to take their showers. Blue cigarette smoke was suspended in the air. Fritz had volunteered to pass out towels for the equipment man and was stacking a pile of warm towels on a shelf when Durocher walked into the room.

"Good job, girls. We just lost a game we should have won. You looked more like a bunch of kids playin' stickball than major leaguers. But what can you expect from has-beens and rejects," yelled the manager, walking into his office and slamming the door.

The players just shrugged and laughed it off, except for one. Arky Vaughan, the starting shortstop, threw his glove against the wall and gave a middle finger gesture toward the door of Durocher's office.

"I hate playing for that son of a bitch," said Vaughan. "Serve him right if I quit baseball."

Fritz lowered his head, embarrassed for Vaughan. He is acting like a spoiled child, he thought.

CHAPTER TWENTY-TWO

VILLA DEL MONTE
SANTANDER, ESPANA
14 JUNIO 1943

J ust after dark, a long, black Mercedes sedan drove into the courtyard of an isolated villa nestled in the Spanish countryside. The driver hopped out and ran around the vehicle to open the right rear door. A smallish man in civilian clothes emerged into the moonlight. Except for his driver, Admiral Wilhelm Canaris had come alone to the meeting. He told his driver to wait with the car and began walking toward the villa's entrance.

Two men materialized out of the shadows carrying Sten guns and pointed them in the Admiral's direction. One of the men held up a hand in the universal stop sign.

"I'm sorry, sir, but I have to search you for weapons before you go in," he said, in British accented English.

"Go right ahead," said Canaris, also in English, and raised his hands above his head.

After a thorough pat-down, Canaris was shown into the great room of the main house of the villa. A fire was crackling in a stone fireplace and the French doors to the patio were shut and bolted. Sentries had been posted around the outside of the villa to guard against inquisitive ears. Two men were there to greet the Admiral. Both were in civilian clothes.

"Welcome, Admiral. It is a pleasure to meet a worthy opponent. I am Stewart Menzies and may I introduce Mr. William Donovan."

With his thinning hair and mustache, slight build and tweed suit with waistcoat, Menzies looked more like a clerk in a London counting-house than the head of the British Secret Service. Donovan was stockier, middle-aged and clean-shaven. He wore a perfectly tailored, blue double-breasted pinstripe suit. He was the Director of the Office of Strategic Services, the American espionage agency. The three men shook hands and took seats on the plush furniture.

"I must say," said Donovan, "I was surprised that you requested this meeting. What would stop us from making you our prisoner and taking you back to London for interrogation?"

"Nothing except honor and the fact that I am no longer your enemy."

Menzies lit a cigarette, rose from his seat and walked to a drink cart. He poured three fingers of single malt Scotch whiskey in each of three glasses and handed them around.

"Your message said that you have a proposal for us to consider. We would be delighted to hear it," said Menzies after resuming his seat.

Canaris crossed his legs and took a sip of the whiskey.

"Gentlemen, speaking for numerous senior German army officers, we have had about enough of Adolf Hitler. He has led our country into a disastrous war that threatens our very existence. Resistance groups have formed in the officer corps. Many are actively plotting the assassination of the Fuhrer," said the Admiral. He took another sip of whiskey and paused.

Menzies and Donovan exchanged glances. There had been rumors of plots against Hitler in the German officer corps, but this was the first confirmation that the rumors were true.

"I am here to ask for an armistice between the Western allies and Germany, to bring this disastrous war to a close. My peace proposal is this. After Hitler is dead, I propose a ceasefire between Germany and the Western Allies, but with the war against the Russians tocontinue. Joseph Stalin is just as big a monster as Hitler. We cannot allow him to win and gobble up Europe," said Canaris, and put his glass down on a side table.

"How do we know you will be able to deliver?" asked Donovan.

"You will just have to trust me, but I have delivered before," said Canaris, and turned toward Menzies. "In 1940, when Hitler was poised to invade England, I knew the invasion would be a disaster for world civilization. You British had nothing that could have stopped it. Had Hitler conquered England, a new dark age would have descended over Europe that could have lasted for decades. I deliberately betrayed my spy networks in England to MI6. You captured the agents and turned them. They began to send endless messages about your island being a fortress bristling with men and guns, which I dutifully passed on to my beloved Fuhrer. Without my help, Germany would have invaded and your war situation would be much darker than it is now."

Menzies nodded his head. It was true, he knew it. He looked over at Donovan, who also nodded.

"This 'peace plan' is a little above our authority," said Menzies "We will let Winston and Franklin chew on this one. We will let you know.

You monitor our signals traffic. If you hear the message, 'the corn is green,' then we need to meet again."

In the rear of his car, after the meeting, Canaris thought about what had been said and his next moves. Abruptly, he smiled. What he had told Menzies about his networks in England wasn't quite true. He still had a small cabal of three highly placed agents in the British government who kept him apprised of what the British were up to.

Canaris turned his mind to the anti-Hitler resistance. After their little talk in February, Oster had gotten busy. He began recruiting anti-Nazi dissidents into the Abwehr. Among them were Diedrich Bobhoffer, a protestant minister, and Hans Von Dohnanyi, a prominent German lawyer. Oster formed a resistance group within the organization, using it as a cover for their activities. Besides plots to kill Hitler, the group tried to smuggle as many Jews out of occupied Europe as they could. Ironically, it was helping Jews and not assassination plots that got Oster in trouble. In March, he, Bonhoeffer and Von Dohnanyi had smuggled fourteen Jews to Switzerland, disguised as Abwehr agents. But they made mistakes and left a paper trail. The Gestapo got wind of it and investigated. Bonhoeffer and Von Dohnanyi were arrested. Oster was dismissed from his job at the Abwehr, and put under house arrest. Canaris missed his friend. It was sad, but the same would happen to him if Hitler wasn't done away with, and quickly.

Before he was sacked, Oster had provided another resistance group with British explosives and detonators. The group was headed by Oberst Henning Von Tresckow, assigned to Wehrmacht, Army Group Center on the eastern front. This group had made two attempts to kill the Fuhrer so far.

The first attempt had occurred on 13 March. Hitler had flown into Smolensk to visit troops in the area. Just before the Fuhrer took off for the return trip, Henning Von Tresckow asked Oberst Heinz Brandt, who was on Hitler's staff and traveled with him, to carry a package to an old friend at Hitler's Wolf's Lair Headquarters. Von Tresckow told Brandt that the package contained brandy. In fact, it contained five kilos of plastic explosives and an acid pencil detonator. It was set to go off thirty minutes hence. Brandt readily agreed and put the package in the unheated storage compartment of the plane.

The bomb didn't go off. Apparently, the detonator froze solid in the unheated compartment. Von Tresckow had a devil of a time getting the package back after the plane landed, without the plot being discovered.

The second attempt had occurred on 21 March. Hitler had been scheduled to visit the Zeughaus Berlin, an old armory on Unter Den Linden, to look at captured Russian weapons. A member of Oster's group, Rudolph Von Gersdorff, there to greet the Fuhrer, had two packages of plastic explosive in his pockets.

Shortly before Hitler's arrival Von Gersdorff went to the men's room and activated ten-minute time fuses and placed them in the explosives. He planned to approach Hitler when the explosives were about to detonate and envelop him in a bear hug. When the explosives detonated, he and the fuehrer would be blown to bits.

Hitler entered the building but did not spend the expected ten minutes looking at the Russian arms. Instead, he had seemed bored and left after two minutes. Gersdorff had rushed to the washroom and deactivated the fuses just in time. The Admiral knew there were other assassination attempts in the planning stage. It was only a matter of time before one of them succeeded. The question was, would it happen before someone discovered his own complicity in the plots? Canaris sighed deeply. In the end, all the attempts on Hitler's life and his peace proposal were probably futile. He was not a fool. He knew that Churchill and Roosevelt would be reluctant to accept his offer of a separate peace. But peace with the Russians wasn't possible after the crimes the SS had committed in their country. The Admiral felt dread in the pit of his stomach that events had progressed too far, and that the Fatherland's destiny was one of utter destruction.

CHAPTER TWENTY-THREE

SPANISH CONSULATE
180 EAST 58TH STREET
MANHATTAN
NEW YORK CITY
JUNE 18, 1943

It had been nearly a week since Keller had arrived in New York. He had flown over on the regularly scheduled flight from Lisbon, Portugal. Customs had been no problem. All he had to do was show his Spanish diplomatic credentials and he breezed through. His papers identified him as Juan Antonio Garcia, a low-level Spanish diplomat.

Since Keller was assigned no duties at the New York Consulate that he had to pretend to do, he could come and go as he pleased. He decided to take a room on the premises. There were rooms that were maintained for visiting officials. The staff gave him a wide berth after the first day. His Spanish was crude, like from some backwater of South America. When coming into his presence, the Spaniards would avert their eyes or walk away. They didn't like the aura around him. One of the Spaniards, a clerk, expressed it as, "el olor de la muerte," the smell of death.

During the week he had been in New York, Keller had taken time to get reacquainted with the city. He went back to his old neighborhood and looked around. He didn't try to find people he knew. That wouldn't be smart. They might call the FBI. He ate hot dogs and hamburgers again, his favorite foods from his childhood. He was disgusted to see Jews and negros walking around free. Someday, he told himself, after finishing with the Russians, the SS would deal with American Jews and niggers. Keller knew just how to handle them.

By week's end, Keller decided it was time to get started. He knew he should plunge into the Job the SS had sent him to do, but he had something personal to do first. It wouldn't take long and then he would find out about the Abwehr spy ring. He had plenty of money. The SS had given him five thousand dollars in ten and twenty dollar bills. It was counterfeit, of course, but very good counterfeit. There were some Jews in Sachsenhausen concentration camp who did excellent work.

The first thing he needed was a gun. Keller hadn't brought one with him in case he was inadvertently searched at Customs. In New York because of the Sullivan Act, a pistol could not be bought without obtaining a permit for it first. He supposed he could ask around in some rough neighborhood looking for someone to sell him a pistol, but he decided he didn't need to.

Keller went to Penn Station in Manhattan and bought a railroad ticket to Philadelphia. He sat in the club car, smoking and drinking beer the whole way. Sitting across from him were two American soldiers in uniform. One of the soldiers had a short cast on his right ankle and a cane propped against his seat. Two rows of medals adorned his chest. He was obviously a wounded veteran, back from combat. He was talking to a slightly younger soldier. His uniform was shiny and new with no medals. Keller listened to their conversation. The veteran soldier was talking about the North African campaign that had ended a month ago in an allied victory.

"We landed at Casablanca and Oran and some other places along the North African coast. The French fought us at first but gave up pretty quick. The planning for the landings had been poor so everything was fucked up. But we soon got our shit together and moved against the Germans. The Krauts kicked our asses at Kasserine Pass, but we learned a few things and began pushing them back. The British were squeezing them from the east and soon the heinies were bottled up in Tunisia. The Africa Corps surrendered on May 13th. Us GIs in the infantry knew the jig was up as early as May 1st. We started taking tons of prisoners and they were in poor shape. A lot of the krauts we took said they were fed up with Hitler and were glad they were taken, prisoner."

Keller's eyes bored into the soldier's face. He was fuming inside but he kept his face passive and said nothing. Soon after that, the train entered the 30th Street station in Philadelphia. Franz wandered around downtown Philadelphia until he saw the three hanging balls of a pawn shop.

A sign over the door advertised the place as BELLS JEWELRY AND PAWN. Keller went in and saw a bored-looking man leaning on the glass front counter. He was about forty with slicked-back hair and a thin mustache.

"What can I do for you?" asked the man.

"I need a pistol, a small one that will fit in my pocket."

"Come on round here, we got tons a guns," said the proprietor and led him to a section of the glass case.

On display inside the case, were about twenty handguns. They were almost evenly split between revolvers and pistols. The revolvers ranged from a giant Single Action Army Colt in .45 caliber to a small nickel .32.

There was a similar spread between the autos, from a Government Model .45 to a tiny .25 auto.

"I's you", said the pawn broker, "I'd stick with a revolver. There are no safeties to worry about, you jus' pull the trigger an' it shoots. The autos also have a tendency to jam."

Keller nodded his head and pointed to one of the revolvers.

"Let me see that one," he said.

The pawn broker took the gun from the case and put it on top of the counter.

"Excellent choice. Colt Detective Special .38 snub nose. I got it from a police detective who was fired from the force for takin' bribes from pimps."

"How much?" asked Keller.

"Twenty-eight fifty. With a box a shells at one fifty, the grand total is thirty dollars."

Keller nodded his head and pulled out a roll of cash from his front pocket. He peeled off two twenties and handed them to the Ppawn broker. After ringing up the sale on the cash register, the Broker gave him back a ten, put the revolver and box of ammunition in a brown paper bag and handed them to Keller, who left without another word. Keller walked back to the station and caught the return train to New York with his new revolver tucked in his waistband in the small of his back.

At four p.m. the next day, Keller took a cab to Foley Square. He idled on the sidewalk across the street from 500 Pearl Street, the United States Courthouse and office building for federal agencies. At five p.m. the building started to empty of people. After about fifteen minutes, Keller was starting to get concerned; maybe his man had been transferred or didn't work there anymore. Then he saw him. His name was William Stephenson.

After his stepfather had been arrested for spying in 1941, Keller's mother had been apprehensive about her immigration status. She and her son had never become United States citizens. She was right to be concerned. A notice came in the mail ordering them to report for deportation. Mother and son had gone to see the immigration officer who was handling their case. His name was William Stephenson.

Keller's mother had pleaded with Stephenson to let her and her son stay in the country. The official had curtly and coldly replied that that would not be possible. Keller's mother had then tearfully begged to be allowed to stay until her husband's trial was over. Again, Stephenson replied with a curt, "no." Keller tried to comfort his mother, but when he looked up at Stephenson the official was smirking at them. Right then and there, Keller swore he would kill Stephenson one day. He didn't know when he would get the opportunity, but somehow he would get revenge. Then this job for the SS had come up and it was like the answer to prayer if he believed in God, which he didn't.

Keller followed Stephenson as he walked southeast on Pearl Street. A few blocks later the INS official entered a parking garage. Keller hung around outside. After a few minutes, Stephenson emerged driving a green, 1937 Chevrolet sedan with New York plates. Keller watched him drive away west.

The next day Keller rented a car at a service garage. It was a beat-up 1934 Ford coupe. Despite its battered condition, it ran just fine. Keller showed his diplomatic credentials to the garage attendant. They were all he needed. He hadn't driven since he was a teenager when his stepfather had taught him. It felt awkward at first but he soon got the hang of it. At four p.m. he drove to 500 Pearl Street. He circled the block for twenty minutes until a parking spot across from the courthouse opened up. Keller parked the car and waited.

At five-fifteen Stephenson emerged from the federal building and began walking toward the parking garage. Franz let him get to the end of the block, then started his car and followed. As he was driving by the garage, he saw Stephenson enter. Keller rapidly circled the block and emerged pointing the other way on Pearl. When Stephenson's car emerged, he followed it closely.

Stephenson drove west to Centre Street where he turned right. He then made a left on Canal and another right on Riverside Drive. Keller settled in behind him. At one point, Franz had to run a red light to keep Stephenson's car in sight. A policeman on foot shook his fist at him. Stephenson stayed on Riverside Drive all the way to the New York suburb of Yonkers, where he turned left and ended up on a quiet street called Glenbrook Avenue. The green Chevrolet pulled into the driveway of a neat suburban home. It was white with blue shutters and small. The government must not pay their henchmen very much, thought Keller. He kept driving.

Keller found a business area. He parked in front of a hardware store and went inside. For five dollars and nineteen cents, he bought a pair of canvas work gloves and a hunting knife, complete with a leather sheath embossed with the Boy Scout emblem. Back in the car, Keller drove around until he found a half-empty diner. He went in, sat in a booth and ordered the blue plate special and coffee. It was six-thirty. It didn't get dark until around nine. He had two and a half hours to kill. After consuming his food, Franz sat and sipped cup after cup of coffee and chain-smoked Chesterfield cigarettes. The waitress didn't mind, the place wasn't busy. Keller could see why. The meatloaf had been overdone and the coffee was weak. Keller spent the time mentally savoring the revenge he was about to exact on William Stephenson.

He left the diner at a quarter to nine. There was still a little twilight, but it was getting dark fast. He drove to Stephenson's street and parked a block away from his house. There were only a few streetlights on the stree., It was obvious the developer had installed the absolute minimum street lighting required. It was good for Keller, the darker the better.

Franz approached Stephenson's house on the sidewalk. He looked around, it was now fully dark and there didn't appear to be anyone out and about. He walked up the driveway. Keller could see a closed garage ahead and a side door with light spilling out onto the driveway. Ducking below the windows, he approached the door.

It was a hot night and the door was standing open. The screen door, however, was closed. Keller looked inside and saw that the room was the kitchen. He could hear the tinny-sounding voices of a radio program coming from the room beyond the kitchen. Franz stood and listened for a moment. The program was Dick Tracy. He remembered listening to it as a child.

Keller reached over and grabbed the handle of the screen door. He gave it a gentle tug. It was locked. He looked through the crack between the screen door and the sill. He could see a thin wire crossing the gap about mid-way up the door. Probably a common hook latch, he thought. Much easier than a bolt latch. Keller put on his gloves and took the Boy Scout knife from its sheath. As silently as he could, he put the blade of the knife into the gap at the edge of the door and lifted the latch. There was some resistance, so he applied more pressure. The latch gave way and opened with a tiny clatter. Keller froze. He moved again when there was no change in the sound coming from the living room.

Keller eased the screen door open very slowly for fear that the hinges would squeak. There was no sound. Apparently, Stephenson kept up on the maintenance of his house. Once the door was open wide enough, Keller slipped inside. He inched toward the doorway to the living room, taking out his gun.

Keller peeked through the doorway. The family was gathered around a large radio console. Stephenson was sitting on a chair reading a newspaper. A pretty blond woman was sitting on the sofa looking at the radio, listening to the program. A girl, about ten and also blonde, was seated on the floor at the base of the sofa.

Keller whirled around the edge of the doorway into the room, with the gun in his hand.

"Everyone be very quiet or I shoot the child," said Keller menacingly.

Stephenson jumped up from his chair and the paper fell to the floor. He had a shocked look on his face. The woman reached down and gathered her daughter into her arms and pulled her up onto the sofa.

"What do you want? Please don't hurt my family," pleaded Stephenson.

"Remember me?" hissed Keller. "Remember how you humiliated my mother and me?"

Stephenson looked puzzled for a second and then recognition dawned on him.

"I remember. Look, fellah, I was just doing my job."

"Do you have a basement?" asked Keller.

Stephenson nodded. The blonde woman had her fist to her mouth, Franz thought she was about to scream. "If you scream I will shoot you all," said Keller in a surprisingly matter of fact tone. He pointed the gun back at Stephenson.

"Everyone down in the basement, you first," motioning with the gun at the INS man.

Keller followed the family down the stairs into the basement, keeping the gun inches from the woman's head. Stephenson snapped on the light as he passed the top of the stairs. The basement was small with a low ceiling and was cluttered with junk on homemade shelves. A layer of dust lay on everything. The family stood facing him in abject fear. The woman took her daughter's hand and pulled her behind her own body.

"Why are you doing this?" she asked, again close to hysteria.

"You want to know why? I'll tell you why…"

While Keller was distracted, talking to the woman, Stephenson moved abruptly and fast as a cat. He grabbed an old rusty, unsheathed sword from a shelf. In an instant, he lunged at Keller. Keller shot him in the head, but Stephenson's forward momentum carried him onward and caused the point of the sword to stick Franz in the fleshy area of his midsection above and inboard of his right hip, penetrating about four inches. Keller grunted with pain and shoved Stephenson's body away. The sword fell to the concrete floor with a clatter.

Stephenson's wife opened her mouth to scream and Keller shot her through the mouth. The young daughter backed away from her dead mother and ran a few feet to the corner of the basement. She sat down and covered her head with her hands and arms. Keller walked over to her, smiled, put the gun to the back of the girl's hand and shot her, the bullet going through her hand into her brain.

Franz Keller looked down at the three bodies and felt immense satisfaction. After a moment, he became aware of a pain in his side. He looked down and saw blood welling from his wound, running down his leg and pooling on the floor. He was concerned. That old sword must have been a family heirloom, he thought. It is old and rusty and there was no telling what germs were lurking on it. I could get tetanus or some other infection.

Keller gave no thought to the mother and daughter he had just killed, although they were not even a part of his grievance with Stephenson. Since he had been a boy, Keller had been indifferent to the feelings and suffering of others, only concerned with his own well-being. The one exception was his Mother. These traits were what had made him such an efficient Jew Killer for the SS. Psychiatrists had a name for people like him, Psychopath.

Keller knew that he would have to stop the flow of blood from his wound and do it soon. Leaving the bodies of Stephenson and his family where they had fallen, he climbed the stairs to the ground floor and continued upstairs to the bathroom, leaving a trail of blood on the hardwood floors.

In the medicine cabinet beside the sink, he found a box of gauze pads. Taking the full stack of pads, Keller pulled up his shirt, put them over the wound in his side and applied pressure. He was starting to feel a little woozy. The direct pressure succeeded in stopping the flow of blood. Franz found a roll of adhesive tape in the medicine cabinet. He took a washcloth hanging from a towel bar, folded it into quarters, put it over the gauze pads and secured it with the tape. To keep it tight, Keller wound the remainder of the roll of tape around his body and over his makeshift bandage.

Keller looked down at his clothing. His suit jacket, shirt, and trousers were saturated with blood. He stripped off his clothes and threw them in a pile on the floor. He got one of Stephenson's shirts from a dresser drawer and put it on. It was tight across the shoulders and long in the sleeves, but it would have to do. A suit from the closet fit him about the same.

Keller looked at himself in the bathroom mirror. His skin was extremely pale and there were dark circles under his eyes. A dangerous amount of blood had been drained from his body and he was unsteady on his feet. He walked back into the bedroom and retrieved his money, wallet and knife, leaving behind his bloody clothes and gloves in a pile. Leaving the house the way he had come in, Keller staggered back to his rented car.

During the drive back into lower Manhattan, Keller found himself about to pass out several times. He slapped his face to stayconscious. He parked the car outside the closed garage where he had rented it and took a cab to the Spanish Consulate. During the ride, the cab driver became concerned with Keller's appearance.

"You okay, buddy?" the driver asked.

"Yeah, I'm okay. I just had too much to drink and my dinner didn't agree with me."

Keller let himself into the side door of the Consulate and stumbled to the sanctuary of his room.

CHAPTER TWENTY-FOUR

STEINS CAMERA SHOP
447 WEST 46TH STREET
MANHATTAN
NEW YORK CITY
JULY 10, 1943

It was already hot at ten am when Fritz Hofmann walked into Stein's Camera Shop. The weatherman on the radio said the heatwave would last only for a few more days. Fritz hoped so. For the last week, people all over the city had been sleeping on their fire escapes and kids had been cracking open fire hydrants to bathe in the spray. The firemen had been lenient, taking their time in shutting off the water. The movie theaters, cooled by refrigeration, were packed. They were some of the few places where people could escape the heat.

Stein was behind the counter, glaring as he always did. Hofmann wished he could make the older man understand that his situation wasn't Fritz's fault, they were both in the same trap. Fritz was in a hurry. There was a game at Ebbets Field today and he wanted to get there early. He only came to the camera shop to check if there were messages to him from the Abwehr.

Fritz bypassed the counter and went into the back room. There, he ran face to face into another man. He was short and slim, with a bushy mustache that hung down from the corners of his mouth. He wasn't wearing a suit but was dressed in a short-sleeved, green checked shirt, that hung outside his slacks. Fritz was instantly, warily on guard.

"You must be Friedrich Hofmann, my companion in crime," said the man in a heavy Irish brogue.

"Who the hell are you?" asked Fritz.

"My mother had me christened Michael Brian Flynn forty-one years ago in the auld sod. I do the same thing you do for our Abwehr friends across the sea."

Fritz relaxed a little. He had been told he had a counterpart. but why was he making contact now? He smiled at the man."I was told we shouldn't meet with each other," said Fritz.

"Aye, we shouldn't, but I have a special reason for breaking that rule. Let's go across the street, have a cup a tea, and talk about it," replied Flynn.

He had a relaxed, friendly manner, but Fritz saw that his eyes were cold and wary. They left the camera shop and walked to a small café around the corner. The place was almost deserted and they took seats in a booth in the rear of the room where they could talk without being overheard. Once the waitress had served their drinks, tea for Flynn and coffee for Fritz, Flynn looked him in the eye.

"Are you one of those fanatical Nazis or just a loyal German?" he asked as he was stirring milk into his tea.

Fritz considered for a moment how he should reply. Was the question a trap? Was the Abwehr checking on his loyalty? Then, he decided, what the hell, just answer truthfully.

"I'm neither," said Fritz "I'm an American. I was born here. My father dragged me to Germany in nineteen thirty-seven. By forty-two I was fighting on the Eastern Front. I had almost resigned myself to dying there when the Abwehr offered me this chance to get out of Russia. But I do my job well for them. What about you?"

"Durin' the Great War, I became enamored of the dashing aviators and their flying machines. I left County Galway and joined the Royal Flying Corps. I ended up flying bombers, Handley Page HP.12s, great ungainly things. I got out in 1919, just in time for the Irish Rebellion. While I was off fightin' for the IRA, the black and tan bastards raided our village. They shot my father and burned our cottage down around my mother. I shot the police inspector in charge of the bastards that killed my mum and dad a few days later and left Ireland with a price on me head. I kicked around the world doin' whatever flying jobs I could. Mostly I was in South America. In late 1940, I heard the Yankee airlines were short of pilots because many of their veterans were bein' drafted into the military. I went to New York and was hired by American Airlines. I work as a relief co-pilot and fly all kinds of different routes. I was recruited by the Abwehr in 1941." Flynn took a sip of tea and continued.

"I have nothing against the Americans. The only problem is they are on the same side as the bloody Brits. There is an old saying, 'The enemy of my enemy is my friend.' Well, the fookin' British are my enemy and that's why I'm doin' this. But it's getting hard for me, what with all the horrible things the Nazis are doing to civilians in this war. Their treatment of the Poles reminds me of how the Brits treated my people, the Irish. "

"Okay, now that we know each other's life histories, why are you making contact with me?" asked Fritz.

"Do you have a gun?"

"No, why would I need a gun?"

"I suggest you get one. I got a message from the Abwehr a few days ago, and they told me to relay some information to you. It seems Heinrich Himmler has gotten wind of our little spy operation. He is sending one of his fookin' SS assholes to America to check us out. The one they are sending is supposed to be a right mean bastard."

On the subway to Flatbush after leaving the cafe, Fritz thought about his situation. His double life was already fraught with danger. It looked like it was going to get more dangerous. Should he follow Flynn's advice and arm himself? If by some misadventure he was caught by the police with a gun in New York he could go to jail, and he couldn't afford that. He was enjoying himself. He loved his job with the Dodgers. He got to travel around the country and see places he had never seen and his feet had finally stopped hurting from the operation in Germany. Working for the Abwehr was actually a minor part of his routine. Maybe he could continue doing what he was doing until Germany lost the war and then just fade into obscurity.

Fritz decided against getting a gun. After all, why should he have to fear the SS? He was doing the job the Abwehr told him to do so he should be okay. He thought, however, that he needed a plan in case everything fell apart. He remembered a class at the Abwehr training school about how to obtain a false identity. It was ridiculously simple, and he decided he would get a new identity just to be on the safe side.

If the spy ring was discovered by the FBI or compromised by the SS and he had to run, Fritz would find it hard to leave Hannah Rosen. They had now been out together many times. It was all very innocent, he just took her out to dinner and dancing. Fritz didn't kid himself, Hannah was way out of his league. But deep down, he harbored fantasies about marrying her after the war was over. It was ridiculous, but it didn't hurt to dream.

When Fritz got to the ballpark, he could sense that the atmosphere there was tense. As he was putting on his uniform, Fritz heard Arky Vaughan talking to a group of players.

"I tell you boys, that was a shitty thing that son of a bitch did," Vaughan said angrily.

Fritz sat down beside Augie Galan on a bench and whispering, he asked him what was up.

"Durocher and Bobo Newsome got in a shoutin' match a few days ago about a pitch Bobo threw to Vince DiMaggio in a game. Durocher suspended Bobo for the rest of the season for sassin' him. Durocher then went and said bad things about Bobo to one a the sportswriters. It was in an article in the paper this morning. Arky is fit to be tied with Durocher," said Augie. Bobo Newsom was a pretty good pitcher who had kicked around baseball for years and had been picked up by Brooklyn.

Fritz looked at the clock on the wall. It was a few minutes to one, nearly time for the players to go out and do their pre-game warm-ups. Arky Vaughan suddenly stood up and strode angrily towards Durocher's office. He threw the door open and it banged against the outer wall. Everyone in the locker room could hear the conversation that took place through the open door.

"What you want Vaughan and whaddya mean slammin' my door like that?" yelled Durocher.

"Did you make those comments about Bobo that were in the paper today? asked Arky.

'Sure I made 'em. So what. The bastard won't make the pitches I tell him to make. What? Did he crybaby to you?"

Vaughan left the office and slammed the door. He went to his locker and started stripping off his uniform. None of the other players said a word. When he was dressed in his street clothes, Arky went back to Durocher's office again, carrying his uniform and spikes. He flung open the door to Durocher's office again. Fritz could see Leo jump up in fury.

"You can take this stuff and my contract and shove it up your ass," shouted Vaughan and threw his uniform and equipment on the desk. He stalked out of the office and then out of the locker room. Durocher stormed out of his office and over toward the rest of the players. His face was a mask of wrath.

Any a you other has-been, prima donna's got anything to say?"

Without looking at Durocher, most of the other players began to take off their own uniforms and change into street clothes.

"This is a fuckin' mutiny," shouted Leo and stomped out of the locker room.

Fritz was stunned. What had brought this on? These guys were acting like children. They were used to playing for Durocher and knew how he could be. They had the best job in the world and should be grateful for it.

Durocher came back accompanied by the Dodgers General Manager, Branch Rickie. Rickie had a hangdog look on his puffy cheeks. His bushy eyebrows were furrowed in a frown. The expression on his face was akin to that of a constipated person who hadn't had a bowel movement for a week. He was wearing a rumpled suit with the waistcoat unbuttoned and a cigar clamped in his teeth. The two of them went to Durocher's office and closed the door. Almost immediately Fritz heard shouting, angry voices. The argument went on for about five minutes, and then the door opened. Rickie came out by himself and walked over to the group of players standing around in their street clothes. "Look, you men are professionals," said Rickie. "You can't do this. It's bad for the game of baseball and it's not fair to the fans who have come out to watch you play. Be reasonable. Get your uniforms on and get out on the field."

Rickie's conciliatory tone suddenly changed. Now there was steel in his voice. "If you don't play, none of you will ever work in professional baseball again."

The naked threat hung out there. It was real. Rickie had the power to do just what he was threatening to do. The players grumbled but put on their uniforms and went out to the field.

"Where's Vaughan?" asked Ricky.

"He's sittin' out in the right field stands with Bobo," said the equipment man, who had left the room and came back. Richie threw his cigar on the floor and walked out.

Fritz expected that both Vaughan and Newsom would be immediately traded to another team. Since he had been with the Dodgers, he had been amazed at the unstable nature of the life of the average major league baseball player. They came to the team and might stay for years or be gone in days, traded to another team. They were like chattel and the owners could trade them on a whim. For doing what those two had done, Fritz figured it was only a matter of time before they were both traded away.

The emotionally hyped Dodgers went out that day and slaughtered the Pirates 23 to 6. Al Glossup hit two home runs. By the seventh inning, Arky Vaughan was suited up in uniform and sitting in the home dugout.

CHAPTER TWENTY-FIVE

SPANISH CONSULATE
180 EAST 58TH STREET
MANHATTAN
NEW YORK CITY
JULY 15, 1943

Franz Keller sipped his coffee and perused a copy of the Daily News. He flipped the pages looking for news about the triple murder in Yonkers. On page seven he found a small article. It said that police were still investigating and were confident they would get their man. Keller smiled. That was just lies to placate the public. If they were going to arrest him, it would have already happened.

The day after the murders, all the papers had run the story in banner headlines. They called it "the open door murder case" and played it up for days. The public was in an uproar. Illicit sales of firearms spiked and people slept with their doors and windows shut and bolted despite the heat. After two weeks, when no suspect was arrested and with no further leads apparent, the newspapers wound it down and moved on to something else. About every week or so they would print a small article in the back of the paper, restating the police's promise to catch the killer.

Keller put down his coffee cup and gingerly felt the wound on his right side. It was still tender to the touch but a whole lot better than the night of the killings. When the taxi had let him off at the consulate, he barely had the strength to stumble to his room and collapse on the bed. He had slept for thirteen hours, waking up weak and feverish.

Keller had cornered the maid and sent her out for bandages and aspirin. He threatened the terrified woman that if she said anything to anyone, he would kill her children. The woman hurried out and brought back enough Iodine, gauze and tape to treat a platoon of men in combat.

For the next five days, Keller lay on his bed alternately sweating and freezing. For a spell, he didn't know how long, he was delirious. The wound festered and he thought that he probably was going to die. Then, gradually, he started to get better. He regained his appetite and his strength began to return. Now he felt he was definitely going to live. The wound still hurt like blazes when he turned at the hips or inadvertently bumped it, so he knew he had some more recovery time ahead of him. But all the pain has been worth it, thought Keller. I have paid back that son of a bitch for the way he treated me and my mother. Once he finished this job for the SS, he would kill the prosecuting attorney who had put his stepfather in jail. But, Keller had to put that out of his mind for now. This morning he had received a message from the SS, impatiently wanting to know about his progress in New York. Keller wrote a reply. He told them that he was watching the camera shop trying to identify the Abwehr operators and that he would have more information soon. He sent the message out in the diplomatic bag.

From the tone of the SS message, Keller realized that he couldn't waste any more time. He didn't have the luxury of lazing about until he could make a full recovery from his injury but must get on with the job. He dressed in his one remaining suit. Stephenson's suit had long since been burned.

Keller went downstairs and cornered Carlos Breyer in his office. To get the information he needed all he had to do was ask. But, Keller didn't do that. He enjoyed intimidating people. He walked up very close to Breyer and looked down at the ridiculous looking little man. Keller grasped the front of the Spaniard's shirt and wrenched him to his feet.

"I am Untersturmfuhrer Keller from the SS. I want the address of the camera shop being used by the Abwehr as a base of operations."

"It is at 447 West 46th Street," croaked Breyer, in terror.

'I want you to continue the same routine as before. You will pick up and deliver messages, but you will let me see them first. Is that clear?"

"Si, Senor Keller."

Keller left the consulate. He took a taxi to the intersection of 46th Street and Seventh Avenue. He got out, paid the driver, and walked east on 46th. He strolled by Stein's Camera Store. He noted that it was a small business that shared a building with several other small storefronts. At the end of the block, he turned and walked back, but this time he took off his hat and went into the store. It was a dim space and had a glass counter with a row of cameras for sale. Behind the counter was a stoop-shouldered, middle-aged man wearing a yarmulke. The Jew met him over the counter.

"Yes, may I help you?"

Hate boiled up inside Keller. Yes, he thought, there is something you can do for me. You can die. If you knew how many of your brethren I have dispatched to the nether world, you would be cowering in fear. But Keller didn't say what he was thinking. Instead, he asked an innocuous question.

"How much do you charge for developing?"

"Fourteen cents a roll for twelve and twenty-three cents for twenty-four."

"Thank you, that is good to know. Good day."

Keller put his hat back on and left the store. Outside on the sidewalk, he surveyed the buildings across the street. A little down the block to the east, he saw a commercial building containing numerous small businesses on four floors. One of the windows on the third floor, fronting the street had a "vacant" sign posted.

When Keller walked in the door of the building, he saw a stairway leading to the upper floors and a hallway beside it stretching into the guts of the building. A sign in the shape of an arrow directed him to the building office down the hall. He went in without knocking. Behind a desk, with his back to the window sat a very fat man. He was bald except for a small fringe of hair above his ears. He held a sandwich in his right hand that was on its way toward his open mouth. When he saw Keller, he reluctantly put the sandwich down.

"Help you?" asked the fat man.

"I'm interested in the vacant office on the third floor," said Keller.

"Thirty bucks a month, first two months in advance. Price includes utilities, 'cept hot water 'cause we ain't got any. We'll throw in your company's name in gold on the door. What business you in?"

"Import, export. May I see the office?"

The fat man rummaged around in his desk drawer, came up with a key and tossed it to Keller.

"Be my guest. Last tenant left some old junk furniture. If you don't want it, I'll have it carried down to the basement. Go on up, I ain't climbin' them stairs."

Keller took the key and walked up the stairs to inspect the office. His side was starting to hurt bad and he felt exhausted. He would soon have to stop for the day. The office was one large room. A cheap plywood divider separated it into a reception area and an inner office. A desk had recently stood in the reception area. Franz could see four impressions in the dirty linoleum floor where the legs had been. He went into the inner office. A battered wooden desk stood near the window with a cracked leather office chair behind it. He moved over to the window. When he stood off to the right of the window, he had an unobstructed view of the front door of Steins Camera Shop. Keller moved the desk and chair, grunting with pain from his side. He succeeded in positioning the desk and chair so he could sit in the chair and observe the door of the camera store in a resting position with his feet up on the desk.

Keller went back downstairs and rented the office. With the key in his pocket, he returned to the Consulate. The next morning, he was back and began his vigil. He didn't leave except for noon meals and trips to the washroom down the hall. A sign painter came and painted his phony company name on the door. Several times in the first few days someone knocked on the door. Keller figured It was either door to door salesmen or someone who wanted to import or export something. He ignored the knocks.

One day as he was entering the building, the obese manager confronted him and asked if he would be interested in some female companionship. Keller thought, why not? He nodded to the man. A half-hour later there was a knock on the office door. Keller called for the person to enter.

The prostitute was tall for a woman and slim. She was on the cloudy side of thirty-five and sported heavy makeup that didn't quite disguise the ravages of a hard and dissipated life. She was clad in a green dress with the buttons undone down the front showing a bit of cleavage. She entered the room and closed the door.

"Hi," she said, "I'm Maizie."

"How much?" asked Keller.

"Ten bucks."

Keller took a ten from his roll and lay it on top of the desk. Maizie came toward him and hiked up her dress. During the sex act, Maizie maintained a bored, deadpan expression on her face. When they were done, Keller made arrangements for her to return every Wednesday morning. She picked up the ten dollar bill and left without speaking.

CHAPTER TWENTY-SIX

FBI, NEW YORK FBI FIELD OFFICE
500 PEARL STREET
MANHATTAN
NEW YORK CITY
JULY 19, 1943

Special Agent Ted Miller walked down the corridor leading to the Assistant Director's office. Mr. Byrnes had called a meeting of all agents assigned to Counter-Espionage. His path would take him past the door to the secretarial pool and Hannah Rose. Even after all the time that had passed and all the rebuffs, Ted was still mooning over her. During the day he was able to displace her in his mind by keeping busy on his investigations. In the evenings it was a different story. He would be reading or eating and the image of her face would suddenly pop into his consciousness. At various times he would try to get angry with her. Ted would tell himself that he was well rid of her and that if she didn't want him then he didn't want her, but it was all useless. He was still hooked on her. At night when he slept he would have erotic dreams featuring he and Hannah that would cause him to have to change his bed linen in the morning.

Today Ted decided to walk by the secretarial pool without looking

THE ADMIRAL'S SPIES | 243

in. As he approached the door, he steeled himself. But as he was passing the door his head turned of its own volition and he saw Hannah seated at her desk.

Their eyes met and Ted abruptly stopped. When Hannah first saw him, her face lit up in the beginning of a smile. It then abruptly changed to one of sadness. She broke eye contact and turned away. Ted hurried on.

But, he had seen something in the moment before Hannah had turned away from him. It was, dare he say it? Longing? *She still cares for me! I know she does.* Ted cursed the Jewish religion. She couldn't be with him because of some archaic taboo about intermarriage with gentiles. He shook his head angrily and went on into the office of AD Byrnes.

On June 20th, there had been a sensational triple murder in a suburb of New York called Yonkers. A man named William Stephenson and his wife and daughter had been brutally murdered. Because Stephenson worked as an official in the Immigration Service, and thereby was a federal employee, the FBI had been called into the case.

The perpetrator had shot all three people, including a child, but in the melee, one of the victims had stabbed him with an old Civil War sword. The perpetrator had lost a lot of blood and left his bloody clothing at the scene. There were no witnesses and little evidence except the bloody clothes. Agents began to look into Stephenson's personal life to see if someone had a grudge against him.

A week later the report from the FBI crime lab on the perpetrator's bloody clothing came back. It said that the suspect had a blood type of O positive, which was useless. Half the population was O positive. The report went on to say that the clothing was German! The lab people had determined that the suit was made of horsehair and according to a hidden label, had been made by the Hansel-Echo Company in Germany.

When the agents in the field office got wind of the report, it caused wild speculation about Nazis skulking around New York. Rumors flew back and forth. Some of them, as usual, outrageous. One said Stephenson had stumbled upon a nest of German spies and they had killed him before he could betray them. Another said that Stephenson was a Nazi spy himself and he was killed because he was disenchanted with the Germans and was planning to go to the FBI.

Ted was caught up in the exciting speculation. The report had revived his interest. Dietrich's last words, the arrest of the woman in Washington and now this. The evidence was building that he was right in his speculation that there were Nazis sneaking around New York.

Assistant Director Byrnes called the meeting to order. There were about thirty agents in the room. There weren't enough chairs so everyone stood in a semi-circle in front of Byrnes' desk.

"I have called you here to clarify the Bureau's position on the murder of William Stephenson," said Byrnes and paused for a moment to scan the agent's faces. "It is the position of the Bureau that the murders were a crime of passion. They were no doubt committed by a German immigrant, possibly because Stephenson was involved in the deportation of someone dear to him. The murders were not the result of espionage activity."

Byrnes folded his arms and glared at the group of young men. An agent in the front row raised his hand and asked a question.

"How do we know it wasn't spy activity?

Byrnes' frown deepened.

"Special Agent Considine, Director Hoover has assured me

personally that there are no enemy spies operating in America at the present time. I will give you leave to go to Washington and tell him he is wrong, face to face. Do you want to do that?"

The agent shook his head.

"I didn't think so. Now get back to work and let us have no more talk about spies. The black market is our main concern now," said Byrnes and dismissed the meeting. The black market was indeed a problem. As shortages had gotten worse, even patriotic people had begun to patronize illicit sellers for daily necessities.

When Ted was leaving, he again walked by the secretarial pool. Hannah was away from her desk and nowhere to be seen.

As he continued down the hall, Ted thought about what Byrnes had said. He didn't buy it. Hoover was wrong. There was an undiscovered German spy network. He could feel it in his bones. But what could he do about his suspicions? He could do a rogue investigation, without backing from the Bureau. To do that he would have to bring in his partner, Bill Parker, on his suspicions. If they were caught conducting an unsanctioned investigation, it would be Parker's job as well as his that would be on the line. Ted couldn't risk that. Not yet. It frustrated him that the Bureau didn't see it as he did.

Back in the Counter-Espionage office, Parker asked Ted if he could use the desk for a while to write out a report. Miller nodded and pulled out his cigarettes and lighter. As he fired up, he noticed that he had only one Lucky Strike left in the pack. He left the FBI office, rode the elevator down to the lobby of the building and went to the kiosk just inside the front door. Ted asked the crippled man manning the kiosk for two packs of Luckies.

'Sorry, Mac, I don't have any. Most of the production is going overseas to the troops. What's left is being gobbled up by black market assholes. All I got left are Rameses."

Ted shook his head, he had tried Rameses cigarettes before and didn't like them. They were terrible tasting. He walked out the front door. Approaching the curb, he looked both ways for uniformed cops. When he didn't see any, he jaywalked across the street toward a drugstore on the corner. A cabby honked at him. It wasn't that he was about to hit Ted, but New York cabbies just liked to sound their horns. Ted entered the drug store but they didn't have Luckies either. He put a half dollar on the counter and settled for two packs of Old Gold cigarettes. He didn't like them as well as he liked Luckies but they were better than Rameses.

The headlines of a newspaper on a rack nearby caught his eye. Ted handed three cents to the clerk and bought the paper. He walked outside and stood on the edge of the sidewalk and scanned the front page.

Two days before, the Battle of Kursk had ended on the Eastern Front. It was the greatest tank battle in history and the Russians had been victorious. There had been horrendous loss of life on both sides. Another article was about a freighter storing 1800 captured German mines blowing up in Algiers harbor, killing hundreds. The cause of the explosion was undetermined. A little article near the bottom of the page caught his eye. It said that the uprising in the Warsaw Ghetto was over. The Germans had brutally suppressed it, killing all the Jewish fighters, and were in the process of demolishing the buildings, looking for hidden Jews.

The war news made Ted aware of the men in uniform all around him. The sidewalks were crowded with people, but the uniforms stood out from the civilian clothes. Ted could spot the combat veterans, and it wasn't just because of the ribbons on their uniforms. The men who had been in combat had a whole different demeanor than the others. They walked warily, with watchful old men's eyes. Ted had no way of knowing what they had gone through, but it must have been horrible. Miller had heard one such veteran talking to another on the subway. The soldier had said he would never believe what a politician said ever again.

Ted turned his attention to the civilians bustling by him. They were all ages, sexes and sizes. Somewhere in this great mass of people were some enemy spies working against his country. The trick was in finding them.

When he got back to his desk, Ted saw a package wrapped in brown paper sitting front and center on his blotter. Parker was nowhere to be seen. He looked at the return address and saw that the package was from Aubrey Swensen. Ted smiled. Aubrey had been his FBI partner for almost four years in Chicago before Miller was transferred to New York. Ted had fond memories of their time together.

He tore off the wrapper and opened the box. Inside was Swensen's "Hand Cannon" pistol in a leather shoulder holster and a box of Remington "Kleen Bore" .45 caliber cartridges. There was also a folded note. Ted opened it up and began to read.

"Machine Gun Miller get this! My uncle just died and left me a hardware store in a town in rural Minnesota. I'm leaving the bureau and embarking on a career in big business. Old J. Edgar will just have to struggle on without me. Since I won't have much use for the hand cannon where I'm going, I have decided to send it to you. With it, you will be able to knock down a charging grizzly bear. Do they have grizzlies in New York? Well, no matter, use it with my blessings. If you're ever around Higby, Minnesota, look me up. I'll treat you to some Swedish beer."

"Your partner, Aubrey Swenson."

Ted lifted the revolver from the box and pulled it out of the holster.

The blue was worn off in places, especially around the muzzle and the front of the cylinder, and the grips were nicked and worn, but the big handgun was clean and lethal-looking. Ted took six of the huge cartridges from the box of ammunition and loaded the revolver. He took off his coat and struggled into the shoulder holster. Pulling out six more cartridges from the box, he dropped them in his right coat pocket. With the gun in place and his coat back on, he was aware of the heavy weight of the big revolver. Ted figured he would get used to it. He unclipped the belt holster of his .38 revolver, withdrew it and locked it in his drawer of the desk.

Ted usually followed FBI regulations. He wasn't a rebel but after learning about the shenanigans going on in Washington with the Director, he decided to bend the rules. If J. Edgar Hoover could have a homosexual lover and blackmail everyone in Washington, then he could carry the "Hand Cannon."

CHAPTER TWENTY-SEVEN

ABOARD NEW YORK CENTRAL RAILROAD

OHIO STATE LIMITED

NEAR HARRISBURG, PENNSYLVANIA

JULY 19, 1943

The blue haze of cigarette smoke was so thick in the hot Pullman car, that it was difficult to see from one end to the other. When someone walked down the center aisle, the smoke would form little eddies in their wake. The smoke had nowhere to go because all the windows were closed. The car was positioned in the forward part of the train and though it was hot, the passengers didn't want holes burned in their clothes by burning cinders flying in the windows. Except for some groundskeepers and office staff, the train contained the entire contingent of the Brooklyn Dodgers National League Baseball team.

The players sat around in their traveling clothes which were invariably suits and ties. Dixie Walker, Augie Galan, Frenchy Bordagaray and Paul Waner were seated at a narrow table playing a spirited game of low ball poker. Arky Vaughn, Dolf Camilli, Mickie Owen, Al Glossop and other members of the team lounged in their seats, reading or dozing.

Fritz Hofmann sat among them. When around the team, he had

ditched his nickname Fritz and was called Fred because German-sounding names weren't currently very popular. The players had accepted him as one of their own. Sitting one seat away, Bobby Bragan, the backup catcher, was smoking a Camel and trying to persuade Fritz to double date with him.

"I tell you, Fred, in Cincy, the Baseball Annies are three rows deep outside the locker rooms after a game. This is prime midwestern, corn-fed pulchritude. After the doubleheader day after tomorrow, while these old bastards are soakin' their feet an' suckin' on oxygen, let's you and me snag two of the best lookin' Annies, an go out on the town."

Bobby had said it loud enough that it prompted a response from Paul Waner in the poker game. At forty, he was the oldest player on the team.

"That's the trouble with you young whippersnappers today, you got no respect for the wisdom of yer' elders," Waner said, in a mocking old man's voice.

"Oh, you're elderly all right, but I don't know how much wisdom you've picked up, what with you bein' beaned so many times," replied Bragan, He was joking about the age of the team. Of the eight position players in Durocher's usual lineup, the average age was 32.8 years, which was very old for a baseball team.

This problem was mitigated by the fact that the other teams were in the same boat.

"Whatcha' say?" asked Bobby.

"I dunno," replied Fritz," I'm kinda sweet on someone right now."

"Think 'bout it. Yer' girlfriend will never know," said Bragan.

Fritz was depressed. He usually enjoyed the good-natured bantering between the players, but not this evening. The pressure of being a liar and a spy was starting to catch up with him. There were too many things that could go wrong, resulting in him being caught by the FBI and executed in the electric chair. Hannah had told him on one of their dates that the FBI had no suspicions of the espionage ring. They thought they had caught all the German spies in America. Fritz wasn't so sure. What if the FBI were on to Hannah and were feeding her false information while they closed in on the agents? It was hard for Fritz to believe that the FBI could be that incompetent. He had had this feeling lately of impending doom.

Joe Medwick came through the door at the front of the car. The brash outfielder was known as a smart-ass and jokester, but he also had a hair-trigger temper and would fight at the drop of a hat. He looked toward Arky Vaughan.

"Arky, I was just near the baggage car and I heard a lot of clucking. You didn't bring the family chickens along on this trip, did you?" asked Medwick

Vaughan's ears got red and his jaw set, but then he relaxed and smiled. Joseph "Arky" Vaughan had been born in the little town of Clifty, Arkansas, thirty-one years before. His family moved to California when he was seven months old. He wasn't the hick his teammates made him out to be. He was a quiet guy and was considered a good player and teammate. Because the other players liked him, they kidded him quite a bit. Everyone was surprised he was still with the team after starting the July mutiny. Bobo Newsom had already been traded.

"Thanks, Ducky, but those aren't my chickens. I shipped mine ahead to the hotel," said Arky, in a calm voice.

The smile instantly left Medwick's face. Early in his career, he was at spring training in Florida and was swimming in a hotel pool. A woman there observed him dog paddling around and remarked that he swam like a duck. The nickname stuck.

"Arky, you know how I hate that name. Call me Muscles. That's my nickname. Muscles Medwick, has a nice ring to it, don't it?"

"Sorry, Ducky," said Frenchy Bordagaray, from the poker game," you'll have to build some muscles 'fore we can call you that."

"Maybe you can answer one a them Charles Atlas ads on the back of Popular Mechanics," said Augie Galan.

Medwick got red in the face and stormed out of the car toward the rear of the train.

No sooner had he left than the door leading to the front of the train flew open and a furious Leo Durocher burst into the car. His eyes surveyed the interior for a moment until his gaze fell on a player named Al Pittman, a tall rangy utility outfielder with bushy eyebrows and a prominent Adam's apple. He had been traded to the Dodgers from the Giants at the start of the season. Leo roared, "PITTMAN, YOU SON OF A BITCH, I GOTTA' BONE TA' PICK WITH YOU," and marched down the aisle with his arms swinging like Popeye the Sailor. Pittman, not knowing what was going on, jumped into the aisle and started to backpedal. He was brought up short by the door at the end of the car. Durocher ended up with his right index finger inches from Al's nose.

"Dearie Mulvey was riding in her forty-foot fuckin' limousine down Third Avenue yesterday. . ." said Durocher. Dorothy "Dearie" Mulvey was the socialite owner of the Brooklyn Dodgers. She had inherited the team when her father died, but the old man had hedged his bets and also made her husband co-owner. Even her loving father could see that "Dearie" was a bit of a dingbat.

". . . and she picked up her glasses on a stick and looked out her left window. She saw a poster with yer' ugly mug in a Dodger uniform advertising Rameses Cigarettes. Are you with me so far?"

"Sure, Leo," replied Pittman

"Shut up! Then she looked out the window on the other side an' saw another billboard with, Guess who?, Mister Al Pittman with a shit eatin' grin advertising Picayune cigarettes. Dearie was outraged and thinks you're a liar and the worst son of a bitch since John Wilkes Booth. She thinks this could reflect badly on the team, even though we both know Brooklyn fans are too dumb to notice something like that. She came down hard on Rickey and he just dumped a shitload a' crap on my head. What possessed you to do such a stupid fuckin' thing?" asked Leo and stood back with his arms folded. Pittman had his hands up, palms out in a defensive position, and his Adam's apple was bobbing up and down rapidly.

"Well, Leo it's like this. I have kinda' changed my smoking habits. I smoke Picayunes in the daytime and Rameses at night," said Al with a tentative smile, blissfully unaware of how stupid he sounded.

Durocher ignored the rising laughter from the other members of the team and launched again at Pittman.

"Don't give me that crap. Both those brands taste like yer' smokin' rolled up horseshit. I know the brand you smoke. You smoke Camels. What this is about is you bein' a greedy bastard. You couldn't pass up the money from the second cigarette company. How much was it?"

"Two hundred bucks," replied Pittman, sheepishly.

"Well, if you do something' stupid like this again, I will trade you to the Mexican league and you'll have to ride a burro to the ballpark every day," said Durocher, and abruptly stalked out of the car. Pittman, embarrassed, soon followed him. He had to walk a gauntlet of Dodgers, laughing and making wisecracks.

The bantering continued until the porters came in and pulled down the hinged beds on the wall and fitted the canvas sleeping curtains. The four poker players moved to the club car to continue their game. The rest slipped into their berths. Everyone was free to choose when to sleep and the quantity of alcohol they wanted to consume. Unlike a lot of the other teams, the Dodgers didn't have curfews or restrictions on drinking alcohol while on the road.

At 9:30 the next morning the train arrived in Cincinnati. The players got off the train and onto a small bus that would take them to the hotel. Fritz stayed to help carry the team equipment. He and the equipment man loaded the mound of gear in the back of a Ford pickup truck. They didn't have to worry about the player's luggage. The hotel had sent a truck and three negro porters to take care of that.

They took the gear out to Crosley Field, the home stadium of the Reds, and stashed it in the visitor's locker room. Fritz got to the hotel around noon. A bunch of Brooklyn players was sitting around a big round table in the hotel dining room having lunch. When they saw Fritz, they waved him over. Due to a fluke in the Reds schedule, the players would have the rest of the day off and the next day but would play a doubleheader on Wednesday.

After lunch, Fritz hailed a taxi in front of the hotel and asked to be taken to Spring Grove Cemetery. He had two dead drops to service. The driver let him out on Spring Grove Avenue in front of the cemetery office. He walked about a hundred yards into the graveyard until he reached a particular grave.

The headstone was old and worn but the inscription on it was still legible. It read, JOHN MILLS, 1821- 1894. There was a metal foot marker on the grave. It was loose. Fritz knelt, pulled it out and reached in the hole. He retrieved a waterproof metal tube. He opened it and found some rolled up pieces of paper. Fritz took a quick look at them. They were labeled as production figures from January to June 1943. A list of companies followed. Fritz recognized some of the names, Crosley Auto, Delco and Ravenna Ordinance, among them. He put the papers in his pocket and replaced the box.

Fritz walked another fifty yards to another grave. There was a similarly old and worn stone. This one said MARY ALICE PITTS, BELOVED WIFE AND MOTHER.1830-1902. There was another metal box. This one was empty. He replaced it and moved on. That completed his task for the Abwehr. Now he would do something for himself.

For the next hour or so Fritz wandered around looking at the tombstones. At last, in a part of the cemetery with more recent burials, he found what he was looking for. Fritz gazed at a gravestone. The inscription read CARL DAVID REED. JULY 6, 1920- DECEMBER 22, 1923. BELOVED SON. Fritz wrote down the name and birth date and walked back to the cemetery office. He used a payphone and called a cab to take him back to the hotel.

The next morning around ten, Fritz walked from the hotel to the Cincinnati city hall, only a few blocks away. Down a marble-floored hall, he found the County Clerk's office. He filled out a form requesting a copy of the birth certificate for Carl David Reed, born July 6, 1920, and with two dollars in his hand, took it to the clerk at the service window.

The clerk, a harried-looking woman in her forties looked over the form. "Do you want a certified copy?" she asked.

Fritz nodded.

"That will be one dollar more, three dollars total," said the clerk.

He paid the money and the woman went away. About ten minutes later she returned with the document enclosed in a tan-colored envelope. He walked out with no questions asked. Fritz laughed inwardly. He had learned how to do this in the Abwehr training school. The birth certificate was the key to a new identity. With it he could obtain a Social Security card, a driver's license, even a passport. If things got too hot, he could take the suitcase full of Abwehr money sitting in his closet and disappear into the heartland of America.

The first game of a doubleheader started at two p.m. the next day. The Dodgers were flat and couldn't seem to score. The Reds pounded them, scoring eleven runs. Durocher pulled his pitcher, Kirby Higbe after he had given up three runs in two innings. He put in Johnny Allen who lasted four innings and gave up seven more runs. For the rest of the game, the Dodgers manager sat and glared at Allen in the dugout. The team was in second place, four and a half games back of St. Louis and Durocher didn't want to fall any more behind. Rube Melton pitched the final two innings and gave up another run. The Reds won 11 to 1.

When the team went into the locker room after the first game. Durocher entered and stared angrily at them for a minute, shouted, "bullshit," then went in the visiting manager's office, slamming the door.

In the second game the pitching was marginally better, but Brooklyn started to hit. Ed Head started the game but was pulled by an angry Durocher after giving up seven runs. Leo was pacing the dugout like an angry panther. Les Webber and Rube Melton closed it out without giving up any more runs. The Dodgers won 9 to 7.

After the game, Fritz was approached by Red Corriden, the first base and hitting coach for Brooklyn. Nicknamed "Lollypop" by the Dodgers players, he had been a player, minor league manager and major league coach for all his adult life, breaking in with the St. Louis Browns in 1908. He was in his mid-fifties and was of medium height and a little chubby, but he knew his stuff about hitting. "Lollypop" put his arm around Fritz's shoulders.

"Leo wants you to start takin' daily batting practice, buddy boy," the coach said. Corriden called all the players buddy boy.

"Me? He wants me to practice batting?" asked an incredulous Fritz. His job had nothing to do with that part of the game.

"It's probly' cause of all the injuries we been having, Durocher thinks we might need you to pinch-hit sometime."

It was true, the Dodgers had experienced a string of injuries, not to the starting players thank goodness, but to the bench warmers. Sprained ankles and pulled muscles accounted for most but some were more serious and would have the players unavailable to play for some time. Durocher said it was "the baseball Gods fuckin' with me again." Whatever the reason for Leo's decision, Fritz was thrilled. The next day his name appeared on the active roster to replace one of the injured players. There was no fanfare.

Every game day from then on, Fritz would catch for batting practice as usual. Then Bobby Bragan would come out, don his catcher's gear and catch while Fritz had his swings. "Lollypop" Corriden would stand off to the side smoking a cigar and giving Fritz pointers. Sometimes the advice was colorful.

"Ya' got yer feet spread too wide buddy boy. Yer not straddling' a fat whore, yer feet should be directly under yer shoulders," or "yer holdin' yer arms too high. Ya look like my sister Josie wadin' through a puddle."

In the next few weeks, with Corriden's coaching, Fritz's batting improved way beyond what he thought was possible. He still had trouble with off-speed pitches, but that was improving too. Fritz was enjoying working out with a bat, but he told himself that he probably would never get the chance to bat for the Dodgers in a real game.

CHAPTER TWENTY-EIGHT

SAVOY BALLROOM
596 LENOX AVENUE
HARLEM
NEW YORK CITY
AUGUST 13, 1943

The odor on the darkened, block-long dance floor was a peculiar mixture of tobacco smoke, cheap perfume and human sweat. The ceiling was painted pink and the walls were mirrored. The huge dance floor was packed with writhing dancers. They were a mixed crowd of white and black. Different colored spotlights roved the darkened room and would pause on a particular couple to showcase them if they were good dancers. Cab Calloway and his band were on the bandstand, belting out a swing rhythm. The dancers were doing a version of swing called the lindy hop by the whites and jitterbug by the black people. The wild gyrations of their hips in performing this dance had caused the swells uptown and The Woman's League for Decency, to call it obscene. Cab himself stepped forward and started to sing.

"The hi-de-ho man that's me.

How'd you like to blow your top?

Dig yourself some fine ree-bop.

Hi-di-hi, he-de-He Oh, the hi-de ho man that's me.

Hi-de, hi-de-hi, hi-de, hi.

Hey-de, hey-de, hey-de, hey.

He-de, he-de, he-de, he.

Hi-de, hi-de, hi-de, hi."

Hannah Rosen and Fritz Hofmann stopped dancing and left the floor. They were close to physical collapse. They had already danced to "Minnie the Moocher" and "Kickin' the Gong Around," before "Hi-De-Ho." Doing the Lindy Hop was incredibly strenuous. They threaded their way to their tiny table near the back of the room. Fritz asked Hannah if she wanted another drink. The music was so loud he had to shout in her ear. The Savoy wasn't a place for conversation. Hannah shook her head, No. As she caught her breath she asked herself how she had come to this place in her life. She had deliberately alienated the man she loved and was going out with another who she really didn't care about.

She had to admit though that Fritz was a decent guy. He had finally told her his real name. He had never made a move on her and was nothing but sweet and kind. Still, in the back of her mind she didn't trust him. Their dates were exclusively dinner and then dancing. Hannah loved to dance. It gave her an escape from the real world. When she was on the dance floor, she could almost forget the mess that was her life.

Fritz Hofmann had also given Hannah insights into the German spy operation in America. Back when she started working for them, she had been warned by the Germans that they had people watching her to make sure she didn't hold back any vital information she heard. That she now knew was a lie. Fred had told her that the operation was limited in scope. There was no one watching her. As a result, she had made the decision not to turn over any more useful information. It was a remote risk to her parents but she couldn't continue to help the Germans.

The strain of all this was starting to affect her physically. This morning she had found another grey hair as she was getting ready for work. Grey hair at twenty-three! There were also little worry lines beginning to form around her eyes. Hannah wasn't overly vain but she wasn't blind either. She knew she was beautiful and attractive to men, but she made it a point to never purposely use it to gain a material advantage. Still, she didn't like to see her beauty begin to fade because of strain. Hannah cupped her right hand at Fred's ear and shouted over the din.

"It's getting late. Please take me home."

Fritz nodded and they rose and threaded their way toward the entrance. They walked through the lobby, with its enormous chandelier, down the wide staircase and onto Lenox Avenue. Under the bright lights of the marquee, Fred took Hannah's hand.

"There is something I need to talk to you about," said Fritz.

Hannah disengaged her hand and stood back warily.

"What is it?"

"Hannah, I know you don't trust me. That's okay, but you have nothing to fear from me. I received a message recently that the SS is sending an agent to spy out Abwehr operations in the United States. Apparently, the SS and the Abwehr don't get along. I haven't seen any sign of him yet, but when he shows up things could get dicey very quickly. If that happens, I have made contingency plans to disappear. I will go somewhere neither the SS or the Abwehr will ever find me."

Fritz paused, thought for a moment and continued.

"I want you to come with me so you will be safe. I know you don't have feelings for me but I couldn't live with myself if something happened to you."

Hannah frowned but said nothing. Fritz was talking about something called the Abwehr. What was that? She had never heard the term before. Was that what the German spy agency was called?

"I couldn't bear to leave you to the tender mercies of the SS. You have no conception of how brutal and inhuman they can be. You wouldn't have to love me or have physical relations with me. Just come and let me protect you," said Fred. He was so earnest and looked so vulnerable that Hannah felt pity for him and decided to let him down easy.

"I cannot. What about my parents? If I go with you, they will die. I can't allow that to happen," replied Hannah. She didn't tell the rest of the truth, that she didn't want to commit to a man she didn't love. They were silent on the taxi ride home to her uncle's apartment. As he walked Hannah to the front door of her building, Fritz broke the silence.

"Just forget what I said. We will continue on as before. After all, it's just dinner and dancing. What can that hurt."

Hannah nodded and he got back in the taxi and drove away. She let herself into the lobby and climbed the stairs to her apartment. She let herself in with her key. She saw her uncle Moshe asleep in his chair with a newspaper on his lap and his mouth open. Sitting on the sofa near him was Aunt Rachel. She was working on the Times crossword, something she did every evening. She looked up.

"Hello my Hannah, how was your evening?"

"It was fine, Aunt Rachel," said Hannah and smiled. She loved her aunt. She had been very kind to her since she came to America.

"I like your young man Hannah, but he is not a Jew. Do you think that is wise?

"You have nothing to worry about. We just both like to dance. It's nothing serious," said Hannah, and went to her room.

As she was brushing her hair, Hannah thought about what Fritz had told her about the SS agent. To have an SS monster on the loose in New York was a chilling prospect. More chilling was the thought that he might come after her. The reports of SS atrocities in Europe that came to the FBI had made her sick to her stomach. But, she thought, why would the SS care about me? I am doing the job I have been forced to do. But, just suppose he did come after me? What could I do? I could buy a gun, but guns are illegal in New York and it was a great risk to carry one. Besides that, I have had no experience with guns. The SS man would probably take it away from me and shoot me with it.

New York was a crowded place. There were a few locations where one was alone. She decided that from now on, she would keep to crowded places. If confronted, she would scream her head off.

CHAPTER TWENTY-NINE

INTERSECTION OF FIFTH AVENUE & 46TH STREET

MANHATTAN

NEW YORK CITY

AUGUST 18, 1943

I n August 1943, there were about seven million residents in the New York metropolitan area. A person living in the city could go his or her whole life without running into a relative or friend from another neighborhood in a chance meeting. The odds against it happening were very high. There were just too many people in the city. But every year people did defy enormous odds. The odds of winning the 150,000 dollar prize in the Irish Sweepstakes were several million to one, about the same as being struck by lightning, but someone won every year. A man featured in Ripley's Believe It Or Not had been struck by lightning seven times. Dubbed "The human electrode," he had the burn holes in his body to prove his claim.

When Fritz Hofmann left his rooming house that morning, he had no idea a chance encounter that would profoundly alter his future, and that of several hundred others was to happen that day. The laws of probability were so against it that, in later years one of those involved, Ted Miller, would chalk it up to divine intervention. Fritz was turning the corner onto 49th Street from Fifth Avenue when the equivalent of lightening striking for the seventh time hit him in the form of a shout.

"FRITZ, HEY FRITZ!"

Fritz turned and instantly recognized the stocky figure of his brother, Eb, running toward him. Eb was older looking, his hair was shorter and he was wearing the uniform of a sergeant in the Marines.

The two brothers met in the middle of the sidewalk and hugged. They did a little circular dance in their excitement. Breaking the huddle, they stood back and looked at each other. Fritz noted that his brother had a double row of ribbons on his chest and a diamond-shaped, blue patch on his left shoulder. It had white stars on a big number 1 made out in red. In vertical letters on the number was the word, GUADALCANAL.

"Eb, what the hell are you doing in New York?" asked Fritz.

"I'm up here on a seventy-two-hour liberty. I'm now stationed at the Norfolk Navy Yard. What about you? I thought you were in Germany with the old man."

"No, I didn't go. I bowed out at the last minute," said Fritz, looking away and to his right. Eb gave him a strange look. Fritz knew immediately that his manner in answering the question had made his brother suspicious. He hurriedly asked a question to try to cover up.

"Look at you, all those medals. Where did you serve?"

"I was on the Guadalcanal and Cape Glouster. I got a bug called malaria. It settled in real deep and became chronic. The Navy doctors said I wasn't fit no more for combat and sent me back to the states. What 'bout you? What are you doing?"

"Eb, you won't believe it. I work for the Brooklyn Dodgers as a bullpen catcher."

"The Brooklyn Dodgers, as in THE Brooklyn Dodgers? Major League Baseball?"

"You bet, it's the best job I have ever had," replied Fritz.

"How did you escape the draft."

"I'm 4F, I've got flat feet.

"Flat feet? You never had flat feet. Remember when we were kids before Mama died. You had to try on 'bout a hundred pairs a shoes to get a pair that would fit your high arches."

"That was years ago. They just fell over time," replied Fritz. Again, the way he answered made his brother frown.

"Listen," said Eb," why don't we find a place and get a beer and catch up?"

"I would like to but it's after twelve. I have to get to Ebbets Field for a game. Why don't you come along with me? I can get you free tickets and I'll introduce you to the players."

"Sorry, I can't. This is the last night of my liberty and I have a date with a beautiful dame. I'm sposed' to meet her at four when she gets off work."

"That's too bad. Listen. I live at 1567 Sheridan Avenue in the Bronx. Look me up when you're in town again. We will really catch up then."

The two brothers hugged again and Fritz headed toward the Rockefeller Center subway station.

When Fritz hurried, later than usual, into the locker room at Ebbets Field, all thoughts about his brother evaporated. The first thing he heard was shouted voices coming from the manager's office. The voices were familiar. They were Leo Durocher and the team's GM, Branch Rickie.

"Why can't you be a player-manager? It might increase the gate. In case you haven't noticed, we are eighteen and a half games behind the Cardinals. We need something to generate some excitement," said Rickie.

"I can't play. I got acorns in my elbows," replied Durocher.

"Acorns, what the hell is that?"

"Acorns, you know, bone chips."

"How long have you been growing acorns in your elbows?

"Couple' a years now."

"Then why the hell didn't you get an operation in the off season to take the acorns out. You could have planted 'em in your back yard and had a coupl'a fuckin' oak trees."

The door banged open and Rickie stormed out.

This wasn't their first or even tenth argument. It was getting to be a regular routine. It was a symptom of a losing team. The St. Louis Cardinals were blowing out every other team in the league. Being so far behind, made it hard for the players to generate enthusiasm in their play. Having Durocher insult them and throw fits made it harder still. The starting players were suited up and lounging around the locker room. They were subdued except for Arky Vaughan, who had a big smile on his face.

While he was pulling on his uniform shirt, Fritz asked Arky what he was smiling about.

"Well, I'll tell you, Fred. It seems our manager, Mister Leo Fuckin'

Durocher, got drunk last week and gave an interview to a writer from the Daily Worker. It's a house rag for the Communist Party. Now this alone would get him in trouble with Kennesaw Mountain Landis, but the Great Leo went further. He said major league ball should recruit negro players to replace the good players who are in the Army, but they couldn't do it 'cause of baseball's policy excluding negro players. Commissioner Landis got all hot an' bothered an' issued a press release denying there was a policy barring negros. Landis is fit to be tied with Durocher. I hope the bastard gets fired."

"You think it will ever happen? Negro players I mean," asked Howie Schultz.

The players talked it over and agreed to a man that black men would never play in the major leagues.

Just before the game, Fritz went to the bullpen to warm up Whit Wyatt, the starting pitcher. He was a big rangy right-hander. A Georgia native, he had been in the big leagues since he broke in with the Tigers in 1929. If it wasn't for the war he would be sitting on a porch in Georgia drinking mint juleps. Today his throws had surprising power, making loud pops as they slammed into fritz's mitt.

"Got a pretty good heater today, Whit," said Fritz.

"Ah'm feelin' fine today, Freddie. Let me at them Pirates."

The game started around two in the afternoon. The stadium was only one-third full, about eleven thousand people. The fans seemed lethargic, not nearly as loud as usual. Whit's fastball was indeed good, but not good enough to prevent the Pirates from drawing first blood, with a run in the top of the second inning.

At the bottom of the third, however, the Dodgers exploded. Frenchy Bordagaray led off and worked Pirates pitcher, Max Butcher, for a walk.

Arky Vaughn then hit a ground ball single to right field. Frenchy stopped at second.

Dixie Walker was next up and hit a ground ball to the pitcher. He bobbled the ball and it rolled about six feet away from him. Everybody was safe and the bases were loaded for Brooklyn with nobody out. Augie Galan hit a dribbler to first base. The first baseman threw home for a force-out at the plate. The bases were still loaded.

Leo Derocher could be heard swearing at Galan from the dugout.

Billy Herman was next up. He worked the pitcher for a three-two count and hit a hard ground ball to first base. The first baseman let it go under his glove into right field, for an error. Frenchy scored. Dixie scored. Galan went to third base and Herman to second.

The Pittsburg manager called for an intentional pass. They threw Gene Hermanski four wide ones and he trotted to first base. The bases were loaded again.

Howie Schultz dug his feet in at the batter's box. He spits on his hands and swung his bat a few times. On a two, two count he sent a screaming single into center field. Galan scored. Herman scored and Hermanski moved to third base. Bobby Bragan was up and swung at a pitch low and outside the strike zone. He hit a ground ball to second base and was thrown out at first. However, Gene Hermanski scored on the out.

It was a big inning for Brooklyn but Derocher wanted more. With two out Frenchy stepped in again. The Dodgers had batted around in the inning. On a three-one count, Howie Schultz suddenly took off from second base, trying to steal third. He was out by a good six feet, ending the inning.

Derocher was out of the dugout like a shot. He was yelling at

Schultz.

"What the shit did you do that for? I didn't signal you to steal!" Derocher continued on but his voice was drowned out by the boos of the Dodger fans. Even the fans were getting a little tired of Durocher's antics.

The Dodgers picked up another run in the fifth and held off the Pirates for a 6-4 win. It had been a good, scrappy game; The kind of a game where the players would go out for a few beers afterward to celebrate in a normal season. Instead, there was silence in the locker room. The players showered and left one by one with hardly a word.

CHAPTER THIRTY

NEW YORK FBI FIELD OFFICE
500 PEARL STREET
MANHATTAN
NEW YORK CITY
AUGUST 18, 1943

Special Agent Ted Miller was returning to his desk from the men's room when he saw a Marine sergeant sitting and talking to Special Agent Bill Connor. He was sitting in front of Connor's desk with his barracks cap pushed to the back of his head and was speaking forcefully. He was smoking and flicking the ashes from his cigarette into an overflowing ashtray on top of Connor's desk. The Special Agent had a skeptical look on his face. Ted noticed there was a double row of ribbons on the Marine's chest. This was a veteran. More than likely he had participated in the hellish fighting in the South Pacific.

Ted loved the Marines. He stopped and put his foot up on a nearby chair. Leaning on his knee, he listened to the Marine talk.

"I tell you, something ain't right. I'm walkin' down the sidewalk an' I see my brother I haven't seen in years. I run up to him and he acts all jittery. The last time I seen him, he was headed back to Germany with my asshole, alcoholic old man. Then he tells me that he is 4F 'cause he has flat feet. Fritz never had flat feet. In fact, his arches were so tall it was hard to find shoes to fit him."

"Sergeant, I think you may be exaggerating. You said before that your brother works as a catcher for the Brooklyn Dodgers. Are you seriously suggesting that one of the Dodgers is a Nazi spy?" asked Connor, with sarcasm in his voice. "Did your brother give you his address in New York?"

"Yes, sir, 1576 Sheridan Avenue. Look, I know I probably shouldn't have come here. I feel like I'm betraying my brother, but Fritz is up to something an' I think it has something to do with the Germans."

"What's he look like?"

"Six feet, slim, athletic, with light-colored hair."

"Alright, alright," said Agent Connor with raised palms, "I'll call Immigration in Washington and check on this. Before today, when was the last time you saw your brother?"

"May twenty-second, nineteen thirty-seven. The old man was all excited about havin' passage back to Germany."

"What are the full names of your father and brother?" asked Connor, with a pencil poised over a pad of paper.

"Engle Hofmann and Friedrich Hofmann. I used to be jealous of my brother because he was named Friedrich, while I was saddled with Eberhard."

Connor pulled his telephone toward him, lifted the earphone and put it to his ear. He jiggled the cradle a few times and the operator came on the line.

"Get me Immigration in Washington please."

While Connor was on the phone, Ted engaged the sergeant in

conversation.

"I see you're wearing the Marine First Division patch. Were you at Guadalcanal?"

"Yes, sir, I was. Went through the whole campaign, then fought on Cape Glouster. I did my share. I caught malaria though. I get these spells that put me flat on my ass. That's why I'm here and not still over there. Chronic malaria, the docs call it. I'm not fit no more for combat. I got a soft billet at the Norfolk Navy Yard," said the Sergeant.

They continued talking until Connor, who had been leaning back in his chair with the phone to his ear listening to the conversation between Ted and the sergeant suddenly sat up and said, "Yes Ma'am." He listened for a full minute and then hung the earphone on its cradle.

"On June sixteenth, nineteen thirty-seven, your father Engel left the United States bound for Germany. There is no record that Friedrich went with him. See, sergeant, it's just as I told you. Your brother is in the clear," said Connor.

"I still think something is screwy," said the sergeant.

"You seem to believe your brother is mixed up in something with the Germans," said Ted. "What makes you so sure?"

The sergeant looked at Ted. He had an open, honest face.

"I'm sure because of one thing sir. I know when my brother is lying."

The Marine walked out after being rebuffed by Agent Conner. Actually, it was more of a swagger than a walk. Marines seemed to carry themselves differently than other servicemen.

Ted went to his desk and wrote down the address the Marine had given for his brother and sat back, deep in thought. The FBI was used to this kind of thing. They got hundreds of these tips every week. But something in the sergeant's face, the obvious sincerity, gave him pause. Despite himself, Ted believed him. His instincts were nudging him to follow this up, especially after all the unexplained shit that had been going on. It all had to be connected somehow.

First, there had been Dietrich. Then the woman was arrested in Washington and the Stephenson murders. Now, this might be further proof that there was something going on right under the FBI's nose. If there truly were Nazi spies operating in the highest government circles, would they have the ability to alter government records? Did Friedrich Hofmann leave the country, return as a spy and then have his Immigration record altered? He knew it was a long shot that this meant anything, The Marine sergeant might be imagining things, but it should be looked into.

What could Ted do about it though? He knew if he went to his superiors with this, they would laugh at him. Then an idea came to him. Why couldn't he do a little digging on his own? He could leave his partner out of it. Besides, Bill Parker had told him he was sick of hearing theories about Nazi spies and didn't want Ted to talk to him about it anymore.

As he was considering this, one half of his brain was telling him he was a fool for sticking his neck out and causing trouble. If Mr. Byrnes was convinced that the Bureau had caught all the spies, then he should play it safe and go along with him. If he was caught using his authority to do a rogue investigation, he would be canned from his job. This mental tug of war went on for some time.

Ted internally debated whether his suspicions about an undiscovered spy ring were plausible. Yes, damn it, not only plausible but likely. He could feel it in his gut. Should he stand by and let the situation continue, maybe endangering the lives of young American

274 | D. W. DRAKE

soldiers, Marines and sailors fighting in the war? Hell, no!

But still, he hesitated. Was what he was thinking about doing worth losing his job and suffering the disgrace that came with it? Ted rubbed his eyes with the heels of his hands. Then his mouth set in a hard line. He thought about why he had joined the FBI in the first place. It was to protect people from murderous criminals like Dillinger and "Pretty Boy" Floyd. The Nazis were worse than all the criminal gangs put together. Miller was privy to intelligence reports of what was happening in German-occupied Europe. The Nazis were lining up defenseless men, women with babies, old people and young children and shooting them down like animals. Anger built in him. Now, these same beasts had come to undermine his country and perhaps one day bring the same horrors here.

But, damn it, this was HIS country. These were HIS people, the very ones he had sworn to protect. Well, the Nazi sons of bitches had gone too far, and he wouldn't allow them to get away with it. Ted knew without bragging that he was a formidable opponent. He was a tenacious investigator and was very dangerous when the guns came out. He would root out these evil bastards, even at the price of being cashiered and living in disgrace. If SAC Byrnes was too dim-witted or too afraid of J. Edgar Hoover to act on obvious facts, then it was up to him.

Ted got up from his desk and headed toward the office of Assistant SAC Milton Turley. As he passed the door to the secretarial pool he glanced in. Hannah wasn't at her desk. Turley was in his office reading reports. The sleeves of his shirt were rolled up and his tie was loosened, something he wouldn't be able to get away with if he worked at the Washington headquarters. Ted knocked on the doorframe and Turley told him to enter.

"What is it, Ted?" I hope it's not some new crazy theory about Nazi spies, said Turley.

"Mr. Turley, I haven't taken any vacation in years. I was wondering if I might have a week off to take care of some personal business?"

Turley thought for a moment.

"Sure, I guess we can spare you. Go ahead. Stop by personnel and tell them would you?"

The next morning Ted left his apartment building and hailed a taxi. He told the driver to take him to Grand Central Station. He walked into the huge building and bought a ticket on an express train to Washington. Ted looked at the departure time on the ticket and then his watch. He had ten minutes before the train departed. He was fortunate enough to buy a pack of Luckies as well as a copy of the Times at a kiosk and boarded the waiting train.

The train was packed with people. The only seat he could find was inboard of an enormously fat man smoking a cigar. Though the seats were usually wide enough for three people, Ted was barely able to squeeze in beside the man's huge bulk. Ted looked around him and saw a sea of uniforms, representing every service branch. Almost everyone was smoking, so Ted lit up a Lucky and added to the thick cloud of smoke in the car. He looked around him at all the smokers. It was really a nasty habit. Every public place had floors littered with stepped on cigarette butts. The rank, stale tobacco smell permeated every place people gathered. Everybody's teeth were yellow. Maybe he should quit, even if he wasn't doing it for Hannah. He unfolded his newspaper and looked at the front page.

The Quebec conference between Churchill and President Roosevelt had ended. The two leaders once again pledged mutual cooperation in the war effort. Ted started to read further but got bored and switched to another article. The RAF had raided Berlin with seven hundred bombers, inflicting heavy damage. About time, thought Ted. The Nazis are getting a taste of what they have done to Allied cities.

The Russians were on the offensive and had kicked the Germans out of Kharkov, wherever that was, probably somewhere in Russia. The Nazi tide was definitely on the ebb. Adolf Hitler had appointed Heinrich Himmler as interior minister of the Reich. Hitler said it was to enforce more discipline within the country. Did this mean the Germans were starting to crack? Ted certainly hoped so.

The train arrived in Washington around noon. Ted left the station and took a cab to 500 12th Street S/W, the Immigration Service headquarters. After wandering around in the big building, he found himself at a service window in the records department. A plain, severely dressed young woman greeted him.

"Yes, may I help you?"

Ted showed his FBI credentials. The young woman's eyes widened.

"I need to see the file page for a man named Engle Hofmann exiting the United States on June sixteenth, nineteen thirty-seven."

"You want to see the actual file? I can give you the information on the file right here."

"Yes, I need to see the actual file."

"I'm sorry, Miss Pettibone would never allow it."

"Can I talk to your supervisor?"

"Yes, just a moment."

The clerk went away and returned a few moments later with another woman who looked just like her, only a little older.

"This gentleman is from the FBI," said the first clerk to the second," he wants to see the actual exit file for June sixteenth, nineteen thirty-seven."

"I'm afraid that will not be possible," said the older clerk," Miss Pettibone would never allow it."

"Could I talk to Miss Pettibone?" asked Ted, getting a little annoyed.

"Pardon me for a moment. I will see if she is available," said the older clerk and walked away. She returned a minute later.

"Please go through the door to your left," she said.

The older clerk met Ted on the other side of the door. He followed her down a hall toward another door, this one open. He could see a woman sitting regally behind a desk in the room. In her fifties, she had a prim face devoid of any makeup. Her hair was pulled tightly into a bun at the back of her head and she wore wire-rimmed glasses.

Eugenia Pettibone was a fifty-two-year-old spinster who lived alone in a Washington flat with only two cats for company. In charge of the records department of the Immigration Service, she ruled her fiefdom with an iron hand worthy of Uncle Joe Stalin. She was also a pedant and was notorious for correcting other people's grammar. Miss Pettibone looked at Ted's credentials and invited him to sit.

"I am afraid that it will not be possible for you to see our physical records," said Miss Pettibone.

"I'm involved with an invest…"

Miss Pettibone held up her hand and stopped him.

"Do not say I'm, say I am."

Ted was starting to get angry but held his temper.

"I am conducting an investigation involving espionage by enemy agents in the United States. It is important that I see the physical records for exit from this country on June 16, 1937, of a man named Engel Hofmann. The reason I have to see them is classified top secret and you do not have a need to know why."

Miss Pettibone gave him an icy stare for a full fifteen seconds and Ted returned one just as frosty. Finally, she looked away and threw up her hands. "Oh, very well," she said, and called to the older clerk, who was hovering outside the door.

"Mary, show this gentleman the file in question."

Ted left Miss Pettibone in a snit and followed the clerk into a huge room filled with filing cabinets. Just inside the door of the room, the clerk greeted a small, severely dressed, mousy looking woman, seated at a desk. "Hello Esther," she said as she walked past. She then led Ted to a cabinet about a third of the way down the fourth row. She wrenched open a drawer and thumbed through some papers one by one. Finally, she started to pull a paper from the file. Ted stopped her and asked to examine the file's position in the cabinet.

Ted pulled out the record for June 16, 1937. Sure enough, there was Engle Hofmann's name. He also pulled out the sheets of the day before and the day after. He lay the papers side by side on the top of the cabinet and examined them closely. The paper for June sixteenth was just a tiny shade lighter than the other two papers. He pulled out two other records for the same week. They also didn't match the shade of the paper for June sixteenth. He held the different papers up to the light. The watermark on the file for June sixteenth was different from the pages before and after. The paper used for the record for June sixteenth was from a different vendor. Ted was stunned. The file had indeed been switched. He thanked the clerk, who carefully restored the files in the cabinet. Ted left the building and took the two p.m. train back to New

York.

§

When the man left the file room, Esther Cohen asked her coworker, Mary, who he was and why he was examining the files.

"He's an FBI agent. He wanted to examine the file on the exit of a man named Engle Hoffmann who left the country on June 16, 1937."

As she was speaking, Esther felt the blood drain from her head and thought she was going to pass out as rising panic gripped her.

"Esther honey, are you all right? You suddenly turned white as a sheet."

Esther's mind was reeling. She feared her spying activities were about to be discovered. What should she do? Should she put a message in her drop for the Germans? Her biggest fear had always been for her sister and her nieces, trapped in Germany. Now it looked like she had failed to protect them and they would be turned over to the SS. Esther couldn't decide what to do. Mary was standing there looking concerned. She had to tell her something.

"I just became ill all of a sudden. I think need to go home and rest."

Miss Pettibone was summoned. She agreed to allow Esther to go home, but not without a parting shot.

"You may go, Miss Cohen, but remember, when you are not here, others will have to do your work."

Esther Cohen retrieved her sweater and purse and rushed for the door.

§

On the train, Ted ignored those around him and thought about the implications of what he had discovered. Hofmann couldn't have switched the records himself. That meant others were helping him and that confirmed in Ted's mind that there was indeed a spy ring operating in America. Whoever the persons were in the group, they had an enormous reach to be able to alter government records. What he was dealing with was much more sinister than he had thought. The problem was that he couldn't go to his superiors with this information. He could get in a lot of trouble for what he had just done. He was on his own. The next logical step was to start surveillance on Friedrich Hofmann. That he would do the next day.

CHAPTER THIRTY-ONE

ABWEHR HAUPTSITZ
TURPITZUFER 76-78
BERLIN, DEUTSCHLAND 20 AUGUST 1943

It was late in the evening and Berlin was dark. Blackout regulations were in effect and those few people out and about were hurrying to their destinations with worried glances at the skies. The earlier optimism about Germany's chances of victory in the war had receded to be replaced by a gnawing fear in the pit of the stomach that all of this wasn't going to end well. All the luxuries Berliners had enjoyed earlier in the war had disappeared and now food was rationed. Yesterday evening, seven hundred British bombers had appeared over the southern suburbs of the city and unleashed a torrent of bombs. There had been heavy industrial damage in the Templehoff area and over eight hundred people were killed. The Luftwaffe surmised that a navigational error by the British had caused them to bomb in the south and not in the more heavily populated center of the city, which was obviously their intended target. If they had, many more people would have been killed. The majority of Berliners now disbelieved the rosy predictions of Dr. Goebbels and knew that hell from the skies would soon be upon them.

In the Abwehr headquarters, most of the staff had gone home to their beds. The only people in the offices were the Kriegsmarine guards, radio operators, a personal aide and Admiral Wilhelm Canaris. The Admiral sat in his private office with the door closed. The overhead lights were off. The only illumination in the room came from a small, shaded desk lamp.

He closed the cover of his diary, in which he had been writing. He stood, locked the diary in his office safe and sat back down behind his desk. The Admiral conceded to himself that keeping the diary was a foolish thing to do. It incriminated him in treason to Adolf Hitler and the Third Reich. The reason he kept the diary was rooted in personal vanity. Canaris knew that if Hitler wasn't removed soon, he would be exposed and arrested by the Gestapo. He had far too many links to groups of conspirators plotting to assassinate the Fuhrer. So, it was a race. Who would win? Would dissident German officers succeed in killing Hitler, or would the Gestapo suddenly come rushing in and haul him off to interrogation and torture? He kept the diary to show future generations of Germans why he was doing what he was doing. He was not a traitor to his country. On the contrary, he was a patriotic German. Hitler and his Nazi thugs had hijacked a great nation and dragged it down to the sewer. Examples of their depravity were numerous. For instance, although rail transport was desperately needed to supply the Wehrmacht, the government had continued to use train after train to transport Jews to the death camps. The Nazis had descended to such a level of barbarism as to defy belief.

Canaris picked up a report from the top of his desk. It was a transcript of a speech that Heinrich Himmler had recently given to an assembly of his SS murderers. He began to read from the transcript.

"I shall speak to you here with all frankness of a very serious subject. We shall now discuss it absolutely openly among ourselves, nevertheless we shall never speak of it in public. I mean the evacuation of the Jews, the extermination of the Jewish race. It is one of these things which is easy to say. 'The Jewish race is to be exterminated,' says every party member. 'That's clear, it's part of the program, elimination of all Jews, extermination, right, we will do it.'"

"And then they all come along, the eighty million good Germans, and each one has his decent Jew. Of course the others are swine, but this one is a first class Jew. Of all those who talk like this, not one has objected, not one has stood up to it. Most of you know what it means to see a hundred corpses piled up, five hundred, or a thousand. To have gone through this and yet, apart from a few exceptions, examples of human weakness, to have remained decent fellows, this is what has made us hard."

"For we know how difficult we should make it for ourselves, if, after all the bombing and depravations of war, we still had Jews in every town as saboteurs and agitators."

The Admiral couldn't read any more. He threw the transcript in the waste can. The gall of Himmler to still call himself and his depraved thugs, "decent fellows." This criminal state must be ended, either through the death of Hitler or an Allied victory.

Canaris had heard nothing back from the Allies about his offer of a negotiated peace. He had to assume that the offer had been rejected. The Admiral almost wept at the thought of what would happen to his beloved country. Germany would be defeated and utterly crushed.

He had been in contact with Oberst Count Claus Von Stauffenberg, the leader of the largest resistance group in the German military, since Hans Oster had been arrested. Stauffenberg said there were several attempts on Hitler's life in the planning stage. The Fuhrer had to die, if for no other reason than revenge for what he had done to the Jews and gypsies. The first would take place in November, three months hence.

284 | D. W. DRAKE

Hitler was scheduled to review new Wehrmacht uniforms. Mayor Axel Von Der Bussche, tall, blonde, blue-eyed and very Aryan looking, had agreed to model the uniform for Hitler and then blow himself up next to the Fuhrer with a hidden bomb. For Germany's sake, Canaris hoped it would work. Von Stauffenberg had told the Admiral in confidence that if all else failed, he personally would make an attempt to kill Hitler.

In the meantime, Canaris decided he would act as if arrest by the Gestapo was imminent. The first thing to be done was to destroy any material in his possession that would aid the regime in the prosecution of the war. He reopened his safe and took out a thick folder containing his most secret files. Placing his waste can in the middle of the floor, he took documents from the file, placed them in the waste can and set them on fire. Included in these documents were information on the American research into an atomic bomb, the "ultra" secret and the new American proximity fuse for artillery. Any secret information that would be of use to Hitler and Himmler went up in smoke.

As he watched the documents burn, he thought about what to do next. The American operation would have to be dismantled. Should he do it now or wait? Canaris had learned from his spy in Himmler's office that the SS had got wind of the Abwehr network in the United States. They had sent a particularly brutish thug to America to investigate. The Admiral had sent a message to his courier agents, warning them. He sincerely hoped they heeded his warning. Sitting in his chair looking at the ceiling, Canaris decided It was time to shut down the American network. He picked up his telephone and dialed a number. A sleepy voice answered.

"Do you recognize my voice?" asked the Admiral.

"Ja, I do."

"Execute Operation Omega."

CHAPTER
THIRTY-TWO 416 WEST 46TH STREET
OFFICE 3C
MANHATTAN
NEW YORK CITY
AUGUST 20, 1943

Franz Keller snubbed out his forty-second Chesterfield cigarette of the day in an overflowing ashtray. The office was a mess. The floor was littered with cardboard Chinese take-out containers, cigarette butts and paper coffee cups. Keller had declined the cleaning service that the building superintendent had offered. He picked up the full ashtray from the top of the desk and dumped the butts onto the floor beside his chair. He wrinkled his nose in distaste. The place smelled like a garbage dump.

Keller had been watching the camera shop for a little over thirty days, not including Sundays when the store was closed. Although his SS bosses were sending him curt messages, wanting progress, he had been patient. The camera shop did a fairly good business, with people going in and out all day. It had taken Franz this long to identify two men whose frequency of visiting the store indicated that they were Abwehr agents.

One was a small man with a bushy mustache, in his early forties, who sometimes wore a pilot's uniform with golden wings on the left breast. The other was a young, sandy-haired man. He was tall and slim, appeared very fit and always wore a suit and tie.

Keller was now almost positive that these two were Abwehr agents and was pretty sure they were the only ones. No one else visited the store with the same regularity except for Carlos Breyer. He had made up his mind this morning that he was going to follow the next one of the two that entered the shop.

Keller was bored almost out of his mind, sitting at his perch day after day watching the door of the camera shop. He was sick to death of seeing fat, sassy Americans bustle by, completely oblivious to the titanic struggle going on in the rest of the world. Keller's countrymen in Hamburg and Berlin had to dig themselves out of the rubble every morning after a night of British bombing, while New York had yet to see one bomb fall. Keller hoped that one day, waves of Luftwaffe bombers would appear out of the Eastern skies and blast Times Square out of existence.

Keller perked up. He had just seen the little man with the mustache enter the camera store. He grabbed his hat off the top of the desk and hurried toward the door. The rapid movement caused his wounded side to ache and he put his hand there to cradle it. It was outwardly healed but still gave him pain. The old sword must have nicked a nerve when Stephenson stuck him with it.

He hurried down the stairs and stationed himself in front of the office building. It was after four in the afternoon on a cloudy, hot, humid day. Sweat began to run down his face as he stood in the doorway recess, chain-smoking and waiting for the Abwehr agent to appear.

After about a half-hour the small man came out of the store and walked west on 46th Street. Keller followed. He didn't worry about the man seeing him the sidewalks were crowded with people. The mustached man turned north on Ninth Avenue. He appeared to be aimlessly walking and would stop often to look into display windows. He turned right on 50th Street, walked the long block to the 50th Street subway station and started down the stairs. The SS man hurried to catch up. When he reached the bottom of the stairs Franz saw his quarry entering a southbound train car. Keller fumbled for a nickel to get through the turnstiles and had to run to get on the same car as the little man before the doors closed.

The southbound trains contained fewer people than the northbound ones, so both he and his quarry found seats. The man with the mustache stared straight ahead and didn't look in Franz's direction.

When the train reached the 14th Street station the man Keller was following got off, climbed the stairs to the street level and walked leisurely two blocks to Union Square Park. He bought a newspaper from a boy on the corner, found a bench near the fountain and sat down. The man opened the paper and started to read.

Keller found a bench around fifty meters away and also sat down. He was drowning in sweat. His quarry looked as cool and comfortable as if he was sitting in a theater cooled by refrigeration.

The small man continued to read his newspaper. He read every word. When he finished a section, he would carefully fold it and place it on the bench beside him. Finally, he got up and walked east on 14th Street to Third Avenue and turned right.

For the next two hours, Keller followed the man south on Third Avenue. The mustached man walked as if he was out for a stroll and not with any purpose. He led Keller through the Bowery and Chinatown, at one point buying a hot dog from a street vendor and eating it seated on a fireplug. A little further along, Keller's target stopped and examined the neckties of a sidewalk peddler, until a policeman showed up and the peddler ran away. Keller was getting frustrated. His feet and his wounded side hurt. He was hot and sweaty and he had to piss really bad. He knew he couldn't stop anywhere to relieve himself because he would lose his quarry.

As the two men approached the Brooklyn Bridge, Franz saw that the street they were on ran under the approaches to the bridge and came out on the other side. Foot traffic had thinned out considerably and he could see a fog bank rolling in from the water. He increased his pace and shortened the distance to the man he was following so he wouldn't lose him in the fog.

His target seemed to walk with more purpose now. The man was twenty meters ahead of Keller as he passed under the Brooklyn Bridge. On the other side of the bridge, he abruptly turned left and Keller lost sight of him. Just then swirls of fog engulfed Keller, cutting his vision considerably. The SS man broke into a run. He passed under the bridge and wheeled left. After a few steps, he stopped. The little man was nowhere to be seen. Keller's vision was cut down to just a few meters and the fog was getting thicker by the minute.

He found himself in an area of closed commercial buildings and the Brooklyn Bridge cable towers soared over him on the left, their tops disappearing into the fog. Keller continued on but knew he had lost his quarry. He was trying to decide what to do next and had just passed the opening to an alley when he heard the sound of someone clearing his throat behind him. He whirled and saw the little man with the mustache standing before him three meters away. He had a small, dark, automatic pistol in his right hand and it was pointed at Keller's chest.

"D' ya mind telling' me why you'd be following' me? D' ya think I'm an amateur? I've been followed by the bleedin' British MI5 and they are experts. I spotted you within a block of the camera store."

Keller drew himself to his full height. "I have been sent by Reichfuhrer Himmler to investigate an Abwehr operation in America. There is suspicion that it may have been infiltrated by Jews."

The man with the mustache smiled and shook his head. "Then you'd be the fookin' SS man we were warned about."

"I am SS-Untersturmfuhrer Franz Keller."

"Why din' ya just walk up and ask me?"

"I didn't know if you were a Jew or not."

The little man chuckled at this. "No, I'm not a bleddy Jew. If I were, you would be lyin' in a shiny pool of blood right now."

"Why does the Abwehr associate with American Jews?" asked Keller.

"You don't know? The whole network is made up of Jews, 'cept fer meself and the baseball player. Th' agents are Jews. They work for us 'cause we're holdin' their families hostage in Germany."

"The SS would never work with Jews. We kill Jews."

The little man thought for a moment. When he spoke again, his voice had a hard edge. "I've heard about how you SS bastards murder women and children in Russia. You know, come to think of it, I'm tired of workin' fer German filth. I resign."

Keller was enraged at the insult. He started forward and the Irishman pulled the trigger on his gun. But instead of a shot, there was a click. The gun had misfired. Keller grabbed the man's arm and the gun clattered to the pavement. He pulled the Irishman toward him, intending to get him in a bear hug and subdue him.

The Irishman shot an elbow into Keller's side, the same side where he had the stab wound. A white-hot jet of pain exploded into his brain, causing him to release his grip and the Irishman darted away.

The pain immediately released a towering rage inside the SS man. He pulled his revolver from the small of his back and shot the little man in the back at a range of two meters as he was running away. He fell and Keller smiled as he stood over him and shot him five more times in the head.

The Nazi looked around. He didn't see anyone in the thick fog but knew the shots would draw people fast. He put his gun back in the small of his back, picked up the Irishman's little pistol and slunk away. Keller hurried back north, trying to put as much distance between himself and the bod, as possible. When he got to an area where there were more people about, he stepped into an alley and urinated against a wall. Feeling relieved, he examined the Irishman's gun. The fool had neglected to pull back the slide and chamber a round when he had loaded the pistol. It was a mistake that had cost him his life. Keller dropped the gun into his coat pocket, hailed a taxi and rode to the Spanish Consulate.

He was covered in sweat and his clothes smelled musty but Keller didn't stop to clean up. He went straight to the radio room, the most secure room in the building. There was a telephone there that bypassed the local New York switchboards and was connected directly to the international operator. The telephone was in a small office with a glass door. Franz went in and closed the door. He lifted the earpiece and gave the operator a telephone number in Barcelona Spain. It was the number his SS superiors had given him to report in an emergency. It took ten minutes for the connection to be made. Finally, he heard a series of clicks and the sound of ringing on the other end of the line.

"Hola, puedo ayudarte," said a voice in bad Spanish. Keller replied, also in Spanish.

"This is Juan Garcia, I have important information."

"Report," the voice said with authority.

"Our cousin's enterprise has all Jewish employees. Our cousin is keeping the employees' relatives safe somewhere in the homeland. The employees work hard out of gratitude that their relatives are kept safe. There are two supervisors who relay the work product to the home office. One of these supervisors was tragically killed today. The one remaining supervisor should have information about the employees and their addresses as well as their mailboxes. Please tell me how you want me to proceed."

There was a pause on the line while the other party thought about what Keller had said.

"Remain by your telephone until you hear from me. What is the telephone number where you are?" the voice asked. Keller read off the number on the base of the phone and the man in Barcelona clicked off the line.

Keller hung up the earpiece and stood. He looked through the glass door and saw the radio operator lounging in his chair smoking a cigarette. Keller opened the door and called to him.

"Bring me some food and coffee. I cannot leave the phone." The radio operator looked back at him with surprise.

"But ,Senor, it is after ten. The cook has gone home."

"I don't need cooked food. Sandwiches are fine and coffee, lots of coffee."

"But, Senor, I cannot leave my post."

Keller became angry and threatened the man in a menacing voice. "If you don't do as I say, I will shoot you right where you sit."

The radio operator jumped up and fled the room, repeating, "Si, senor, Si, senor."

He was back inside twenty minutes with a tray containing a pot of strong black coffee, a cup and two cheese sandwiches. Keller attacked the sandwiches, finishing each in two enormous bites. He then slurped the coffee, chain-smoked and settled down to wait. It was after midnight before the phone rang. He picked up the earpiece and put it to his ear.

"Senor Garcia," said the voice on the other end of the line, "We have decided to take over our cousin's enterprise. You will confront the supervisor and find out all he knows. You will then rehire him or discharge him if he proves difficult. You will do this as soon as possible. You will be in charge until we can send someone more senior to take over. In the meantime, we will resettle the employee's relatives in a more appropriate place. Do you understand my orders?"

"Si, senor," replied Keller. The line went dead.

Keller stumbled to his room. He was exhausted. He needed a shower and bed in the worst way. Confronting the, what did the Irishman call him? Oh ,yes, the baseball player would have to wait until tomorrow.

CHAPTER THIRTY-THREE

670 COURTLAND AVENUE
APARTMENT 2D
SOUTH BRONX
NEW YORK CITY
AUGUST 20, 1943, 11:45 PM

It was a small apartment in a fairly modern building. The super knew his job and kept the place immaculate. The interior of the apartment, by contrast, could not be described as anywhere near immaculate. The furniture looked like it had been carried in and dumped with no thought to placement. There were no pictures on the walls, there were dirty dishes in the sink overflowing ashtrays and empty brown beer bottles lined up on the coffee table. Women marry men knowing they are slobs but thinking they can reform them. It's usually a hopeless task. Living in cheerful squalor is ingrained in the male half of humanity.

Special Agent Ted Miller sat in an overstuffed chair in a pool of light from a tall floor lamp. He had been there for a long time mulling over his suspicions about spies and what he had learned so far in his private investigation. His thoughts were a jumble. He had suspected the existence of an undiscovered espionage ring in the United States for close to a year. But, all the evidence he had to go on amounted to only tempting little tidbits.

That is, until recently. Ted now thought that he might be getting closer to cracking the case. He circled back and started at the beginning when his suspicions were first aroused.

The first piece of evidence was the spy Dietrich's last words. He had told Ted, "You will never catch them, no one would ever suspect them." Dietrich was saying outright that there were people the FBI would be interested in but would never suspect. What kind of people would never be suspected of being Nazi espionage agents? High-level politicians? Military officers? Citizens of neutral countries? To say nothing about refugees from Nazi oppression. There were Poles, Czechs and Greeks coming out New York's ears. What about Jews? No one would suspect them of working for Hitler after the oppression they had suffered at his hands.

Wait a minute. The woman that was arrested in Washington had a Jewish name. Ted had initially thought she was probably a communist, working for the Russians. But what if she wasn't a Red and was spying for Germany. Why would she do it?

Ted remembered from his FBI counterintelligence training that there were only three motivations to make a person betray their country. The first was an ideology, a person so zealous for a cause that it would override his or her loyalty to their nation. But it was hard to imagine a Jewish refugee from the Nazis being a follower of national socialism.

The next reason to betray one's country is money. A person lets greed erode his patriotism. Ted had heard all his life how Jews were greedy and dishonest. Miller thought this was bullshit. People were people and there were good and bad in all groups. To think that because

296 | D . W . D R A K E

of an accident of birth one group was worse than another morally, was the wisdom of a fool. Jews were pretty much like everyone else. It was possible that the woman in Washington was motivated by greed, but he didn't think so. The risks were too high for any amount of money. The punishment for espionage was death in the electric chair.

The third motivation for spying against one's country was blackmail or threats of physical harm. A person is discovered to be an embezzler or sexual deviant and the enemy uses the information to blackmail that person to work for them. Threats of physical harm could be not only against the person but also against their loved ones.

Ted sat forward abruptly, inadvertently knocking over a half-full bottle of beer on the table beside his chair. "SHIT!," he yelled and retrieved the bottle before all the beer inside had spilled out on the carpet. Ted chided himself for the vulgarity he had just uttered.

You must control yourself better, he thought. What if something like this happened in public and you swore like that? He shook his head in disapproval It wasn't seemly and he resolved to never let it happen again. He looked at the spot on the carpet where the beer had spilled. Almost all the liquid had been absorbed into the carpet. He shrugged and sat back down in the chair.

He struggled for a moment to regain his train of thought. Where was I? Oh yeah, what if the Nazis are blackmailing American Jews with threats against their relatives in Germany? With their past record, the Nazi bastards were certainly capable of such a monstrous thing. It was the most obvious answer as to why a Jew would spy for Germany. And the most obvious answer was usually the right one. As one of Ted's Ohio State professors used to say," if you walk in a room that is knee-deep in horseshit, look for a horse, not a zebra."

His new theory accounted for all the evidence. Such a network of reluctant Jewish spies would require a support person, probably more than one, to carry messages back and forth, smuggle them out of the country, and maybe to act as an enforcer in case any of them got out of line. Maybe the murder of the Immigration official had been committed by one of these support personnel. Perhaps the Immigration man had stumbled upon some information that threatened the operation. Ted asked himself, where do I go from here? His deductions seemed logical. It was a good theory.

Ted sat forward again and rubbed his face with the palms of his hands. Just listen to yourself, he thought. Maybe, perhaps, what if, it was all supposition. He might be right but then again, all his deductions could be just so much bullshit. One thing he was sure of, If he went to Mr. Byrnes with this, Byrnes would first laugh and then get angry. He would then transfer Ted to the Aleutian Islands to open a one-man office to investigate fish thefts.

The only solid leads he had centered on Friedrich Hofmann. Ted had followed Hofmann for the last two days. On the first day, Ted waited outside the address on Sheridan Avenue. He watched the tenants leave the house for work. A tall, athletic man who fit the description given by Hoffmann's brother came out. Ted followed him. He led Ted to a camera shop on West 46th Street and then to Ebbets Field in Flatbush. Ted bought a ticket for the game and spotted Hofmann in a Dodger uniform walking around in front of the home dugout. After the game, Hofmann had gone home to his rooming house.

Yesterday, Ted had watched Hofmann leave his boarding house and walk south on Sheridan. Miller waited for twenty minutes and approached the house. The front door was open and he saw a woman in her fifties wearing an apron and mopping the floor in the entry hall. Ted stepped inside, took out his FBI credentials, held them out in front of him and called to the woman.

298 | D. W. DRAKE

"Excuse me, ma'am, I'm with the FBI and I need to talk to you."

The woman gave him a surprised look and hurried over to him.

"The FBI! You want to see me?"

"Yes, it's about one of your tenants. Friedrich Hofmann."

"I have a Fred Hofmann. Is that who you mean? He's a nice boy. Works for the Brooklyn Dodgers. Always pays his rent on time."

"Yes," said Ted, "that's him. He's not in any trouble. He is being investigated for a security clearance and an important government job. I need to see his room. You must assure me Mrs. Ah. . ."

"Taylor."

"Mrs. Taylor, you must not tell him I was here."

Mrs. Taylor looked at him for a moment, then nodded her head.

"Just let me go and get my passkey," she said, and hurried away.

She returned in under a half minute and led Miller upstairs to a door halfway along a hall. She put the key in the lock and swung open the door. Ted entered and Mrs. Taylor started to enter after him. Ted stopped her.

"Please wait in the hall, Mrs. Taylor. I'll just be a moment," said Ted, and closed the door in her face.

The room was neat. The bed was made and there wasn't any clutter about. He checked the small closet first. There was a suitcase on the top shelf. Ted took it down, undid the clasp and looked inside. There were two cameras sitting on top of what looked like banded stacks of money. Ted examined the cameras. They seemed ordinary, had no film in them, and he put them aside. The money looked like it was newly printed, just like Dietrich's, and appeared to be thousands of dollars. He returned the cameras to the suitcase, closed the catches and put the case back on the top shelf. Ted checked under the bed and carefully lifted the bed mattress and looked under it. Nothing.

Then he saw a book on the floor beside the bed. He picked it up. It was a copy of <u>Northwest Passage</u>, by Kenneth Roberts. Ted remembered that Dietrich had a book by the same author in his room. Ted then noticed there was a pad of paper on the floor that had been hidden by the book. He picked up the pad. There were impressions on the top page. Ted held the pad sideways to the light and studied the impressions. They were the same as Dietrich's, groups of numbers. Then it hit him. It was a code, and the book was the key to deciphering it. "Got you, you bastard," said Ted out loud.

He replaced everything and left, closing the door. He again admonished Mrs. Taylor not to tell Hofmann he had been there and left the house. Ted went to Ebbets Field at three o'clock and waited around outside until Hofmann left after the game. He then tailed him home.

Ted decided that Hoffman was the key to everything. He had a suitcase full of money, was using a code to communicate with someone, and had his immigration record altered by someone, presumably another spy. If he could somehow get a solid piece of evidence, some fact that couldn't be explained away, his FBI superiors would have to listen. Ted yawned and stretched in his chair. He must sleep. He had to be outside Hoffmann's rooming house early.

CHAPTER THIRTY-FOUR

1567 SHERIDAN AVENUE
WEST BRONX
NEW YORK CITY
AUGUST 21, 1943

Fritz Hofmann bounded down the stairs. His stomach was growling with hunger. He entered the dining room and saw the other roomers digging into scrambled eggs and fried potatoes. This was an unbelievable treat. Breakfast usually was oatmeal and coffee. Fritz had just sat down when Mrs. Taylor entered from the kitchen with a platter piled high with more eggs and potatoes. Before he could help himself, his landlady took his plate and filled it with a steaming pile of food. She set it down in front of Fritz and said, "There you are, Fred," and looked at him strangely.

Fritz shrugged and tucked into his food. Women are screwy sometimes, he thought. Another boarder, Miles Simpson, had a newspaper in front of him and was talking about a murder.

"It says here that the murdered guy was a pilot for American Airlines."

Fritz lost his appetite immediately. His fork came to a stop in mid-air. "Does it give his name?" asked Fritz.

"Yeah, says here his name was Michael Flynn, forty-one years old. He was a pilot for American Airlines. They found him near the Brooklyn Bridge pumped full of lead. It says here the police think it was a crime of passion," replied Simpson.

Fritz went pale. He dropped his fork and fled the table without a word to the other tenants. He ran up the stairs to his room. Once inside, with the door locked, he began to pace. It was too much of a coincidence that Flynn could have been killed by a street robber. It had to be connected to the Abwehr operation. The only time he had talked to Flynn, the Irishman had warned him about an SS man coming to spy out the operation. If it was the man from the SS who had killed Flynn, and he was pretty sure it was, then he could be next. It was time to disappear. Every instinct told Fritz to grab his suitcase with the money and Carl Reed's birth certificate and vanish.

But he was reluctant to go. He had a date with Hannah tonight. They were going back to the Savoy Ballroom. He wanted to see her one last time and try to persuade her to come with him. He decided he had to take a chance and stay for one more day.

Fritz took his suitcase down from the closet and checked that the Abwehr money was still there. He threw the cameras onto the bed, put on his hat and, carrying the suitcase, went down the stairs and out to the sidewalk. Fritz walked to the 170th Street subway station.

On the way, he checked that no one was following him. He didn't spot a tail but he knew he was really bad at detecting surveillance.

Fritz took the subway south to Times Square and walked east to Grand Central Station. When he entered the cavernous building it was packed with people, mostly servicemen in uniform. Looking around, he saw a bank of lockers against one wall. Fritz weaved his way through the crowd and opened a locker with a key protruding from its lock. He slid the suitcase into the locker, put a dime in the slot and locked the door, pocketing the key.

He left the station through the west door and walked north on 6th Avenue to 46th Street and turned left, stopping often to check behind him, to see if he was being followed. When he reached Stein's Camera Shop, he discovered that the place was locked with a closed sign on the door. Fritz figured Stein had also seen the article in the paper and had gone to ground.

Fritz found a small diner. He sat in the back, facing the door until nearly twelve, sipping coffee. Then he left the diner and caught the subway to Ebbets Field.

§

When Ted Miller saw Hofmann emerge from his rooming house carrying the suitcase, he was afraid that his quarry was going to skip town. Ted presumed that the suitcase still contained the stacks of money. When Hofmann entered Grand Central Station, Ted became alarmed that he would lose the man in the crowds. Hofmann could hop a train for anywhere.

Ted moved closer to Hofmann and prepared to arrest him in the middle of the hustle and bustle of the huge building. Then he saw Hofmann place the suitcase in a locker and head toward the exit. Ted backed off again. Miller gave him a long lead but kept Hoffmann in sight except when he turned corners. He was pretty sure his quarry hadn't spotted him.

Hofmann stopped at the same camera store he had visited the other day when miller was following him. Ted wrote down the address, the store had to be connected to the spy ring. The store was closed and locked and Hoffman walked away from it.

Ted was surprised when Hofmann picked up another tail as he left the camera store. The man following Hofmann was a stocky man in a grey suit. He had a cruel-looking face that reminded Ted of a cheap gangster thug. He was an amateur at surveillance, however, remaining too close to the man he was following. Who the hell was this? Ted asked himself. Who would want to follow Hofmann except him?

Hofmann sat in a small café and sipped coffee for over two hours. Around noon, he rode the subway to Ebbets Field, the crude-looking man, and Ted shadowing him all the way.

A subdued group of players greeted Fritz when he walked in the Dodger's locker room. He asked Augie Galan why everyone was so glum.

"Durocher and Rickie just had another argument. They left the door open an' we heard everything. Rickie wants Durocher to trade some more high salary players to save money. He said attendance was down and they had to cut back. To his credit, Durocher argued back, but it didn't do any good. All the fellas r' wonderin' who's gonna get the ax next."

It was another sign of a losing team. At the start of today's game, the Brooklyn team would be seventeen games back of the Cardinals. The boo birds were out at every home game now and, what was worse, the fans weren't coming to the games like they did last year. In late July, two well-liked players, Dolph Camilli and Johnny Allen had been traded to the Giants for some low salaried players. It put a damper on the spirit of the others on the team.

Durocher had changed too. Before he was loud and aggressive. Now he was silent most of the time but seethed with resentment and anger.

The feud with his shortstop, Arky Vaughan, had turned more ugly. The two didn't speak, ever.

Fritz shook off the gloom when he walked onto the field. The sight of the ballpark always lightened his spirits. When he was warming up the starting pitcher, Hal Gregg, some of Fritz's gloom returned. Hal's curveball wasn't working and his fastball was just mediocre.

The game started off okay. The Brooklyn pitcher managed to retire the Cubs in the top of the first inning without any score. In the second inning, the roof fell in. The Cubs started pounding the ball to all fields. It was one of those games where the ball was be hit just out of the reach of the fielder. Little Texas Leaguers would fall in for hits. The Cubs pitcher, Lon Warneke, was on his game, but even when a Brooklyn batter made solid contact, the ball was hit right at somebody and was caught.

At the bottom of the ninth inning, with two outs, the Dodgers were down thirteen zip. Frenchy Bordagaray went to the plate and hit a two-two pitch for a triple in the left-field corner. Fritz thought it was a nice hit but a little too late to matter. He had no idea that he was about to participate in something memorable.

Durocher called Howie Schultz back from the on-deck circle, looked down the dugout at Fritz and yelled.

"Hofmann, get in there and bat for Schultz."

Fritz didn't move. He was frozen. He thought, did he just say what I heard him say?

"Hofmann, did you hear me? Move! Bat for Schultz."

Fritz was up and moving. He picked up his bat from the line of them arrayed in front of the dugout and walked tentatively to the plate. As he walked, he looked around at the stadium. The stands weren't as full as earlier in the season but there were still lots of fans waving and cheering. The grass looked greener than usual and the colors of the Cubs players' uniforms strikingly vivid. He heard the announcer say his name on the loudspeaker.

"Now batting for Schultz, Fred Hofmann."

Fritz entered the batter's box and swung the bat repeatedly as he got himself set. He looked out at the Cubs players. The pitcher, Lon Warneke, was studying him. The infielders were crouched with their gloves close to the ground and Fritz could see Frenchy leading off from third base.

Fritz felt a tinge of fear. Warneke was the Cubs star pitcher and was on his way to winning twenty games this year. Fritz thought back to the last time he had played in a baseball game, back in Wheeler's Mill. He had failed that day. Would he fail again? Please God, prayed Fritz, don't let me make a fool of myself.

The umpire crouched down behind the plate, raised his padded shield and pointed at Warneke to begin. The big man wound up and fired a fastball right down the middle of the plate, knee-high. The pitch seemed unbelievably fast to Fritz.

"STEERIKE ONE," called the umpire.

The pitcher wound up again and let fly. It was a curveball that broke low and outside. The next pitch was another curveball, also out of the strike zone. Warneke slammed the ball into his glove in frustration, then walked around behind the pitcher's mound rubbing the baseball and talking to himself. Then he strode back to the pitching rubber and set himself.

Fritz just knew the next pitch would be a fastball. Call it intuition, or an angel on his shoulder whispering in his ear, he knew it would be a

306 | D. W. DRAKE

fastball in the strike zone. His concentration tunneled down to the pitcher's right hand. As the ball left Warneke's hand in a blur, Fritz started his swing. The ball roared in belt high and on the outside part of the plate.

Fritz's bat met the ball right on the sweet spot of the barrel. The loud crack and the jarring up his arms told him that he had made solid contact. He tore off toward first base, with everything he was worth. He saw the Cubs first baseman, Phil Cavarretta, leap high in the air, but the baseball sailed over his outstretched glove into fair territory down the right-field line.

As he approached first base Fritz saw the first base coach, "Lollypop" Corriden, windmilling one arm and pointing at second base with the other. Hofmann rounded first running as fast as he could. The operation on his feet had slowed him down and his feet still hurt a little when he ran hard, but he ignored the pain and chugged toward second base with everything he had.

As Fritz started his slide into second, he looked up and saw Eddie Stanky, the Cubs second baseman, who was crouching over the base, bring his glove up in preparation for catching the ball. Fritz felt his spikes contact the side of the base a half-second before he felt the slap of Stanky's glove on his leg. There was a cloud of dust so he couldn't see anything for a moment.

"SAFE," yelled the umpire and the crowd roared.

Fritz stood, dusted himself off and took deep breaths to get his wind back. He felt as elated as at any time in his entire life. This was as good as being reprieved from combat in Russia. He had just doubled against one of the best pitchers in baseball. I have proved myself, he exulted inwardly. I can play in the big leagues. Whatever becomes of me from now on, I will never be the same man.

Al Pittman then struck out to end the game and strand Fritz on second base. But it didn't matter to Fritz. His walk from the field into the locker room was like walking on air, so great was his elation. Many of his teammates came up, slapped him on the back and congratulated him.

It was during this walk that Fritz realized something. There had been other more experienced players that Durocher could have used to pinch-hit. Hofmann's chance at-bat was a gift from the manager to him. He felt a feeling of overwhelming gratitude to Durocher wash over him.

When he entered the locker room, Fritz went directly to the door of the manager's office. He knocked and was rudely told to come in. Durocher was sitting behind his desk in a particularly pissy mood after losing the game thirteen to one.

"Whaddaya want, Fred?" asked Durocher, his voice gruff. He was sitting sidewise from his desk, with his feet propped on a trash can, looking at the wall.

"Mister Durocher, I just want to thank you for giving me the chance to hit today."

Durocher swung around to face Fritz and held up his hand in a signal to stop.

"Do you fuckin' think that I put you in today because I like you an' wanna help you? Well, I don't like you. I don't like any a' you assholes an' yokels on this team. Everything I do here has one object, to win ball games. I put you in to see how you handle pressure. This collection of ignorant hicks and clowns they call a team had already lost the game, so I could afford to experiment with you. You did okay. Maybe I can use you in the future, maybe not, but it will be a judgment based on what's good for the team and not that I'm queer for you, got that? Now get the fuck out of my office."

As Fritz was turning to leave he glanced back at Durocher and saw that he had the beginnings of a smile on his face.

CHAPTER THIRTY-FIVE

FBI NEW YORK FIELD OFFICE
500 PEARL STREET
MANHATTAN
NEW YORK CITY
AUGUST 21, 1943

Hannah Rose glanced at the clock for the third time in the last ten minutes. She saw it was five minutes to five. She put her supplies away and covered her Royal typewriter. It had been a slow day in the office, Mr. Turley had taken the day off and there was very little typing that needed doing. Since lunchtime, Hannah had sat at her desk and watched the clock inch its way through the afternoon. Faye Carson, a long-time government worker who occupied a desk next to Hannah, had perfected the art of sleeping with her eyes open and sitting upright, but Hannah didn't think she could ever learn to do it.

"It's really simple sweetie," Faye said, "just prop yourself up on your elbows and stare at something across the room. Then, just let your eyes go blurry and just like that, you're asleep."

Hannah had laughed and said," Thank you, but I might slip and hit my chin on the top of the desk."

The minute hand on the clock didn't move smoothly, it lurched a tiny bit every minute. When it made the final jerk to straight-up five o'clock, chaos erupted. It was as if one had stirred a nest of water moccasins. Everyone was up and moving, including Hannah.

The subway car was packed, as usual, on Hannah's commute north and she had to stand. With the rocking of the train, a man standing beside her repeatedly let his hand brush against her backside. She looked at him. He was a salesman type in his forties with a sweaty, red face. Hannah had learned a lot since coming to New York. She leaned over and whispered to the man.

"If you touch me again, I'm going to start screaming that you're a subway pervert and those two soldiers over there are going to beat you until you cannot stand."

The man looked at her with guilty eyes, then scowled and turned away from her.

It was hot in the apartment when Hannah let herself in with her key. She saw Uncle Moshe and Aunt Rachel through the window. They were sitting on cushions on the fire escape to avoid the heat. Both waved to her as she passed the window on the way to her room.

Inside her room, Hannah looked at her watch. It was almost six. Fred would be here at seven. That gave her an hour to eat and get ready to go out. She smelled her armpits to determine if she needed to bathe. It had been another hot, humid day and the odor told her she would need to take a bath. She stripped to the skin and put on her robe from its hanger in the closet. Hannah padded across the apartment to the bathroom. She closed and locked the door to prevent anyone from barging in and seeing her naked.

She plugged the drain in the big claw foot tub and turned the taps to start the water running. While she was waiting for the tub to fill, Hannah shucked off her robe and examined her naked body in the full-length mirror that was screwed to the wall.

She was twenty-three now. She no longer had the budding body of a teenager but the fully developed form of a woman. Her breasts were full and her pink nipples jutted outward, away from the centerline of her body. Her waist was slim and her belly flat. She turned sideways and saw that her bottom was round and firm. The legs weren't bad either.

Hannah had looked at other women and she knew she was very good looking. It's too bad that I am probably destined to be a spinster, she thought. If I continue to feel the way I do now, no man would ever love this body. Maybe I will someday meet someone besides Ted that I can love, maybe not. The future will tell.

Fritz Hofmann had fallen in love with her, she could tell, but she could never be his wife. She didn't feel about him the way she felt about Ted. Fred was nice and kind, and a good dancer, but that was all he was.

An hour later Hannah was ready when Fritz rang the bell. She was excited that they were going back to the Savoy Ballroom. She could already hear the music of the band in her head. She was wearing a green pleated dress that would give her freedom of movement on the dance floor, and low heeled shoes to keep her from breaking an ankle. As she and Fritz dashed down the steps to the waiting cab, she didn't notice two men in separate positions on the block. One was standing across the street sheltering in a doorway. The other was down the block standing beside a parked car.

§

Ted Miller watched Hannah Rose scamper down the stairs with Friedrich Hofmann, get in a cab and drive away. He was stunned. He felt like a mule had kicked him in the stomach. The blood rushed to his head and he felt faint. He had to steady himself by putting his hand on the fender of a parked car. When he had tailed Hofmann to Hannah's apartment building, he had wondered why he had gone there. Ted had hoped that Hofmann was going to visit another tenant of the building, but he had gotten an ominous feeling in his gut.

Ted turned and stumbled down the sidewalk like a drunken man. How could it be, he thought, that his Hannah, the woman he loved and had been pining for, was involved with a German spy? Then the realization hit him. She was a spy, too! She was working right in the bosom of the FBI! Hannah was Jewish. Did she have threatened relatives in Germany? So many questions were swirling in his head.

What hurt the most though, aside from the spying, was that she seemed to prefer Hofmann's company to his. If she was in trouble, she could have come to him for help. Maybe Hannah really didn't care for him. Maybe she was just toying with him. Miller's hurt and resentment turned to anger. The bitch has been playing me for a sucker, he told himself.

Ted knew he was now through with Hannah and the whole situation. He didn't care about Nazi spies, the FBI or anything. All he wanted to do right now was to find a place to get blind drunk. He stumbled into a basement bar. The place was dark inside and smelled of stale beer and cigar smoke. Four patrons were slumped over their drinks at the long mahogany bar. The emotionally shattered FBI agent slid onto a stool and waved the bartender over.

"I want three double bourbons lined up right here," he said, pointing to the bar top in front of him.

The bartender took one look at his angry face and said, "sure pal."

Ted stayed in the bar for an hour and a half, drinking shot after shot. His emotions were wildly gyrating from hurt and pity to intense anger, at Hannah's betrayal. He was well on the way to being blind drunk when he stumbled out of the bar and took the subway home.

§

Hannah and Fritz walked down the wide stairway from the Savoy Ballroom at around ten pm. Both were exhausted and perspiring in the humid night air. There had been a no-name band playing tonight, but they had turned out to be very good. Hannah's pulse was still throbbing from the music.

"You wanna get a Coke or something?, I'm thirsty," asked Fritz.

'Okay."

Hannah looked at him and smiled. He had been as excited as a little child when he had picked her up. All he could talk about on the way to the Savoy was his being allowed to play in a baseball game and getting a hit. She was glad for him. At least good things were happening to somebody.

They walked south on Lennox Avenue toward an all-night diner in the next block. There was still moderate foot traffic even though it was late. As they were passing the mouth of an alley, a stocky man with a coarse face emerged and rushed up to them. Hannah looked down and saw he had a stubby gun in his hand and it was pointed at Fred's midsection.

"I need you both to come with me now," said the man in a menacing voice.

Fritz reacted instantly. He shoved the man backward with all his might while shouting, "Hannah, run!"

Hannah turned on her heel and took off, dropping her purse to the pavement. She ran as she had never run before. She ran a block and then zigzagged over to the next block. Finally, she could run no more. Hannah stopped, bent over, put her hands on her knees and gulped air. The few people about were black and they eyed her curiously. She knew she had to get off the streets. She saw a bar a half block away and headed toward it.

The inside was long and narrow with a long wood bar running almost the full length. Two elderly black men were sitting on stools at the bar having a bleary conversation over shots of bourbon. A heavyset, bald bartender took one look at her and asked, "You alright, lady?"

"Yes, I am fine. Do you have a telephone here?"

"Yeah, it's in the back."

Hannah sidled up to the bar.

"Could you possibly lend me a nickel to make a phone call? I seem to have lost my purse," Hannah asked the bartender. The bald black man hesitated a moment, then smiled. He reached in his pocket and handed her a nickel.

"Here you go."

"Thank you. I will pay you back."

The bartender made a dismissive gesture and went toward the other end of the bar. Hannah walked to the back and entered a booth with a pay telephone on the wall. A big phone book lay precariously on a small shelf. Hannah quickly looked up a number, put in the nickel, dialed a number and put the receiver to her ear. She heard distant ringing and when a person answered, Hannah, spoke urgently.

"This is Hannah Rosen. Do you remember me? Good. I am in trouble. Can you come and pick me up? Yes, just a moment."

Hannah leaned out of the booth and called to the bartender.

'What is the address here?"

"301 West 142nd Street."

Hannah repeated the address into the phone and hung up. She stayed in the shadows at the back of the bar, fearful that the man with the gun would find her. After about ten minutes she flushed with relief when she saw a black 1935 Studebaker Land Cruiser, with Herb Johnson at the wheel, pull up on the street outside. Herb was warily looking all around. Hannah ran out of the bar toward the car. Herb reached across the seat and opened the passenger door. When she was safely inside, he gunned the motor and sped away.

'Hannah, what the hell is going on?" asked Herb, concern written on his brown face.

"A man with a gun is after me. I must get home and get my aunt and uncle out of our apartment. I dropped my purse when he pointed the gun at me and it has my address in it."

"Maybe we should go to the cops. They will protect you."

"No, no police," replied Hannah. The police would ask too many questions about why this had happened. She knew instinctively that it had something to do with the Germans.

Twenty minutes later Herb stopped the Studebaker in front of Hannah's building and set the brake. Hannah raced up the stairs. Herb followed her after retrieving a baseball bat from the back seat. Thirty seconds later they were standing in the living room of Hannah's apartment, trying to explain to her incredulous aunt and uncle why they had to get away from the building right now.

"I can't explain now," said Hannah," but we all have to get out of here."

Behind her, the door to the apartment exploded inward with a crash and splinters of wood from the jam flew across the room. The same ugly man with the gun that had confronted her and Fred outside the Savoy rushed inside. He grabbed Hannah by the hair and twisted, while at the same time pointing his revolver at the three other people.

"You, all of you in there," he snarled, gesturing toward the bathroom with his gun.

Herb looked like he was going to fight. He was holding the bat threateningly

"Get in there or I kill her," said the man with the gun.

Herb slowly dropped the bat and the three people backed into the small bathroom and the assailant pulled the door closed. Turning to Hannah, he backed her up against a wall.

"Where's your boyfriend, Jew?" he hissed near her ear.

Looking over the man's shoulder, Hannah saw Fred Hofmann appear in the open doorway to the apartment. Her eyes widened. The man with the gun saw her expression, let her go and whirled just as Fred charged at him. Up came the gun and there was a loud explosion. Hofmann went down clutching his side. Hannah's abject fear was instantly transformed into a rage. Without thinking, she leaped on the gunman's back and started to pummel his head and scratch at his eyes. The stocky man overpowered her deftly, plucking her from his back with ease, but not before her nails left parallel, bloody scratch marks across his left cheek. He put a hand to his face, and when his fingers came away bloody, it seemed to enrage him. He backed her against the wall again. He put the gun in his pocket and came out with a wicked-looking knife, the blade gleaming in the light. He whirled Hannah around so that her back was to the door.

"This is how we treat Jew bitches in the SS," he said with a cruel grin and brought the knife up over his head, preparing to plunge it down into the side of Hannah's unprotected neck.

Another gunshot echoed in the room, this one much louder and deeper than the first. A heavy .45 caliber lead bullet, fired from the doorway of the apartment, crossed the room traveling at 960 feet per second, generating a tremendous 460-foot pounds of energy. The bullet hit the man holding the knife just under his right eye with the force comparable to a speeding freight train. It was deflected slightly upward by the edge of the eye socket and started to tumble through the brain, leaving a three-inch wide tunnel in its wake. As the bullet exited, it carried most of the back of the man's head with it. A bright red gush flew into the small hallway behind him, spattering the walls with Aryan brain matter and Nazi blood. The smile was still on SS-Untersturmfuhrer Franz Keller's face as he collapsed onto the floor like an inanimate object, which of course he now was.

Hannah whirled around and looked down the smoking .45 caliber bore of the Hand Cannon. Coming into focus behind the gun was the determined face of Ted Miller, his square jaw firmly clenched and his mouth set in a grim line. Hannah stumbled, as if in a trance, across the room and collapsed into Ted's strong arms, sobbing.

'Hannah, what the hell is happening here? Who was that man?"

"He's a German SS bastard and he has killed at least one man here in New York," said a wounded Fritz Hofmann from the floor.

Things got hectic after that. Within a few minutes, there were ten New York cops in the apartment building. Within thirty minutes, FBI special agents arrived and ushered the cops out. An ambulance and young doctor arrived from Belleview Hospital. The doctor bandaged up

Fritz Hofmann. He had a clean through and through wound to the lower abdomen that apparently hadn't hit anything vital. When AD Byrnes arrived, Fritz began to talk to him, while the doctor bandaged his wound. He laid out the entire Abwehr spy operation for a shocked Byrnes.

Everyone in the apartment during the shooting was taken to the FBI office on Pearl Street, except for Fritz, who was taken, under guard, to Bellevue Hospital. Byrnes went into his private office and conferred with Director Hoover in Washington by telephone. Fritz told the agents interviewing him at the hospital where to find the list of Abwehr agents in the book in the Public Library. An agent rushed out to get the head librarian out of bed to open up the building. Within an hour the FBI had the list.

Phone calls were made to FBI special agents all over the eastern half of the United States, interrupting their slumber. By ten o'clock the next morning most of the Jewish Abwehr agents were in custody. By the end of the week, all were in custody. The last to be arrested was Esther Cohen. She was finally tracked to a friend's house in Maryland where she had been hiding since she fled the Immigration Service file room, after Miller's visit there.

Two FBI agents went to Stein's Camera Shop. Stein was missing and the place was closed and locked so they had to make a forcible entry. In a locked cabinet in the back room, they found a coded message labeled "Friedrich Hofmann." At the FBI field office, using Fritz's instructions, an agent used the copy of Northwest Passage, which had been recovered from Hofmann's room by two other agents, to decode the message. The message read:

"Ceaseoperationsinformagentsinplacedestroyallincriminatingeviden ceabandondrops."

With all the hullabaloo, no one paid much attention to Ted and Hannah sitting in a corner of the office on a small sofa. Ted had his arm around her and she was still shivering with shock.

"Why did you do it, Hannah?"

"I was forced to do it. They are holding my Mama and Papa hostage in Germany. They said that if I didn't cooperate with them they would turn them over to the SS and they would die. Do you hate me for what I have done?"

"No I don't hate you, I love you. I have been crazy about you for a year. I don't care about the spying or anything you have done. I will wait for you as long as it takes. Do you love me?"

"Oh, my God, Ted, I think I have loved you since the first moment I saw you on the way to that meeting," said Hannah, softly.

Hannah had a sudden thought, "Why did you come to my apartment tonight?

"I was following Hofmann. I saw you leave with him and went out and drank for hours. I was very hurt and angry and thought you had betrayed me. I came to your apartment to give you a piece of my mind."

Hannah's eyes lowered and a tear rolled down her cheek.

"You were right to be angry. I did betray you as well as my aunt and uncle and this wonderful country. I deserve whatever they do to me."

Ted lifted Hannah's chin and looked into her eyes.

"Hannah, you were a frightened young woman who was presented with an impossible choice. You acted the way you did because you loved your parents and were human. The law might criticize you, but I won't."

They kissed. It wasn't a kiss of lust but one of tenderness.

"I feel so sorry for my parents. The SS will kill them now," said Hannah, her face a mask of sadness.

CHAPTER THIRTY-SIX

KONZENTRATIONSLAGER BERGEN-BELSEN
BELSEN, DEUTSCHLAND 22 AUGUST 1943

Bergen-Belsen was a large concentration camp located on farmland between the small German towns of Bergen and Belsen, hence the name. Consisting of rough wood barracks and small factories, it was surrounded by a high fence of electrified barbed wire and guard towers with SS men holding machine guns at the ready. Bergen-Belsen was designated work and holding camp by the SS, as opposed to a death camp. The designation was misleading. The inmates were provided with only the equivalent of thirteen-hundred calories a day. In reality, it was slow motion extermination by starvation. The prisoners, reduced to little more than walking skeletons, stumbled about their assigned tasks with gray, emaciated faces. By contrast, the SS personnel and their auxiliaries were pictures of health. Sleek and well-fed, they strutted about the camp with their heads high.

One such SS-man was SS-Untersturmfuhrer Willi Schanz, but he was a bit too sleek and well-fed. Rolls of fat overflowed his belt and his bulging neck almost obscured the collar of his uniform. His heft combined with his short stature presented almost a comical impression. But there was nothing comical about Willi Schanz. He was a bully and a sadist and delighted in the brutality he inflicted on the helpless prisoners. At the moment he was chugging across the large open area in front of the camp administration building. His small pig-like eyes were showing worry and he was in a hurry. The camp Commandant, SS-Hauptsturnfuhrer Adolf Hass, had summoned him urgently. Schanz marched into the Commandant's office and shot his arm out in the Nazi salute.

"Heil Hitler."

The Commandant returned the salute.

"Heil Hitler, Shanz. I have a little job for you. In the woods south of Suderburg there is a Jagdschloss containing about one hundred Jews. They are being guarded by a detachment from the Kriegsmarine. Take ten SS men and twenty auxiliaries, go to Suderburg and bring those Jews back here. We have need of them. I want them alive but if you have to shoot one or two of them to ensure their cooperation, that is fine. Any questions?"

"Nein , Herr Hauptsturmfuhrer," replied Schanz.

In the Commandant's outer office, Schanz studied a large map of Greater Germany hanging on a wall. Using his right index finger, he traced the route he would have to take to Suderburg.

An hour later, a convoy of gray painted Mercedes and Opel trucks containing Schanz and his men roared out of the main gate of the camp. They couldn't travel directly west to Suderburg as there were mountains and wild forests in the way. Instead, the convoy traveled south to Celle and then northwest to Suderburg. About two-and- one-half hours after leaving Bergen-Belsen, the convoy negotiated a narrow road through woods and the lead truck stopped at the gate to the hunting lodge compound.

The naval guards were at their posts. Schanz climbed down from the cab of the lead truck and waddled toward a sailor manning a drop bar gate. Schanz was met at the gate by a junior naval officer. Schanz gave the Nazi salute. The naval officer returned a conventional military salute, which annoyed the Untersturmfuhrer.

"I have orders to take the Jews housed here into SS custody. What is your name.?" asked Schanz.

"I am Obersleutnant Zur See Franzel. Feel free to take any Jews you find in the compound."

Franzel then gave a signal for the bar at the gate to be raised and stepped aside. Schanz got back in the cab of the lead truck and the convoy drove into the courtyard of the hunting lodge. The SS Troopers and their lackeys jumped from the trucks and fanned out inside the barbed wire.

Inside the building, they found the kitchens with food items lying around in various stages of preparation, rooms full of three-tiered bunks and a library with a pitiful collection of books. But, there were no Jews.

Schanz was furious. He stalked back to the main gate and confronted Franzel.

"Why didn't you tell me the Jews were gone?"

"I make it a practice to never to presume to tell the SS anything. Would you have believed me if I had told you?" answered the naval officer.

"Where are the Jews?"

"I really don't know. Some Wehrmacht officers showed up here yesterday with orders from the general staff. They took all the Jews away."

"You could be in serious trouble for this ,Franzel."

"My men and I are detailed to work for the general staff. Why would I be in trouble for following orders from my lawful superiors?"

Schanz turned away, his round cheeks red with anger. He would now have to go back to Hauptsturmfuhrer Haas and report failure. He was apprehensive, others had been demoted for less. The fat little Nazi threw a tantrum and kicked the tire of a nearby truck.

CHAPTER THIRTY-SEVEN

FEDERAL COURT HOLDING CELLS
500 PEARL STREET
MANHATTAN
NEW YORK CITY.
AUGUST 28, 1943
9: 28 AM

Hannah Rosen sat on the thin mattress of the bunk of her cell, a picture of dejection. She thought about her future or lack of it. She faced exposure as a German spy, a trial and execution in the electric chair. On top of all that, her parents in Germany were probably now dead. Everything she had done had been for nothing.

Ted was the one bright spot. He came to see her often and seemed much more optimistic than she. Every time she thought of him saying he loved her, her heart would melt and she would almost die of longing for him. But he hadn't come to visit her in two days. She was beginning to worry that he had come to his senses and abandoned her. She wouldn't blame him if he had.

The outer cell doors clanged open and a matron appeared. She was dressed severely in all black. She opened Hannah's cell door with a large brass key.

"Come on Rosen, you're wanted upstairs," said the matron.

The woman escorted Hannah to the FBI offices upstairs. Hannah didn't look in when they passed the secretarial pool. She was too ashamed. She was shown into the Assistant Directors' office. Mr. Byrnes was seated behind his desk.

"Come in, Hannah. Please sit," said Byrnes and dismissed the matron.

When they were alone, Byrnes folded his hands on top of his desk and looked Hannah in the eye. He was looking very uncomfortable. He took a deep breath and spoke.

"Hannah, you will not be prosecuted for your actions on behalf of the Abwehr. You are going to be released."

Hannah looked at him, stunned, "I'm to be released?"

"Yes, but in return, you must sign these papers attesting to the fact that this entire incident has been declared top secret, Director's eyes only, and you can never disclose the events of the past two years to anyone, ever. If you violate this agreement, you will be liable to execution as a spy. Do you agree to sign?" asked Byrnes.

Hannah's head bobbed up and down in agreement. She quickly signed the papers. Byrnes then stood up.

"Hannah, you are free to go. Obviously, you can't work here anymore. You will have to find other employment."

In a daze, she stumbled into the outer office and into the arms of Ted Miller. The two clung to each other, oblivious to the other people around them. Finally, Hannah stood back and looked up at Ted's face.

"What is going on?" she asked.

"Director Hoover is very embarrassed that there has been a German spy ring operating in the country since 1941, right under his nose. He is afraid that his enemies in the government will use the information to force him out of his position. So, he has decided to cover the whole thing up. Everyone will be released. I just got back from Washington. I was summoned there for a private meeting with Hoover and Clyde Tolson. The three of us sat around like old pals. Tolson even served me coffee. Hoover said I should have gone over Byrnes's head and brought my suspicions directly to him. He would have acted on them," said Miller.

Hannah saw the look of skepticism on Ted's face and asked, "You didn't believe him?"

"Not for a minute. I think he is looking for a fall guy in case this whole thing blows up in his face and becomes public. He acted pleasantly but I could tell he was very agitated underneath. If this case is ever exposed to the newspapers, I think Hoover is going to blame the whole thing on Assistant Director Byrnes. Oh, I almost forgot, I stopped by to see your aunt and uncle this morning. This came for you yesterday."

He handed her a sealed envelope. The printing on it said it was an international telegram. Hannah tore it open and unfolded the sheet of paper within. She read:

"Deine mutter und ich sind sicher in Malmo Schweden, Papa."

Tears rolled down Hannah's cheeks. She hugged Ted.

"Oh Ted, my mama and papa are alive and safe in Sweden."

Miller spun her around in celebration, then pushed her out to arms-length.

"I have just one question to ask you, Hannah Rosen. Will you marry me and have a bunch of screaming brats and still love me when I'm old and gray with a pot gut and I can't hear very well?

Hannah was so overcome with emotion that she didn't trust herself to speak. She nodded her head vigorously and leaped back into his arms.

The three women from the secretarial pool were standing in the doorway to their office bawling like babies, the scene was so romantic. Mr. Byrnes opened his door and saw the couple embracing. He cleared his throat.

"Ted, could you step in here a moment?"

Miller left Hannah's arms, went into the assistant director's office and closed the door. He stood before his boss.

"Ted," said Byrnes," Do you think it wise to continue a relationship with that woman? After all, she is a German spy".

Ted looked at Byrnes with a twinkle in his eye. He couldn't resist.

"Mr. Byrnes, how could she be a German spy? You have told me many times that there are no enemy spies operating in the United States, we have caught them all."

10: 30 AM

Leo Durocher sat in his office under the bleachers at Ebbets Field. He had a pencil in his hand and was working out the lineup he would use for the next Dodger away game. The team was going on the road for the balance of the season. As far as Leo was concerned they might as well cancel the rest of the season. The Cardinals had the pennant won. He hoped that Rickey wouldn't fire him for the team losing so badly. His finances weren't in the best of shape right now.

Durocher lowered his pencil and thought about the Hoffman kid. He hadn't shown up for another game. That made six he had missed. After the first two, Leo had sent "Lollypop"Corriden to Fred's rooming house looking for him. The landlady said that Hofmann had disappeared suddenly, taking his suitcase with him. Durocher wondered what was going on. Then he sighed and made a mental note to stop by the front office and fire Fred's ass. Saving another forty dollars a week will make Rickey happy. It was a shame though, he liked the kid. He had been an eager worker and didn't give him the lip some of his prima donna players did.

The upcoming 1944 season was shaping up to be even worse than this one for finding talent. Several of the younger Dodger players had received draft notices that Rickey had gotten deferred until the end of the season. Durocher had intended to give Fred Hofmann a good long look in spring training next year.

2: 40 PM

Fritz Hofmann lay in a private room in Belleview Hospital with his left wrist handcuffed to his hospital bed and watched the big shot FBI man named Byrnes walk out the door. He was surprised and elated but still in disbelief. Byrnes had said he wasn't going to be prosecuted for spying for the Germans! Fritz had been forced to sign some papers and Byrnes had turned to leave with a look of distaste on his face.

Fritz's thoughts were interrupted by the New York policeman who had been guarding his door breezing in. "This must be your lucky day," said the cop. The officer threw an envelope with Fritz's belongings on the bed and proceeded to remove the handcuffs from his wrist and leave the room without another word.

At four pm, Fritz was abruptly discharged. He was given a bottle of aspirin and an admonition to avoid strenuous activity and keep his dressing clean and dry for two weeks. He found himself outside the

330 | D. W. DRAKE

hospital on the sidewalk.

Standing in the afternoon sun, Fritz didn't know what to think. He had expected a trial and execution and couldn't believe he was now a free man. But he still couldn't believe his luck. His natural pessimism was asserting itself as a cloud of doubt drifted in to displace his sunny thoughts. What was to stop the government from changing their minds and picking him up again. If he ever went to trial he would be convicted, because he was guilty, and he would be fried like a pork chop in the electric chair. He shuddered at the thought. No, he was still in danger and could still wind up dead. His instincts told him that his best course of action was to put as much distance between himself and the east coast as he could, as fast as he could. As much as he loved his job with the Dodgers and the future prospect of playing for them, he couldn't stay in New York. Fritz still had the key to the railroad station locker in his pocket. He had told his interrogators that it was the key to his locker at Ebbets field.

He took a cab to Grand Central Station, retrieved his suitcase from the locker and bought a ticket on the first train to Chicago. When he got there, he would decide where to go from there. Looking out the window as the train departed, he thought about Hannah. He still loved her but knew he had no chance. He had seen how she looked at the tall, rugged-looking FBI agent.

He glanced up at his suitcase on the rack above his head. It carried the Abwehr's money that he had decided was now his to keep. It also contained something else. Concealed under the lining on the inside of the lid was a certified copy of the birth certificate of Carl David Reed. Friedrich Hofmann, also known as Fritz and Fred, all-American boy, German soldier, traitor, Nazi spy and major league baseball player for the Brooklyn Dodgers, was about to cease to exist.

EPILOGUE

FRITZ HOFMANN

When Fritz arrived in Chicago, he couldn't decide where to go next so he continued on west until he hit the Pacific Ocean. He settled in Los Angeles, California. He assumed the name of Carl Reed and kept it for the rest of his life. Saving his Abwehr money, he went to work for Lockheed Aircraft in Burbank, assembling bombers. At the end of the war, he was laid off with thousands of other workers.

Fritz then used his stashed money to form a partnership with another man building little cracker box houses for returning GIs. His business took off like a rocket and he helped develop the San Fernando Valley. He became a wealthy man, got married and had two children. Whenever his pessimistic nature tried to assert itself, he would remind himself that he hadn't been executed as a traitor. He considered every day of the rest of his life a bonus.

In 1955 Fritz discreetly hired a private detective to find his brother Eberhard. The report came back that Eb had died the previous year from liver complications of the malaria he caught on Guadalcanal in 1942.

When the Dodgers moved to Los Angeles in 1958, Fritz became a season ticket holder. For the rest of his life, he attended almost every Dodger home game. He could be seen in his seat five rows back from first base. He always wore an old Brooklyn Dodger baseball cap. He died in 1996.

ARKY VAUGHAN

Vaughan refused to report to Dodgers spring training for the 1944 season. He decided he would rather quit than play for Durocher. He sat on the porch of his California ranch house and brooded for three years. In 1947 he returned to the Dodgers and batted a respectable .325. He was released from the team after the 1948 season when his batting average plummeted. He retired for good. Arky died in 1952.

Arky Vaughan was elected to the Baseball Hall of Fame in 1985.

LEO DUROCHER

Durocher went on to manage in the major leagues until he retired in 1976. He managed for four ball clubs and had a winning percentage of .540.

In 1945 he ran afoul of Baseball Commissioner "Happy" Chandler, for hanging around with gamblers and crooks. Among them was Benjamin "Bugsy" Siegel. When admonished by the Commissioner, Durocher told him to butt out of his personal affairs.

In 1947 Leo had a public row with Larry Macphail, the owner of the Yankees. The spat was fodder for the tabloids for months and included allegations of rigging games. The allegations were nothing more than over-hyped allegations but Durocher lost the public relations war and was suspended for a year.

1947 also saw Durocher and Branch Rickie conspire to break the baseball color barrier. They called a young phenom up from the minor leagues. He happened to be black. His name was Jackie Robinson. When some of the Dodgers players balked at playing with a black man,

Durocher gathered the team together and made a short speech.

"I do not care if the guy is yellow or black or if he has stripes like a fuckin' zebra. I'm the manager of this team and I say he plays. What's more, I say he can make us all rich. And if any of you cannot use the money, I will see that you are all traded."

Durocher died in 1991 at the age of 86. He was inducted into the Baseball Hall of Fame in 1994.

1943 BROOKLYN DODGERS.

Besides Leo Durocher and Arky Vaughn, three other players on the 1943 Dodgers team were eventually inducted into the Baseball Hall of Fame. They were Billy Herman, Joe Medwick and Paul Waner.

ADMIRAL WILHELM CANARIS

In February 1944, Heinrich Himmler finally amassed so much circumstantial evidence of disloyalty against Canaris that Hitler removed him from the leadership of the Abwehr. He was put under house arrest though, instead of the prison that Himmler wanted.

During the SS reign of terror following Count Von Stauffenberg's failed attempt on Hitler's life in July 1944, a search of the Admiral's home resulted in the discovery of his diary. He was sent to Flossenburg Concentration Camp. In early April 1945, when Hitler was shown excerpts from the diary and realized how he had been tricked, he flew into a rage and ordered Canaris executed.

On 9 April 1945, Canaris, along with Hans Oster, Deidrich Bonhoeffer, Karl Sack and Ludwig Gehre were ordered out of their cells in Flossenburg. They were led naked through taunting SS guards to heavy wire nooses and hanged. It took many years before the truth finally came out that the Admiral wasn't just another Nazi, but a

German patriot who gave his life opposing Hitler.

J. EDGAR HOOVER

Hoover remained Director of the FBI until he died in 1972. Immediately after his death, by order of the President, the contents of Hoover's private safe were confiscated and destroyed. That night, politicians all over Washington partied. The booze and the hookers flowed freely.

Hoover had never married and he was buried next to his long-time friend, Clyde Tolson.

HEINRICH HIMMLER

In May 1945, after the Fuhrer's death and the collapse of the Nazi regime, Himmler was caught by the British while disguised as a common soldier. He killed himself with a cyanide pill before he could be interrogated. Despite his murdering millions of people, to the end of his life, he considered himself to be a decent man.

CARLOS BREYER

In early 1944, Breyer was recalled to Spain due to pressure from the American State Department. They wouldn't tell the Spaniards the reason; they just wanted him gone. Carlos stayed in the Spanish Diplomatic Service. In 1966, he was appointed an ambassador to a small banana republic in South America. The Generalissimo of the republic was also a short man. Like Carlos, he wore platform shoes. The two got along swimmingly.

HERBERT JOHNSON

Herb abandoned his driving school shortly after the war. He partnered with his cousin in a wholesale cleaning products business. He made good. He took care of his ailing mother until she died in 1952, then married and had three children. Herb and Hannah Rosen Miller remained friends for the rest of their lives.

RACHEL AND MOSHE ROSEN.

Hannah's aunt and uncle remained in New York until Moshe retired. Then they moved to Israel. The shooting in their apartment was the most exciting thing that had ever happened to them in their whole lives. They were very irked that they couldn't tell anyone about it.

TED AND HANNA MILLER

Ted and Hannah were married a week after her release. She was pregnant eight weeks later. Ted remained in the New York field office of the FBI until August of 1946. During this time, he waged a one-man campaign to get Hannah's parents admitted to the United States. He was rebuffed at every turn. Congress, especially members of the Democratic Party from the south were averse to allowing Jewish refugees into the country. We already have a problem with the negros. They argued. Why import another problem?

Ted finally went to his friend, Federal Judge Hiram Potter. The old judge got on the telephone with a crony of his in the State Department. The State Department man's wife just happened to play bridge every Tuesday with the wife of a senior Immigration Service official. In typical Washington style, the skids were greased.

On March 22, 1946, Yakob Rosen and his wife Anna, walked down a gangplank in New York harbor into the waiting arms of their joyful daughter, Hannah. Their son-in-law and grandson were also there to greet them. Edward Miller was two years old. He had Hannah's dark hair and beautiful eyes and his father's square jaw. He stood, wide-eyed, holding his father's hand, wondering who these strange people were.

336 | D. W. DRAKE

Ted learned in August 1946 that he was to be transferred to the Oklahoma City field office. He suspected that Hoover had personally ordered the move as punishment for Ted making so much trouble for him. Rather than accepting the transfer Miller resigned from the FBI, marched downtown and Joined the New York Police Department. Over the years, he worked his way up in the ranks and became one of the city's top homicide detectives, with the rank of Lieutenant.

Meanwhile, Hannah devoted herself to their growing family. They had a total of four children, three boys and a girl. In their little house in Queens, she coped with having two children at a time in diapers in an era before disposable diapers were available. Her parents lived with them and Anna was a tremendous help. They had a typical life. Ted would complain that she nagged him and Hannah would rage at him for leaving his dirty underwear on the bathroom floor. After repeated tries, Ted quit smoking in 1948. Hannah never got over her love affair with bacon.

Over the years Ted generally voted Republican. Hannah was a staunch Democrat after she became a citizen. When Ted really wanted to get her goat, he would comment to her that his vote canceled hers out every election day.

They had arguments, but they didn't usually last long. When Hannah got angry, her eyes would flash with fire and color would spread up her cheeks. At those times Ted would look at her and she was so achingly beautiful that he would surrender and the two would head for the bedroom.

In 2003 their family threw a party for their sixtieth wedding anniversary. As their children, grandchildren and great-grandchildren serenaded them, Ted looked at Hannah. The years had taken their toll but even now there were hints in her appearance that she had once been a great beauty. Ted didn't see the old woman beside him. Instead, he saw the young and beautiful Hannah of 1943. Hannah likewise didn't see a wrinkled, turkey necked, gimlet-eyed old man. She saw the wavy-haired, young Ted with his square jaw and lopsided grim that had stolen her heart all those years ago.

"Any regrets?" asked Ted.

"None," replied Hannah, "though I wish you weren't so messy."

Hannah died of a heart attack in 2006. Ted, unable to cope with life without her, followed her six months later.

All in all, by any objective measurement, the union of "Machine Gun" Miller and the "Ice Princess," was a good and enduring one.

THE COVER-UP

The secret of the German-Jewish spy ring was kept. The Jewish agents were only too glad to keep secret the fact that they had spied for Nazi Germany. In the FBI, the truth was only known to the leadership and a small number of special agents and office workers. J. Edgar Hoover cowed everyone who knew about the whole incident into silence with threats and intimidation. They were forced to sign non-disclosure agreements. In later years, after Hoover was gone, the involved FBI agents, long since retired, kept silent about the spies. They thought the entire incident would stain the FBI reputation if it was revealed.

In 2010 an elderly patient in a New Jersey nursing home began telling wild stories. Her name was Naomi Gershon. She announced to everyone around her that she had been a German spy in the U.S. State Department during World War II. The stories were surprisingly detailed and entertaining. The staff, other patients and her son, on his weekly visits, listened to her but gave no credence to the stories. The thought of a Jewish woman spying for the Nazis was just too ridiculous to entertain. Everyone was sure that the tales were just the fantastic ravings of a senile old woman.

THE END

AUTHOR'S NOTE

Thank you for reading my book. If you enjoyed it, won't you please take a moment to leave me a review at your favorite retailer?

Thanks!

D. W. Drake

Sign up for email updates and receive free advance reading copies, updates on new releases, special offers and bonus content. You can contact me directly by email: dwdrake@savanatpress.com

You may also sign up at: www.savanatpress.com

Made in the USA
San Bernardino, CA
11 June 2020